ABOUT THE AUTHOR

Lexie Winston has been an astronaut, rock star, princess and time traveller. In her dreams. But none of the dreams have lived up to what becoming an author has been like. She gets to live in a world of pure imagination, and her heroines get to do the things she's always wished she could.

When not writing books, Lexie is a mother of two gorgeous teenagers and the wife to a patient and understanding man. They live in Western Australia and are lorded over by a black toy poodle. She loves camping, reading and if her Kindle was stolen, her world would explode.

And you can find all links at

www.lexiewinston.com

OVATION

LEXIE WINSTON

ALSO BY LEXIE WINSTON

The Collectors Division

(Paranormal Reverse Harem Series)

Guardian

Guardian's Blood

Guardian Ascending

Collector's Division Omnibus

Neighpalm Industries Collective

(Enemies to Lovers Reverse Harem)

Abandoned Girl

Broken Girl

Tormented Girl

Wanted Girl

Cherished Girl

Loved Girl

Superficial Girl - Jacinta's Story Part 1

Superficial Girl - Jacinta's Story Part 2

Neighpalm Industries Collective 1-3

Neighpalm Industries Collective 4-6

Seductive Sins Collection

(Reverse Harem Series)

Glorious Gluttony

Gangs, Guns, and Glory

Glory Glory Hellelujah

Crowning Glory

What's the Story, Morning Glory?

(Seductive Sins Omnibus)

Galaxy Circus

(Sci-Fi Reverse Harem Series)

Apprentice

Stagehand

Whisperer

Mama - Galaxy Circus Novella

Performer

Ringmaster

Interlude

Spectacle

Ovation

A Night Most Wicked - Galaxy Circus Novella

Broken Promises

(Dark Poly Romance Series)

Secrets Kept

Lies Untold

Trust Broken

M.I.T.H.O.S

(Contemporary RH)

Spies Like Me

Spies Like Us

Storm View Stories

(Contemporary Standalone RH)

Ice Me Out

First published by Neighpalm Publishing in 2024

Ovation

Mobi format: 978-1-7636228-3-8
Print: 978-1-7636228-4-5
Cover design by Raven Ink Covers

Editing by Elemental Editing

I decided not to add a glossary in this book. I had complaints whether I put it in the front or the back. So if you need a refresher on our cast of characters the main ones are listed on the next page. Everything else you can find by scanning the QR code which will take you to my website Galaxy Glossary

MAIN CHARACTERS

Lila Adams
Caspian
Link
Saxon
Xavier
Echo
Maxsim
Tirrian
Silac
Nikos
Ghosie
Brannock
Zeydan

CHAPTER ONE

Lila

"John, William, Eric, come quickly. Liliana is awake."

There's a beat of silence as Xavier's words sink in before the room explodes into chaos. All three of my grandpas, who were fully focused on Vivian, turn their attention to Xavier.

"She's awake?" Tears well in my eyes at the hopefulness I hear in John's voice.

"Yes, come quickly. She's asking for you and muttering about Vivian." Xavier gestures in the direction of their wing. He looks completely frazzled and not like the put together warlock we all know and love.

"Should I chase after her?" Saxon asks, looking in the direction Vivian just went.

"No!" William shouts, running his hand through his hair. It's grown out a bit over the last few months, and he is definitely in need of a new buzz cut. It's sitting kind of funny from all the tugging he does. "No, definitely not. If Liliana wants to see her, then we can always send her another message. We don't know enough yet, not to mention Phillip and Fiona's conversation that Connor overheard."

"Come on." Eric takes off using his enhanced speed. John and William follow quickly behind him, and I turn to look at Zeydan through the window. He's watching the children, but his tails are bristling with agitation and his head is cocked like he's listening to something.

He turns to look inside the window, and his eyes glow with power.

"I should tell him," I say quietly, biting my lip.

I'm still a little unsure about where we stand. He mated me, and I can feel the small slice of his soul inside me, but it's a one-sided bond. I haven't sealed him to me yet, and despite his protests that Liliana is like a sister to him, there is no blood between them. What if there was something more once upon a time? They are as old as dirt, so it wouldn't be beyond the realm of possibility that they had a fling in the past.

Before I can make a move, though, he disappears, only to reappear directly in front of me. "She's awake." He doesn't phrase it as a question, so I just nod. "I thought I could feel a remnant of god power." His brows furrow in confusion. "But I could have sworn it was a remnant of death power I felt, not life. Now that I'm inside, though, I can feel the gentle wave of life."

"Will you go to her?" I ask, and he shakes his head as Ghosie walks outside to round up the children. His fur will protect him from the cold better than any of the others. I hear them squealing and giggling as they refuse to come inside.

"No, not yet. Are your grandpas with her?"

"Yes, they went immediately," I reply as the cats and Ghosie wrangle the children and herd them inside. They are starting to get whiny now, and all of them protest loudly.

"Then I think warm baths and bed are in order." Nikos is quick to scoop Hali up as she ducks around Echo, trying to get outside again. She starts to scream. I'm not sure where she gets her temper from—certainly not me.

"That sounds like a good idea." Caspian gets Jack while Tirrian and Brannock grab the other two girls. Silac swoops in and lifts Typhoon, who is quick to snuggle into his chest. That baby is such a snuggle rabbit and has his daddies wrapped around his little finger. They all disappear in the direction of our wing, and the noise dies off.

The cats shake off their fur, flinging droplets of water everywhere, and I glare at them. They have the grace to look sheepish before slinking over to the fireplace, making themselves comfortable in front of the flames.

"Are you going to go up there, Lila?" Saxon asks as he starts to pack up the games. Ghosie and Zeydan join in, Zeydan putting away the deck of Go Fish cards, while Saxon stacks the blocks of Jenga together.

"Not yet. I don't want to overwhelm her. It will be a big shock for her, and I'll let the grandpas, Link, and Xavier explain everything to her before I join them," I tell them as I grab the Twister mat and fold it, placing it and the customized spinner back in the box. I head over to the table with the Clue game and put away all the pieces as well as the cards and packs of Guess sheets. Once finished, I stack the boxes on top of each other, making a mental note to take them all back to the ship with us when we go.

I don't meet any of the guys' looks. I don't want to see what they think. I'm not technically hiding, but I know once I go in and meet my grandma, everything is going to unravel. We will know the truth that I'm certain has been staring us in the face.

I'm not paying attention to what's going on, caught in my thoughts, as I sit on the sofa in front of the fire. Echo puts his big head in my lap and gives my hand a lick. I absently stroke his mane, and he makes a weird, rumbling kind of purring sound that's soothing, but I hear the others talking quietly in the background. I watch the flames as they lick over the logs, the sight combined with the warmth emanating from it slightly hypnotic.

I feel the sofa sag as someone sits next to me

"Talk to me, Lila." Saxon puts his arm around my shoulders and tucks me against his side. I snuggle into his large body and sigh.

"What do you want me to say?" I ask, not really sure what the problem is. We were having an awesome family evening playing games before Vivian interrupted. There was no way I was going to let her through to sit with Liliana, even before she got spooked. I need the cousins to wake up so I can pump them for information as well.

"Why aren't you racing to meet your grandma?"

I shrug as much as I can while trapped in his arms. "I don't know. What if she's disappointed? I don't remember meeting her in any of my memories. I must have, right? She only went missing a few months before my parents were killed."

"Lila, why would she be disappointed? From what I understand, they loved you and your parents very much."

I shrug, having no idea why I feel this way. Meeting my grandpas was the best thing that ever happened to me, so why wouldn't meeting my grandma be the same way? "Maybe because her identity is so up in the air. I don't want to become attached and realize we got it wrong."

Saxon nods and gives me another squeeze. "I can understand that. After what you've been through, it's no wonder you hold everyone at arm's length. Come on, why don't we get some sleep? It's probably going to be in short supply over the next few weeks. I'm sure if they need you, they will come get you."

Saxon stands up and tugs me to my feet. I go reluctantly. I know he's right, but my gaze drifts to my grandpas' wing of the house. There's a whirl of emotions inside my body, I'm sure I won't fall asleep quickly. I look at both cats and find them asleep in front of the fire. It's weird, considering they love the snow and ice so much. You would think it would be too hot for them, but nope, they are snuggled together and purring contentedly, so I leave them where they are. They will probably wake up and go back outside at some point.

As we head to my bedroom, Ghosie and Zeydan follow. Both stop at my room and give me a kiss good-night before heading to the room they share. Neither of them press to stay with me—Zeydan because he can feel everything that's going on, and Ghosie because of his fur. We don't sleep in the same bed because we'd spend all night fucking and wake up more exhausted than rested. Hopefully one day, we can figure out a way to fix his problem. I know how touch starved he is, and I make a mental note to spend some more time with him, even if we do end up horizontal.

Now that we're all mated, I feel slightly more settled, despite only having half a mating with Zeydan and not having Brannock fully locked down. As I strip and climb into bed, I promise to finish the Skarrian bond with both of them as soon as possible. I'm sure that will help resolve any lingering doubt.

Saxon climbs in behind me and snuggles against me, and I sigh with contentment. I tip my head, offering him my neck. He cups my breast with one hand while the other slides down to gently circle my clit as he laves his tongue over the thick vein that pounds with what he needs.

"Bite me," I murmur quietly, a slight whine in my tone. I'm feeling all kinds of needy, and being loved on by one of my mates will hopefully settle the rolling turmoil of my emotions.

He doesn't make me beg, and as he slides his fangs into my neck, he enters me from behind and lazily thrusts his fat cock in and out in time with his pulls of blood. My body sings, and my mind soars as my orgasm rolls through me like a gentle wave, erasing all worries and doubts and focusing my attention on the delicious sensations he's wringing from my body.

When he finally fills me with his cum, he sweeps his tongue over the two fang marks in my neck, sealing them so I don't continue to drip blood. His hips lazily continue to roll, his cock not losing his erection despite him already finding his release. He keeps me on edge, plucking at my nipples and teasing my clit until I'm a begging, pleading mess once again. I hear the door to our room open and close, and I know one of my other mates has joined us.

"It looks like you're taking very good care of our mate," Caspian rumbles, and I peel my eyes open to look at my first mate.

"Want to join us?" Saxon asks, and I watch with a little giggle as Cas quickly tears off his clothes. I don't get to continue to watch the show, though, because Saxon pulls out of me, and I whimper at the loss of his thickness.

He rolls me over and murmurs, "Patience, my sweet. I'm just getting us in a better position. Cas will stuff you full again and keep my cum deep inside you."

My pussy throbs at his dirty words as he pulls me flush against his chest, lifting my leg so it's over his hip and giving Cas easy access.

Saxon leans in and takes one of my nipples into his mouth, giving it a slow suck before piercing it with his fangs. His venom flows through my system, pushing me toward orgasm again, and I pant and squirm, but he holds me tightly.

"Stuff our wife full. She's a needy wench," Saxon tells Cas as I feel him get onto the bed. I expect to feel his legs against mine, so I'm shocked and delighted to feel his tentacles caressing my skin instead. The little suckers place tiny kisses everywhere they touch as his arms wrap around my body, pinning me between the two males.

"Bite me, Lila, and drink your fill while your husband takes care of your carnal needs," Saxon instructs as one of Cas's tentacles inches toward my pussy and slides through Saxon's cum which is dripping out of me.

"Can't let this go to waste," he mutters behind me, pushing it back into my body. I gasp as its thickness pushes into me, throwing my head back and closing my eyes.

"Uh-uh. Pay attention to me." Saxon grabs my chin and forces my head back down. He releases a claw on one of his fingers, and my eyes widen as he slides it across his pec. The scent of his blood reaches my nostrils, and my mouth waters as my own fangs click into place. I lean forward just as Cas removes the tentacle from my pussy and pushes it into my asshole without prep. I groan and struggle against the intrusion, but they hold onto me while Cas forces it in.

"Good girl, taking your mate deep into your ass," Saxon croons, pulling my head down so I can lick the blood trickling down his chest. I lap at the wound as I feel another one of Cas's tentacles enter my pussy. It's a lot, but I need it. I want to get lost in desire and be a dripping, sated mess, used and abused and stuffed full of cum. It triggers a part of me that wants to be permanently full of my mates' cum. I want them to tie me to the bed and use me as a cum receptacle so I don't have to think about anything more than when my next dose of cum would be coming. That life would be simple.

My mind becomes a messy haze as Cas fucks me in both holes while I drink from Saxon, but then Saxon pulls away, and I sob, trying to get his blood. Cas rolls into a half reclined position, his back against a pillow, and takes me with him, leaving me double stuffed. My eyes roll back at the sensations coursing through my system. They've kept me on the edge of coming for a long time, and I'm practically begging for it. Saxon follows, straddling us. Blood continues to run down his body from the cut, and he uses it to coat his cock, sliding his hand back and forth as he gestures for me to open my mouth.

"Let your mates fill all your holes, and we'll let you

come," he tells me, and I eagerly open my mouth. He grabs my head and fucks my mouth with reckless abandon. All I can do is breathe through my nose as Cas's tentacles thicken inside me and fuck me harder as well. It doesn't take long before I'm flying into space, my mind clearing of everything but the bliss they are wringing from my body. Saxon fills my mouth, and I swallow his seed as quickly as I drank his blood while Cas fills both of my holes with his cum.

We collapse into a messy, sweaty, cum-covered heap, and I couldn't be happier.

CHAPTER TWO

Lila

The following morning, I find myself alone in my bed. Cas and Sax helped me bathe after our sweaty fun times, and I slept like a baby, the two of them having fucked all my immediate worries away. When I wake alone, though, all my concerns come barreling back like an out of control freight train.

Today is another busy day of auditions, and I didn't get a chance to talk to Link about the onboarding of all the crew yesterday. Today, Malik is arriving from Fluxx with the rest of the shifters in the crew, and I'm sure Cas will like to be there to meet him. We also need to start shifting any personal items we want to take with us back to the ship. It will be at least a few months before we return to Skarr after we resume our previous schedule.

That's not even taking my grandma and all the

information she might have to share with us into consideration. As much as I want to pull the sheets over my head and hibernate, I don't. I throw them back and get up, grabbing another quick shower to help me wake up so I'm ready to face everything today is going to throw at me.

The living area is suspiciously free of children and mates. Usually, it's a hive of activity, and the strange silence puts me even more on edge. I make my way to the kitchen to get some coffee, hoping to run into someone there. Instead, I find my grandpas waiting for me. I'm instantly on alert. This seems too organized to be a coincidence.

"Good morning?" I ask cautiously, and although they look tired, all three of them seem like the weight of the world has been lifted off them.

"Lila." John smiles at me, a genuine one without strain that I haven't seen since I first arrived at the circus. "Grab some coffee and come sit. We want to talk to you about a few things."

I don't move, my heart starting to race with anxiety. Eric lifts the mug in front of him and sends it over to the counter using his telekinesis. I blink in surprise. I often forget they also have powers. It's been a while since I saw him use it.

"Stop panicking," he says as the cup lowers down. "Can you pour me another one too? It's going to be quite a day."

"Don't be an asshole, Eric. Can't you see she's already spiraling?" William scolds his brother before coming over to me and taking me by the arm. "Lila, everything is okay. Get your coffee and listen to what we have to say."

"Where is everyone?" I ask, letting William lead me to the coffee pot. He takes a clean mug out of the cupboard, placing it into my hand before filling it and Eric's.

"Link and Xavier are in their bedrooms. They spent most of the night checking on your grandma and cousins. We told them to get some sleep. The rest made themselves scarce. I think they all have errands today, and they are going to wrap up the auditions for you and make sure your rooms have been remodeled as requested. The ship is scheduled for departure tomorrow, and we need everything to be situated as soon as possible. Kinga and Andre are looking after the children. They are heading to a playground to let them run off some excess energy. I think they were going to build some snowmen and try their hand at tobogganing. Kinga and Andre aren't too keen on the cold, though, so I'm not sure how long that will last," Eric tells me, chuckling. I guess being cold-blooded in cold weather wouldn't be much fun. I know Tirrian grumbles repeatedly about it as well, even though he has internal heat he can access.

"Okay," I reply, feeling a little less anxious now that I know everyone is fine. "How are Phillip and Fiona?" I ask as William guides me back to the table, and I take a seat next to John.

"They are stable, but it might help if you give them

another healing session. Link said you should be able to now. We're hoping they will wake soon too."

"Of course," I agree. I don't like them, but I don't believe they need to suffer either, so if I can help ease that suffering, then I will gladly help.

"We need to find out what happened to them. I have a feeling everything is related now that we know Lili's story."

"She told you what happened?" I ask, and the three of them nod solemnly, though I can see the fury blazing in their eyes.

"Yes, we know everything."

"And?" I prompt, but William shakes his head.

"Liliana asked if she could meet you. She wants to explain it to you herself."

"She wants to meet me?" I ask, my voice quiet.

"Oh, Lila, nothing would make her happier. You were the light of her life for the first few years. Every time we came to Earth, she would stay with you and your parents. It was only that last time that she didn't come with us, which was strange within itself."

"And is she the goddess of life?" That's the most burning question I have, and I brace myself as the three men exchange glances.

"Yes, she is," John confirms, "which I can assure you comes as a surprise to us all, her included."

"She didn't know?" I ask, unable to hide the shock in my voice.

"No, but I'll let her explain it to you. First, we need to talk to you about something else." His brow creases, and the tension that he's been carrying for so long returns. I look at the other two, and both of them appear serious as well. My stomach rolls as I consider what they might need to talk to me about.

"Okay," I say hesitantly, cupping my mug with both hands so I don't squirm like a teenager who was out after curfew.

"Relax, it's nothing bad." Eric waves a hand at me, but it isn't particularly reassuring. I've come to learn his oh-shit-o-meter is definitely broken.

"No, not at all. In fact, I'm hoping you will be happy for us," John adds, and I feel some of the tension drain away from me. John is usually the most uptight, so if he's relaxed about whatever they want to tell me, then it can't be all too drastic.

"Lila, we've decided to retire early. Having Lili back just highlights how much we've missed out on, and we're ready to move on to the next phase of our lives." William crosses his arms and leans back in his chair, keeping his steely gaze on me. My heart starts to race. "We hoped to hand the circus over to your parents, but that isn't possible, so it's your turn. Now that you have a solid mating circle, we think all of you are perfectly capable of taking the Galaxy Circus by the reins and making it something special."

"What do you mean?" I need explicit clarification before I start my small, possibly large, meltdown.

"We won't be joining you when the ship leaves for Earth," William says, voicing the words I had been dreading, and I feel nauseous.

"But, but..." I'm kind of lost for words.

"Take a deep breath, Lila." Eric chuckles, and I want to shove my foot up his ass. "You've got this. We wouldn't be handing it over to you so soon if we didn't think you could cope."

My breathing comes even faster, and I feel a little lightheaded. I lean my forehead onto the table, and Eric chuckles.

"We'll only be a screen call away, but we want to make up for lost time. If this has proven anything to us, it's that time is not guaranteed."

I breathe in through my nose and out through my mouth a couple of times and get myself under control. "I can completely understand that, but it doesn't make me panic any less. I don't think I'm cut out for such a huge responsibility. Hell, I can't even take care of three babies, not to mention the two new ones, let alone a gigantic corporation like Galaxy Circus."

"Maybe not yet, but you have a group of men, most of whom have been trained to take over their parents' companies or rule. Between the thirteen of you, I have no doubt that this company will flourish."

Everything they say would make sense to someone sane and rational, but to me it just sounds like blah, blah, blah. None of it is penetrating the panic. "But what about the orb? What are we going to do with that? Surely it isn't safe now that the Syndicate suspects we have it."

"Ah, yes, the orb." William's tone has me lifting my

head and looking at him, my previous panic a small drop in the ocean of the panic his tone now causes me.

"What? What do you know?" I demand, and the three of them exchange another one of those all-knowing glances that makes me want to pull at my hair and scream. How can a glance speak so loudly yet say nothing?

"We now know the origin of the orb. Liliana told us everything, but again, it's her story to tell," John says solemnly.

This time I can't hold in my annoyance, and I stick my tongue out and blow him a raspberry. The three of them chuckle again. Assholes.

"Fine, then what are we waiting for?" I ask, standing up. "Where's Zeydan? Should he be here for this?" I ask as the grandpas follow my lead and stand with coffee mugs in hand.

"He's sitting with her now. She was asleep when we left her, but we didn't want her to wake alone."

"She remembers him?" I ask as I follow them into their wing of the house.

"She does now," John confirms as we reach the bedroom area. "Why don't you pop in and fix the twins first? She needs as much rest as she can get."

I scoff. "Are you sure about that? From what I understand, she's been resting for the last twenty odd years."

"She wasn't in stasis that whole time," William tells me, and I hear fear in his voice. "She's only been in stasis for the last few years, and that was on and off. It was only recently that her captives finally broke her and she admitted where the orb was. She held out despite what they tortured or threatened her with, but they finally broke her once they brought in a new Syndicate member who had leverage she couldn't stand against." The fear is replaced with blazing hot fury. I wonder what finally broke her.

I go to ask, but William shakes his head. "It's not important right now. We need to take one step at a time."

With those mysterious words, he walks away, leading me toward the room the twins were stashed in.

I huff out another breath of annoyance and follow them, leaving my coffee behind. Damn men didn't even let me finish it before they began demanding my attention. Luckily I filled up on my husbands last night.

I pass through other rooms, shivering at the cool contrast to the rest of the house. None of these rooms have their heating switched on. There is no point in heating rooms that aren't being used, and we've been gathering in the middle of the mansion.

Some of the furniture is still covered with dust cloths, but I guess if they are staying, then they should probably do something about that.

William reaches the room next to the one my grandma is in. "Xavier and Link moved the twins here when Vivian first arrived yesterday. We left them here just in case she decides to return."

"Not that we're ever going to let her see Liliana,"

Eric growls, and I blink at the aggression in his voice. Sure, none of them ever showed any signs of affection for her, but this is bordering on psychotic fury. I suspect there is more to this than what meets the eye, especially after Vivian scurried away like a rat yesterday.

"No, we definitely won't be," John agrees. "Why don't you change your form before you go in? I'll grab you a robe from one of the guest rooms." He moves farther down the hallway to do just that, but I hold up my hand.

"No need," I tell him. "I just need a couple of slits in this shirt." I point to the one I'm wearing, tap into my warlock power, and use it to create what I want, then I let the change wash over me. I feel my Celestian wings push through my skin, the sharp burst of pain expected and bearable now, although I still flinch.

All three of them gape at me in amazement. "I thought you had to be in a specific form to use specific powers. Isn't that what Oshan said? How did you just use your warlock powers?"

I shrug. "Turns out I'm a special snowflake. I can access powers without needing to be in that form."

The three of them exchange another one of those glances that drives me fucking nuts.

"Maybe Lil was right," John murmurs, but before I can ask about what, William flings open the door to the twins' room and strides in, the other two hurrying after him. Cowards.

I head into the room, shooting death glares at my

three grandpas who huddle against one wall. I make my way between the two hospital style beds that have my cousins lying in them. They are both hooked up to heart monitors and have electrodes on their temples monitoring their brain activity as well as IVs keeping them hydrated.

I frown down at them. Both are much paler than normal, which makes the cuts and bruises I couldn't heal stand out even more. I have no idea what happened to them, but I have a gut feeling that Htaed wasn't responsible for it all.

I let the power seep into my hands and hold them over Fiona, watching her cuts and bruises fade. She has some internal bruising on the brain too, which I manage to heal, reducing the swelling. Hopefully that is all that's keeping her asleep. I then do the same for Phillip. He has the same kind of brain swelling, but I can't find any external trauma that may have caused it. Neither of them had contusions or lumps on their head. It's almost like they both suffered some kind of concussive force like an explosion, but there was no evidence of that in the barn.

The power recedes, and I brush a hand over Phillip's forehead, pushing back a lock of hair that fell into his closed eyes.

His eyes flutter at my touch, and I yank my hand back, unable to escape the surprised yelp that leaves my mouth.

"Is everything okay?" John asks, stepping forward. Despite Phillip and Fiona being assholes to me, they are sweet with the grandpas and have a fairly good rela-tionship with them. I think I just made them feel threatened, and I probably would have felt the same way if the situation was reversed.

"I think he's waking," I reply as a groan leaves Phillip's mouth, and he lifts a hand to his head. The four of us wait patiently despite wanting to pounce on him and demand answers. Even an asshole like Phillip deserves a little leeway.

CHAPTER THREE

Lila

"**F**uck, I feel like I got stomped on by Viggy," he mumbles.

"You're not totally wrong," I reply, and he flinches.

"Lila?" he asks as his eyelids flutter like he's trying to open them.

"Yeah, take it easy. Don't force it. I healed you, but you were both pretty banged up. There's probably going to be some residual exhaustion," I tell him quietly, but he doesn't listen and struggles like he's trying to get up.

"Whoa, Phillip, just calm down." John comes over and pats his great nephew's foot, trying to reassure him.

"Fiona?" he asks, managing to crack his eyelids open. I wave my hand and dim the lights, using my

Celestian powers, and it seems to help as he blinks a couple of times and looks directly at me.

"She's over there. She hasn't woken yet, but we are hoping it will be soon."

He swings his head in the direction I point, wincing before heaving a sigh of relief when he sees his sister and settles back against the bed once more.

"Phillip, what happened to you?" Eric steps a little closer. I see him shudder and grimace, then his jaw sets in a stubborn line.

"We can protect you," William tells him, and I see the tension in his jaw ease ever so slightly. "Just tell us the truth."

The room is deadly quiet except for the beeping of the various monitors. William reaches over and turns the sound off on Phillip's and patiently starts removing the leads. There is no point in disturbing Link when he's been up all night. I see the exact moment Phillip decides he's done keeping secrets and wait patiently for him to blurt out everything.

"Did you know that animal persuasion or animal affinity is not my and Fiona's strongest power?"

I scoff. "That's not really any surprise. Htaed was a menace."

He grimaces and nods. "Yes, unfortunately his mind was not stable enough to deal with our powers. It turned him a little mad. Because they aren't the strongest, we have to press them hard upon an animal to get a response, and sometimes it doesn't work well."

"So if that isn't your strongest power, then what is?" John prompts.

"The ability to withstand pain. Both Fiona and I have an extraordinarily high pain tolerance and rapid healing."

I frown skeptically, thinking of the state we found them in. They weren't healing at all. "Are you sure?" I ask doubtfully.

"Our powers became clear when she and I survived the accident that killed our parents. We were sent to live with our grandparents. Our grandpas were always very careful to have us regularly checked over by a doctor since we would hurt ourselves and not even notice, but when they died, things changed. Grandmother didn't pay us much attention and left us alone frequently—that is, until she discovered we were a good way of taking out her frustrations. Vivian has an uncontrollable temper. Usually she would just break things, but one day, Fiona jumped up to stop her from breaking a photo of our grandpas, and Vivian hit her instead. When Fiona didn't even flinch, that was the ultimate challenge to our grandma, and she used her as her punching bag."

I gape at him, shocked at his words, and I can tell the grandpas are equally as stunned.

"You're probably wondering why I didn't stop her," he says. "We were only thirteen at the time, and I hadn't had my growth spurt, not to mention the ability to discern a lie is not Vivian's only power. She has many that she doesn't show people, and one of them is the ability to hold someone frozen in stasis."

You could hear a pin drop in the silent room.

"She would immobilize us until she worked through whatever was angering her then release us and leave us to heal. Our power to heal is slow, but we were able to recover from all the damage. If you hadn't found us, we would have eventually healed. It isn't the first time she beat us as badly as that."

"What were you doing at the sanctuary?" Eric asks, but before Phillip can answer, a moan from the other bed has us turning to look at Fiona.

She's so pale, she's almost translucent, but she manages to open her eyes, and she glares at her brother. "What are you doing?" she mutters, her voice rough from disuse.

"I'm telling them the truth. She tried to kill us this time, and I'm not willing to die for the wicked she beast. None of the things she told us will come true. She's delusional, and I won't let her drag us down with her. You know she will."

She runs a finger over the now closed gash that probably would have scarred her face if I hadn't interfered. She meets my gaze when she finds only smooth skin.

"Thank you," she tells me, and I can see in her eyes that she means it. "Can someone help me sit up? I want to face my humiliation head-on."

William gives her a hand, stuffing another pillow

behind her back, and I pass her a glass of water, which she quickly chugs.

She waves a hand at her brother, gesturing for him to continue his story, so we turn our attention back to him, but I keep an eye on her. I want to see her reactions too. I reach out with my warlock powers, trying to get a feel for both of them. They could be excellent liars, but surprisingly, all I feel is humiliation and regret.

"We were at the sanctuary because we know we fucked up with Htaed. We wanted to make it up to you, so we were working on a new act with the mini steggies. Vivian tracked us down to make demands, and when we refused, she beat us then released Htaed. I'm pretty sure she meant for him to kill us, but I don't know if he got bored after taking a swipe at us, or if we managed to drive him off, but he lost interest and started in on the steggies. Vivian had left by then. I'm sure she thinks we're dead," Phillip says flatly.

"What did she want you to do?" I press, and it's Fiona who answers.

"She's been obsessed with some object for years, claims that you guys guard the legendary orb of power and commanded us to find it. It's why she pushed for us to be in the circus to begin with. She wanted us to find it. For a while, we were able to put her off. We told her we needed to establish trust, but she started to lose patience, so we had to make some effort to look like we were searching for it. It's why we freed Viggy on Earth. She has contacts there, and they reported it to her. We told her we were able to search the ship while everyone was distracted with that."

"It's also why we helped the warlock and Vilaxian bitches release Saxon from stasis. We are sorry for that, by the way." She looks at me, and I'm surprised to see she means it.

"What was the mean act about then? I got the distinct impression you didn't like me."

Fiona rolls her eyes. "Vivian had spies aboard the ship who reported to her. We needed to make it look like we were actively working against you since that was her goal. If we couldn't find the orb, then we were supposed to get rid of you so the Adams brothers had no choice but to hand the circus over to us."

I gape at her, my mind blown by everything the two of them are telling us.

"She's evil, Lila. No compassion or empathy exists inside her whatsoever. She puts on a good show in public, but in private, the monster she is shows through." Phillip looks as broken as his sister does, and I can't help but feel sorry for them. It could easily have been me if I had been placed with the wrong foster family.

"Well, you don't ever have to return to her. As far as she knows, you perished in that supposed dino attack. We can make an announcement of the sort and then give you new lives if you want." William is in planning mode. "Alina and Marcus's house is still available on Earth. It would be good to have another family member on the planet to help with alien management and to run the safe house again, especially now that Aura is no longer there.”

“I think they want to return if we deal with Agent Smith. Susie said as much,” I tell him, and he nods.

“That would be great. Aura would be on the West Coast, and your parents’ place was in Connecticut, so we’d have people on either side of the continent.”

The twins exchange a glance. I wonder if they have some kind of twin telepathy, because it seems to drag on forever before Fiona nods. “I think we’d like that, but I would like to request a change of identity. I don’t want grandma to be able to find us.”

A growl rumbles deep in Eric’s chest. “Trust me, that will not be a problem, but we can arrange new identities for you with our Earth lawyers. You just let us know what names you would like to use.”

“We had no idea Vivian was like that. Why didn’t you ever come to us?” John looks at the twins with anguish in his eyes. “We would have helped you.”

Phillip shrugs. “Trust is not something that comes easily to us for obvious reasons. The person who was supposed to love and care for us turned us into their punching bag. We think she actually had our grandfathers murdered once Liliana disappeared, paving the way for her to coax you three into a bonding with her. She was obsessed with the circus and certainly didn’t mourn them in private, even if she put on a good show in public.”

“Well, we know she had a hand in what happened to Lili, and she will pay for her treachery, but it’s probably a good thing you both went along with her plans. I don't think she would have hesitated to get rid of you either," William tells them.

"Do you think she killed your parents too?" I ask and have a sudden shocking thought. "Do you think she had anything to do with the deaths of my parents?" Again, you could hear a pin drop as the room descends into sudden stunned silence.

Another rumble erupts from Eric's chest, one worthy of a dragon. "I'll kill her myself." He puts his hands together and cracks his knuckles.

"I don't know about your parents, but maybe, since you were supposed to die too. She was livid when we told her you had been found. I'm just glad we were nowhere near her, because I'm not sure we would have survived that temper tantrum." Fiona grimaces at that thought before she continues, her despair clear. "But I don't think she had anything to do with our parents' deaths. It was a random car accident. A drunk driver slammed into our car, killing them instantly. Phillip and I survived because of our gifts, but it was close. We were in the hospital for weeks afterwards, our grandpas barely leaving our sides until they could bring us home."

The pang of sympathy that rolls through me is almost crippling. All the animosity I felt toward them is gone in light of their story. I don't blame them in the least for protecting themselves, and I forgive them for everything. I just hope we can move forward and create a solid family bond, because there is no way I'm going to let them go back to being treated like that. "I'm so sorry you've had to live with this for so long, but I promise we will make sure you never have to again." All three of my grandpas nod, murmuring their agreement.

The relief radiating from Phillip and Fiona is staggering, and my warlock powers pulse inside me, begging me to absorb such strong emotions, but I remember Xavier's rules. Consent is always necessary, so I clench my jaw and don't absorb it from them. "You should both rest a little longer. The ship isn't leaving until tomorrow. Is there anything you need us to retrieve for you? I can send Xavier to your place to get it so you don't have to chance running into Vivian."

They exchange a glance. "It would be nice if we could go get our things," Fiona says, and I look at my grandpas.

"Can we create a diversion to make sure she isn't home so they can do it?"

They exchange one of their mysterious glances, and I can practically feel them using telepathy to communicate, even if I can't hear them. William turns his gaze to me and stares—I know he's thinking and not trying to see through me—before nodding.

"Actually, I think we have just the thing. I need to speak to Brannock about it first, but I will let you know," William says secretively, and I frown but refrain from questioning them. They'll tell me what they are planning when they are good and ready and not a second before.

"Then I'll speak to Xavier as soon as he returns. You two stay in bed until he does. You're healed, but it won't hurt to get some sleep and a good meal. I'll bring something up to you in a little while." I turn to leave, but before I can get very far, Phillip's hand shoots, out and he grabs my wrist. I look down at it before meeting his eyes.

"Thank you, Lila. We don't deserve it, but I hope you can forgive us for our treatment of you." I feel all kinds of awkward but pat his hand before removing it from my wrist.

"It's fine. I could have been in the same kind of situation if I hadn't been placed with kind families."

He leans back, and his eyelids flutter closed, his exhaustion weighing him down. I move out from between the beds, and Fiona's eyes follow me the whole way. When I get to the doorway, I turn to look at her. She mouths, "Thank you," before she also closes her eyes. I sigh and make my way out of the room, my grandpas trailing behind.

I lean against the wall outside their room, closing my eyes as I ponder another problem that has been added to our shoulders.

"Lila?" The voice has me cracking one eye open to find Zeydan looking at me from the doorway of my grandmother's room. "Are you okay?" he asks, but he obviously knows the answer, because I see sympathy in his eyes. I shake my head but push off the wall and walk toward him.

"No, but I will be." He opens his arms, and I walk straight into them and sag against him. He holds me tightly, and I feel a small amount of my worries ease just from his touch.

"Lilessa... Sorry, Liliana would like to see you now," he says quietly, and just like that, all my nerves come back to me with a vengeance, and my body stiffens as I pull away from him.

I nod and brace myself for the next emotional kick in the teeth. "Lead the way."

CHAPTER FOUR

Zeydan

My mate stiffens in my arms and pulls away. I would love to spirit her away and hide her from all her problems. My planet would be the perfect place to hide, but that's not going to happen anytime soon. I've lived away from company for a long time, and it is taking me a little bit of effort to adjust to all that my life has become. I yearn for when life was simple, but I was hiding, not wanting to face the fact that all is not right in the galaxy and the planets my brothers and sisters crafted with such love. Even when they forgot about their creators, we still watched over them despite being limited in power. I feel like we're on the verge of something big, and this is exactly where I need to be for now.

After my conversation with my sister, I'm even more sure of this. When Lilessa told me her story, the fury I felt was all encompassing. Being betrayed by one of our own is a kick in the gut I never saw coming, but my anger is not the focus at the moment. I shove it down and move out of the way to allow my mate to enter the room and meet her grandmother for the first time. I need to put aside my own emotions so I can support my mate while she copes with her own. I can feel how fragile she is at the moment, despite the brave face she wears.

"We're going to leave you to it. We heard her story, and I think she would like to tell you it herself," John says to Lila as she pauses to see if they are coming.

"Yes, I need to make a call or two and get Brannock back here to make a plan to deal with Vivian," William says.

"Are we going to kill her?" Eric asks, and I frown.

"Despite our lack of power, killing her will not be easy," I tell them, and Lila frowns, her confusion evident. "Even if you succeed, she will eventually reincarnate."

"Not if I have anything to do with it," a steely voice calls from inside the room, and Lila and I turn to face the owner of that voice. "Come closer so I can see you," my sister calls to my mate. The Adams brothers send her away with encouraging nods, and I follow my mate into the room, closing the door behind us.

My soul sister is reclined on the bed, looking paler than I remember, and there's a certain fragility about her that shocked me to the core. I may be half the deity I used to be, but she barely has a spark of her previous power. She smiles that same serene gentle smile that I remember, though, as her eyes roam over my gorgeous mate, taking in everything.

"Come closer, sweetheart, I don't bite. We were just discussing the possible whereabouts of our brothers and sister. We are going to need them if we are going to get our powers back." She pats the bed next to her when Lila hesitates. I watch as my mate steels her spine and goes over to the bed, lowering herself into the spot my sister pointed out. "Look at you, you're just as gorgeous as your mother." She looks between the two of us and rolls her eyes.

"For god's sake, Z, sit down and stop hovering. We're both big girls and will be fine. She might not remember me, but we were very good friends once upon a time."

I huff at my sister's attitude but do as she says and take the seat I previously sat in, pressing my knee to my mate's in silent support as my sister continues talking, reaching for Lila's hand and taking it in hers.

"Imagine my surprise when I finally woke up and found my soul brother patiently waiting for me to wake with my own mates." She doesn't peel her eyes away from her granddaughter, and Lila squirms under her scrutiny. A small grin kicks her lips up, and her eyes sparkle. "Still can't sit still, I see. Now forgive me, but my story is a long and tedious one, so I hope you don't have somewhere you need to be."

Lila shakes her head. "No, Gigi, I don't." That

small grin on my sister's face turns into a blinding smile, and her eyes glitter with unshed tears.

"You remember?" she asks, and Lila shrugs.

"A little. I remember calling you Gigi, and mostly, I remember feeling loved and safe with you. My memories are so foggy from that time. Xavier's parents said they may eventually return but not to force it. Every now and then, I get snippets of a feeling, but that's it, nothing substantial."

My sister's blinding smile drops, and I can't help feeling sorry for her. "Your parents?" she asks, and Lila shrugs like it's not a big deal, but I know that isn't how she feels.

"Same."

Liliana sighs and nods decisively. "Well, I guess I should start at the very beginning, and eventually, we will get to your parents. Does that sound okay?" Lila nods, and Liliana's brows dip into a frown.

"My story starts a short time before the war between the Una's and Aza'axians. You know about that, right?"

Lila nods. "Yes. Over the orb of power of which the Galaxy Circus now guards."

Liliana's eyes turn a little unfocused, like she's remembering a time long past, and nods. "Yes. I believe fate had a hand in the Adams' ancestors becoming the guardians of the orb and your grandfathers being my mates, but that happens a little later in the narrative. When my brothers and sisters created the galaxy, we were worshiped, as was our right. We created planets and filled them with life, both sentient and non-sentient. We spent time on each of the planets, gifting our worshipers with good fortune and luck as well as granting favors and basically being benevolent benefactors. Each of us was a master of our domain—life, death, water, fire, air, and earth."

She gestures to me, acknowledging my element. I think back to that time and remember I was happy, but nothing like I am now. Something was always missing in my life, and now that I have met my mate, I know it was her. My happiness then was but a small meteor in the sky compared to what I now feel.

"We were happy, or so I thought, but I was wrong, and I paid for it dearly, as did my elemental brothers and sister because one of us was far from happy."

"Vivax," I growl, and Liliana nods.

"Yes, our sister of death. Death brings sadness, but without it, there can be no renewal, and it's an integral part of the circle of life, but Vivax came to resent her powers. She created life, but instead of nurturing her creations, she frightened them, and they came to fear her. Instead of changing her ways, she reveled in that fear, and her creations became more and more terrible. She started avoiding spending any time with us and always had excuses why when we asked her to. The final straw was when she created a race capable of subjugating others and feeding from their turmoil and pain. We decided to have an intervention. Although we didn't like to interfere with one another's creations, she had gone a little too far. That race was wicked, and I had a vision of them spreading throughout the universe, destroying everything we worked hard to create. The remaining five of us believed we could convince her to unmake them," Liliana says wryly, and I roll my eyes and snort.

"Boy, were we delusional."

My sister nods, her mood becoming somber. "Yes, we were, because by then, Vivax resented us immensely and had been making plans to get her revenge as she desired. She flat out refused to unmake her creations, and none of us could do it because we didn't have a hand in creating them."

"Revenge against what?" Lila asks, sounding confused, and I don't blame her. We hadn't actually done anything to Vivax, but in her paranoia and impending madness, she believed she was a victim. Even though we were not responsible for her creation or her powers, she decided to hold it against us.

Liliana shrugs her shoulders. "Something she supposed we had done to her. She blamed us for her having death magic, which is ridiculous since none of us know where or how we came to be, we just were, but she claims we stole all the 'good magic.'" Liliana makes quotation marks with her fingers.

I huffed at the sheer ridiculousness of her accusations then just as I do now. She was like a small child having a temper tantrum when we confronted her, but little did we know, she had spent some of the time she was avoiding us crafting a plan that blindsided us all.

"We appealed to our creators, praying day and night for some guidance, and Sanshia

was gifted a vision that said if we combined our powers, we could unmake that race. So that's what we did, but it backfired on us. When we went to the planet to unmake it and its creations, Vivax was waiting. She stood aside without an argument, and that's when I should have known it was a trick, but we thought our sister was finally coming to her senses. When we started channeling our power into the core of the planet, Vivax redirected our powers into a crystal that none of us had ever seen before. It was capable of absorbing and storing power, and we could feel it stealing everything from us—not just draining us, but actually stealing it completely."

Lila is listening with rapt attention, and her mouth rounds in awe as Liliana continues her story.

"When Lilessa realized what was happening, she was able to cut us four elementals off and banish us, sending us far away from the planet, her power always being slightly greater than ours as the goddess of life," I chime in, remembering finding myself flying through the vast expanse of space, confused and alone. "When I finally came to my senses and returned to the planet, I couldn't find her or Vivax. There was a huge crater a mile wide where we had stood. When my brothers and sister also returned, we searched for days, but there was no sign of either of them."

Lilessa nods, and a tear trickles down her cheek, but I don't even think she notices because she's so wrapped up in remembering what happened. Lila reaches for her hand again and gives it a squeeze.

"What happened?" she prompts, and Liliana startles before wiping away that tear.

"When I managed to release the others from the pull of the crystal, I cast a spell to entrap Vivax in her own treachery, hoping if she was trapped as well, then she would end it, and all of our power would return to us, but that isn't what happened. Once she was ensnared, she was drained as well. I was horrified. Both of us were going to die, completely drained of our power."

Lila gasps, her eyes wide as she leans forward ever so slightly, completely absorbed in the tale.

"Vivax fought, but it was too late. I knew we would reincarnate, but I had to ensure that the orb now full of our power didn't fall into the hands of the same race that we were trying to destroy, because that would have been a disaster. I summoned the most enlightened race I created, the Una's. They had the ability to become vapor and travel through space at great speeds. I entrusted them with the protection of the orb, making them promise to share the power that the crystal now contained with the universe, and I was confident they would. Their core makeup didn't contain avarice or lust for power. Vivax fought the whole time, going so far as to attack me with all her remaining death power, but our powers were never meant to be used against one another, and it was the final death blow. It backfired, and she exploded, the blast taking me with it because I had lost all of my own power and was incapable of shielding."

"But wouldn't the Una's have been destroyed as well?" Lila asks. She shakes her head.

"No, because they were able to travel as vapor, so they were unaffected by the destructive blast. I'm assuming they retrieved the orb once the crater we created cleared."

"Why didn't the orb get destroyed as well?" my mate asks, and I can tell she is dying to ask more questions and is barely restraining herself.

"Because it contained the full power of the goddesses of life and death as well as half the power of the four elemental gods. It is indestructible, which is why it had to be guarded."

"That's why the Una's couldn't destroy it and had to pass its care on to the Adams family at the end of the war when their race was decimated," I add, and Lilessa nods.

"Yes. The war was a miscalculation on my behalf. I had no idea that would happen, and my heart weeps for the Una's. Maybe once I have my power back, I can help repopulate their planet. They were a favorite creation of mine, so gentle and unassuming, and it's why they ended up decimated—they weren't built for war."

"So what happened to you? Did you reincarnate? How did you come to be my grandmother?" Lila stands up and paces across the carpet, all of her questions bubbling to the surface. I get up to soothe her, but Lilessa waves me down and watches her grand-daughter pace. "Is Vivian actually Vivax?" She spins around, her hand on her hips, and I can't stand it anymore, so I reach out and drag her into my lap, nuzzling at her neck to calm her with my touch. She sighs and sinks into me, and I feel smug satisfaction. Despite our one-sided bond, I can still help balance her emotions.

My sister beams at the two of us. "You two are so cute," she murmurs before the joy in her eyes fades and she answers Lila's question.

"Yes, Vivian is Vivax, and she is the person who trapped me in that box." She pauses and reaches for a glass of water on the side table. Lila jumps up and passes it to her, and Liliana takes a sip through the straw. I can tell she's starting to struggle, but I know she's determined to tell Lila everything, so I keep my mouth shut. Lila doesn't sit back down, instead wandering around the room. Her nervous energy would be endearing if the situation wasn't so serious. Eventually, she just leans against the wall and focuses on Liliana again.

"This was not the first time we died during our existence. All of us have a time or two," she tells Lila, and I chuckle. During times of boredom, we often dared each other to do crazy things, knowing we would always reincarnate. "But it was the first time that we didn't have any knowledge of our former lives when we reincarnated, and we were babies instead of fully formed beings like in the past. Vivian and I were born as twins to a Skarrian family, and neither of us retained any of our former knowledge. Fate must have played a hand in my life though. Your grandpas courted me, and we mated, and until I was captured and tortured, I didn't know any different."

"But Vivian did?" Lila asks, and Liliana shakes her head.

"Not to start with, I don't think. We were never super close, since she always considered me competition. She wanted the Adams brothers for herself, and when they started courting me, she became jealous, and we grew even further apart. But then she met her mates, and I thought she had gotten over her issues. We spent time together with our families. We were both pregnant, me with Marcus and her with Mitchell, Fiona and Phillip's father. Things were good, but as the boys grew up, we saw less and less of them. We were, of course, traveling with the circus, and when we were back on Skarr, we saw Mitchell and his fathers, but Vivian was always busy. She was sitting on the Skarrian council in our family seat. Technically, it was my seat, as I am the oldest, but with my commitments to the circus, it was easy enough to let her take it. It made her less resentful as well, or so I hoped, and to start with, it worked, but she kept asking me weird questions—questions I didn't think anything of because they never really made sense at the time. Every time I returned to Skarr, she asked if I had new powers or remembered anything from our past, wanting to know if the circus was a front for something else."

"She remembered?" Lila slides down the wall and pulls her legs up against her chest, wrapping her arms around them and resting her chin on her knees.

"Yes, and I still had no clue. I demanded to know what all the questions were about. By this time, she had custody of Phillip and Fiona. They are three years older than you, Lila, so they would have been about seven. Mitchell and his wife were killed in a car accident, and I wasn't able to make it back to Skarr for the funeral. Vivian decided she was going to bring the children to visit Earth and that it would be a good distraction for them all, so instead of traveling to Earth with the pod, I waited and was going to teleport down with them when they arrived."

"But that obviously didn't happen," Lila remarks, and my sister shakes her head.

"No. When I met her shuttle, she was the only one on board. She hit me with a stun gun and kidnapped me. I'm not sure where we went, but I was kept in a cell. When I demanded to know what she was doing, she told me everything. I didn't believe her at first, I thought she had a mental breakdown, but then she started torturing me, which eventually triggered my memories to return and activated my immortality again. She would hurt me, and I would heal, but I refused to tell her what happened to the orb. Hell, I didn't know what happened to it then. All I knew was that it was in the hands of the Una's when we died that day, so of course I wasn't any help to her, but she couldn't let me go because I knew she was after the orb now. She wanted her powers back and was going to keep mine and our fellow gods' powers as well..." Liliana trails off, and I can see the toll this is taking on her, so I pick up where she left off.

"She orchestrated your parents' death then offed her own husbands because, by then, she heard rumors of the Una's meeting with someone on Skarr, and they were pointing to the Adams family and Galaxy Circus. She was going to convince the Adams brothers to take her as their new mate, and then she would have free rein of the circus to find the orb. When that didn't work, she started the Syndicate and planted people within the circus, including the twins. She thought that getting rid of Alina, Marcus, and you would make the twins the next heirs. She wasn't aware that the protection of the orb is tied to the Adams' blood, but she hadn't counted on you surviving. When she found out, she was furious. Her plan had to be paused until you surfaced and she could get rid of you again."

"But you proved to be more powerful than she expected, though I am not surprised. You carry the genes of a god, so you were always destined to be more powerful, and to have such a large and powerful mating circle to protect you hindered her at every step."

"Why put you in stasis?" Lila asks, and Liliana shrugs.

"She was worried that if I got close to the orb myself, then I could take my powers out of the orb and leave hers trapped—or keep hers for myself." She scoffs like it's ridiculous. "Like I want more powers. I would have been happy for her to keep hers, but I know that sentiment wasn't returned."

"So when and why did you finally admit the circus and the Adams had the orb?" Lila asks, and Liliana closes her eyes, but before she does, I can see the uncertainty in her gaze. I had a feeling she was hiding something, and this just confirms it.

She swallows and takes a breath, and when her eyes open, there's no sign of any turmoil. "Vivian and Agent Smith of the Earth facility Area 51 became allies. I'm not entirely certain how, but she told me about his special project."

When I heard about this, I felt ill, and I was ready to track this man down and flay his skin from his body, but the Adams brothers told me they have plans for him.

"Special project..." Lila sits up and looks more alert. "I wonder if that was what was behind the door we couldn't access," she mutters to herself, and Liliana nods.

"Agent Smith has been detaining aliens and has a breeding project. He's trying to breed his own army to be able to take over the world. They threatened to start killing the children and add you to their program. They said you had no powers and were completely helpless. I'd already lost so much, and I knew there wasn't much chance for me to be released, but I also didn't want your grandpas to suffer again. Losing me and then your parents would have been hard enough to come back from, but losing you on top of that would have broken them…"

Lila nods her agreement. "Yes, I think you're right. When John was ill, I was so worried about them."

"You can't let her get her hands on the orb."

"But how are we going to stop her?" Lila asks, and my sister and I exchange a glance.

"We're going to return everyone's powers to them. We just need to track down our other sister and brothers," I explain, and Lila frowns.

"Even Vivian's powers? And how, exactly, do you plan to find your other siblings? They've managed to stay hidden for hundreds of years."

Liliana shakes her head. "No, Vivian's not trustworthy. We would be stupid to put faith in her again, but our siblings' powers can't stay trapped in the orb either."

"So what are we going to do with them? Can someone else become the god of death?" Lila asks.

Liliana nods. "Yes, it should be possible for someone of the same bloodline."

"So Phillip or Fiona?" Lila asks, frowning. "I'm not sure they would want to do that. They seemed pretty keen to start new lives on Earth."

"Yes, possibly, but being one quarter divine may not be enough. You could do it, Lila," Liliana says, and I feel helpless as Lila turns pale. I had much the same reaction, but when I argued with Liliana, she pointed out that we didn't have much of a choice unless we wanted Vivian to take her powers back.

"Fuck no," Lila says, shaking her head vehemently. "There has to be another option."

"There isn't. You're the only one left with the bloodline after the deaths of your father and theirs," Liliana replies, tears welling in her eyes. "I'm so sorry, my sweet girl. I would take them if I could, but I can't be both the goddess of life and death."

CHAPTER FIVE

Brannock

We leave Lila at the Adams' family home and split up in the morning. We know she needs time with her grandparents without any interference from any of us, so we use the old divide and conquer creed to finish up all the jobs that need to be done before the ship leaves Skarr tomorrow.

Link and Xavier spent the night looking after the twins and making sure Liliana was okay when she first woke. Now, after a nap, they are returning to the ship to finish welcoming the rest of the crew and performers. Nikos, Echo, Maxsim, and Caspian are spending the day purchasing play equipment and supplies to create a kid friendly environment, as well as buying school supplies Link requested. The Adams have made it known that the ship will now be family friendly, and crew and performers with families are welcome to bring them aboard if they wish. Kinga and Andre are in charge of keeping the children occupied. I do not envy them that job in the least. The three kraken babies are taking a little time to get used to being separated from their parents, while the two merbabies aren't as concerned, not having the undivided attention from all of their parents for months on end. When they asked if I would like to join them, I quickly came up with a random excuse as to why I couldn't. I love our babies, but they are exhausting.

Ghosie is finishing up the auditions with Susie and Magenta's help, leaving Silac, Tirrian, Saxon, and myself to make plans to rescue Chloe once we get back to Earth. Saxon and I take point, as we are both familiar with the layout of Area 51.

"Chloe is being kept in a different area than the containment cells the Adams usually collect detainees from," I tell him as he brings up a map of the facility in the war room of the big ship. This is the best place for us to plan because there is enough room for us, as well as all the information we need with the touch of a button. I frown as I study the schematics of the facility and jab my finger at it.

"This is missing a whole wing. Obviously Smith is hiding this from you. There is a door here" —I point to where it should be— "and there is a whole wing of cells that are more like living quarters. The beings kept there are used as breeding experiments. Smith is hoping to breed his own army of aliens to do his bidding." The room is silent, and I look up and see the four of them gaping at me with wide-mouthed shock.

"Seriously? And you didn't think to tell us this before?" Tirrian growls, smoke drifting out of his nose.

I shrug my shoulders. "It hasn't been relevant until now. There was nothing we could do about it until we prepared to go back to Earth. The Adams were not going to detour from their goals of fixing John and then retrieving their wife from stasis," I say blandly, not feeling guilty in the least. My own child is being held captive, and I still knew it wasn't going to make a difference to them. I do understand though, because I would have felt the same way in their place. After all, as far as they knew, I was a detainee who had committed a crime.

The dragon continues to growl at me, and I lose my shit, slamming my hands down on the table and glaring at him, my spines bristling with my mood.

"Don't forget that my daughter is locked behind those walls. They want to breed her. Believe me when I tell you this has been harder on me than anyone else."

Tirrian closes his eyes and takes a deep breath before opening them and giving me a nod. "Yes, you're right. I'm sorry. Please forgive me, my friend. The thought of forced breeding is a trigger for my dragon for some reason."

"It's a trigger for all of us." Silac shudders. "Heck, I can relate. Being forced to marry Kinga was the same kind of violation. Thank fuck for Lila." He grabs a pen and draws on the tablet on the table, adding the wing to the diagram and labeling it, as well as circling the access door.

"Okay, so we need to get through that door. It shouldn't be a problem. Xavier should be able to teleport us all in there, but it might be a moot point. Once we take over the facility and round everyone up, we can just force Smith to let us in and free the captives." Saxon shrugs like it's no big deal, and normally, he would be right.

I shake my head. "Smith has a failsafe on that wing. The second he expects an incursion, he will press a button, releasing a toxic agent which will kill everything inside that wing of the facility. If he can't have them, no one can."

"He's going to suspect something the minute we return earlier than planned, isn't he?" Tirrian looks to me for confirmation, and I nod.

"I would guess so. There is no reason for us to return to Vegas since you already did those performances. If the circus was going to resume its tour, it would be in Asia."

"Okay, so we need to provide a decoy for him. We will need to set up to perform in Singapore while the rest of us plan a sneak attack on the base," Silac suggests.

"Smith will still be on high alert. It doesn't make sense for you to return too quickly, and he will be suspicious and quick to pull the trigger," I warn them, my panic about my daughter's safety making me anxious.

"Hey, easy, man." Silac grabs my shoulder and gives it a squeeze. "We have the warlock. There is nothing Smith can do to us that Xavier can't counter. He is only human."

Before I can reply, the door to the war room opens, and the Adams brothers enter. "What are you doing here?" Saxon asks in surprise. "We thought you would be doing the family bonding thing this morning."

William claps Saxon on the shoulder as John and Eric take a seat at the large conference table, looking at the schematic we have displayed. "Liliana asked to speak to Lila alone. We wanted to talk to Brannock about something." He looks at me, and I feel my eyebrows jump in surprise.

"Oh?" I ask, curious about what they want.

"Before we get into that, what's going on here?" Eric gestures at the schematics before rubbing his hands together gleefully. "Are we planning the attack on Smith?"

"Yes. We are just trying to work out the logistics." I explain what I just told the others, and the brothers exchange one of those glances that I know drives Lila mad. I'm almost certain the three of them can speak telepathically.

"We may have a solution to that problem. We now know that Agent Smith is a member of the Syndicate," William announces, and some of the things I overheard him say finally makes sense.

I nod. "Yes, I can see that. Recently, he became even more smug and gleeful, and he bragged about having some very good friends in very high places. He said it would allow him to become a very important man on Earth."

"Agent Smith is the reason our wife gave up the location of the orb," John states before the three of them tell us their wife's tale. I know I'm not the only one of us who is stunned with the information. "She said that Vivax told her about all the aliens he is holding for his breeding experiments and that they would start executing them one by one starting with the children unless she told them where they were. They also said they would take Lila because she was powerless and add her to the rotation."

My mouth drops open in horrified shock at the thought of them killing my daughter.

"Liliana caved, not willing to risk that they would go through with the threat. She decided that we would be able to protect it, even if the Syndicate knew, especially with all the powerful people aboard the ship," John explains, waving his hands around in agitation.

"Although she had no memory of why, she was the one who organized to have the powerful children of the ruling families of Westalin, Aquilia, Vilax, and Fluxx on our ship. She said she had a vision. Although she was drained of her goddess abilities and reincarnated as a Skarrian, one of her gifts was occasional visions. She thinks it was her powers trying to return to her, especially because she was so close to the orb for so long." William is looking at the blueprints of the base where Silac added the new wing to the drawings. "What's this?"

I share the information with them, and Eric slams his hands down on the conference table much like I just did. "We need to kill that rat."

"We were just saying we need to find a way to get him out of the office, but he barely ever leaves," Tirrian says, and William smirks.

"What if he is summoned to a Syndicate meeting in space?"

"Huh?" Silac sounds confused, but Saxon's eyes widen, and he nods his head before turning to me.

"You still have that communication device we confiscated from the Madovian?" he asks me, and I nod.

"Yeah, I continue to send false reports. No one knows she didn't survive. I keep telling them I'm lying low until the circus is recalled."

John rubs his hands together with glee. "Good. It's time to send a message saying you have been recalled and are rejoining the circus. Say you have a lead on where the orb is being kept after your nest mate used her powers of persuasion on Dylan."

"Then a few days later, you are going to message them and say you found the orb and arrange a meeting, telling the Syndicate you want more money or something. The Madovians are a greedy and mercenary race, so it won't be out of the ordinary."

"But then what?" Tirrian asks, smoke drifting out of his nose as his wings rustle restlessly against his back.

"Then the Syndicate will gather to squabble over the orb, getting them in one place, and we can take them all out in one fell swoop and rescue all of the detained aliens in Area 51." My heart starts to race with excitement. This plan could actually work, and we won't have to risk anyone's lives.

"And let me guess, you're going to let Lila change into her Madovian form to spring the trap." Tirrian crosses his arms and glares at us.

"She wouldn't want it any other way." Saxon tries to placate him, and Tirrian growls.

"Of course she wouldn't, but it doesn't mean I have to like it."

"We will send a couple of you with her. She can parade you around on leashes. You know how Madovians like to do that. Xavier can glamour you to look different, but they won't even blink at her having a man or two by her side," William suggests.

"Probably you and Silac. Both of you are reptiles and ideal breeders for a Madovian," Eric points out sneakily, and it has the desired effect. We all watch as Tirrian visibly relaxes and the smoke stops pouring out of his nose.

"How are we going to manage both incursions at the same time though? I doubt Lila will want to miss the one on Earth, and I'm certainly not going to. The circus pod is the only one that can land on Earth. If anything else tries, it will get shot out of the sky," I point out, voicing a possible problem.

"That can't be true though. Aura got those Jelliads onto Earth somehow," Eric replies, and William sighs.

"I suspect they teleported them down, which isn't beyond the realm of possibility from a cloaked ship in space. We will use the big ship to do the same thing, but we need to start the setup process so if there are any spies that manage to slip through the cracks, they will think it's just a circus show as normal."

"If we don't teleport directly to the base's landing platform, they won't even know we are there," Saxon says, but I shake my head.

"They have infrared sensors covering the outside of the base, and all the cameras inside have that capability," I warn them, but Tirrian just smirks.

"I'm pretty sure our warlock can take care of all those things."

"That's true. Smith has never managed to capture one despite trying to. He desperately wanted to keep Xane, but he knew that would probably be an error in judgment. What about Smith? How are we going to get him to leave the base?"

"I suspect he has a way. Liliana said that he and Vivian struck a deal when he gave up the information on the alien children, which allowed him to attend the Syndicate meetings in person. She said Vivian was furious, and that he's a disgusting slug of a male and she would kill him if she could, but he actually has something she wants." John takes a seat at the table. The three Adams men are restless and have been standing this whole time, ready to get some revenge on behalf of their wife.

"Did Liliana say what that was?"

Eric shakes his head and drags his hands through his long hair in agitation. "No, but she was simultaneously pissed and smug about it. I can't wait until we can take care of her."

"And how are we going to do that?" I ask him, and they exchange another one of those maddening looks.

"It won't be easy, but Liliana knows a way," John says vaguely, and I feel a prickle of anxiety.

"First you need to deal with Area 51, and then you can use a shuttle and rendezvous with us at the location of the Syndicate meeting. We will go ahead and scout for the best place," William instructs, and Saxon's eyebrows jump.

"Aren't you coming to Earth with us?" he asks, and the men shake their heads.

"No. Congratulations, you all just became equal owners of Galaxy Circus. We are retiring." John sounds practically giddy with excitement while my mouth drops open in shock. Lila's other mates look just as surprised as I do.

"You're retiring?" Tirrian repeats, sounding bewildered.

Eric scoffs. "You didn't think we were going to waste any more time now that we have our wife back, did you? Heck, we're still young, and I want to spend the rest of our years enjoying life while not being in a constant state of worry. At least you guys will have it easy now that the orb of power is going to be dealt with."

William and John glare at Eric as he drops another bombshell. "Orb of power?" Ghosie asks.

"We haven't gotten that far with all of them yet," William tells his brother, who just casually waves him off.

"Pfft, it's not like they are going anywhere. Even Brannock, who hasn't completed the mating ritual, is in it for the long run. Anyone can see that." He turns his attention back to us. "Long story short, the Adams family ended up with the orb of power at the end of the war. The circus guards it, and Liliana, who was the goddess of life, is going to use it to get her powers back and deal with Vivian who was the goddess of death. We just need to track down the other elemental gods. I'm not sure how we are going to do that."

He drops that bombshell casually, and although I'm still in shock and I can see that Tirrian and Silac are too, Saxon doesn't look as surprised. I'm guessing he probably already knew about the orb. He has been mated to Lila almost from the beginning, so I'm sure it's already come up in conversation.

"That has to be why my father was so insistent that someone from our family needed to be in the circus and why so many royal families have offspring performing in the circus."

"Yes, Liliana was insistent many years ago that we needed to foster good relations with some of the bigger races. She claims she didn't know why at the time, just that she had a vision that insisted it happen. We think it was so Lila would have all the protection she needs against the Syndicate. Let's face it, no matter who the members are, none are going to be more powerful than the ones she has in her harem," John says, confirming what Link suspected.

"Okay, we will come up with a plan, discuss it with the rest of our family, and let you know. We have that one stop at Vilax that we can't avoid. Lila insists we go forward without anything hanging over our heads, and that is the last problem we need to deal with," Tirrian informs the three men.

"Yes, and then we'll head directly to Earth. I think Magenta would be the right person to put in charge of organizing the circus in Asia while we make our stealth attack on Area 51."

"No alien gets left behind, and you need to make it crystal clear to the authorities that they can't let this happen again. We will install one of our own at their base to coordinate with them. No more human liaisons," William says firmly, and we nod.

"Agreed. I actually have a friend who might be interested in the position—obviously not the one who sold me out. He will be dealt with while we're there, I'm almost certain he didn't get what he bargained for and ended up in captivity with a collar around his neck like I had. Another one of my teammates would be the perfect fit. He's as tough as nails but has the right kind of compassion and isn't judgmental, so he would judge a person by their actions, not their species."

"I think you need to coordinate with Aura once you get underway. They will want to take back the Pleasure Inn from the aliens Smith installed in there. Stay out of that, it's none of our business, and they can take care of that mess themselves. We have too much on our plate to get involved," Eric instructs.

"And with their combined powers, they should have no trouble overthrowing their enemies. They wouldn't have been able to even get that far if Mark and Susie hadn't been involved last time. Xane should have just fogged their minds and sent them on their way," William grumbles, and I cough uncomfortably.

"That was my fault. I had that collar on and had to do what Smith demanded. He threatened to unleash my berserker side if they didn't cooperate. They did what they had to in order to protect their clients and staff."

"Smith will go down, I promise. Let's see how brave he is when he's faced with a wrathful mate posing as a Madovian. I bet she eats him right up." Tirrian snickers, and Silac blanches.

"Let's hope that's all she does to him." The rest of the men wince at the thought of what Madovians like to do to men, but to be honest, that would be the perfect karma for a man hellbent on breeding his own army.

CHAPTER SIX

Lila

My grandmother's last words leave me shaken and distressed, and I feel tears well in my eyes as I shake my head. "But why me? Why can't you give it to Phillip or Fiona?"

"Oh, honey..." My grandmother tries to get out of bed, but she's still weak, and Zeydan jumps up to stop her. "Well then, you go and hug her," she snaps at him, almost making me smile as he rolls his eyes and resettles her before scooping me up. He returns to his chair and settles me in his lap, stroking my hair and whispering words of reassurance to me.

"But I'm only a quarter divine as well," I argue. "I'm no more divine than them." I feel Zeydan stiffen underneath me, and not in the fun way.

"Well, actually, you're a little more divine because

you're mates with Zeydan and now hold a small sliver of his divinity within you."

"I'm sorry," he whispers and presses a kiss to my hair as I mull over the bomb they just dropped on me.

"But between the two of them, they are like half divine. Can't you split the power between them?" I know my words are selfish. Phillip and Fiona would like to start over on Earth far away from the trauma that has been inflicted on them over the years, but I still voice it because hell, I don't want it either.

"Are you really sure they are in the right head space to be divine? After everything they experienced at the hands of their grandmother, maybe they might be a little twisted inside," my mate remarks as he continues to try and soothe my distress.

"I think about how Viggy always flinched from their attention. I know they said it was because they had to push their will to get him to respond, but I don't think it's just that. I think the cattle prods probably didn't help either. I guess it would take strong personalities to withstand the kind of treatment they have without letting it change them, and I really don't think Phillip and Fiona are all that strong. No, it would probably be better for them to be on Earth far away from any kind of divine power." I slump even further into Zeydan's arms, feeling completely defeated. "What will I have to do?"

My grandma shrugs. "You get the power to cause or stop death and all the creation power involved with being a divine being, although I'm almost certain you have some of that power. Zeydan told me you can use the powers of different forms without changing into that form. I think that comes from your divine power. It shouldn't be possible."

"Does that make me responsible for all the beings she created?" I ask, thinking about the Aaz'axians. I should be able to correct their curse. That makes me sit up, and I feel a little spike of excitement at the thought.

"I mean in theory, yes, but they survived these last seven hundred years without any interference from the divine creator."

"How come you didn't reincarnate immediately?" I ask, voicing the question that has been floating around in my mind.

My grandma smirks at me. "How old do you think your grandpas are?" she asks, and I shrug. I haven't really thought about it, but then I gasp.

"Don't tell me they are seven hundred years old?"

Zeydan chuckles, and his body shakes beneath me. "Stop teasing the girl," he scolds, and my grandma giggles like a schoolgirl.

"No, you're right, we aren't quite that old. I guess it took five hundred years for us to recover from the blast that killed us, and even then, our memories and past lives were forgotten. We were reborn on Skarr a little over two hundred years ago."

I gape at this information. I knew they were my grandpas, but I assumed they would be in their seventies, not in double centuries.

"Skarrians are a long-lived race. It's why our birth rate is so low. It's a trade-off to keep the population controlled. You can only give birth once every twenty to fifty years. The female has a fertile period, and during that time, she must have sex with all members of her mating circle to fertilize her egg. Mating circles will disappear for weeks at a time to make sure they conceive during that period, because it's a long wait between cycles, and it's heartbreaking if it doesn't take." Her eyes are sad, and I'm assuming since my father is their only child that she has experienced this disappointment before.

"Then how did I get knocked up with Cas's eggs? Then there is Nikos as well." I'm confused.

"Because they are a different species, it can be circumnavigated. The Skarrians who have other species in their mating circles tend to have more children than the ones that are pure Skarrian." She claps her hands together, and her eyes brighten. "I can't wait to meet all my great-grandbabies. The boys tell me I have five now. I just wish Marcus and Alina were here. They would be so excited to be grandparents."

A wave of sadness washes over me, and we're both quiet for a moment, lost in our thoughts. Zeydan just holds me, giving me comfort through his touch, but then Liliana shakes her head and claps her hands together, making me jump. "Okay, enough sadness. I am so happy for you both, but I noticed the bond is only one-sided. Lila, why didn't you claim Zeydan like he claimed you?" She cocks her head to the side inquisitively. It's almost animalistic, and I kind of blanch. Her stare is so intimidating. I can definitely see the divine inside her even if she only has a drop of her former powers.

"But, um, ah…" I stumble over my words, reluctant to mention we haven't fucked five times.

Her eyes sparkle, and she grins. "Ah, okay, but that is the Skarrian way. You don't need to do it like that. All you have to do is take a sliver of your own divine power and push it into him."

"Divine power?" I ask, still not sure what she means.

"Yes, that ball of power sitting deep inside your core. You may think it's your Skarrian power, but I can assure you, it's more than just that. At the moment of release, grab a pinch and thrust it into Zeydan, and you will be fully bonded in only the way a divine being can be. I plan on doing it to your grandpas as soon as I get my power back." I scrunch up my nose and shudder at the thought of them having sex, and she giggles again. Her laughter makes my heart soar, knowing the four of them have another chance at life. I understand now why they are choosing to retire.

"Go take care of that. I need to rest a little more, and I know the ship leaves tomorrow on a rescue mission to Earth. One of your mates has a child that needs their parent, and Smith needs to die. Another grandbaby to spoil, even if she isn't so small." Her eyes turn hazy, and she stares vacantly for a moment.

"Gigi..." I push out of Zeydan's arms, but he catches me before I can get far.

"Wait, she's having a vision. Don't disturb her." He doesn't haul me back to his lap, but he does hold my hand as he stands up as well.

It doesn't take her long to come back to us, but as her eyes clear, she nods decisively. "Yes, we have much to do before our lives can return to normal. Your mates will fill you in on everything else." She turns her attention to Zeydan. "One of our brothers is about to make a reappearance. Be kind to him, he has missed you as much as you missed him, and you have all suffered alone for too long. It is time for our family to reunite."

After those cryptic words, which we don't quiz her on, she settles down to rest a little longer as Zeydan and I make our way back to the main living area of the mansion. I'm all kinds of shaken up over everything I have learned and need a moment to process it all before I can even think about shoving some of my divinity into Zeydan.

I make myself coffee, and I feel his eyes on me although he remains silent while I run over everything in my brain. I bring my coffee over to the sofa and throw myself onto it, taking a sip of the hot beverage. "That was all... Wow, just wow. I'm kind of speechless," I mutter as Zeydan steps in front of me, his bushy tails fanning out behind him as he looks down at me with concern.

"I can imagine you're feeling a little overwhelmed," he says, and I scoff.

"You think? I don't know where to start or what to do to fix it all."

He crouches down and spreads my knees, pushing between them, his eyes locked on mine. "I think you need to let your mates help you. Don't take this burden on by yourself."

"Oh, I wasn't planning on it. It's too much for me to even contemplate keeping to myself. It's time for a family meeting."

"Also, your grandpas made it sound like they have an idea on how to deal with Smith and the Syndicate. We should probably talk to them."

I look around the room and groan as all the other things that need to be done before the ship can leave flood my mind. Before I can voice my worries, Xavier stumbles out of our wing, his hair in disarray and eyes watery with sleep. He's wearing a pair of sleep pants and nothing else, and my mouth waters at the sight of him, but I stuff that down. He grunts a greeting at us before heading directly to the coffee machine. My eyes widen with surprise as he pours a big mug and takes a sip. Xavier usually avoids coffee. He doesn't need the artificial stimulation because he gets that from absorbing emotions.

"Are you okay?" I ask him, and he screws up his nose, looking grumpy. "*Phoeall*, you are a loud projector, and the last hour has been quite uncomfortable, as everything you have been feeling has bombarded me."

I wince and open my mouth, but he just waves an

impatient hand. "Do not apologize for feeling all of those emotions. It was a lot for you to discover. It's my own fault. I was so tired, my normal shields slipped."

"Are you going to be okay?" I ask him, and he nods. "Yes, I need to feed. My stores are unusually low. When I heard your grandmother's story last night, I shielded the house. I didn't want Vivian returning and ambushing us while we were asleep or distracted."

Link appears before I can thank my warlock mate. He doesn't look quite as disheveled as Xavier, and he managed to dress himself. He's wearing his circus uniform and has brushed his hair. "Where is everyone?" he asks, giving me a kiss on the cheek before he, too, helps himself to the coffee. I think I've been a bad influence on my mates, since all of them seem to have picked up the habit.

"Finishing off all the jobs we have to do before the ship leaves tomorrow," Zeydan tells them. "We need to meet them up there this afternoon. All the performers should have arrived by then, and your grandpas are announcing their retirement and you taking over, and they want a full show of support to push down any dissenters," Zeydan explains, and my eyes widen. He and my grandpas are obviously making plans without me. I'm okay with that as long as they keep me in the loop and don't spring shit on me.

Xavier puts his coffee down on the table. "Sounds like we have a plan then, but if that isn't until this afternoon, then I can think of a good way to spend the next couple of hours." He beelines directly to me, tugs me to my feet, then throws me over his shoulder. My mug goes flying, as does the coffee in it, and a loud screech leaves my mouth.

"Xavier!" I scream, but the mug and coffee pause mid-flight, Zeydan having stopped the disaster. The coffee flows back into the cup, and the mug settles on the coffee table as Xavier strides toward my bedroom. "Are you two coming?" he asks. "I need a top up, and I can't think of a better way to do it."

I lift my head and see Link smirking at us. He gives me a little finger wave. "I'll take a rain check. I'm meeting Mark and Susie on the ship to give them a tour of the med bay and introduce them to the anatomy files of all the new species they will be seeing. Both of them have a lot of work to do."

"Wait." I smack Xavier's ass. "Just put me down for a moment." He pauses but doesn't lower me. "Are they really going to travel with us?"

Link nods. "Yes, it looks that way. I think they will probably travel back and forth from Celestia regularly. His parents aren't ready for him to disappear again now that they have finally found him, but they also understand he needs to spread his wings, so to speak."

"But what about Aura and their family?"

Link shrugs. "I'm not sure, Lila. You'll have to ask Susie about that. I didn't feel like I could pry since I only really just met them."

I huff out a little breath of air, and Xavier takes this as his cue to keep going. "Come on, god man. You can come play. I'll be as full as can be if you fuck her," Xavier calls over his shoulder, and I watch as Zeydan stands up and follows us at a slower pace. I would think he was reluctant, but the heat in his eyes says the opposite. Hopefully I can shove a bit of my own divinity into this man and lock him down tight.

CHAPTER SEVEN

Lila

In the bedroom, Xavier slides me down his body, and the two of us watch with awe as Zeydan joins us, stripping down, his naked chest on display, wearing only that skirt I so enjoy. Xavier makes a hissing sound, and when I drag my eyes away from Zeydan, I see my warlock's mouth is open with surprise.

"Sexy isn't, he?" I smirk at my warlock.

"Yeah," Xavier is slightly speechless which makes me giggle

Zeydan smirks and winks at the warlock before he scoops me up, laying a heated kiss on me.

I wrap my arms around his neck and my legs around his body as he walks over to my bed. He stops to throw me down, but I hang on.

"Wait," I say, sounding slightly breathless from the kiss. "Where is my divinity inside me? How do I feel it, take a piece, and shove it into you?" I ask him, and Xavier lets out a small whistle.

"I don't know what the two of you are talking about, but it sounds like a fun time," he comments as he slouches indolently into the chair in the corner of my room, his voyeur hat firmly on his head.

"Lila is a quarter deity, so she can bond with me like I bonded with her. She needs to find that well of godly power inside her and take a small piece then shove it into me."

"Godly power?" That get's Xavier attention, and Zeydan nods without looking away from me.

"Yes, Liliana thinks that is why Lila can access her forms' powers even if she isn't wearing the right one."

"Well, that makes sense. Oshan was insistent that she would splice herself if she even attempted that, but it seems to come to Lila without any trouble."

Zeydan focuses on me, and I feel his power expand and sink into me. I moan, because it feels all kinds of good, and I wriggle against him, but his hold on me tightens. "Focus, Lila," he instructs, and I attempt to do what he says. His power probes at something inside me that seems to swell. My body feels tight, and it throbs with electricity as he caresses it. "This is your divine power. It is quite substantial, way more than I expected." Zeydan sounds surprised, but it's all I can do to remain focused.

My nipples are tight, and my pussy is wet with need, and all I want to do is grind against him. I try to kiss him again, but he turns his head.

"Try to grab a piece of it," he tells me, and I groan but attempt to do what he says.

Closing my eyes, I focus inward, pushing past the voices of my various creatures and forms, going deeper inside myself than I ever have before. Searching for the elusive power, I almost give up, but eventually, I can see a rolling ball of pure white power, with a small sliver of green mixed into it.

"Is this it? Is the green your power?" I ask him, poking at it and feeling the calm, serene aura Zeydan exudes. It has a grounded, solid impression, which is the very essence of my earth elemental god.

"Yes, that's it," Zeydan encourages as I poke it with a metaphorical finger. "Now take a small piece about the size of a coin. You don't want to take too much because then you will be giving it to me, making me more powerful and you less. It's a fine balance."

I pinch off a small amount.

"Yes, good. That's the amount you need, and when we climax, you need to shove it into my body."

Now that I know where it is, handling it is a piece of cake. I let the small amount I grabbed rejoin the mass, then I open my eyes and focus on the god in front of me. He's smiling at me, and I see love in his eyes.

"I can't wait to feel your power inside me. I bet it's a beautiful, chaotic, brilliant mess."

I should feel insulted at that, but he isn't half wrong. He kisses me as he lays me down on the bed. I start to wrestle my clothes off, but magic washes over me, and suddenly, I'm completely naked, as is Zeydan.

He turns to face the warlock, and I sit up so I can see Xavier's face when he notices what Zeydan is packing. "I could have done that," he grumbles good-naturedly, and Xavier grins.

"You were taking your damn time." I watch with glee as his eyes run down the length of Zeydan's body. He isn't in his godly form yet, which is nice because I can still kiss him, but it is still impressive. Xavier's eyes widen, and his lips purse when he gets to the three writhing members. He sits up and moves around so he is behind me on the bed. "I was just going to watch from over there, but I need to see what that looks like going in and out of your cunt," he murmurs as he slides behind me, placing his legs on either side of me, and draws me back so I'm leaning against him.

Zeydan smirks as he puts a knee on the bed, sliding his large hands up my thighs. I drop my legs open as he settles between them, his focus on my pussy which is dripping with need. His tails move behind him in an erotic dance, and his ears twitch. He leans in and sticks out his long, thick tongue. Xavier groans quietly behind me as Zeydan licks a path from my asshole to my clit.

"Holy fuck, does that feel as good as it looks?" he asks as I shudder and moan.

It's hot and wet, and the pressure is delightful as he alternates between circling and flicking my clit to fucking his tongue deep inside my dripping hole.

Xavier wraps his arms around my chest and holds me against him. His own cock is thick against my back as I thrash my head back and forth, writhing under Zeydan's ministrations. My first orgasm bursts out of me, and I scream loudly, my thighs shaking as Zeydan holds them apart, lapping at the mess that leaks out of me while my toes curl.

"So pretty," Xavier murmurs as Zeydan pulls back, licking his lips as he runs his palm over my soaked core before sliding it over each of his three members.

"How does he even fuck you with those?" Xavier asks, intrigued. I can't answer, still breathless from my orgasm as Zeydan's body starts to change. Xavier tenses behind me, and I feel his interest as we watch the god change shape.

"Holy shit..." The words are breathy in my ears as Zeydan's face changes shape. He gets bigger, those golden fronds appear behind him, and his cocks twine together, forming the corkscrew. There's an intake of breath behind me. "How does that even fit in you?" Xavier asks, sounding impressed. It takes a lot to impress my warlock, since he is overly experienced and jaded.

"You'll see," I reply.

Zeydan looks at my warlock over my shoulder. "How involved do you want to be?" he asks.

"All in." He sounds eager, and I roll my eyes, chuckling. My warlock is such a whore. He's lucky he's adorable and he keeps it within the family. He would gladly only be with me because I am his intimate, but why would I force him to do that when I'm happy to share with him?

Zeydan's muzzle turns up in a foxy grin that is decidedly evil. "Be careful what you wish for."

"But I thought you could only fuck your mate in god form?" I put a hand on Zeydan to gain his attention. "I don't want you hurting Xavier."

He leans in and gives me a kiss. "Be still my mate. He is your mate and by extension mine, my dust will prepare him, and he will not feel any pain. Or none that I don't wish him to feel." Zeydan look at my warlock with such desire I see Xavier shiver with anticipation.

His fronds waver and rise above and over me, sprinkling us with gold and green dust. I feel it sink into my skin, the liquid shot of ecstasy flowing through my body, and I arch into Xavier, who also moans and grinds into me.

"Holy fuck," he growls as he stiffens and orgasms at the same time I do. "Ugh, why is my body doing that? My asshole feels like it's dripping cum and fluttering with need."

Zeydan chuckles. "My dust is preparing and reshaping you for my cock as well."

I moan at the thought of watching them fuck. "Yes, please," I mutter, knowing I need to see that.

Zeydan shrugs. "I am willing if the warlock is, but first, I want your pussy wrapped around my member while I paint your womb with my seed as we finalize our bond."

My back grows damp, and I know Xavier has orgasmed again, spilling into his pants. He grumbles, and I feel his magic work, and then his body is as naked as mine is. Being pinned between them causes a sensory overload. I reach for Zeydan as his lower body shifts toward mine, lining up his corkscrew cock, but Xavier grabs my hands and pins them down, circling my wrists like manacles. Zeydan's tongue flicks out, and he nips and licks my nipples as he slowly sinks into my body, his cock winding in like a screw. The moan that leaves my mouth is obscene, and my body shakes and shudders as the gold and green dust continues to sprinkle over me.

"God, yes! Fuck!" I groan as he slides in and out, starting slowly then getting faster until he's hammering into my cunt. It ripples and tightens, my body on the very brink of mind-blowing pleasure. His cock is hard and thick and long, and it fills my pussy perfectly.

"Now, Lila, grab your power and shove it into me," Zeydan commands, and I am powerless not to obey. I pinch off the blinding white power, and as I throw my head back and scream, another orgasm powering through me, I shove the ball into the very center of him.

He bellows, throwing his head back and howling like a wolf, his teeth bared as I feel his hot cum fill my channel. Xavier thrusts against my back, his cock sliding across my skin, and I feel his hot seed paint my back as he, too, succumbs to the intense pleasure of our coupling. I feel him suck in the pleasure like a man starved of oxygen.

"So good," he slurs, releasing my wrists and playing with my nipples as Zeydan slides in and out a few more times, prolonging my own euphoria.

The pleasure slowly subsides, and he pulls out, a gush of fluid flowing from my cunt. He slides two fingers into the mess before shoving it back into me. "My cum stays in your cunt," he growls, and I feel my pussy ripple again as my body shivers. Somehow, he manages to drive those fingers into my corkscrew pussy with no problem.

He slides his hands up my body and lifts me off Xavier, then he moves me to the side. He leans in and whispers, "Are you okay with this?"

I give him a quick nod and kiss him on his snout, pleased that he asked me first. "I can't wait to see you destroy his asshole," I tell him, and he smirks again, making my pussy throb.

"On your hands and knees," he growls at the warlock, and Xavier, who I am almost certain is dominant in all his relationships, swiftly obeys. Huh, I would have put money on the idea that he would have at least protested, but Zeydan is a god, and who doesn't want to be dominated by one of those?

I roll onto my side, running a hand over his beautiful lavender skin, his silver marks swirling. I've never noticed that before, but I guess I've always been distracted.

"Slide under him and suck his cock, my beautiful

mate," Zeydan commands, and I am quick to obey. Although I really want to watch Zeydan's cock plough Xavier's ass, I'd much rather be an active participant. I run my tongue up and down Xavier's length, teasing the tentacles at the base, before wrapping my lips around it and sucking the tip. He groans, and his head falls forward. I feel his breath on my pussy.

Releasing his cock, I slide a little farther back and take one of his testicles into my mouth, rolling it around before releasing it with a pop. I can now see Zeydan's fingers sliding in and out of Xavier's ass.

"Good boy. You take my fingers so well. You're tight, and you're going to feel so good around my cock." Zeydan's dirty talk causes my eyebrows to jump and my pussy to clench. The god has a filthy mouth, who would have guessed?

Xavier groans again, and I watch as Zeydan lines himself up and pushes forward.

"Oh my god!" Xavier sighs reverently as Zeydan's cock screws into his asshole. He throws his head back and bellows as Zeydan starts to fuck into him in earnest, and I wiggle back down, taking his cock deep into the back of my throat, my suckers working against his hard flesh.

"Not going to last," Xavier warns as I hear a slap, and another moan leaves his mouth, his cock jumping inside my throat.

"You will hold it," Zeydan commands as he powers his hips back and forth, the gold and green dust sprinkling all over us again. My orgasm builds again without contact from either of them, but then I feel something between my legs. I gasp and look down, but there is nothing there. I slam my legs together, but I can still feel it deep inside me. Is there a ghost in the room trying its luck?

"It's my magic," Zeydan assures me, and I sigh with relief, let my legs fall apart, and allow him to do his thing.

The magic thrusts in and out of my body, a tendril drifting across my clit, featherlight and tantalizing. My body coils tighter as Xavier's cock kicks again. His precum dribbles down my throat, and I swallow around his length as Zeydan slaps his ass again.

"Come now," he commands as more dust rains down over us, sinking into our skin.

Xavier's body tightens before he moans long and loud, emptying his seed down my throat. His cock throbs, and his whole form twitches with pleasure. I swallow, struggling to keep up with his release as Zeydan also lets out a moan, flooding Xavier's ass with his own seed at the same time my own orgasm detonates. My legs flail as I try to clamp them closed, but Zeydan's magic holds them, and all I can do is ride out the pleasure, my body writhing while Xavier's cock still floods my mouth with cum.

Finally, Xavier stops coming, and I pull away, cleaning his cock with my tongue, catching all his delicious release, before sliding out from under him and collapsing on the pillow. I watch as Xavier falls forward, Zeydan's cock still lodged firmly inside his ass.

Zeydan goes with him, smothering him with his body and whispering words of praise as he strokes his hands over Xavier's skin. I'm not sure I've ever seen anything sexier, and I smile as my eyes drift closed, the feeling of my god mate solid inside my chest. Life is fucking good.

CHAPTER EIGHT

Lila

That afternoon, Xavier, Zeydan, and I teleport to the ship. On arrival, we make our way to the main dining room. It's a fancier version of the one on the circus pod and more like a five-star restaurant than a cafeteria. The crew and performers were ordered to gather there for a meeting with the grandpas.

I find Maxsim and Echo talking to their former streak with Minx, Natalia's sister, firmly ensconced in the middle of them. The three male cats look at her with adoring eyes. There is also a much smaller juvenile female whom I recognize from when we were on Iceen. This is the even younger sister, but I can't remember her name. I brace myself for a little aggression from the two new female cats—after all, it's kind of my fault their mother is dead and her sister is imprisoned and awaiting trial—but she just lets out a little yowl and throws her arms around me, giving me a hug.

"Lila, thank you so much. I can't tell you how much it means to me that you stopped my mother and sister. They were horrible, horrible people. All those omega males, and I couldn't help them."

I pat her awkwardly on the back but quickly step away. There's an unhappy rumble coming from Echo's chest because we're touching. I feel him shuffle closer and press his front to my back. Minx also puts a little more space between us, gesturing to her younger sister. "Thank you for allowing Soshi to come with us. I didn't want to leave her behind now that mother is gone."

I frown at the streak. "It's no problem, but is it really appropriate for a child so young to be living with you? I can't imagine the environment of a new streak is really the place for a child, especially when an omega goes into heat." All that fucking is most definitely not appropriate for a child of ten, but I'm being careful how I speak around her young ears.

"Soshi has a companion, and they both have their own den in our quarters. Maxsim was kind enough to ensure it was soundproofed when they made the adjustments."

I turn to my mate with a raised eyebrow, because when we used those quarters for our own fun time just recently, it didn't have two separate dens except for the cave we used. They better not have taken our quiet place.

"When Trace informed me that they were bringing Soshi aboard with them now that the ship has been deemed family friendly, I made arrangements for their quarters to be renovated again after they finished ours," he explains. "She will also attend school aboard. Mazlan was rather neglective of her learnings, saying she was only good for breeding, so there was no point in her having any. I'm almost certain she and Brannock's daughter, Chloe, will be on the same level, even though Chloe is slightly younger. While shopping for supplies, we included things for their age group as well as the younger children."

"And where is her companion?" I ask, looking around for another lightning cat. Minx wrinkles up her nose.

"Olga stayed in the den. She wasn't interested in socializing with other species."

A growl rumbles out of my chest. "Well, that kind of attitude won't be tolerated anymore. It doesn't set a good example for her charge." I wave at the small girl who is glaring at me. "If both of them are going to be here, then they have to be tolerant and accepting."

"Please, Lila, forgive Soshi. She has years of my mother's programming to overcome," Minx implores, and I sigh.

"Why are you so kind? How did you manage to avoid becoming your mother's pawn?"

She shrugs. "I am not sure, but I never liked how she spoke to or treated anyone. Natalia was a beast to me, so I guess I made a promise to myself to be better and never to do to others what was being done to me."

"Well, that's commendable," I tell her as Echo's arms wrap around my waist and he plasters his chest to my back. His little baby bump is becoming more pronounced, and I feel it now. It makes me all warm and tingly inside. "Send her companion home. Find a lightning cat who is more tolerant, or maybe you should be looking to another species for her companion."

Soshi gasps and shakes her head, stepping up to Minx. "I want to go home too." She crosses her arms stubbornly, and Minx shakes her head.

"You can't. Nobody was willing to look after you because you're a beast. I had to promise Olga way more money than is normal to get her to agree to come. Your reputation for being Mom's little terror precedes you."

I'm getting impatient now. I don't have time for this shit. "You four will have to look after her for now and keep your carnal activities to a minimum until we can find her a replacement companion. If you go into heat before we can, bring her to our quarters, and she can stay with us." I turn my attention to the small cat. "You better have an attitude adjustment, otherwise life will become very unpleasant for you."

The girl is still glaring at me, but I see tears well in her eyes, and I feel a little guilty.

"Look, I know life probably hasn't been all roses for you, but if you give the circus a chance, you might enjoy being a part of it. Heck, you can even join the act if you want. We would pay you a wage, and that means you would have some money to spend when we stop on planets, or you could save it for your future. Think about it."

Her tears don't fall, and I think I pique her interest with the job offer. I mean, she's still a kid, so it won't be a big part, but making her feel important and special might go a long way in making her feel wanted.

"Maxsim, do you think your mother could suggest a suitable companion?" I ask him, and he nods.

"I'm sure one of my or Echo's siblings would enjoy a change of scenery. We will contact them this evening and have them meet us on Vilax. If none of them want to join us, then maybe a Vilaxian companion would be appropriate too. They can withstand the temperatures of Iceen and would enjoy living in a den."

"I thought they all sort of existed as clans for feeding purposes. Would we even be able to find an individual?"

Fuse nods. "That's a good idea. Some Vilaxians don't join clans and use feeding dens instead, and there are always clan dissolutions and Vilaxians who haven't joined a new one yet, but if you could ask the matriarch first, that might be best."

"Very well. Please let us know if there are any issues. We will inform you when school starts for Soshi."

"And we were just telling them about the children's facilities that were installed before you arrived, so they know they can take her there too," Echo whispers in my ear as he snuggles into my back.

"Great, so we will see you later?" The three of us leave them be and continue to the large, head table. I didn't mention their act because they aren't aware that the grandpas are retiring yet. I will set up a meeting with them later once they know I'm now the boss and their ringmaster.

I stop at a rowdy table of shifters and smile at Caspian's brother, Malik, and two very familiar looking dragons. Both of Tirrian's brothers, Titus and Thorn, are sitting at the table and seem to have made fast friends. Actually, who knows, maybe they knew each other prior to now. They certainly seem to be acquainted with one another.

"Well, hello, I didn't know the two of you were joining us." I look between them, and Thorn screws up his nose.

"We weren't going to, but Tallon is being courted by two dragons, and my mother went into heat, and her and dad are not being particularly discreet about it."

Titus shudders. "I can never not hear the noises coming from their rooms. I am scarred for life. Neither of us were waiting around for Tallon to start up too."

I cough, hiding the burst of laughter that barreled out of my chest. I probably shouldn't be too gleeful, since this could very well be me with my grandparents instead. "I completely understand, but you're going to have to make yourselves useful, no free rides. Do either of you have any experience with children? I am looking for a second nanny."

They both turn pale, and Malik chortles next to them. "Our nieces and nephews are certainly a handful." Malik got to meet them when Caspian and Nikos took them swimming with their family on Fluxx.

"Actually, we were thinking maybe we could help out with the Vilaxian act. Both of us are acrobatic, and we heard that none of your Vilaxians have returned yet, and Saxon will be on his own. You're also missing the Aquilians, which means you'll be down two big acts."

"Where did you hear that?" I demand, crossing my arms, feeling defensive.

"Look around. I overheard it being gossiped about half a dozen times from any number of crew members." Titus waves his hand at the surrounding crew and performers. "Is it not true?"

"No, it's true, but we don't know for sure about the Vilaxians. The Aquilians definitely won't be returning to the show, but I have hired three more acts, and I think Ghosie and Magenta may have hired a couple more today."

"Did I just hear my name?" I spin around to find my magenta-haired friend beaming at me. "We saw some amazing acts, but we decided we had enough for now. But they are definitely on the list if we ned to add more," she tells me, and the rowdy group of shifters quiets down.

When I turn to look at them, all three of them, as

well as the rest of the shifters at the table, are all staring at my friend like she's a juicy piece of steak.

She raises an eyebrow, looking curiously at the three new males. "New meat?"

"Mags, meet my brothers-in-law—Malik, kraken shifter, and Titus and Thorn, pain in the ass dragons." Thorn gives her a wave, but smoke drifts out of Titus's nose, and I hear him rumble quietly. That's interesting.

Malik rushes to his feet and holds out a hand, taking Magenta's and pressing a kiss to the back of it. "The pleasure is all mine." His eyes sparkle with interest, and I want to squeal with excitement, but I control myself.

I expect Magenta to bat her eyelashes and flirt with him, but she kind of just murmurs, "Hello," and gives the two dragons a quick nod before looping her arm in mine and dragging me toward the head table again.

"Who are you and what have you done with my friend?" I hiss as soon as we are out of earshot. Well, maybe not out of hearing range, since they are shifters after all, but we can pretend. Something is wrong with my friend, and I want to know what right now.

CHAPTER NINE

Lila

She shrugs.

"Can't a girl be happy with her own company?"

"A girl can, but not you," I retort, and she sighs.

"I'm feeling a little less enamored with being a Skarrian than I usually am. Seeing you with all your mates makes me want the same thing. Playing the field is getting a little tiring."

"So what are you going to do about it?"

She grimaces. "I kind of thought I had something good here on the ship, but it turns out I was the only person who thought that. None of them have returned. I guess they were only having a bit of fun. Serves me right for getting attached."

"Are you talking about Nixie, Velorina, and Hale?"

She nods.

"Nixie couldn't really help it. She's now crown princess of Aquila, and her mother is a fucking sea snake who's no better than that slug of a father, and has recently imprisoned her. As for the Vilaxians, they are probably going to join us when we stop there on the way."

"They've been dodging my calls. I went to Vilax for a few days to hang out with them, but they were busy with that clan dissolution shit. I spent my time shopping and having spa treatments. Vilaxians have amazing anti-aging spa treatments."

"Well, okay, but there are plenty of other fish in the sea. Two of those shifters for example." I gesture back the way we came.

"Yeah, I'm not sure. If they want me, then they are going to have to do the pursuing. I think maybe I'm just too easy. I need to make them work harder."

I spot someone I recognize and pull Magenta to a stop. "Connor? What are you doing here?" Mags gasps and shuffles behind me. That's weird.

The Skarrian dino keeper smiles at me. "Hello, Lila. With all the mini steggies joining the show, a keeper was needed, so I volunteered. I always wanted to do some traveling." He eyes Magenta behind me with an amused look. "Hello, Mags. It's been a while. You're looking gorgeous, as usual."

She clears her throat and steps from behind me before giving him an awkward wave. "Hi, Connor.

Can't talk, we need to be somewhere. See you around." She practically drags me away.

"An ex?" I ask her, and she groans softly. "Yes, you could say that. That man has a talented tongue, but he was as free with his love as I was. I can hardly hold a grudge for his wandering eye, but when it's on me, I prefer for it to stay focused and not drift. He was seeing a couple of other people at the same time as me, which I wouldn't have minded if I was invited to join the fun, but I wasn't, so I walked away."

"How does that work? If you've already slept with him before, do the five times reset after a certain period of time, or do the times you've already banged count?"

She giggles. "Lila, you are so fixated on the five times rule. You do know it's five mutual orgasms, right? As long as you don't come at the same time, you can bang as much as you like without sealing the mating bond."

I stop suddenly and gape at her. "Seriously?"

She stops giggling, and her expression turn serious. "Did you really think it was five times period?"

"Yes."

"Oh, honey." She tugs me, and I start walking again. "As long as you don't come together, you're fine. They could pull out once you orgasmed and come all over your body, which is one of my favorite ways to avoid sealing the bond. It also keeps my skin silky smooth."

"Well shit. The grandpas weren't all that clear

about it. I guess I don't blame them." I wrinkle my nose at the thought of having to explain it to my grandchildren. It's going to be bad enough giving my own kids the birds and bees talk. Thankfully, most of them will take after their fathers and won't need to hear the Skarrian version of it.

"I guess it's a little too late now anyway. I'm mostly sealed to all of them now except Brannock."

She shudders slightly. "I completely understand why you haven't done that one. Sex with an Aaz'axian sounds brutal." She, of course, hounded me for the details, and I took such glee in her pale face while I gave her all the gory facts. Serves her right for being nosy.

We make it to the front of the room. Echo and Maxsim followed us the whole time, but they stayed quiet, allowing Mags and me to talk uninterrupted. They join my grandpas and other mates on the raised platform. The children are being watched by their nanny and bodyguard. We really have to get another one, or we're going to cause Kinga to run off, or maybe stumble away sobbing with exhaustion.

Magenta leaves me and grabs a seat off to the side as I join my family. My nerves are starting to sing. What happens if the performers and crew aren't happy with the changes? Are we even going to have a circus after this next announcement? I look around the room and notice there are a lot of smiling, happy faces and very few grumpy ones, which is a relief.

I see Aura and their family sitting in the back, and they give me a little finger wave. I really haven't had a chance to get to know them. Maybe it isn't such a bad thing if there is animosity between them and my besties.

Susie and Mark are at a table on the opposite side of the room. Mark has his beautiful Celestian wings on display, and Susie is snuggled up next to him. Susie is my ride or die, and I will take her side every single day. Sitting with them is another blindingly attractive Celestian whom I don't recognize. The three of them seem to be deep in conversation and haven't noticed my arrival yet. The man is the very definition of golden —golden skin, long golden locks tied back at the nape of his neck, and even some kind of golden gladiator outfit that I noticed was popular on Celestia. He looks like a golden archangel warrior from an Earth religion.

"Who is that with Mark and Susie?" I ask my family, hoping one of them knows the answer.

"That is Mark's guardian angel that his parents insisted on sending along with him. Being the crown prince of Celestia comes with responsibilities that are chafing him." Xavier sounds amused. "But he is new to his power, and his parents don't want to lose him again. Aarin is a general in the Celestian army and has been instructed to protect him with his life."

It looks like the conversation turns heated. Susie watches on with wide eyes as Mark and Aarin argue, and eventually, Mark throws his hands up in exasperation. Aarin remains calm the whole time and has an expression of extreme satisfaction on his face. I'm guessing Mark lost that argument. The golden angel turns his attention to the front of the room, and I meet his eyes. He gives me a nod before his attention keeps moving, but then it stops dead. His eyes widen, and he sits up straight, mouthing words I can't make out. I watch as he goes to stand, but a throat clearing next to me draws my attention away from the surprised Celestian.

"If I could have your attention please?" William amplifies his voice to address the loud, overcrowded dining room. The noise slowly settles as everyone turns their attention to us.

"Welcome back! We are so pleased you could all join us once more, and we hope you enjoyed your impromptu vacation."

"Once again, we thank you for your patience while we dealt with a number of personal matters. As you can see, John is back and fighting fit again." Eric waves his hand at his brother, and the crowd cheers and claps. Although we tried to keep his condition quiet, it's not easy on a ship as big as this one, and word got out. He is well loved amongst our staff, and everyone was very worried.

"Thank you." My most humble grandfather blushes at the reaction and gives a nod of thanks before clearing his throat. "But as you are probably aware, we are ready to get underway again. The ship has been fully stocked, and the crew and performers are mostly all here apart from a couple of new acts who should arrive and board overnight, which means we will be leaving as soon as possible tomorrow morning."

There are more cheers and foot stamping from the enthusiastic crowd.

"We hope you make all the newcomers feel welcome. Things will need to change a bit, but we will keep everyone updated on the ship-wide news service and will arrange for rehearsal time as well during our trip to Earth," William informs everyone. "As you all know, we changed our policy regarding families on the ship, and we now welcome everyone to travel with theirs if they wish to. Many of you put in requests for family accommodations, and we have allocated you new rooms if this was the case. We welcome them all and look forward to meeting each and every one of them. New facilities such as play areas and school rooms have also been allocated, and an information packet is available for anyone who requires it. Depending on how many children there are, we may need to hire some more teaching staff, but that will happen as needed. If anyone has any questions, please address them to Lila's mates Ghosie and Zeydan. Both of them have kindly offered to run this program."

This last announcement causes a small amount of muttering amongst the crowd. I'm not sure if it's because Ghosie is a carevasta bear and they don't have the best reputation, or the fact that the rumor that Zeydan is one of the original gods is doing the rounds. We haven't confirmed or denied anything, since it's no one's business.

"I think the fact that I trust both of these males with my five children should speak volumes to you, but we are not a dictatorship, and we welcome constructive criticism, but it better be valid," Xavier calls out, his mist shrouded body shimmering with enough agitation to stop the muttering in its tracks. It's weird seeing him like that, since he hasn't worn it for a long time. I don't know how I feel about it. I know he thinks it intimidates people, and he isn't wrong, but I think seeing his real form would do the same. He claims he's too pretty to be intimidating though. That made me roll my eyes.

"Please bring any of your concerns to the warlock. He will hear you. Moving on." Eric is smirking, knowing full well no one will speak to Xavier. "We have one final announcement. William, John, and I are retiring." The murmurs start up again, but he holds up his hands. "I'm sure you have all heard by now that our wife has been found, and we have made the unanimous decision to spend as much time reconnecting with her as we can. That means we will not have time to split our attention with the circus, but we are very happy to announce we are turning its responsibilities and leader-ship over to our very capable granddaughter and her twelve mates." He waves at the thirteen of us with a game show worthy flourish.

"Lila will now be your ringmaster and boss, and we hope you will give her the respect and courtesy you have always shown us," William growls as stunned silence fills the room. It's kind of awkward, and I resist the urge to fidget.

"Woo, yeah! Congratulations," Malik shouts and

starts clapping, with Thorn and Titus quickly taking up the call, followed by their other buddies who are all from Cas's first act. This quickly spreads, and the applause is thunderous. I'm not sure how sincere it is, and I am certain there will be a number of hiccups as we find our way, but I have hope that this is all going to work out.

"Speech," I hear someone shout, and I glare at Susie who just gives me a wink.

A hand on my back gives me a little shove forward. I'm not sure which of my mates did it, but I will find out and make them pay. I wipe my sweaty palms on my pants and wave.

"Uh, hi. I can't tell you how proud I am to be a part of the great Galaxy Circus legacy, and I look forward to trying my best to fill my grandfathers' very big shoes. It won't be easy, but I hope you help make this transition smooth. Please feel free to approach any of us if you have any questions or suggestions as we take this new step forward."

The meeting breaks up not long after that with food and alcohol flowing, turning it into an impromptu retirement party for the grandpas. They are surrounded by cast and crew alike, so I leave them be. I decide to join Mark and Susie at their table. I want to grill her since I haven't had a chance to yet, so I look around to tell my mates, but all of them have been dragged away and are being monopolized by other people. I shrug my shoulders in defeat, knowing they will find me when they can, then I head toward my friend's table, hoping I can order something to eat and drink as well. It's been a long ass day, and with everything I learned from Gigi, I haven't felt like eating until now.

Before I can get there, I'm waylaid again. I'm starting to get annoyed, but that disappears when I see who it is. "Zala!" I cry out and throw my arms around her. She stiffens, but I don't let her pull away, and eventually, she relaxes and returns my hug.

"Hello, Lila. Congratulations on the promotion."

I pull back and study her, but she doesn't look surprised.

"Did Zamala see something?" I ask, and she just smiles mysteriously. She's obviously been taking lessons from her grandmother, but then the smile drops, and she frowns. "Is everything okay?" I ask, butterflies starting in my stomach. "Did you bring Shiny? Is he okay?"

I can't wait to see my larnuk again. I've been missing him something fierce, even if we only just bonded.

"Yes, Shiny is with my animals. He's a mischievous boy," she tells me with a small grin. "But I have some rather disturbing news. We're not quite sure how, but Zilla has escaped her imprisonment and disappeared."

"She what?" a gruff voice grumbles behind me. "How did this happen?" Tirrian wraps an arm around my waist, and I snuggle into him. Who would have guessed that the asshole would be so touchy-feely? I'm not complaining though.

"We're not sure, but I'm assuming she had some help."

"Zamala couldn't give you any insight?" my mate snaps, and I pinch him.

"Hey, it's not Zala or Zamala's fault."

"I'm sorry, you're right, but it doesn't mean I can't be pissed." He presses a kiss to the top of my head.

"I can assure you Father and I are just as pissed. We traced her to the spaceport, but she obviously jumped a transport and went off planet. She could be anywhere now. She wasn't doing well. Her bond with her larnuk faded quickly, and she was going through withdrawals. She will need to seek medical intervention."

"Or drugs," Tirrian says wryly, and I frown, not understanding what he means.

"Rilunese who end up with severed larnuk bonds often resort to recreational drugs to ease the symptoms and end up addicted to something else. Suva is often used, and while it isn't addictive, they mix it with numerous other synthetic compounds to extend the effect, and that's what makes it dangerous," Zala explains. "Father has put out a galaxy-wide bounty on her, so she shouldn't get very far."

"Well, she isn't on this ship, and that's all that matters." I brush off their concerns, because I have enough problems to worry about without adding Zilla to the list. She's someone else's problem now. "I'll come and visit Shiny as soon as I can," I promise the larnuk mistress, then I say my goodbyes before heading in Susie's direction again.

Tirrian stays behind. I'm sure he will grill her for more information, and I'm okay with letting him handle that. I have twelve mates, and I need to spread the responsibilities out, otherwise I'm going to be spread too thin and have a nervous breakdown before we even arrive in Earth's orbit.

CHAPTER TEN

Caspian

"**B**rother!" Malik cheers, holding up his bottle of beer and saluting me with it. The rest of my act cheers as well as I take a seat at the table they have commandeered. It's rowdy, and most of them have enjoyed an alcoholic beverage or two. I smother a grin. They will feel a little under the weather tomorrow morning. I'm pretty sure it will be the perfect time to announce a rehearsal to rework our act, but I'll let it be a surprise.

"Sit and tell us what being mated is like. Is it all it's cracked up to be?" Thorn demands, the dragon prince slurring his words.

"Of course it is. Lila is an amazing woman. My brother got really lucky." Malik slaps me on the back, and I cough with surprise. "Now tell us about that beauty she was with earlier. What species is she? Is she single? What does she do in the act, and can you assign me to assist with it?"

I gape at my brother. I've never heard him speak so enthusiastically about a potential paramour in my life. He usually likes to play it cool and let them come to him. Titus elbows him hard, and Malik spits out a mouthful of beer.

"Forget about squid rings. Tell me, does she like dragons?"

Thorn just rolls his eyes and shakes his head. "Jesus, what has gotten into you two?" he mutters. "Just moments ago we were checking out all the available singles on the ship, and now you are focused on one. Boring."

"I think she's my mate," they both announce and then look at each other in shock.

"No, she's my mate," my brother argues, shaking his head.

"No, my dragon insists she's ours. The minute her scent hit our nose, we knew." Titus shoves Malik, who shoves him back. Titus stands up and tackles him, and the two of them hit the ground and start rolling around, wrestling.

I sigh and look at Thorn. "What the fuck?" I ask him, and he shrugs.

"They are always like this. They just need to fuck and get over it." He rolls his eyes and turns his attention to the person on his other side.

Oh, huh. So it's like that, is it? I was going to step in and tell them that she's Skarrian, like Lila, so it is possible she's both their mate, but now I'm going to let them go. They need to work out their own shit. It doesn't take long.

I order myself a beer and something to eat, and eventually, they stop rolling around and sit down, both of them adjusting their pants in a way that makes me want to smirk.

"Are you finished?" I ask dryly as they settle into their seats.

"For now," my brother mutters, not meeting my eyes, and I want to chuckle, but I hold it in. I can make him suffer later.

"Do you want me to tell you about Magenta or not?" I ask them, and they lose the sullen fury and perk right up.

"Yes," they say together, and Titus mimes zipping his lips.

"Magenta is Skarrian, and she has a solo act in the circus. Her power is levitation, and she does a pretty thing with silks and then plays a game of dodge ball with the crowd. It's a fan favorite because if anyone hits her, they get to take her out on a date."

"Skarrian, you say?" Malik asks, side-eyeing Titus. "That means she will have multiple mates, right?"

"Possibly," I hedge, not willing to give them any hope. It's fun to see them both deflate. "And she likes females as well. She certainly is popular, but I've never seen her get too serious with anyone. May I make a suggestion?" I continue without waiting for them to reply. "Your beasts are insisting she's your mate, but be careful on how you approach this. They could very well do what mine did to Lila and force the issue. I'm not sure Magenta would be as understanding as Lila if she was mated and knocked up after one night of fun. In fact, your survival would be in question. You also need to be open to the idea that you two may not be the only ones Magenta is attracted to. Remember, she doesn't feel the mate call like you do. She will be attracted, but it won't be as imperative to her."

"You need to woo her," a voice says over my shoulder, and I grin.

"What do you know about wooing?" Malik asks Nikos as he takes a seat next to me. "From what I hear, you tricked Lila into mating you."

Nikos holds up his hands at the aggression in my brother's voice. "While we may have started off as a misunderstanding, I can assure you we are all on the same page now." Gone is the bubble-headed himbo we all knew, and in his place is a calm, sensible man who has embraced fatherhood with open arms. "I'm telling you so you don't make the same mistakes Cas and I did. I suggest you romance her. Bring her gifts, take her out on dates, and hold off on the sex for a little while. Magenta's self-esteem isn't as good as it should be. Many see her as the slutty Skarrian who is good for a few nights but not long term. Don't make that mistake."

Both Malik and Titus stare at the merman with undisguised shock. Yup, the man is surprisingly insightful now that he's not pretending to be a dick.

"He's not wrong. With Nixie not returning and Hale and Velorina being no-shows, Magenta is alone for the first time in a while, and I don't think she felt as casual about the three of them as she pretended to."

"Also, don't turn it into a competition between you. Listen to your beasts but come up with a plan to woo her together. Show her you are willing and happy to be involved in a mating circle. Shifters are notoriously prejudiced against poly relationships," Nikos points out, and I nod my agreement. We did get some disapproving looks from various shifters on Fluxx, including the dragons.

He continues. "You don't have to fuck each other, but you have to be willing to work together to give her pleasure."

Malik and Titus both shift uncomfortably in their seats, and I really don't think that is going to be a problem. In fact, if the two of them aren't fucking by the end of the week, I will take charge of all potty training with the triplets which, let me tell you, has not been easy. Jack likes to whip it out wherever he is.

Nikos continues his wooing tips, which is a hoot. He hasn't had to do any of it. "Buy her pretty things, give her a cute pet name, take her out to dinner or flying or swimming. Spend quality time getting to know her without complicating things with sex. If your animals are anything like this one's" —he gestures to me— "or the dragon's, then they will be difficult and push for more. Talk to them and explain you are in it for the long haul, not just a quick roll in the sheets."

The two males look at me, and I nod my head. "I hate to admit it, but he's right. We have all made many mistakes with Lila, so learn from them and court her right. I don't think she's ever had the pleasure before. She's stubborn, though, so don't let her railroad you, and she will want to break it off after a short period of time. She's conditioned herself not to want more. Don't let her. And he's right, you need to be open to letting others into the relationship, but set ground rules with Magenta. Lila doesn't have any problem with us messing around with each other, not that all of us have explored that option yet, but Magenta is the focus of your circle. She may not want anyone else touching you, so you need to establish boundaries. Her recent fun time involved two other women and one male, and she wasn't opposed to any of them touching each other, but it's better to be sure."

Malik stares at me with wide eyes. "Look at you, being all adultlike and shit. Lila has been good for you. I'm proud of you, bro." He reaches across the table and gives my hand a squeeze.

Before I can reply, my communicator alerts me to a message. It's from Kinga. The children have been fed and wish to say goodnight to their parents. I show Nikos the message, and he jumps to his feet.

"Please excuse us, our offspring are in need."

He takes off toward the exit. Both Maxsim and Echo are heading in that direction as well. Neither of them want to hang around any longer than necessary. Echo tires easily now, and Maxsim gets all growly if someone other than one of us brushes against him by accident.

I stand up and stretch. "Duty calls," I tell them, unable to stop the smirk that crosses my mouth.

"Family looks good on you, brother." Malik reaches over and slaps my hand. "Give my nieces and nephews kisses for me."

"I'll tell them their favorite uncle, Malik, is here on the ship. I'm sure they will insist on visiting you soon."

He grins. "You bet I'm their favorite uncle."

Titus scowls. "Not for long. Once they meet me, I will quickly take the top spot." This draws Thorn's attention.

"Unlikely. Everyone knows I'm the nicest of the dragon princes. Once they see my contribution to their hoards, I'm sure I will quickly become the favorite."

"What did you get them?" I ask, unable to stop my curiosity.

He crosses his arms and smiles smugly. "Unlike the rest of the idiots in my family, I understand that children of that age who aren't dragons probably don't have the innate drive to hoard, so instead of gifting them gold or jewels, I gifted them Squishmallows. They are big enough so they can sleep amongst their hoard comfortably, even as they grow."

"Squishmallows?" Titus asks. He and Malik glare at Thorn in confusion, but I grin and nod with approval. I know what he is talking about. Link explained this phenomenon to me when we were on

Earth. Lila had bought a number of them to put on her bed.

"They are a super soft squishy pillow, shaped like a character or food, that are very popular on Earth. Lila loves them, and I'm sure they will be a big hit with the children as well. I'm impressed. You may just win that favorite uncle title. How did you get your hands on them?"

His grin drops, and he looks around to see who is listening, but no one is paying attention. "I have a contact who does black market runs to Earth and picks up items."

I nod, unsurprised to hear this. We knew there must have been a way on and off Earth that wasn't just through the circus. We should really question Aura about it. I'm sure there are a lot more illegal aliens on Earth than Smith knows, but then again, if he has his own way on and off, he must suspect. The man is most definitely not an idiot.

Malik and Titus glare at the dragon, and Titus elbows his brother none too gently. "You didn't tell me about that."

Thorn adopts a nonchalant expression. "A dragon needs to have his mysteries."

I leave them to argue about what other shit he might know that he hasn't shared with his brother and glance over to where Lila is. She is sitting with Susie and Mark and another Celestian whom I haven't met yet. I consider going over and interrupting them, but I know Lila should probably hang around after such a major announcement and soothe any ruffled feathers. It wouldn't do for her to disappear, because it might make the crew uncomfortable, even if it was to kiss her children goodnight.

I leave her. The four of us should be enough to get the five youngsters to bed without any extra assistance.

When I get to our suite, I hear squeals of delight coming from the nursery. When I arrive, I stop and lean against the doorframe and watch with so much love and joy. Maxsim and Echo are in cat form, and they are giving the three krakens a ride around the room. Nikos is breastfeeding both of his young ones, their water cribs already filled and waiting for their occupants. They will continue to nurse from him for a couple more weeks. Although not as large as a female's breasts, his still remain slightly engorged to provide for his young. I find myself oddly attracted by the sight. Watching Lila pump milk for our young was a massive turn on for me, I just never thought I'd feel the same way about Nikos. I must have a nursing kink. I shift awkwardly as my cock hardens in my pants, not wanting anyone to notice, but of course I couldn't be so lucky.

"I can feel your arousal," a voice whispers in my ear, and I curse the warlock's existence. He chuckles, obviously able to hear my expletives inside my mind. The nosy bastard isn't so insistent on privacy and consent when it comes to Lila's mates. "Now, now, don't be embarrassed, it is quite a stimulating view. I also share your nursing kink, and my mouth waters at the thought of wrapping my lips around his ripe nipples."

Oh, well, okay, I shouldn't be surprised the warlock is so open about these things, since he is a kinky fuck. Lila and Nikos haven't had a chance to be intimate on dry land yet, and although I got to join in last time, I think some of the others are envious that they missed out. We all like to watch any one of us fuck our wife, and it's even more enjoyable to be invited to participate, even if it is restraining her for their pleasure.

Xavier chuckles again and runs a hand down my spine and around my waist, pulling me back against him, his mist form gone now that we are in our private suite. "I just sent our wife an interesting image in her mind. I'm sure it won't be too long until she joins us. Shall we get this wrapped up so when she does, the kiddies are all tucked in?"

He brushes his hand over my cock before pushing past me and swooping down to scoop Jack from Echo's back.

"You need to be more careful with Daddy Echo. Remember, he's having babies too. You are going to have two new siblings to care for in a few months. How about you all jump into bed and get some rest so you can grow big and strong to help us look after them?"

The three krakens are quick to obey. There was a little jealousy to begin with, but now they are the ultimate protectors of their little brother and sister. They scramble into their beds, and Xavier takes Ty from Nik. His tiny tail wiggles with excitement at the sight of his warlock daddy. He really has the children wrapped around his little finger.

Xavier lifts him and rubs his nose against Typhoon's, and the little baby squeals with delight, grabbing two handfuls of hair. Xavier winces and manages to untangle the tiny fingers before giving him a kiss on the cheek and slipping him into his water crib. Typhoon happily swims to the bottom and curls his tail around his body, closing his eyes.

In the meantime, Nikos is dealing with a screaming Hali. She doesn't like the fact that she's separated from her brother in a different crib, but when we put them together, she would keep him awake, so we moved them apart. I can see Nikos's anguish at his daughter's screams and tell he's wavering. I hurry forward and take the screaming child off his hands.

"Hali, sweet girl. If you go to sleep, we can go for a swim in the big pool tomorrow," I coo to her, and this has the desired effect. She gives up on her tears and claps her hands together. These two are not quite as old as the kraken babies, but in human years, they are about eighteen months, according to Mark. Their language skills are developing rapidly, and their comprehension skills are off the charts. Link suggests that they will probably develop as quickly as the kraken babies. It sent Lila into another tailspin, because three teenage girls will be terrifying.

I slide her into her own pod. She swims back and

forth a few times before she settles down at the bottom as well.

Maxsim and Echo curl up between the older kids' beds. They will stay there for a while until all the family members have returned and the suite is locked down for the night before moving to their own bedroom. They each have one, Lila ensured we all have our own space, but they tend to sleep in the same bed.

"How about we get a drink while we wait for Lila?" Xavier suggests before he grabs Nikos by the hand and tugs him out of the room. I follow along behind them. I have no idea what that male has in mind, but I'm curious to see what it is.

CHAPTER ELEVEN

Lila

I approach the table Mark and Susie are at. No one notices me, as they seem to be in the middle of an argument. "I've said it before and I'll say it again, we don't need you tailing our asses across the galaxy. You're only here because my parents insisted on it. They wouldn't know if you did your job or not, so how about giving us a little bit of breathing room?" Damn, Mark sounds annoyed. He's usually so mild mannered, but it turns out he does have some fire in him. His wings bristle with agitation, and I feel a ripple under the skin of my back. It's a weird itchy feeling. One set of wings wants to come out and join the fun, but which one? I brush the feeling away. I'm getting so much better at ignoring the insistent mimic power.

The golden guardian angel doesn't say anything, just smirks at him. Susie is looking between the two men like she needs a bucket of popcorn. Oh, I can't wait to hear all about this, but I won't quiz her about it while the two of them are around.

"Hey, can I join you?" I don't wait for an invite before I pull out a chair and take a seat, swiping my finger over the holographic menu. "I'm freaking starving. I haven't eaten all day, too many emotions wreaking havoc on my system, but all of a sudden, I could eat a horse."

Mark just about leaps out of his seat, but Aarin gives me a welcoming nod.

"Well, if it isn't the boss lady." Susie gives me a sassy grin and a wink. "Better behave now, boys, because we wouldn't want to be tossed off the ship before we've even hit orbit."

"Lila, congratulations on your promotion." Mark leans over and gives me a kiss on the cheek. "Sorry, I didn't see you there."

"I noticed," I say dryly, putting in an order for food and a bottle of rilaxious. "Is everything okay? How about you introduce me to your new friend, since he is on my ship?" I raise an eyebrow, and Mark blushes as Susie giggles, before he waves a careless hand at the Celestian.

"This is Aarin. My parents insisted he accompany us. They weren't happy with me leaving so soon after we were reunited, which I completely understand, but I'm not ready to be the crown prince and settle down. I'm excited about discovering all the galaxy has to offer. Hell, until a few months ago, I was human with absolutely no chance of even going into space, let alone traveling the stars.”

“But you must understand your parents’ position. You are new to your power and vulnerable once more. Although they have seized control of the planet again, there are still rumbles of a democratic rule opposed to a monarchy, and you would be the perfect target for those factions to take out,” Aarin argues casually like he isn’t talking about my friend being assassinated. “Your fathers decided I would be the best person to teach you to protect yourself both physically and with your growing powers.”

“Why you? General Saxon could have instructed me just as he is instructing Lila with self-defense.” I wince at that argument. Apart from our first disastrous attempt at self-defense, we actually haven’t had any more lessons. I’m not even sure how Mark knows about that. I guess Susie filled him in.

Aarin scoffs. “While I respect General Saxon and his very extensive abilities and talents, he is also a married man who is focused on protecting his family, not to mention taking on the responsibility of running this operation. No, it will be me, and I will not hear any more arguments.” Aarin stands up, spreading his wings wide before tucking them against his back. “I will come find you once we are underway tomorrow. We will schedule your training to work around your responsibilities in the med bay. I bid you goodnight. I have an old friend I need to talk to.” He bows to Mark and nods at both Susie and me before turning with military precision and stalking through the room in the direction of the front table.

I stare after him, kind of dumbfounded. "Wow, what a hard ass," I murmur, and Mark groans, slouching down and burying his head in his arms on the table.

"You have no idea," he grumbles, and I shake my head.

"Oh no, I had a perfect view of his ass when he walked away. You could use those cheeks as airbags." I mime cupping them, and Susie cackles.

"That's half of Mark's problem. He pops a hard-on if Aarin just breathes on him the wrong way. Can you imagine what it would be like doing hand-to-hand combat?"

"Susie..." Mark groans and turns his head. "He is my fathers' oldest friend. I can't be lusting after him. He's going to think I'm such a perv."

We watch as he stops in front of Zeydan. Zeydan crosses his arms and glares at the male, and I brace myself for some kind of confrontation, but the two of them stare at each other for what seems like forever before they embrace each other without words. There are manly slaps on the back, and the hug goes on for a long time before they part and start talking quietly to one another.

"Hmm, an old friend of your fathers', right? Are you sure there isn't anything divine about your fathers' friend apart from his looks?"

"I don't think so. No one has ever said anything.

You think he might be a god?" Mark's eyes widen in surprise as he watches the same scene I do.

"I think the god of air may have been hiding in plain sight. What was his original name again? Zeydan told me..." I snap my fingers, and my own eyes widen. "Holy shit, his name was Markit. Maybe he changed it because it was a little too close to yours, especially if he was hiding in plain sight amongst one of his creations."

"Oh my god, now the thought of training with him is even more terrifying," Mark laments.

"Nonsense," Susie scolds him. "He is hot as fuck, and if we can get him to pull the stick out of his ass, he might prove to be more than just protection. Who cares if he's a god? Hell, one of Lila's mates is a god. I bet the sex is off the fucking charts."

I smother the sly grin that really wants to make itself known and change the subject, seeing that Mark is only moments away from a meltdown and Susie isn't doing anything to help. I will grill Zeydan when I get back to my room, but I'd put money on the fact that Aarin is the god of air. One down, two more to go, and we have all we need to take Vivian down.

"Speaking of more than just protection... What happened with you guys, Aura, and their family? I thought you were all in with them."

Mark sits up and puts his arm around Susie, pulling her against his side like he needs the comfort, and their lips turn down.

Susie shrugs. "With my Skarrian powers activating, we had to be careful about not bonding them to us, so we backed off a little. Orgasms are fun, but when the people involved want different things, accidently tying yourself to someone is a recipe for disaster," she explains quietly. They are on the other side of the restaurant and look completely engrossed in their own conversation, but they do have supernatural hearing.

"They want to return to Earth and asked us to come with them, but when we said no, they got a little annoyed," Mark explains. "Not that we could return to Earth anyway, since we burnt our identities when your lawyers faked our deaths. We have nowhere to go and no jobs to return to."

"And that's not even taking into account that neither of us want to. We're excited to travel with the circus and explore all the planets that are new and fascinating to us. None of them were very happy, except Xane. He could feel how we felt and was kind, but the others were not so understanding, so we decided it was better to just make a clean break of it."

Both of them feel incredibly sad, but there's also anger and annoyance at the situation, so instead of giving them empty platitudes, I squeeze their hands and change the subject.

Our food and drinks come as we talk about anything but personal relationships. I don't want to rub how good mine are all going in their faces.

Susie is telling me all about how she discovered her levitation powers and that her and Magenta have been discussing a dual act when an X-rated image pops into my mind, and I just about spit my drink all over the table.

I cough and splutter but manage to keep all the liquid in my mouth.

"Are you okay?" Susie asks, reaching over and slapping me on the back.

I wave her away and swallow my mouthful. "Holy shit, yeah, I'm good," I tell them, my cheeks turning red and my inner creatures all bellowing for me to get off my ass and leave. "Xavier just projected something into my head, and I wasn't expecting it."

"What did he want?" Mark asks curiously, and I want to warn him to be careful what he asks for.

"Ah, the kids are going to bed and would like me to kiss them goodnight," I reply, refusing to tell them that the image was of a naked Nikos wrapped in Caspian's tentacles, his ass being impaled by one while Caspian lapped at the milk leaking from his nipple. Caspian most definitely has a nursing kink, and I'm not sure if that was a real image or one Xavier was making up, but I'm pissed I wasn't invited to play too.

I quickly stand up. "Have to go. There is nothing scarier than three kraken and two mer babies crying in unison. Trust me." Mark and Susie exchange a glance and shudder as I wave my goodbyes and hurry away without a backward glance.

I hear someone call my name, but I don't stop to see who it is. In fact, I call on my warlock teleporting powers and disappear from the main dining area, reappearing in the entrance of our suite. I'm breathing heavily and slightly breathless, and Nikos and Caspian stare at me with concern, but Xavier just smirks.

"Did I miss it?" I demand, and he starts to chuckle.

"What did you do?" Caspian asks our warlock, who just casually slides a hand along the back of the sofa he's sitting on before sweeping his fingers through Nikos's golden locks. Nikos blinks in surprise, but he soon melts into Xavier's touch as he gives them a little yank.

"You want to be a good boy for your mate, don't you, fish man?" Xavier asks, and Nikos purses his lips and rolls his eyes in annoyance. What a brat! When Xavier tightens his grip and gives another tug, he nods.

"Yes," he answers and allows Xavier to drag him closer and kiss him.

"What's going on?" Caspian asks, not looking too upset about the proceedings as I stalk a little closer.

I run my hand through his short locks and lean in to kiss him. Caspian is always so responsive, and he reaches for me as he returns my kiss, but I duck away from his reach.

I'm impatient, and the living room isn't the place to do what I want, so I reach for Caspian and Nikos and teleport the three of us to my bedroom. They stumble slightly, since my teleporting skills aren't as smooth as Xavier's yet.

"Now that was rude," Xavier scolds me, appearing in a flash. I knew he would follow, and I couldn't reach all three of them.

I ignore his pout and circle a finger between Nikos, Caspian, and me. "Do you want to have some fun?"

I think I render them both speechless, but unfortunately, Xavier isn't.

"What about me?" he whines. "It was my idea."

"No, you get to sit on the chair and watch this time. If you're a good boy and keep your hands and magic to yourself, then I'll let you fuck my ass when we're done," I promise him, and his eyes light up and he quickly takes a seat.

"Are you horny, my sweet oyster?" Nikos has recovered from his surprise and is stripping off his shirt, his eyes burning with desire.

"Yes. It's Xavier's fault. He put an image in my mind that has me intrigued," I reply, and Caspian cocks his head to the side as he starts to undress.

"Oh?" he asks, unable to smother his curiosity.

"Hey, don't blame me! I took the idea directly out of the kraken's head," Xavier calls, and Cas's fingers freeze on his buttons.

"My head?" he asks, sounding confused, but then his eyes widen, and a blush makes his blue cheeks turn purple. "Oh." He looks down at his feet.

"Oh no." I step up to him and use a finger to lift his chin. "Don't be embarrassed. I thought it was fucking hot. I want to see that." I project the same image into Nikos's head, and he coughs, choking with surprise as it appears inside his mind.

"Ah, um, yes, I wouldn't be opposed either," Nikos splutters as he hurries to remove the rest of his clothes.

I huff and wave a hand, and their clothes disappear. I hear Xavier's slow clap behind me but ignore him.

"Shift," I order my kraken. I would almost feel bad about how demanding I am, but my creatures are riding me pretty hard, especially my dragon. She wants a nest and hatchlings, but if she can't have them, then she will settle for a good dicking.

Cas's body shimmers, and when it comes back into focus, his tentacles are writhing impatiently as he climbs up onto the bed. I grab Nikos's hand and drag him over, pushing him back. He bounces on the mattress, our mouths clashing together as he wraps his arms around my body. This is the first time we've been naked on dry land, and I rub my body against him, enjoying how it feels. He moans in delight and thrusts his hard cock against my body, his hands roaming over my curves as he rolls us over.

A tentacle creeps across Nikos's back, and he stiffens for a moment, but when the suckers start to activate, he moans and relaxes.

"Feels like a hundred mouths caressing my skin," he mutters into my mouth. I lick his lips and run my own hands over his back as more of Caspian's tentacles wrap around us. I turn my head to the side and find my kraken's lips, our tongues tangling as Nikos squirms on top of me, firmly entrapped by Caspian.

Cas continues to kiss me as he lifts Nikos, suspending him above us. I look up and smile at the sight. "Well, that's pretty," I tell him, and I hear Xavier grunt his agreement. When I slide my gaze to him, he is naked and has his hand on his cock, stroking it.

I roll and dig around in my bedside table for some lube. I know Cas's tentacles secrete their own lube, but if Xavier is going to fuck my ass, then I want some too. I toss him the bottle, which he grabs out of the air with his free hand.

"Get over here," I order him, not wanting to wait to join in the fun, but he doesn't listen. I kind of figured it was too good to be true. He submitted to Zeydan, but I doubted he would take orders from me. Fine, I can wait. I turn my attention back to the other two. Cas has Nikos suspended above us. His back is arched slightly, pushing his chest and cock out at such an appealing angle. I reach up and stroke my hand down his length. He groans as a tentacle pushes past his lips and plunges in and out of his mouth.

"I'm sure he was about to start talking, so I thought I'd shut him up," Cas offers, and I hear Xavier chuckle.

"That's mean. I happen to like his words," I tell him, but he doesn't look sorry in the least. I know it feels good for him to have it sucked on, and he is unrepentant.

Cas shifts him again, his tentacles positioning him so he is lying flat above us, and then he lowers him a little. Nikos gasps, but Cas still has him tightly wrapped. Now his chest is in reach, and I lean up and take a nipple into my mouth. His pecs are still slightly swollen, filled with milk for our children, and it dribbles into my mouth as I suckle on his peaked nub.

Cas moans, and when I look at him, I find him watching with slitted eyes as his tongue sweeps over his lips like he's dying for a taste. I pull away and lean forward, pressing my lips to his, then I fill his mouth with the milk. I hear two groans and look away, finding Nikos and Xavier watching us with hooded eyes.

"Fuck, that's sexy," Xavier mutters and stands up, moving over to the bed. "Your turn," he orders Cas, pointing at Nikos's chest and taking charge. Cas shifts Nikos so he is directly above him, and he lunges for one of his nipples, rolling it around with his tongue before latching on and sucking hard. Nikos moans, and his whole body shudders as precum dribbles out of his cock as it pulses.

"Suck it, Lila," Xavier commands, pointing to Nikos's cock as he trickles lube into Nikos's ass crack. I don't follow his order straight away because I want to watch Nikos's face as Cas pushes a tentacle into his hole while he sucks on his nipples.

Nikos's head is thrown back, and his eyes are closed in ecstasy as Cas's tentacle burrows into his tight ring. He gasps and groans as Cas's tentacle pushes until he has a good portion of it stuffing Nikos's hole.

"Perfect. You are doing so well. Such a good boy." Xavier caresses Nikos's body, circling the nipple Caspian isn't sucking on with his finger. He leans in and licks it before giving it a quick suck as well. His eyes widen in surprise at the taste and amount of milk that leaks out of it. All my guys loved my breasts when I fed the babies, but they didn't nurse for long.

"So good," Nikos mutters around the tentacle in his mouth as the one in his ass starts to thrust in and out.

"Suck his cock, Lila. He won't last very long, I can feel it," Xavier says, and I get up on my knees so I can reach his cock. It isn't an easy angle, and I can't take much of it into my mouth, but I lick and suck the tip while Xavier slides in behind me and uses a finger to lube up my ass. The stretch burns, but I concentrate on Nikos, knowing it will feel good soon. Xavier shuffles in behind me and slides his cock through my pussy, coating it in the mess dripping out of me, before pushing into my ass. He moves slowly until he slides past the ring and then thrusts deeply. I open my mouth and scream, surprised by the onslaught, but he circles a finger around my clit, and soon it feels pretty fucking good.

I return my attention to Nikos's cock, but I feel another of Cas's tentacles push into my pussy, and I shudder once I'm stuffed full of my mates—one in every hole.

I lose track of time as moans and groans and wet slurps fill the room, creating a slutty soundtrack of our fuck fest. Nikos lasts a little longer than I expected, but it isn't long before he shouts and floods my mouth with his cum. It's tangy and salty, and I guzzle it down as my orgasm detonates, and pure fucking bliss runs through my body. Some of his cum leaks out of my mouth, dribbling down my chin. Xavier grabs my chin and turns my head, his tongue catching what I missed. His pace increases as my body clamps down around him, and I feel his cock swell and his body stiffen as he moans and fills my ass with his cum. At the same time, Cas groans loudly, and I feel his tentacle pulse, filling my pussy and Nikos's ass and mouth. He can't catch it all, and it leaks. Cas lowers him and also licks up the dripping cum from Nikos's chin.

"That is fucking filthy," I mutter as Xavier and I watch.

"But so fucking good," he agrees, sliding out of my ass and using two fingers to stuff his cum back in. "Clench, Lila. I want you to drip my cum for hours."

There's no way I'm not going to shower after this, but we can pretend for now as we all collapse in a sweaty mess, Cas lowering a wrung out Nikos to the bed.

His eyes flutter closed, but he has a small smile on his face that makes him look serene. He's well fucked but happy.

CHAPTER TWELVE

Lila

The ship gets under way the following day. A few deliveries and late arrivals held us up, but we are finally on a course for Earth via Vilax. My grandparents said their goodbyes at their estate. They didn't want to leave Gigi on her own, and they promised to see us soon. When I questioned them about that, Saxon assured me he'd fill me in on everything once we were underway.

We just wrapped up a full meeting between the thirteen of us. It's the first chance we've all had to be in the same place for more than a few moments since movie night. Even during the announcement last night, I didn't really get to spend any time with all of them.

I briefed them on my grandmother's story, and to say there were some shocked expressions is an understatement, then Saxon did as he promised and filled me in on the plan. I am highly impressed with it and can't wait to execute it. There were a few half-hearted arguments against me assuming my Madovian form, but they were quickly shot down. Brannock sent the message to the Syndicate posing as the Madovian, telling them she had a lead on the orb and should have it in her hands by the time we get to Earth, which should be in about a week.

After the meeting, I take a seat in the captain's chair on the flight deck, just wanting a moment to really absorb the fact that I am now the boss, but the adrenaline running through my system at the thought of what we have to do is exhilarating, and I'm restless, so I get up and start pacing. Bubby watches me, a silent beacon of support I am grateful for. I know if I wanted to talk, he would listen, but for now, I'm good.

My biggest focus at the moment is the keystone of the plan—the orb, or it's actual location to be precise. When the guys asked me exactly where the orb of power was, I didn't have an answer for them. My grandpas told me they would let me know when the time was right, which is not yet, apparently, but I can't help speculating where. There are so many possible hiding places on the ship, it could take forever to find it, and it also gives me an excuse to ignore the fact that I am essentially going to become the goddess of death when we do deal with the Syndicate. I really don't want that, and I have kept that little bit of information to myself. Zeydan is the only one who knows. I asked him not to say anything yet, and he has respected my wishes for now.

At the moment, he is meditating on the bio level. We cleared it out of any crew, and he's going to try to draw some power and put out a galaxy-wide call for his siblings. Apparently he can send a burst of power that works like a beacon, which should get their attention, or that's what we hope anyway. It turns out I was right, and Aarin is his long-lost brother. He made his home on Celestia and was content to be normal when his own search for Lilessa and Vivax failed. He said he did look for the others a few times over the past hundreds of years, but he could never get past Zeydan's plant and animal defenses. He figured he hadn't wanted to be found, so he let him be.

I suggested he help send the beacon, but Aarin needs air to boost his power, and artificial air from a ship doesn't really cut it. His powers are limited like Zeydan's after Vivax drained them. Before, neither of them needed to be around their element, but after, it's the only thing that will power their magic, but at least they had that.

"Lila." I stop my pacing at the sound of Bubby's voice and look at him. I'd been so focused on putting one foot in front of the other that I had completely zoned out. I look around the flight deck and notice everyone is staring at me with curious faces.

Crap, not the best impression on my first day as captain of this hunk of junk. Yikes, Bubby would probably kill me for calling his precious a hunk of junk despite the cool *Star Wars* reference.

"Sorry, I have a lot on my mind," I explain. "We reworked the show during our meeting, and Ghosie was going to send out a ship-wide rehearsal schedule. I'm just nervous to see what everyone thinks." I'm probably oversharing, but I don't care.

Everyone seems appeased by my explanation, and the scrutiny eases. "We're being hailed by an Aquilian bird of prey, so we've dropped out of warp speed to answer it," Bubby tells me, and I groan.

"Really? Fuck! Seriously, what does that evil hag want now? She made it perfectly clear that Nikos and our children were not wanted. When Nikos tried to contact his friend about her evil plans and his help in saving Nixie, he got no response." Saving Nixie has been added to our to-do list, but not before we take care of everything else. She will be alright in the dungeon until we can get to her. Her mother won't risk assassinating her, otherwise, she could start a civil war, and she doesn't need any extra turmoil.

"One of my contacts tells me Aquilia is on the brink of civil war. The citizens have not taken kindly to the new queen's rule. They say she is no better than her husband, and there are grumbles of a possible uprising," Saxon says from the doorway to the bridge. Standing behind him are Brannock and Tirrian.

All three men join us as Bubby brings up the image of the Aquilian spaceship on the screen.

"We got the alert you sent out. Nikos is also on his

way. He was swimming with the children. Link and Ghosie hurried down to help Caspian with them, so he won't be long."

Suddenly, Zeydan and Xavier appear in front of us, Zeydan's hand on the warlock who stumbles slightly.

"Shit, warn a guy, will you?" he mutters as Zeydan releases him and steps forward, staring at the Aquilian ship.

"Who is on the ship?" Zeydan demands, and I roll my eyes.

"We haven't quite gotten to that yet due to all the dramatic entrances." I don't hide the sarcasm. My men can be such drama queens. "But if it's the sea snake, how much trouble would we be in if we blasted her out of the sky?"

"Probably not a lot if the rumors have credibility, but how would Nikos feel about you killing his mother?" Xavier asks dryly, and I arch an unamused eyebrow at him.

"Probably the same way he feels about the fact that you killed his dad," I snarl, and he raises his hands in defense.

"Hey, that wasn't me, that was my parents."

"Same, same." I turn my back on him and study the ship. "They aren't being particularly aggressive, and they seem to be keeping pace. They hailed us?"

"Yes, but I haven't accepted the message yet. Shall I wait for Prince Nikos?" the communications officer asks.

Just at that moment, Nikos arrives on deck. He's

wearing a vest and pants of what looks like black fish scales, making his skin and hair appear vibrant against the dark colors. It kind of looks like armor, and he must have had it stashed in his little house in the Aquilian habitat to be able to have put it on so quickly. He's also carrying his large shiny trident in his left hand.

He pushes his wet hair back from his face and glares at the screen. "Hail them," he instructs, the perfect picture of royal arrogance. You wouldn't think he enjoyed being milked by his mates last night. I squirm at the memory and sit down, crossing my legs and nodding to the communications officer who looked to me for confirmation.

"Aquilian warbird, state your business. We have weapons locked on you and will fire unless you comply," Bubby demands, and an image pops onto the screen. It's Nixie.

"Stop, please, don't! I'm requesting asylum," she says quietly, not looking at us but off to the side of the screen.

"How do we know you are telling the truth, sister? For all we know, you are on a mission for our mother," Nikos retorts sharply, and that finally has her raising her head. One of her eyes is puffy and swollen with a large, dark bruise around it.

"I'd rather get thrown into the Molstoy Trench than do anything for that sea witch," she declares as another person moves into view. He has long, sky blue hair and matching eyes, with whirls of blue on his chest and neck that look like waves. He has a tattoo of a ferocious sea creature with huge teeth and spines on his right bicep, and he's wearing the same kind of outfit as Nikos. It looks like scale-covered armor, but his is a deep ocean blue.

"Hurricane." Nikos nods his head at the man who I know is his friend, the one Nikos was trying to contact to warn him about his mother's plans and ask him for help.

"Tito?" Zeydan says, and the man turns his attention to my mate. His eyes widen in surprise.

"Zeydan, my brother. Is that you?"

"No, that can't be your brother. That is my friend, Hurricane. We grew up together," Nikos argues, sounding as confused as I am.

"Let us aboard, please, and we can explain everything," Nixie begs, finally looking at me. "I don't expect you to forgive me, Lila. I've been a terrible friend, but I beg you to listen to my story."

"There are four life-forms aboard the ship," our security officer cautions.

"Who is with you?" I ask her, unwilling to give in just yet despite wanting to. The safety of this ship is more important than my friendship with Nixie. She wasn't above putting her people first, and neither am I.

"Hurri's twin sisters are with us. He is their sole guardian since his parents recently died." Her eyes are shadowed, and I bet their deaths had something to do with her mother.

"My friend, I am sorry," Nikos says solemnly and looks at me, his eyes beseeching me to help them.

"Fine, but the war bird is too big to dock in the hangar," I tell them, and Hurri shakes his head.

"If the uprising is unsuccessful, then Nerissa's forces will be tracking us. She will not let us go. We need you to make it look like it was destroyed until we know if the coup is successful and we can return safely. It's better to pretend we are dead until then."

"I'll head to the teleport bay and have them beamed over," Nikos says, but before he can move, Hurri reaches out, clasps Nixie's shoulder, and waves to someone off screen. Two young girls, I'd put their ages at about fourteen, momentarily move into the shot, and then the four of them disappear altogether.

"Hey!" Nikos shouts, sounding panicked, but Zeydan holds up his hand.

"Wait for it," he says, and all of a sudden, they reappear directly in front of us, the packed flight deck getting even more crowded.

Nikos and Nixie hug, while Zeydan and Hurri do the same, and the two teenagers stand around awkwardly.

"How about we move into the war room? There is more space there, and Bubby can get this ship moving again. We are on a deadline to get to Vilax on time, and warp speed is the only way we can do that," Brannock suggests and leads the way, leaving the crew to do what they need to do.

Our guests follow after him, with Saxon and

Xavier close behind. Nikos and Zeydan are deep in conversation with Nixie and Hurricane.

"Can we do that? Don't we all need to be strapped in to jump back into warp?" I ask Bubby, and he smiles.

"I will sound the alert, but the war room seats are equipped with harnesses, so you will all be fine."

"Is someone going to take care of that?" Tirrian points to the war bird that is now back on the screen.

"Are we sure it was just the four of them on board?" I ask my security chief, and he nods.

"No sign of any other life-form. It's clear to destroy."

"Let's move to a safe distance, and then you have the go ahead to fire on it," Bubby tells the pilot and weapons officer.

"Come on then, let's go and see what drama awaits us now." Tirrian holds out his hand, and I take it, then we follow after the others. The warp siren sounds, giving the ship's occupants a five-minute warning to strap in.

In the war room, which is really just a big conference room with a table with holographic capabilities, everyone is taking a seat. As they place their asses in the chairs, harnesses snap out from the back rest and slide over the occupant before latching into the seat. The base of the chairs are built into the floors and can't be moved around, unless you want to swivel in them, but it looks like the mechanism locks when the harness snaps into place.

Zeydan waves me over and gestures to Hurricane. "I'd like you to meet my brother, Tito," he says, and the male holds up a hand.

"I go by Hurricane now. Tito is a relic of a former life."

Zeydan nods his understanding. "Markit said much the same thing. He goes by Aarin now."

Hurricane's eyes light up. "You have seen him?" He sounds hopeful, and Zeydan rocks back on his heels, looking smug.

"He is here on this ship. It will be one hell of a reunion."

"Quickly, take a seat so you don't get smooshed when we jump into hyperspace," Xavier instructs, letting his mist fall away. After giving me a quick kiss, he makes his way to a chair. Ever the gentleman, he guides the two wide-eyed teenagers and helps them into theirs. I can see crushes form and stars in their eyes as they giggle to each other while he takes his own seat with a dramatic flourish.

"So tell us everything," I demand as I take my own seat at the head of the table, Brannock on one side and Saxon on the other. Both of them are on high alert for any misdeeds from our guests. It's good to be queen— I mean ringmaster.

CHAPTER THIRTEEN

Nikos

The ship moves slightly, and the young girls whom I recognize as being more grown-up versions of Hurri's sisters gasp. The preteens they were when Nixie and I left Aquilia are gone, and now they are pretty teenagers who I am sure do their best to drive my friend crazy. Storm and Tempest were such adorable little children and worshiped the ground their much older brother walked on, but they were also cheeky little girls who liked to get up to mischief.

"It's just your ship blowing up," Tirrian assures them, placing himself midway down the table between Lila and our guests. Zeydan also takes a seat on that end, much like Xavier. They are all strategically placed in case those claiming to be friends are actually enemies instead. I approve, but I hope like hell they are not trying to play us false in any way. I'm still shocked at

Zeydan's announcement. How can the man I know and grew up with be his godly brother? Before I can say anything, though, Nixie starts her story.

"After you left, Mother was kind to my face for a few days, but it soon became apparent she was no better than our father. We established a council, people handpicked by me who I knew would be a good counter measure to any decisions she might make—mers who would benefit our people and not just themselves." My sister is most definitely more suitable for ruling than I am, since she is infinitely less selfish. "But as we started making decisions and suggestions on changes to Father's rule, Mother was not happy. Some of the mers who had been loyal to my father decided it was better to follow her and get rewarded than try to do right for the better of the mer people. In the end, she imprisoned us all and became a dictator."

"How did you get away?" Brannock asks suspiciously.

"She promised breeding rights of me to one of the crusty old men. When I was being transported to his estate close to where Hurricane was stationed, he created a diversion and managed to free me."

We turn our attention to my friend, who takes over his part of the story. "I have been a part of a resistance for a while now."

"Hang on, before we get to that, how did you and Nikos grow up together if you are also Zeydan's long-lost brother?" Lila interjects, needing some back story before we go on, and I want to know this information as well.

"Of course, sister, my apologies." Hurricane nods to her, and she gapes at him.

"Sister?" Lila mouths to Zeydan, and he shrugs. I mean, I guess he is her brother-in-law now, if what he says is true, and she seems to accept that.

"When we were damaged after Vivax's plan was foiled, we were scattered amongst the galaxy. A good chunk of our power was gone, or at least the power to create new worlds and races was. Our general powers were still greater than those of our creations, but it made us vulnerable and easy to kill, and we made a decision to go our separate ways and live quiet lives amongst our creations. I chose the Aquilians." His version lines up with Liliana's and Zeydan's stories.

"This is similar to what Aarin told me," Zeydan tells Hurricane, mentioning the Celestian we now know is Zeydan's other brother, the elemental god of air. We were all shocked to learn that. How have they all ended up in the same place together? Ghosie speculated it must be fate playing a hand in all of this. Maybe whoever originally created them is trying to right the wrongs of the universe.

"I lived a quiet life for many years, faking my death and later reappearing on the other side of the planet in a different community, but eventually, some of the mers got suspicious. Nikos's ancestors, who have held the throne for a very long time, were a wily and suspicious lot, and I wasn't able to outsmart them. I was ambushed and killed."

Nixie and the two girls gasp, and their eyes shine with tears. My own heart aches at the thought of my friend being subjected to any pain from my family.

"Go on," I encourage.

"I knew it wouldn't be permanent, but I didn't reincarnate for a good many years, and it was to a family that was part of the inner circle at the palace. Nikos and I were childhood friends. Eventually, my memories returned. I was about seventeen or eighteen by then, but instead of telling anyone, I decided it was better to live as Hurricane. My life was good, and my parents were lovely people. My best friend and his twin sister spent more time in our residence than their own."

He isn't wrong. Nixie and I did everything we could to escape our parents, who were in a toxic marriage and fought constantly when Dad paraded his harem of mistresses in front of my mother. She grew more bitter as we got older, and by the time we were teenagers, she couldn't stand to look at us and vice versa.

"His parents were kind, loving, good people and made us feel like we were wanted. They knew life for the crown prince and princess of Aquilia was not all it was cracked up to be," I explain.

"Nikos was being groomed to take over from Marlin, and Nixie was going to be married off in an alliance that would benefit Marlin. Their parents did not like my influence on their children. Nikos was using his airheaded facade almost permanently by then to fool his father into thinking he was a moldable idiot. Marlin didn't like me around him and ordered me to attend military school."

"Which was exactly our plan," I interject. "I wanted Hurricane as my right-hand man when I took the throne, because there wasn't anyone I trusted more, but then the Aquilians were ordered by the council to send someone to perform in the circus. Dad got it in his head that he could make good political alliances if he sent us. He knew the crown prince of the warlocks and General Saxon were already performing in it, and had been informed that Caspian and Link, although not royalty, had influential families, and we were instructed to make friends."

"That didn't go so well," Lila remarks, and I shake my head ruefully.

"I did not want them dragged into my parents' drama, so I continued my airhead charade and remained aloof. Nixie and I were certain that the pod we were performing with were spies for my parents, so she made friends with the cast and crew."

"You used Magenta and the two Vilaxians?" Lila accuses my sister, unable to hide the hostility in her voice.

My sister vehemently shakes her head. "God, no," she cries and clasps her hands together. "One of us had to look like we were making an effort. If I wanted to stay on my parents' good side, I would have seduced one of the men they wanted me to. No, Mags, Hale, and Velorina was me being selfish and wanting something for myself. I knew it could never be serious though. I was always going to marry someone my parents picked out, and Mags was not on that list. The Vilaxians were eventually going to need a clan as well. It's hardwired into them."

We all look at Saxon for confirmation. "Yes, she is mostly right. A Vilaxian does feel longing for a clan when they are not a part of one." Lila frowns, and he must see her worry, so he picks up her hand and gives it a reassuring squeeze. "The exception being when we find our blood rose. I do not ache for a clan, and even if I did, all of your mates would satisfy that need. It's not just a need for blood, but for emotional ties, and I have that with our family."

Her face clears, and I can practically feel her relief. She turns her attention back to my sister. "Then what?"

Hurricane takes over again. "While in military school, I was invited to join the resistance—one that opposed Marlin's rule and wished for a different leadership. I convinced them that Nikos was not his father and that he should rule instead. We had to be careful, because Marlin had spies everywhere. We were in the process of planning an assassination when the warlocks took care of the problem for us." Hurricane nods his thanks to Xavier, who waves his hand nonchalantly, but before he can reply, the ship makes the leap into warp speed. It shudders for a moment or two, my chest aching as a great force presses down on it. Holy shit, that hurts. Usually I am below the surface of our pool when we do that, and it doesn't hurt anywhere near as much since the water buffers us. It finally stabilizes, and we are all released from the harnesses.

"You're welcome," Xavier says, and Lila rolls her eyes at him taking the credit. I remember he was knocked out during the whole thing.

"We thought things might change once Nerissa was in charge, but then she declared Nikos was an enemy of the crown because he was pregnant and mated to a non-Aquilian. We knew it wasn't going to be different, so we continued our plans for the coup, just changed our main target, but then Nixie was imprisoned, and I knew I had to save her."

Hurricane is staring at my sister like the sun shines out of her ass, and something starts to roll around inside my brain. Before I can voice my thoughts, though, Lila says something that makes my heart skip a beat.

"How long have you known she was your mate?" Lila asks, and he turns to stare at her with open-mouthed astonishment. I am also looking at my mate in shock, unable to compute what she is saying.

"I'm your mate?" Nixie asks, staring at him with such surprise and no small amount of longing.

"Like hell he's your mate!" I jump to my feet, slamming my hands on the table. "Aquilians don't have mates. We choose who we want to be with." I don't have any problem with my sister being with my best friend if that is what she wants, but it has to be her decision. Our parents already tried to take that choice out of her hands, and I won't do the same thing.

"Nikos," Lila cautions and waves a hand to get me to sit back down. I do as she asks, but I won't take my eyes off my friend who still hasn't answered my sister.

"We don't get a choice of who our mates are," Zeydan says quietly.

"But Gigi chose my grandpas because she was reborn as a Skarrian, so why shouldn't it be the same for Hurricane?" Lila argues.

Zeydan bites his lip, and he shakes his head. "I don't know exactly how it works, but I did ask her about that, and she claims that even once she regained memories of her past life, she still felt like all three of them were her mates and that she hadn't made a mistake." He pauses for a moment, like he's thinking about what he should share. "I hope you will keep this between us, but Aarin confided in me that Mark is his mate, which is why he insisted on accompanying them to the circus. Mark's parents are aware that he is the god of air. He didn't die and wasn't reborn, he just changed his name to fit into their society and confided in the royals when he knew they were trustworthy."

"Holy shit," Lila mutters as Xavier waves a hand, and I feel magic settle over me.

"Hey," Tirrian growls at the warlock who just waves him off impatiently.

"Just a little geis so that that information isn't shared by accident." He's looking at the two teenagers in the room, and I understand his line of thought. I guess Tirrian gets it too, because he relaxes again.

I turn my attention back to my sister and best friend, and they stare at each other with stars in their eyes. Hurri holds Nixie's hand like she's the most precious thing in the world to him. I kind of thought my sister was more into females than males, even though I know she has had relationships with both. Lila is frowning, and I guess she has the same thoughts.

"How do you feel about that, Nixie?" she asks, biting her lip with worry.

"Like I'm the luckiest mer in the world. I had given up my crush on Hurri years ago because I thought he saw me as an annoying little sister." My sister sighs as Hurri leans forward and presses a gentle kiss to her lips. I want to gag, but I control myself and instead turn to look at my own mate so I don't have to watch such a gross sight.

"But you said you leaned more toward females," Lila argues, wanting to make sure Nixie really is on board with the mate stuff.

They must stop kissing, because my sister answers. "Usually I do, but Hurri was always the exception. I crushed on him so hard when I was a teenager, but I didn't have the guts to make a move because he was also our best friend." When I look back, she's gesturing to me. "I loved my brother too much to ruin the one friendship he seemed to value over everything else."

My eyes fill with tears at her sacrifice, and the rest

of my anger seeps away. How can I begrudge them any of this?

"I wouldn't stop you from pursuing anything with another if that is your desire. I want your happiness more than anything, and I am not as unenlightened as many of the races of the universe," my friend assures my sister.

"We can talk about this later," she promises him.

"Well, okay then," Lila claps her hands together. "I guess it's welcome to the circus. Will you all be willing to perform in the show?" She looks to the four new arrivals, and Nixie and Hurricane both nod.

"Yes. We talked about this during our journey here. We should be able to rework the performance so it still catches people's imagination." Nixie looks at me. "Especially if we have my niece and nephew involved as well. When can I meet them?" she asks and puts out her hands, making grabby motions.

"I'm not sure they are ready for the show quite yet, and they just finished a swim in the pool when your ship hailed us, but we can go to our suite, and I can introduce you if you want." I stand up and look at my wife, who gives me a small encouraging nod. She knows how much I have longed to have my twin meet our babies.

"What about you two?" Saxon's attention turns to Hurricane's sisters, who have remained quiet this whole time. "Are you going to want to perform in the show?"

"Will we get paid?" Storm asks. Her hair is a darker

shade than her sister's, and she is the feistier one of the two. Tempest is gentler and quieter, and usually lets Storm do all the talking for her.

Tirrian chuckles and gives her an approving nod. Of course the dragon would support that kind of question. "Yes, of course, all our performers do. You will also be expected to attend lessons and continue your education."

"And where will we live?" Storm asks, crossing her arms. I smother my grin at her negotiation.

"Well, there is the Aquilian habitat that still has the two homes in it. Nikos and Nixie's and the one the other pod used," Brannock points out.

"Good, because we do not want to live with our brother if he is going to be doing that all the time." Storm points at Hurricane and Nixie, who are kissing again, and I wrinkle my nose.

"I understand completely. I don't see why you couldn't live in one while they live in the other."

Hurricane breaks off his kiss at my words and glares at me.

"What? It's not like you won't be able to supervise them, it will just be at a more tolerable distance for all involved."

"Who are you to tell me how to raise my sisters?" he barks, and I raise an eyebrow at him.

"I am your crown prince," I snarl, and he smirks.

"Ah, but I am your god." He puffs out his chest, and I roll my eyes.

"We have not worshiped the gods for a long time.

You are a washed-up has-been." The two of us glare at each other, and Lila starts to chuckle with the others joining in until the whole room is filled with laughter.

"Ha-ha-ha, that was too good, but let me stop you both. This is my ship, and I am in charge. I don't care if you're a king, a god, or a warlock. What I say goes." Lila's words have power, and my body shakes as it washes over me. "The girls will have their wishes within reason. You will still be monitored, and until you can prove you are responsible and can be treated as adults, you will have a curfew. Now, I am just about done for the day, and I want to see my babies. How about you join us for some lunch? Tomorrow will be busy while we rehearse the show."

Hurricane bows his head, conceding to Lila's authority—for now. I also agree, secretly turned on by her show of power. I catch Xavier's eye, and he winks at me and mouths, "Hot."

"Why don't we make a family reunion of it and invite Susie, Mark, and Aarin as well?" Brannock suggests, and Zeydan looks at Lila with hope.

"Better make it in the dining room then, because our suite is not big enough for a party like that," she says, knowing it will make Zeydan happy.

"I'll call ahead and book a table." Saxon stands up. "If I make it an hour later, that will give Nixie time to show the others to their new home."

"I'm assuming you all escaped without your belongings?" Xavier muses, standing up, and the four of them confirm this. "Write a list of what you need, and we will source it for you either from Vilax or Earth. Do you have someone you can contact to take care of your things back on Aquilia?"

"One of the trusted members of the resistance was going to pack up my belongings at the barracks and then go to my family home and pack that up as well. Once things are more settled, we can either return there or have them shipped to us."

"We're never going home, are we?" Tempest asks, tears streaming down her face.

Nixie stands up and moves to the girl, gathering her in her arms and holding her while she sobs. "I hope we can one day."

"Well, I don't want to be king," I announce, and Hurricane looks at me with surprise, "so if you are amenable, then I would appoint you as regent until Typhoon comes of age."

Lila looks stunned at this announcement. Of course it hadn't occurred to her that he is in line for the Aquilian throne, and Hali next if he doesn't want it, but heaven help Aquilia if she leads it with her temper. We'd constantly be on the verge of war.

"But that's a subject for another time." Zeydan obviously sees the panic in our wife's eyes and takes action. "Come now, let's celebrate another win for our family."

CHAPTER FOURTEEN

Saxon

The trip to Vilax passes quickly. Rehearsals are in full swing, and Lila is very happy with the new acts and how the show is looking. With the Aquilians back on the program, albeit with a reworked show, and the new acts, it's a longer and more exciting show than we had previously. The only act that hasn't rehearsed yet is mine. Although Thorn and Titus offered to help out, we're still short a couple of fliers. Both Susie and Magenta have offered their assistance, but I will wait to see what happens at home before I give them an answer.

We are docking at the spaceport that sits above Vilax, where they house their own battleships. The main ship is too big to land on the surface, so we will teleport down for the tribunal. I'm staring out the window of my room as the ship maneuvers into position, both my hearts beating faster than normal with my nerves. It's weird. I can go into battle, and my heart rates don't change, but the thought of anything upsetting my blood rose is enough to send my hearts into palpitations.

I haven't been completely honest with Lila. I told her I wasn't worried about this tribunal and that it should just be a formality. Finding a blood rose is one of the only surefire ways of dissolving a clan and really shouldn't have required a tribunal, so then why have we been called for one? My aunt should have sent Estrella and Radella packing. It isn't like we were kicking them out of the circus. They could have stayed with Hale and Velorina and continued performing. They just had to stop their possessive crap. I was never theirs to begin with, and I am most definitely Lila's now.

I sigh and push off the cold frame, heading to my wardrobe. Appearing in front of the Vilaxian queen requires formal attire. I advised the others, and they were sourcing an outfit for Lila to wear, one that is Vilaxian in nature. Xavier assured me that Tinka at one of the ship's boutiques was more than capable of producing something fit for a princess. After all, I am a prince of Vilax, even if I go by my general title.

My parents' clan are advisors to the queen, and I can't wait to see them and my extended family. Although my mother and father may be gone, and I miss them with all my heart, my family clan still considers me one of their own. Xenos is my twin, and we have five more clan brothers and sisters, as well as my aunt's daughters whom we are all close to. They are dying to meet my blood rose, and they should all be in attendance for the tribunal. It is a formal affair and not one that is taken lightly amongst sanguinistas.

I pull out my uniform and dress, making sure my medals are all in place before strapping my sword scabbard to my back. I study myself in the mirror and finger comb my hair. I'm sure Auntie will complain, but I've let my hair grow out slightly since I left military service, and I know Lila loves running her hands through it.

Happy with how I look, I head out into the living area of the suite. The tribunal is an evening affair, and our children are already in bed. We made the decision that only Lila and I would attend the tribunal, and the rest of her mates kicked up a fuss, but I argued it was a Vilaxian legal proceeding and not something that would normally include guests. It would have been different if it was a political dinner or a ball. They all eventually conceded on the promise that if anything went sideways, Lila would teleport us to safety. She can't go as far as the ship in space, but she could get us out of immediate harm, and I could take over from there and find us a place to hole up until we could be beamed back aboard.

The rest of Lila's mates are all lounging around our living area to wish us good luck.

"How do you think this will go?" Brannock asks, taking in my military uniform with wide eyes. "Hell, I haven't seen a Vilaxian in uniform since the war. You scrub up well, General." He tips his bottle of beer at me in a salute, and I nod my thanks.

"I'd like to say it will go smoothly, but I think that's wishful thinking. Estrella and Radella are known for their dramatics. I tried to contact Hale to see if he had any information for me, but he is dodging my calls... as is my brother." I frown. This is what has me the most worried. None of my family are accepting my calls. I haven't been able to reach any of them since I got word of the tribunal. Not even the queen or her staff are responding to my messages. It's radio silent.

"Maybe you should reconsider taking some of us along," Silac suggests, his tongue flicking in and out in agitation. "Xavier could glamour us as Vilaxians."

"That still wouldn't help. You need special clearance to attend a tribunal. Only the queen, her council members, which are my family clan, and the offending parties are permitted." Then an idea comes to me. "And any witnesses if needed."

"So Link could go as your witness. He was the one who had to restrain you, and he has the footage of the two females releasing him from his sedation," Caspian suggests.

I purse my lips in thought. It is perfectly reasonable for me to insist on such a thing. "Yes. I think that would work."

"And maybe you might want to mention that Lila will be taking on the mantle of goddess of death in the near future and, as one of their creations, it would behoove them not to get on her bad side." Zeydan leans against the window frame, much like I had done in my room, his attention split between our conversation and the ship docking. Lila had kept it a secret for a day or two, but she eventually told us about becoming the goddess of death and how terrified she was of it.

"That is good thinking." Ghosie points at the deity. "They can't argue with that."

"But that means admitting we plan on taking care of the current goddess of death, and if Vivax has her spies amongst your people, it could get back to her and mess up our plans." Tirrian is keeping a cool head for a change, which is slightly surprising but not totally unexpected since he is military trained as well.

"Can't we just pretend none of this is happening?" Echo whines, and Maxsim snuggles his pregnant mate closer to his body.

"Lila has been through so much shit. If your aunt refuses your clan dissolution, then I'm not sure she won't go ballistic on them," Maxsim growls. "Are you prepared to go against your family?" Maxsim asks, voicing something that has been plaguing me, but I can answer without hesitation.

"Absolutely. I'm ninety-nine percent sure it won't come to that, but I would walk away from my family without hesitation," I assure him, and a small sound behind me has us turning to look at the hallway to our bedrooms.

I just about swallow my tongue when I see Lila standing there. Her eyes are shiny, and she clutches a hand against her chest. "You would give up your family for me?" She sounds awed, and I use my speed to get to her.

I take her clasped hand and press a kiss against it. "I would do anything for you," I tell her before running my eyes down her body. "You look incredible."

I release her hand, and she uses it to tug at her outfit. "Nobody told me Vilaxian formal wear was synonymous with stripper chic or harem girl casual."

She's wearing my colors, silver and black, and they look gorgeous against her beautiful hair, which she has left long with a loose curl to it. Her skirt is a gauzy swath of material with slits up both thighs, allowing her legs to show every time she takes a step. The bodice is mostly just a bra with beading and a small amount of floaty gauze covering her stomach with a slit through the middle so you can see her belly button. She's wearing a chain around her waist, and a jewel dangles enticingly over her crotch, drawing the eye to it.

My skin itches, and my fangs drop into place. Neither of us have fed from one another for a few days, and I feel the overwhelming urge to sink my fangs into her neck and my cock into her body. A rumbling growl reverberates through my chest, and Lila's eyes widen before she smiles, showing her own fangs to me.

"We probably should have fed before we left," she says, slapping a hand over her mouth. "They are a little hard to control."

"That was deliberate," Link says behind me, and Lila turns her attention to him. I don't think I could form words at the moment to explain why, so stunned I am by her beauty.

"What do you mean?" she asks as I step out of the way and offer her my arm.

"An old Vilaxian tradition, one you may be asked to perform, will be proving to the council that Saxon's blood rose, who was previously not Vilaxian, is capable of sustaining him," Link explains, wincing slightly.

"What do you mean?" Lila asks sharply. She's a smart girl, and I think she knows what he is going to say, but he explains anyway.

"You may be asked to feed him in front of the tribunal."

"But feeding leads to fucking." She looks from me to Link, and I'm still too fucking chicken to say anything. The great General Saxon of the Vilaxian army has been reduced to quivering in fear from his wife's temper. Link glares at me before nodding his agreement to her words.

"Yes, it does."

"I'll have to fuck in front of the whole tribunal, witnesses and all?" Her eyes widen, and she looks at me for confirmation. I nod, resisting the urge to adjust my cock. I'm pretty sure she doesn't want to know how much I like that idea.

"We will have to fuck in front of his family, clan, and aunt? Hell, his brothers and sisters and cousins too?" She sounds appalled. "I'll never be able to look them in the eye again. Fuck it! Let's blow this popsicle stand and take our chances as renegades."

She whirls around, ready to hightail it back to our room, and my heart sinks. Although I said I would give it all up for her, I really don't want to. I don't think it will be a problem, but I want the chance to make sure.

"Lila." Ghosie steps in front of her, not letting her pass, and she won't risk touching him at the moment, so she stops in place.

"Ghosie..." She growls in a very bear-like way, and he just smirks at her.

"You know you aren't going to run away. You are one of the bravest females I know, and if a little fucking in front of Saxon's family is what it takes to prove that you are meant to be together, then I know you will do it."

"But I'll never be able to sit across the dinner table from them at Christmas and look them in the eye," she whines and looks at him with pleading eyes.

"We don't celebrate Christmas," I add helpfully, but she whirls and glares at me.

"Not helping," she snaps at me.

"Hell, if you're that shy, throw up a distortion spell. They will get the gist of what's happening but not be able to make out any details. I bet they aren't really that keen on seeing it either," Xavier says. "You should really talk to your aunt about abolishing that stupid law."

"That's a thing?" Lila asks the warlock, and I feel a prick of hope once more.

"Yeah, it's easy. You just manifest it into being.

Think that you want the image of you distorted and will it to happen." Xavier shrugs like it's no big deal.

"How will I know though?" she asks.

"I can give you a signal," Link suggests.

"Or I can come too. After all, I am a witness and can testify to what my warlock harem members did," Xavier says slyly, and I snort quietly with amusement.

The sneaky warlock worked out a way to come on this trip after all, and from Brannock's and Tirrian's amused smirks, they know it as well.

"Right, okay then. It will be the four of us then. Shall we get moving? The less time we spend here, the quicker we can get on the move again. Brannock has been so patient, but he must be frantic with worry about Chloe." She moves over to him and gives him a kiss on the cheek.

"I'm okay, because I know it will all be over soon, but I have dibs on Smith's head."

"Head, entrails, testicles, whatever you'd like, my love," Lila promises rather bloodthirstily, which is why we all love her so much.

She goes around and gives each of her mates who are staying behind a kiss, rubbing her hand over Echo's belly before stopping in front of Nikos.

"Can you go down and check on your sister for me? I haven't told Magenta that she returned. I swore the bridge crew to secrecy, but you know how things get out. I think Magenta needs to hear the story from Nixie, especially now that Nixie has a mate."

"I'll go now," he promises and kisses her soundly

before slapping her ass. "Your bosom is so bountiful in that top and would look wonderful bouncing up and down as I drive my cock into you," he says with a wink.

She giggles and whispers something in his ear, which has him blushing and nodding before hurrying out of our home, adjusting his cock inside his pants.

"Such a naughty wife," I tell her, and she gives me a wink. I wave my hand at Link and Xavier. "You need formal wear, and we don't have any time."

"It's fine." Xavier waves his hand, and he and Link are suddenly wearing formal attire. For Link, that involves a suit that fits his body like a glove and just about has Lila drooling. For Xavier, his outfit is slightly more exotic. He has on dark purple, wide-legged pants that are also split and show his legs when he walks, all of his purple swirls on display. As for his torso, he is wearing a long vest that is open and shows off all his delicious lavender skin. I growl at the thought of everyone seeing what he usually keeps hidden from everyone's eyes but his family's.

"You're going like that?" I hear Lila ask, sounding almost as jealous as I feel.

He inclines his head. "Yes. Despite this being a private tribunal, I will be wearing my diplomatic hat as a witness. I will honor the Vilaxians with my countenance."

"Do you even hear how arrogant you sound?" Caspian asks, bemused.

"Why is it arrogant when it is the truth?"

Lila shakes her head as Xavier slides an arm around

her waist, drawing her close. He rubs his nose against hers. "You know it is the truth." He releases her and shoves her at me. I grab her as she stumbles. "Now let the Vilaxians see how enamored you are with each other. Link and I will be your dutiful witnesses. Let us make our way to the transport room and beam to the surface. It's time to put those two bitches in their place."

CHAPTER FIFTEEN

Xavier

It is dark when we arrive on Vilax. They only get like seven hours of sunlight a day, which makes it difficult to know what time it is. Saxon informs us it's late in the afternoon and that our tribunal was scheduled for around six in the evening. Time works differently here, but he says that's the basic equivalent to Earth time for Lila's sake.

The receiving room we arrive in is ornate, and Saxon explains it is the palace receiving room. All tribunals are held at the palace as the queen and her council are the only authorities who can dissolve a clan.

We are met by Saxon's brother, Xenos, which is still slightly jarring, because I look at him and see the mirror image of my husband. He greets us with a small formal bow.

"Well, that's a lot less enthusiastic than the last time we met," Lila says dryly. A small frown forms between Saxon's eyebrows. I feel a pinch of concern from our bloodsucker, and his hearts starts to race. He seems to be surprised by the greeting as well.

"If you could follow me, the queen and council are waiting for you." He doesn't wait for an answer before he turns and moves away from the teleport platform. Saxon looks at Lila and gives her hand a squeeze before releasing her. Link and I exchange a concerned glance, but we stay quiet for now. We follow Xenos, Saxon zipping forward to keep pace with his brother. They have a whispered conversation that I can't hear. Damn Vilaxians, able to talk below a warlock's hearing register.

"What's going on?" Lila mutters over her shoulder to Link and me. We remain at her back, guarding her from any kind of rear attack. My power crackles at my fingertips, as I am on high alert for an ambush. Something is not right here. I have visited Saxon at his aunt's castle in the past, and it is usually full of people bustling back and forth. At this moment, there isn't even a servant in sight. I purse my lips at Lila's question.

"I will not speculate, but Xenos has always been a kiss ass to the queen. Don't get me wrong, she loves them both, and as far as I know, Saxon has an extremely good relationship with her, but when she asked for volunteers to join the circus, Saxon was the one who stepped up. Xenos refused, saying it would be beneath him. It split their clan in two. Maybe Xenos has decided to take Estrella and Radella's side. If it would benefit him, he would in a heartbeat."

Lila doesn't like this information, and she hisses her disapproval of Xenos's lack of loyalty. "Have I finally found a brother-in-law I'm going to dislike? I knew I couldn't be so lucky to like all of them." She stops and raises an eyebrow at me. "Remind me, do you have any siblings? I don't remember you mentioning any, and neither did your mom or dad."

I bow gallantly and grin. "Alas, they broke the mold when they made me, and I am my parents only child."

She rolls her eyes, which seems to be a permanent response when we are conversing. Maybe I should have Link check her for an ailment.

She turns her attention to the good doctor. "And you? Do you have any family you haven't mentioned yet?"

He shakes his head. "No, only my mother and father, and you already know how unpleasant my mother can be."

"Mm-hmm," she agrees. "I need to make a folder to keep everyone straight for birthday and Christmas invites. Yours and Nikos's mother, as well as Saxon's brother, will go on the hate list. They only get one chance, and he blew it. I will reserve judgment on the queen of Vilax until I meet her and any other family members you have brought to the table."

I'm about to remind her that birthdays and

Christmas are strictly Earth traditions, but the doctor elbows me, and a whoosh of air escapes my lungs as his elbow digs into my side.

I glare at him. "What the fuck, man?" I snarl, but he nods at Lila, and I notice her eyes glistening as she whirls back to continue forward.

Oh fuck, our wife is upset. Now I'm going to have to kill Saxon's brother. Fuck, I hope he will forgive me. Things are going to be awfully uncomfortable in the marriage bed if he actively hates me, but then I've always enjoyed a violent hate fuck. It makes sex interesting if you don't know whether you will survive to orgasm or not.

We stay silent, and Saxon and Xenos's conversation sounds like it gets more aggressive with hissing and snarling, but try as I may, I still can't make out any actual words. Finally, Saxon throws up his hands and stops keeping pace with his brother, waiting for the three of us to catch up with him. We continue to follow his brother, but at a distance.

"Stay alert. Something is not right, and Xenos wouldn't tell me what's going on." Saxon sounds frustrated, and I can feel how much Lila wants to wrap him in her arms and give him a hug. Our wife is so loving and kind, and I will kill just about anyone to keep her that way.

"I didn't bring any weapons," she mutters, sounding annoyed at herself. "I've gotten pretty good with my lightning whip, and Tirrian and Silac have been teaching me to throw knives."

Aww, isn't that adorable? She wants to go in armed for Saxon. How did we get so lucky? "Never fear, my sweet," I murmur and release a burst of power, conjuring a beautiful sheath of throwing knives on each of her sexy thighs. My cock hardens at the tantalizing sight of weapons being so close to her tight cunt.

She stumbles and looks down, gasping in surprise. Lila turns back and throws her arms around me. "Thank you," she says and gives me a fleeting kiss on the lips before turning forward. I puff my chest out with pride, and I hear Link snort and feel his amusement scent the air.

"Don't be jealous, I haven't forgotten about you. I give gifts to all my loved ones, my sexy cyborg." I conjure him a harness holding a crossbow and a dozen bolts.

I wink at his surprise, and he shakes his head. "Are you taking a leaf out of Nikos's playbook? You sound ridiculous," he mutters, but he pulls the crossbow out and admires the construction before returning it to the holster.

I keep my power sparking at my fingertips, not needing a physical weapon to do damage, but when I look at Saxon, he's frowning.

"I'm not sure we should be taking weapons into our tribunal meeting. We will probably be required to remove them, since we will be in front of the queen."

As we arrive at the door Xenos disappeared through, Saxon frowns. "That's strange, the throne room always has guards at the door. There should be at least two keeping watch at all times." He reaches for his sword, pulling it from the scabbard on his back. Lila and Link also arm themselves as I wave a hand, and the doors burst inwards.

The room is dark and silent, and as we step cautiously into it, I hear a rustling of someone's clothes off to the side and brace myself for an attack.

"It's an ambush!" I scream and blast fire into the air to light up the room so we can see our attackers.

The lights come on and the crowd of people in the room shout, "Surprise," just before my magic hits the chandelier in the middle of the ceiling, launching fragments of glass all over and plunging the room back into darkness.

The silence is even more deafening than before.

"What the actual fuck is happening here? Are we being attacked?" Lila's voice is loud, echoing through the throne room.

We hear someone clear their throat awkwardly. "Ah, not exactly."

A small spark lights up somewhere down the back, and someone lights a candle. Whoever holds the candle walks toward us. I decide to help out with the lights, since I had a hand in destroying the chandelier, and throw some light balls into the ceiling, illuminating a gathered crowd dressed in their finery. The person holding the candle comes into view. It is Sabine, the Vilaxian queen, with her blood rose, Aleister, and their twin daughters, Mehira and Musette.

"Nephew, I apologize for startling you and your

companions. We wanted to celebrate your joining." She looks from Saxon to Lila and smiles. "So we took the liberty of researching Earth customs in honor of your blood rose. Maybe we made a mistake."

Saxon just gapes at his aunt, but a smile spreads across Lila's lips, and I can feel how much she likes what she just heard. Oh, the queen just earned some major brownie points. I bet she went to the top of Lila's like list.

"What?" Saxon stammers like he doesn't understand what she's saying.

"A surprise party. That was the idea. A celebration of your blood rose binding," she says slowly like she's explaining to someone who is learning impaired. She looks at her husband. "Did we damage him when we yelled 'surprise?' Do you think he needs medical help?"

Lila clears her throat and steps forward, curtsying to the queen like she had been instructed. It's low and fluid, as if she's been doing it all her life. "Your Majesty, a surprise party was a lovely thought, and both Saxon and I appreciate it. I apologize for our overenthusiastic warlock." She turns and glares in my direction, and I wince. "I think he thought we were about to be attacked. Saxon may also be a little surprised and confused because we were told we were coming here for a tribunal, and that the clan dissolution was being challenged."

The queen's eyes glimmer with understanding, and she nods before waving a hand and huffing. "Utterly ridiculous and a waste of our time. We denied their claim before it could even be lodged. Both girls were instructed to find new clans or go alone like some of our people choose to do."

"But why all the secrecy? I haven't been able to reach any of you for weeks. I thought you were all dodging my calls," Saxon asks, looking at his family. His brother is still nowhere to be seen. I scan the crowd, looking for him, and spy him skulking in the back. I recognize the people he is with—Hale and Velorina, as well as his own clan members, Kavita and Dante. Velorina and Kavita are all snuggled together, looking loved up, with the men hanging out behind them. My eyes meet Xenos's, and I glare at him. I know why he's avoiding his brother now, but I think he is going to be disappointed that Saxon has no fucks to give about him snapping up his former clan members. Magenta is going to be sad, though, and Lila is going to be pissed. It's probably good that he's on the other side of the throne room.

Aleister chuckles and nods. "We were. You know how bad everyone is at keeping secrets. Sabine threatened anyone who spilled the beans about the surprise with new recruit training for the first semester at the military college. You know how painful that is. None of us were willing to break it, so it was easier to avoid your calls."

"So no tribunal?" Saxon asks, looking around.

"No, silly, just a fun party for you and your blood rose." Mehira waves her hand around the room. "We have so much fun planned." The twins are younger versions of their mother. Actually, because they stop aging once they reach their majority, the three of them could pass as triplets if not for the wealth of experience in Sabine's eyes.

"If Prince Xavier could maybe fix the damage he caused, then we can get the fun started," Musette says dryly. I wince and wave a hand. The damaged chandelier reforms and casts a bright glow across the room once more. We can see decorations and tables set for dining, as well as a great big "Just Married" sign spread across the room.

I bow to the queen with a flourish. "My apologies, Your Majesty. I was just trying to protect my loved ones." Link follows suit, while Saxon gives his aunt a kiss on each cheek before hugging his uncle.

Sabine narrows her eyes, looking at me thoughtfully before turning her gaze to my wife. "Yes, I can understand that, but from what I hear, your wife is perfectly capable of taking care of herself. Come, Lila, let us take a seat. Our guests are dying to meet you. My nephew can introduce you as they take turns making excuses to visit the head table."

"It would be my pleasure, Your Majesty." Lila inclines her head gracefully, and Sabine tucks her hand into Lila's elbow and shakes her head.

"None of that 'Your Majesty' nonsense. You may call me Auntie Sabby. That goes for both of you as well," she instructs Link and me. She leads Lila ahead of us. Link and I offer Musette and Mehira our arms to escort them, as Aleister and Saxon follow closely behind.

"Good job on the chandelier. Pity it wasn't permanent," Musette whispers in my ear. "We hate that thing, but Mom thinks it's elegant."

I look up and wrinkle my nose at the gaudy monstrosity. "I can arrange for it to have another accident if you want," I offer, and she squeezes my arm.

"You were always my favorite friend of Saxon's."

We both know she means lover. We never hid our relationship from either of our families, and we spent a number of delightful breaks from the circus holidaying here or on Westalin. Our families are great friends in private. In public, we pretend to be more distant so other nations don't worry we will gang up on them and take over the galaxy, although my parents, Sabine, and Aleister often joke about it when they have a few too many drinks.

My gaze catches on Xenos again, who is staying back. "What is going on with that asshole?"

She follows my gaze and purses her lips in disapproval. "Just his usual duplicitous behavior, trying to one-up his brother." She huffs. "I don't know what his problem is, but the minute Hale and Velorina returned, the three of them wooed them like you have never seen anyone being wooed before. They are joining his clan. Last I heard, they were courting Radella and Estrella as well."

"They aren't!" I gasp, unable to hide my shock. "That will hurt Saxon more than anything else he has done in the past. They actively tried to hurt Lila when they released him from sedation. They hoped he would kill her."

She nods. "Yes, he doesn't realize it, but he has gone too far. He has lost Mother's good graces. First, by refusing to join the circus when she requested him to, and now this. She had to threaten him to get him to cover for Saxon when he was incapacitated. She said she would remove his titles and estate."

"Seriously?" I can't believe what I'm hearing. They have never been super close, but Saxon always hoped Xenos would lose his jealousy as he got older and more mature. I guess that still hasn't happened. When Lila hears of what he has done, he will be shit out of luck, even if he changes his ways. Lila, like me, is a champion grudge holder. Xenos will never wiggle his way back into her good graces, and I bet the minute he hears that Lila is now in charge of the circus, he will try to suck up to her. It's a super important position in the galaxy, and while not royal, the reach of her title is quite significant—not to mention she is the granddaughter of the goddess of life and the future goddess of death, supreme leader of the Vilaxians.

I smirk at the thought, and Musette squeezes my arm. "What do you know?" she asks.

"Ah, my dear Musette. Watching Xenos scramble to get back in his brother's good graces is going to be amusing. That is all I am willing to say," I tell her as we take a seat at the head table, and I lean back to enjoy the festivities.

CHAPTER SIXTEEN

Link

The tension drains out of my body now that I know the tribunal isn't happening. I have met the royal family in the past, so sitting at the head table with them is no hardship. Mehira is pleasant company, and she gives me a running commentary after dinner as all of Saxon's family clan members pass the table, trying to win favor with the queen, Saxon, and Lila.

"Most of them aren't bad, they are just terrible bootlickers. They are only council to the queen because her brother and his wife were. That's Saxon's parents' clan. Mother couldn't bear to replace them after their deaths, so she continues to put up with them. They have been slightly helpful over the years, but mostly they are pompous, self-righteous assholes. Mother has been contemplating electing a new council, and they heard about it, hence the fawning." She waves a contemptuous hand in their direction, taking a sip of her blood wine. "The only one that is half bearable is her." She points to a beautiful woman with pin straight, long black hair down to her ass. She is standing slightly apart, watching the proceedings with a blank face.

"That's Saxon's clan sister, Vanity. Horrible name, but like I said, her mother is an idiot. She prefers to go by Van. She is a little bit of a lone wolf. Many have petitioned to have her in their clan, but she prefers to remain by herself and make use of the feeders and donor bags."

"Do you know why?" I ask, feeling intrigued.

She shakes her head. "I'm sure she probably doesn't enjoy all the jostling and scheming involved in establishing a clan hierarchy. Musette and I feel the same. Both of us would rather hold out for a possible blood rose than join a clan. We see how devoted Mother and Father are to one another and want what they have."

I nod my head in complete understanding. "Have you had any luck yet?" I ask, and she pouts.

"No, but we travel around Vilax regularly. Mother gives us different diplomatic missions in the hopes we might find them in the general population like she found Father, but I think with Saxon finding his with Lila that maybe we need to look beyond the Vilaxian population. Fate has a funny way of putting blood roses in each other's paths, and neither of us have even had an inkling of ours."

"You may be right. It's good that you aren't closed-minded and bigoted like some of your people." I think of Radella and Estrella and how they reacted to Lila being Saxon's blood rose.

Mehira sniffs and waves her hand. "Those two were always full of self-importance. They thought they were above their station because they were in the same clan as the queen's two nephews. You should have seen their heads nearly explode when they were trying to decide which twin to follow when the clan dissolved." She giggles evilly.

I think about telling her that they are welcome on the ship if they so choose, since Saxon's act is short quite a few fliers, but I need to run it by both him and Lila first. He may not want them aboard. Family can be difficult despite the obvious close relationship they have.

Musette stands up and claps her hands, gaining everyone's attention. "Let the games begin," she declares, and there is a flurry of activity as tables in the middle of the throne room are cleared away, leaving a group of chairs placed back-to-back.

"What's happening?" I ask Saxon's cousin, who just smirks with undisguised glee.

"When Mother and Musette were researching Earth party traditions, they discovered that games are regularly played at them. They decided it would be fun to play a few here as well."

I frown as I try to remember my own Earth

research. I can only remember party games being a staple of children's birthday parties, not whatever this one is supposed to be. We watch as most of the members of Saxon's family clan gather around the chairs. The only ones not taking part are his brother and the people gathered around him. His two clan members, Kavita and Dante, are with him, but so are Hale and Velorina.

"What is going on there?" I ask Mehira, and she growls as her gaze finds what I'm referring to.

"Xenos is not being very loyal to his brother. He is making a huge mistake, because Mother has taken note and is not amused," she replies mysteriously.

Music starts to play, and the clan members begin to dance around the chairs in a large circle. They are writhing and twitching in what I think is supposed to be dance moves, but they almost appear like they are having a fit of some kind.

"What's going on?" I ask, confused at what I'm seeing. I turn when I hear my wife laughing. Her eyes sparkle with amusement, and she claps in time to the music.

"This is called musical chairs on Earth," she explains to Saxon and me. "The aim is to dance around the chairs as the music plays, and when the music stops, you need to sit on one of the chairs."

I turn back to the spectacle, count the chairs, and compare it to the number of clan members. "But there are less chairs than people," I point out, and she nods, grinning.

"That's the point. The people who don't manage to sit in the chair are out."

"Oh fuck," Saxon mutters, and my eyes widen as the music stops and there is a mad dash for the chairs. It all happens in a blur of motion, the movement too fast for us to make out due to Vilaxian speed. All of a sudden, someone goes flying through the air, hitting the floor and sliding a distance. Then, there is snarling and cursing as a fight breaks out. Fists fly as blows are exchanged. Lila's mouth drops open as a chair is smashed over someone's head.

"Vilaxians are incredibly competitive, and nobody likes to lose," Saxon says flatly. When the movement finally stops, there are two blood-covered family members—one groaning from being thrown across the room, and one knocked out completely.

The music starts up again, and the chair winners all stand up and continue to dance, stepping around the losers. A couple more chairs are removed, and the injured Vilaxians are escorted off the floor by the queen's guards.

"Well, that was..." Lila trails off, and Sabine claps her hands.

"Highly fucking entertaining. We should include musical chairs at all of our functions," she exclaims, congratulating Musette on the wonderful idea.

Musette preens, and Mehira snorts and rolls her eyes. "My choice of game is so much better." She sits up straight, her wine glass forgotten, wearing a determined look on her face.

Fuck, I had forgotten how competitive the twins are. This surprise party, while a sweet idea, is quickly devolving.

Once musical chairs is over, and the injured losers are all taken care of, we get up to mingle for a little while. Saxon doesn't stray far from Lila, and I find myself caught up in a conversation with the head of Saxon's family clan—or I guess the head now that Saxon's dad passed. He is a pompous fool who likes to toot his own horn, as Lila would say. I'm barely paying attention, instead keeping an eye on my family. Both Saxon's and Lila's expressions are looking a little strained at their individual conversations. Xavier, of course, seems like he's having a blast. I'm sure he's causing as much mischief as possible.

"Next game. This was my pick," Mehira shouts as something is lowered from the ceiling. The gathered crowd cheers as the object comes into view. It is a large, star-shaped thing that looks to be made up of an organic material. I find Lila, who is smiling and nodding her head. She obviously knows what this is.

"It is time for the penisata," Mehira announces and waves a hand. A guard comes over holding a blindfold and a wooden stick. "It is filled with wonderful prizes for those of you quick enough to get them."

Lila's smiles drops, and she frowns slightly. I search through my data banks in the hopes I can figure out what a penisata is.

"Who will do the honors in going first?" Mehira

asks, and there is a jostle amongst the partygoers as they all fight to go first.

Instead, she waves Saxon forward. "As the guest of honor, it shall be your turn first," she declares.

Saxon shrugs and smiles good-naturedly, and he allows her to blindfold him before she passes him the stick. She spins him three times and then faces him toward the hanging object.

"Go," she cries as I finally figure out what this game is. She pronounced it wrong. It's a piñata, and it involves taking turns hitting the object with the stick until it breaks open and candy and prizes spill out.

"Where did you find a piñata?" I ask Musette, who is glaring at her sister.

"Oh, we have black market contacts. They smuggled us one from Earth," she says as Saxon takes a swing and misses. The crowd jeers, his brother the loudest of them all, and I can see his jaw set with determination. Shit, Saxon isn't immune to the Vilaxian competitiveness.

Something occurs to me. "So that's a regular Earth piñata, and it hasn't been reinforced for Vilaxian strength?" I ask her, and she cocks her head to the side and shrugs.

"I don't think so."

I turn back to see Saxon lift the rod once more and cry, "Wait!"

It's too late. He swings with determined precision. The stick hits the piñata with such force, it is knocked off the string and becomes a lethal projectile, flying across the throne room at super speed. There are screams and shouts as people duck and move out of the way of the deadly flying object. Luckily, no one gets caught in the path, and it smashes harmlessly against a wall where it shatters into a million pieces, the insides sliding down the wall in a musical tinkle. It looks like they filled it with coins and gems, and not the usual candy like on Earth.

There's a quiet pause as everyone stares in shock before chaos descends as there is a mad dash toward the prizes. People scramble around the floor, trying to fill their pockets. There is more bloodshed, hair pulling, and bitch slapping than a catfight in a warlock's harem.

"Holy shit." I shake my head at the carnage, but again, the queen claps her hands.

"This is the best party we have ever had. We will be the talk of Vilax."

"Your mother is quite insane," I mutter to Musette, who shakes her head with an amused smile.

"No, not really. She just likes to keep them all on their toes. She isn't wrong, though, this is fun. Seeing such pompous assholes fight over such petty things really is glorious. They are going to be so ashamed when they sober up and realize how they behaved."

"That's devious," I remark.

Lila is pulling the blindfold off Saxon and congratulating him on a job well done. She sees me watching her and gives me a subtle wink. I chuckle as Xavier approaches us. He's frowning, so I instantly go on alert. I know he was scanning minds today for nefarious plans.

"What's going on?" I ask him.

"Xenos is going to try to get a reaction out of Saxon. He's annoyed that Saxon hasn't even noticed that Hale and Velorina are with him and his clan again."

Musette scoffs. "Of course he is. He isn't happy because the attention isn't on him. He's happiest when Saxon is off world because all the focus can be on him. He was so angry when the others decided to go with the circus. I am surprised he's actually forming a clan with them again. I'm sure it isn't for the right reasons."

"He's going to flirt with me to try to get a reaction out of both Lila and Saxon. Do me a favor and take them away. Ask to see his bedroom or something. Keep him occupied while I deal a blow to Xenos's ego."

"Will that cause a problem with the queen? We don't want to upset Saxon's aunt," I ask him, and he and Musette exchange a glance before bursting into laughter.

"My mother will think it's entertaining. She lives for drama now that Vilax is at peace. It feeds her need for war without bloodshed. Saxon will be the only one hurt. Go distract him. I will make sure the bloodshed isn't life threatening," Saxon's cousin insists.

"His life, not mine," Xavier growls, and his fingers spark with lightning.

I sigh, knowing there is no talking him out of it.

He is offended for his lover and wife and will not take the insult lying down.

I look around the room and find Saxon and Lila standing off to the side. I hurry over to them just as Xenos makes his way to Xavier. He practically slinks like a cat, but unlike Saxon, who unknowingly exudes sexual charisma and lethality from his pores, Xenos kind of looks constipated and awkward, like he's trying too hard.

I reach Lila and Saxon at the same time as I hear Xenos greet Xavier. "It is a great honor to be in the presence of the warlock. It would be my pleasure to show you around the palace if you would like." Xenos puts his hand on Xavier's arm.

A rumbling growl comes from Saxon's mouth, and Lila hisses.

"What is that asshole up to?" she spits out, her eyes locked on Xenos's hand.

Instead of shrugging him off, Xavier looks down his nose at the hand on his arm. "You dare to touch me?"

Xenos doesn't take a hint at the obvious threat.

"Oh, I can do way more than just touch you if you'd like. I heard your sexual appetite is great. Have you ever been bitten by a Vilaxian before? Or a whole clan?"

Saxon stiffens, his rumbling growl getting louder.

"Oh, he did not just suggest that," I mutter in disbelief. I can't believe the audacity of Saxon's twin. He must know that Xavier and Saxon have been lovers before. I know they spent time together during our downtime.

"What's going on? What's so bad about what he said?" Lila asks me.

Saxon's entire body vibrates like he's barely restraining himself from lashing out at his brother. "Being bitten by a whole clan is taboo. It is dangerous to the bite recipient because all the clan members are drinking from them, and it floods their bodies with so much venom, they don't know they are dying until it's too late. Mentioning it in polite company is foolish. There is an underground trade for such practices, and bite junkies are usually the victims," I explain to Lila as she wraps an arm around Saxon's waist to distract him

"Bite junkies?"

"Vilaxians who are addicted to venom and its properties," Saxon says through gritted teeth.

Musette and Mehira, who are both still standing with Xavier, look shocked, their eyes wide and lips pursed with disapproval. Musette mutters some words to Xenos, but he ignores her, keeping his eyes locked on Xavier.

"Come now, I bet Lila would love a tour of the palace and to see your childhood bedroom." I step in front of Saxon, blocking his view of what's transpiring.

Lila frowns. "What about X?" she says, and I shake my head.

"He will be fine. He told me he will take care of this and that we are to take care of our guy. Remember, he hasn't eaten. I bet a bit of blood will help cool his temper. He's hangry," I tell her, and she loses interest in Xenos, knowing Xavier will cut the idiot to shreds, and shifts her concern to Saxon.

"You're right. I'm feeling a little peckish myself. The blood wine was barely enough to alleviate my hunger." She jumps onto the idea of distracting Saxon beautifully. I wonder if Xavier said something telepathically to her.

It works, because Saxon's attention turns to his blood rose at the mention of her hunger. "Come on, I will find us somewhere a little more private to feed."

As I follow the two of them out of the room, neither of them looking backward, I realize the party has devolved and turned into a bit of a feeding orgy. Party favors in the form of blood donors have been brought in, and the feeding and fucking portion of the night has begun. No wonder Xenos approached Xavier, foolish though he may be. I'm sure once Xavier puts Xenos in his place, he will find us.

We wander quietly through the dimly lit palace, only coming across an occasional servant. Most of them are attending the party. Finally, Saxon opens the door to an opulent yet slightly musty room. He crosses the large expanse and throws open a pair of curtains before opening the set of doors leading onto the balcony, letting in a burst of fresh night air. It has a small chill to it, and Lila shivers in her barely there outfit, which was not out of place. In fact, it was a lot more demure than most of the females' outfits.

When he turns back to face us, his eyes are glowing

red, and his fangs are on display. "Oh wow," Lila says, then she turns and stalks toward me, her eyes red and fangs beared. She waves a hand, and my suit disappears, leaving me naked.

"Lila?" I ask, wanting to make sure she's okay.

She gets to me and leans in to whisper, "Just go with me. I promise it will feel good."

I relax. I trust her with my life, and I hate that Saxon is upset, so I'll let her lead the way.

"Are you hungry, my sweet?" She turns her head to look at Saxon as she runs a finger down the pulsing vein in my neck. I shiver at her touch, and my cock starts to harden. I love the feeling of Lila's fangs in my neck, and it looks like I'm about to feel Saxon's too. I can't wait.

CHAPTER SEVENTEEN

Lila

I beckon Saxon over to us, and he only hesitates for a moment, his lips pursing in surprise before his eyes hood and he stalks over to join me as I pin Link against the wall. Saxon runs his tongue up Link's neck. Link's head flops back against the wall, and he closes his eyes and moans as I do the same thing on his other side. I reach for his long length, wrapping my hand around it and pumping my fist up and down. He jolts as his knees buckle at my touch before he locks them in place. I lean in to kiss my cyborg, but Saxon threads a hand through my hair and yanks it to the side. He licks a line up my neck before turning my head so I can kiss him. His fangs nick my tongue, and my blood pools into our mouths. He groans and laps at the blood, swallowing it down. I'm panting and breathless once he pulls away.

"Get on your knees," he orders, his voice guttural, his red eyes blazing with desire. I quickly obey, dropping to the ground. I wait patiently for him to give the next order, but he kisses Link instead. I watch in awe as he dominates the cyborg, their mouths mashing violently together. There's a dribble of blood that trickles from their lips, and I know Saxon made Link bleed for him. I groan at the thought. Link's blood is so delightfully fizzy and energizing.

I don't want to wait, so while Saxon is distracted, I run my tongue over Link's femoral artery, plumping it for my fangs, but before I can bite into it, Saxon's hand is back in my hair, giving it a sharp tug.

"No, Lila," he scolds and yanks my head away from Link's thigh.

I groan, and my nipples tighten in delight. Fuck, sometimes you just want to be treated like a plaything. Use me like a fidget toy and push all my buttons.

"You will wait," he orders. "Suck his cock first. Make your mate feel good, and then you can feed."

Suck his cock? Yes fucking please. Saxon uses his grip to guide my mouth to Link's cock, holding my head in place.

"Use her mouth like your own private glory hole," he commands Link, who obeys with a groan. I open my mouth wide, and Link slides his cock into my mouth, my fangs scraping along the sensitive skin as he glides smoothly in and out. It's not enough to make him bleed though, just to give him a bit of pain to counter the pleasure. It's an exquisite point to balance on.

I use my tongue, sweeping it across his length, but mostly I just breathe through my nose and put my hands against his thighs so I don't over balance. His thrusts start lazily, but he builds up momentum. As he gets faster, he occasionally stops with his long length deep down my throat. I struggle slightly, the intrusion making my eyes water and spit run out of the side of my mouth, but just when I think I can't take it any longer, he pulls out and lets me gasp for breath.

"Look at the mess you are making of our wife," Saxon says, pressing kisses to Link's chest and nibbling on his pretty nipples.

I gaze up at them, knowing I must look like a hot mess, but they groan in unison as I meet their eyes.

"Fuck, she looks good like that... like you ruined her," Saxon praises. "You need a reward for doing such a good job. Put your mouth back on his cock, Lila, and make sure you don't spill a drop," Saxon instructs. I desperately want to watch, so I do as he says, but I keep my eyes on what they are doing.

I suck and slurp on the tip of Link's dick as Saxon sinks his fangs into his neck. Link stiffens and then lets out a long, guttural moan as Saxon's venom starts to work while he gulps mouthful after mouthful of Link's blood. I know it won't be long until Saxon's venom has Link spilling into my mouth, and I consider biting his cock so I can have a cum and blood smoothie, but Saxon's hand is back in my hair.

"Don't you dare bite him." He gives my hair a sharp tug, and I decide not to disobey. I hear him start to lick Link's blood, and my core throbs, desperate for something to fill it. Well, I can't drink his blood, but that doesn't mean I can't get myself off too. I start to slide a hand down to play with my clit.

"No, Lila." Saxon slaps me on the ass, and I let out a muffled squeal. "You will wait. Make your husband feel good first." I can't pout because Link's cock is in my mouth, but I want to.

I'm soon distracted by a loud shout, and then Link thrusts deep and spills down my throat. I swallow quickly to keep up, but it's a lot, and some of it leaks out, the fizzy, tart taste tickling my taste buds. Once he finishes, I use my tongue to clean him before licking my lips and using my finger to catch what I missed. I'm about to stick it in my mouth when a hand clamps down on my wrist, and Saxon brings my finger to his mouth. He licks Link's cum, and his eyes widen at the taste of it. I smirk at him, and he glares at me and my brattish behavior.

"Now, wifey, you weren't particularly well behaved. You were selfish and wanted your pleasure before your husband got his. Time for us to punish you."

Before he moves, he checks on Link to make sure he isn't woozy from blood loss. Although Link looks dazed, he recovers quickly and waves Saxon off.

"I'm fine, and I want to watch you punish our wife," he says, pushing off the wall as Saxon bends down and scoops me up before striding over to the extra-large Gothic bed that takes up most of the room. He tosses me on it, and a breath of air escapes my mouth as I land.

"Watch? Oh no, I think it's going to take both of us to punish her. Get over here," Saxon orders as he climbs up and crawls across the bed, his cat-like prowl making my pulse hum with excitement.

"You tried to take care of your greedy cunt yourself," he says as he leans over me. "That is our job. Now we're really going to make sure it's taken care of." He bares his fangs and hisses at me, and I just about swoon with excitement. Yup, there is something officially wrong with me. I mean, we all knew it, but this just cements it. Goosebumps break out across my skin, and my breathing increases. I turn my head, giving him access to my throat.

He doesn't take it. Instead, he lifts me up and nods to Link to slide underneath me. Link does so, and Saxon lowers me onto him, his skin cool against my overheated flesh. I lean back, sitting on Link, his hard cock resting in my butt crack.

Saxon rearranges us so Link's dick is notched at my entrance. "Can you make that a little thinner? We don't want to split our wife in half," Saxon asks, and when I look down my body, I watch in awe as Link's cock lengthens but gets slightly less girthy.

Saxon nods. "Perfect, now fill her," he barks, and Link thrusts into me. I gasp as he bottoms out, my eyes watering at the slight pinch of pain. Link's hands come up, one sliding to my breasts and tweaking my nipple while the other circles my clit. I pant before moaning as his cock begins to vibrate inside me.

Neither of them really give me time to adjust, because when I look down again, Saxon has grabbed a bottle of lube and is coating his own thick length with copious amounts until it glistens in the low light. Tossing the bottle to the side, he notches himself at my entrance and slowly starts to push in next to Link. He stops suddenly, his eyes widening with surprise when he feels Link's cock vibrating.

"Whoa, that's intense," he mutters, and I grunt.

"Try being me," I tell him, and he pinches my nipple, and I squeal.

"Hush, you are being punished. Be a good girl and take your mates' cocks." He pushes farther inside, sliding back and forth and going deeper with every thrust. Link groans and moves his hands to my hips, holding me still for Saxon.

He is finally in, and my cunt is stuffed full of my mates. Link holds still as Saxon slides back and forth, gliding his cock along my upper walls and Link's cock, and all three of us groan obscenely.

"Feels so good," I say, and Saxon's eyes blaze with hunger. My fangs throb, and I feel my venom leak from the tips.

"Such a good girl. Now we're going to fill you so full of our cum, it's going to leak out, but we aren't going to let it. When it tries, we will stuff you full of our cocks again, over and over, until your belly rounds with our babies."

God, I want that too, but I know my protection will stop that from happening for now. It's fun to pretend though.

"Yes, please, fill me with your cum. I want your babies," I beg, playing along. Both men growl, and my body vibrates with a shiver at the sound.

My words set them off, and together, they wreck my pussy in a coordinated dance. They thrust in unison, pushing the elasticity of my cunt to its limits. It's pure fucking heaven, and I feel so many sensations that my mind short-circuits, and I float.

Saxon bites into my neck, and I find myself back in my body, screaming as my orgasm races through me like an out of control freight train.

He drinks, and the sucking sensation feels like it has a connection to my clit. I writhe in ecstasy. Link's hands are clamped hard on my hips to hold me in place, and I'm sure there will be fingerprints tomorrow as evidence of such deviant pleasure.

Finally, Saxon releases the suction and seals the wound. I can't wait any longer, and I strike. My fangs sink into his throat, and I guzzle his blood down, sending my venom surging through his body. He shouts and starts to piston into me as the vibrations in Link's cock increase. I swallow mouthful after delicious mouthful of his life essence as the two of them fill my womb with their life forming seed. It's warm as they paint my insides with their cum, both of them groaning obscenely as their cocks pulse and jump inside me, my cunt rippling as it milks them dry.

Xavier eventually joins us, the three of us snuggled up in bed with me between the two males. He strips and climbs in behind Saxon, pressing a kiss to his lips before leaning over him and doing the same to me.

"What happened with Xenos?" Saxon asks reluctantly, staring up at the ceiling and not meeting anyone's eyes.

"Don't be jealous, my love. The only fangs marking up this pretty skin are yours and Lila's." He pauses for a moment. "And maybe Silac's. I wonder if I could survive a naga bite." He taps his lips thoughtfully, and Link snickers with amusement.

"Some of Lila's other mates and forms have teeth too. What about Nikos's?" Link runs a finger over the scar on my breast, and Xavier shudders.

"Pass, they are a little too sharp for me. He can keep them to himself."

I giggle, feeling my cheeks heat. "I like them," I admit, and he reaches over Saxon and slides his hands under my arms, pulling me toward him before situating me on top of him.

His naked body is warm against mine, and he

grinds his cock against my core as he kisses me. I moan as his hands stroke over my naked back, one hand slipping between us. He plunges his fingers deep into my pussy, thrusting a couple of times, and I squirm and groan as he strokes over my G-spot. He's just teasing me, though, because he pulls his fingers out and slides them into his mouth, sucking and licking Saxon's and Link's combined releases.

"Hmm, delicious," he says, and I blush even harder.

"Fuck," Link mutters, and I watch as he reaches down and adjusts his cock, which must have hardened again at the filthy act. My warlock does know how to work a room.

"Anyway, the moment you left the throne room, Musette told her mother that Xenos offered me a clan feeding. Sabine was beyond livid. Your aunt really knows how to throw a spectacular tantrum. She practically destroyed the throne room."

Saxon winces. "Ah, yes, it is a regular occurrence. Her temper is hot, but it usually runs its course fairly quickly." His lips turn down in a scowl. "My aunt could not ignore the fact that he offered something so taboo, one of our very strictest covenants, in front of so many witnesses."

Xavier nods. "Yes, and the punishment for feeding from one person as a clan is death. It really is that taboo." I guess he said that for my sake, because the rest of them seem to know all of this.

"So did my brother die?" Saxon asks flatly. He's

bracing himself for the worst but not willing to show how devastated he is that it's come to this.

Xavier sighs and grabs his arm, giving it a squeeze. "No. It is only through the grace of the queen, and my deviously spectacular mind meddling powers, that Xenos and his clan live to see another sunrise."

My warlock husband is not lacking in self-esteem, that's for sure, but I feel a wave of relief burst out of Saxon and decide to let the ego stroking go for now.

"What happened?" I ask, almost as addicted to drama as Sabine is, especially when someone who has hurt or upset my mates is getting their comeuppance.

"I muddled the minds of everyone else but Sabine, Aleister, Musette, and Mehira so they wouldn't remember hearing Xenos proposition me. This is the only thing that saved him and his whole clan from death. Sabine sentenced him and his clan to twelve months at the Coldsummit Barracks without a reprieve."

Saxon groans and puts a pillow over his head.

"What are the Coldsummit Barracks?" I ask. Link looks as uninformed as I am.

"Coldsummit Barracks is an outpost in the Blood-born Mountain. The military uses it to train troops for cold weather combat. The snow never melts there, but teams only ever spend a few weeks there at a time because it is so miserable and there is nothing else around it for miles. All supplies have to be shuttled or teleported in. Usually, it is kept unmanned at any other time, unless someone needs to be punished, but a month is the longest punishment most have to endure. To be sent there for twelve months... Well, I'll be surprised if no one dies or goes insane during that time." Saxon sounds mournful, his voice slightly muffled by the pillow still over his head.

"Yes, I was impressed by Sabine's ruthlessness. She certainly deserves her reputation as one of the most respected rulers of the galaxy. I think death probably would have been kinder," Xavier agrees.

I feel a slight pang of sympathy for Hale and Velorina. I bet they wished they hadn't been seduced by whatever Xenos offered them now. On the other hand, though, screw them. I wonder if I can convince Sabine to send Radella and Estrella too. They did have a hand in the whole Saxon sedation debacle as well. It would be the ultimate punishment for them to have to listen to those two complain the whole time. I'll speak to her in the morning about it.

"Oh, my dear, your deviousness is such a fucking turn-on." Xavier grins at me, obviously plucking the thought from my mind, before giving me another kiss. I can taste Link's and Saxon's cum on his tongue, and I lick his mouth for more of it. His hands start to roam, but I'm worn out and worried about Saxon. I wiggle off Xavier and worm myself between him and Saxon, wrapping my arms around Saxon's body. Xavier spoons me from behind. Link also moves closer to Saxon, taking the spot I was in, and puts a reassuring hand on him. I smile from the knowledge that my mates want to look after each other as well as me.

"Let's rest. As fun as tonight was, we really need to get to Earth. I won't make Brannock wait any longer. Xenos made his bed, and now he must lie in it. Hopefully he will spend the next twelve months reflecting on his issues and he'll emerge a changed man. I want you to have a good relationship with him, but not at the expense of your mental health. Family who plays mind games like that aren't family at all," I murmur, pulling the pillow off Saxon's face so I can see his pretty eyes.

"No, and who needs him when you have a new one who loves you to pieces?" Xavier grins and caresses Saxon's cheek. "Because we do love you."

Aww, fuck. How cute is that? I feel like birds need to be chirping and fireworks need to be exploding over our heads at that declaration, so I make them. I wiggle a finger and cast the magic into the air. All three of them gape at the sight that now appears above us.

"What the fuck?" Xavier exclaims, and all three of them turn to look at me.

I shrug, not feeling embarrassed at all. "It was a real Disney moment," I explain, knowing they don't have a clue what I'm talking about, but I don't care.

I close my eyes and let my mind drift. It was great to meet Saxon's family. His family clan was a bit much, and I felt like they were looking down on us, but I really don't care. His blood family, minus Xenos, likes us, and that's all I care about. It will be funny to see their faces once I take on the mantle of goddess of death though. I might force them to worship my ass. I need to find new and creative ways for that to happen. Maybe they need to stand on one leg and fast for twenty-four hours to prove their devotion.

Now that this whole issue is behind us, I'm ready to hand Smith his ass. He's going to wish he never fucked with the Galaxy Circus.

CHAPTER EIGHTEEN

Echo

I'm jittery and impatient, and I've been wide awake for hours, worrying about Lila and the others and how their visit on Vilax is going. In the past, something like this wouldn't have bothered me, but the further along I get in my pregnancy, the more I worry about my loved ones. Previously, all I worried about was Maxsim and me and surviving the next day, always on alert for Natalia to attack, and now that is no longer an issue, you'd think things would be easier, but it really isn't. Now I have a lot more loved ones to worry about.

Our five little bundles of energetic joy make my heart swell with emotions. I can't imagine how I could love anything more, but the thought of our own flesh and blood babies is low-key terrifying. What if something goes wrong? What if I'm a bad father? When I expressed my feelings to Maxsim last night, he laughed so hard he would have fallen off the bed if it were off the ground.

How could he be so insensitive? I rolled over and didn't speak to him for the rest of the night, but it meant I didn't get my daily dose of sex, and now I am irritable and horny, which is not a good combination in a hormonal person. I want to be knotted or locked, and I'm kind of jonesing for it. These pregnancy hormones are no joke.

Huffing, I sit up in our nest. Maxsim's quiet snores tell me he's still fast asleep, and I'm still annoyed at him. He tried to talk me around when he realized I was upset, telling me I was going to be a wonderful father and that I already was with our current babies, but it was too late. I need Lila. She is the only one who will understand. Or is she? Nikos! He would understand too. I quickly climb out of the nest and leave the room, the change in temperature making sweat trickle on my fur. Our room is kept at subarctic temperatures, especially for us, so it always takes me a moment to get my bearings and for Xavier's spelled pendant to work.

Once my temperature is regulated, I head down the hallway that houses all the bedroom doors, going to the very end. The children's nursery was deliberately placed far away from the rest of the bedrooms just in case the soundproofing didn't work in any of them. There is nothing more disturbing than walking in on your parents copulating, especially if it's a group bonding experience. I still shudder at the memory of seeing my own omega father getting railed by the rest of my parents. I stick my head in just to check. They have been known to get up and wander around the suite in the middle of the night, but all five of them are tucked safely in their beds and water pods.

Smiling, I close the door again and make my way to Nikos's room. I knock on it and wait. It doesn't take too long before he opens it completely naked, his hair a tangled mess and his eyes blurry with sleep. He blinks at me for a moment before opening the door wider and letting me in.

I enter without a word, hurrying over to his bed and climbing in. It smells like him, like spicy, salty margaritas, and I bury my nose in the pillow. He stares at me before shrugging and returning to bed, climbing in next to me.

"What's wrong, little pussy?" he asks, rolling onto his side and arching an inquisitive eyebrow. "It is very early for you to be awake in your state."

I freeze. "My state?" I ask, snarling a little.

He holds his hands up in defense. "You're growing two living beings. I remember how exhausting it was," he explains, reminding me why I am here. He has been where I am.

I sigh. "Sorry, I'm a little irritable, and it's making me irrational. I had an argument with Maxsim. He pissed me off."

His eyes brighten with understanding. "Ah. It is alright, sweet kitty cat. People who are not so knowl-edgeable about how being pregnant feels can make the mistake of speaking before truly thinking about what they are saying." He runs a soothing hand over my head and down my shoulder.

I close my eyes and start to purr at the sensation, wiggling a little closer. My perfume begins to fill the room with my need, and I wince in embarrassment. When I crack my eyes open, he is looking at me with knowing eyes.

"You would like your fins stroked, no?" he asks, and I frown.

"Huh?"

He shakes his head and chuckles. "What I mean is that the pretty kitty needs to be stroked? Am I right?"

I bite my lip before nodding. "I'm so freaking horny. It's basically a permanent state."

He nods with knowing eyes. "I remember it well. I spent most of my pregnancy aching for Lila since I was being held prisoner by my father with no relief in sight. I understand very well."

He's quiet for a moment, and I look everywhere but at him.

"Would you like me to take care of your need? I can't lock or knot you like your alphas, but I bet I can make you feel good and take off the edge until Lila can get back or Maxsim removes his head from his ass."

I gape at the merman. Gone is the silly airheaded prince he always portrayed, and in his place is a male who looks at me with desire and want in his eyes.

"No need for reciprocation. I would just be happy to help you out—if Maxsim won't bite my head off, that is," he promises. "If not, I am happy for you to snuggle in here until Lila returns."

He waits patiently for me to decide. My body is already joyfully accepting the offer, my blood rushing to engorge my cock and make my asshole throb with need, but my mind is at war. Lila wouldn't care one little bit about me taking Nikos up on his offer. She would probably pout that she wasn't here to join or watch, but Maxsim's reaction is another thing.

He has been much more relaxed since I became pregnant, and even liked my suggestion for Link to join us during our next heat, but we haven't really discussed playing with anyone else in our mating group. He didn't outwardly reject it, though, when Lila was talking about it during our last time together. I reach down and grab my cock through my loincloth. It aches something fierce, and although I know I could take care of it myself, I do like the idea of Nikos lending a hand.

"I can see you are conflicted. How about I go wake your mate and have him take care of you instead?" he suggests, starting to get out of bed. He doesn't seem upset. Instead, he is perfectly understanding.

"He laughed when I told him I was worried about being a bad father."

He stops and turns back to face me, no amusement on his face at all.

"Ah, well that was pretty stupid of him, wasn't it? I completely understand. I have had the same feelings, and I am sure he feels the same way too, but Echo, he probably laughed because you have taken to father-hood more naturally than most of us. You protect and cherish our babies like they are the most important things in the galaxy."

"They are," I reply. "I would give my life for them."

He nods. "Exactly. You have nothing to worry about. Trust me, okay?" He reaches out and strokes his hand over my fur again, and I push up into his touch. "Maxsim laughing was not okay, and you are entitled to feel hurt. He will grovel to you when he wakes and finds you are not in bed with him. All will be right again." He drops his hand and rolls to face the ceiling, closing his eyes. "Sleep here for now, and Lila will be back soon."

I snuggle into his side, and he lifts his arm, putting it around my body. My cock rubs against his naked skin, and I groan. "I would like you to take care of it for me, but I need to talk to Maxsim first," I say, and he nods.

"How about you just stroke it, and I will stroke mine at the same time?" he suggests, tossing his blankets back, revealing his erect cock dripping with fluid. I stare at it in the low light of his room. In this form, he has scales over it, but they lie flat against his skin. It is nice and girthy, and my mouth waters at the thought of feeling it in me. My asshole throbs, and I reach down and tear off my loincloth, tossing it to the floor. Stroking myself to completion is not cheating, and lots of people use visual aids to assist them. That's what porn is, after all.

I roll onto my back so I have full access to stroke my length, but I keep my eyes firmly locked on him. I watch him fist his cock in his hand and match his tempo as he strokes it up and down.

He mutters dirty words to me that have me panting and almost begging him to fuck me, but I clamp my teeth down and tighten my grip, furiously tugging on my dick. It doesn't take long before we both spill our seed all over our hands. I desperately want to lean forward and lap up his release, but instead, he climbs off the bed and heads into our shared bathroom. When he returns, his eyes shine with pleasure, and he passes me a cloth before cleaning up his own mess.

Once we are clean, he tosses both in a nearby clothes basket before climbing back into bed. He crawls over me to return to his spot, his naked body brushing across mine in the process, and I moan quietly. He stops and looks me in the eye. "Next time, I'll come down your throat and you will come down mine," he promises, and I squirm at the idea of sixty-nining with the gorgeous merman.

He returns to the position he was in and drags my body against his. My itchy need has settled, so I close my eyes and fall asleep, blissfully thought free.

axsim finds me snuggled up to Nikos the next morning. I see his nose twitch, obviously scenting the spilled cum in the basket, but instead of roaring and losing his shit, he thanks Nikos for taking care of me before apologizing profusely. He says laughing like he did was insensitive of him, and he should have reacted differently. I can't believe he is being so mature about all of it, and I secretly wonder if maybe he got his own advice from somewhere.

I assure him nothing except seeking our own pleasure occurred, and he actually gave me a blanket green light to go further with any of the others if I ever wanted to in the future. I am tucked firmly back into his side and still speechless when Lila and the others return from Vilax.

They don't return alone. Saxon's cousins, Musette and Mehira, are with them. Both of them begged their mother to do some galaxy travel, and she approved it. They are going to be the new fliers in the Vilaxian act, along with Saxon's clan sister, Vanity. The cousins are loud and excited to be on the ship, giving all of Saxon's mating group big hugs and welcoming us to the family. It's kind of sweet and so very unlike our quiet, watchful Vilaxian, and it's nice to see him lighten up when they tease him.

Vanity, on the other hand, is quiet and subdued

and hangs back. She is very much like her clan brother. She greets us politely but doesn't get involved in any of the chatter. I watch her and notice she has sadness in her eyes. I hope being in the circus will eventually change it.

On the way back to our suite, Saxon tells us that she decided not to join a clan. She doesn't like the politics involved and decided she preferred to drink from a donor. All three girls will be drinking donor blood or from volunteers. Lila has sent out a ship-wide invitation, and I'm sure they will have no shortages. All three of them have the beauty of a Vilaxian. Musette and Mehira hope to find their blood roses while on their travels, and I have my paws crossed for them.

Although they put on brave faces in public, the four of them are in subdued moods when we return to our suite. At first I panic, thinking that the clan dissolution was denied, but they reassure us everything is fine. Despite wanting to spirit Lila away to our den, we gather with the others in the living area while they tell us what happened.

Nikos feeds his twins, my own pecs aching at the sight. I can't wait until I can do that for my babies. The kraken babies love on the four who had been gone for the evening, despite them being asleep the whole time they were gone, but they quickly grow bored, and Ghosie sets them up with some blocks to distract them. Now there is a male who has excellent fathering instincts. I can see the longing in his eyes, and I know when Lila decides to give him a cub, he will also love and protect it like the fiercest mama bear in the galaxy.

Lila laughs when she tells us about the surprise party that the queen arranged to celebrate their mating, explaining the concept to those of us who don't know about surprise parties, which is basically all of us but Brannock who lived on Earth. We all laugh when she tells us about Xavier killing the chandelier when he thought they were under attack.

"Luckily they didn't do a cake that had someone inside it or they would have been killed!" Lila chuckles.

"You have cakes with people inside them?" Ghosie asks, his bright fur paling ever so slightly as he swallows nervously, his attention turning from the children to Lila. "Is this something I need to worry about when we get to Earth?"

We all wait silently for her response as she looks at us with a small frown on her face.

"Seriously?"

"I thought some of the galaxy species we created were barbaric, but we don't bake people in cakes," Zeydan mutters.

Brannock bursts into laughter, making me jump in fright. Maxsim rubs my arm soothingly and growls at the Aaz'axian who is in his human glamour. He seems more comfortable in it than his real form, but who am I to judge?

"Sorry," he apologizes, his loud chuckles lowering in volume. "They don't bake people in cakes. Sometimes they will have a fake cake and have someone jump out of it as a surprise for the person whose cele-bration it is."

I purse my lips, trying to imagine it inside my head.

Lila nods. "Traditionally, it's a pretty girl or guy without many clothes on as a surprise for the birthday boy or girl."

I glance at my mate, and he appears as bewildered as I do. "Huh?" I look back at Lila.

She stammers and blinks and looks to Brannock for help. He gets up and goes over to the tablet that controls everything in our suite. We watch quietly as his fingers run across the screen, and then he hits a button, and the big viewing window turns into a screen and an Earth movie plays on it. We all watch as a dark, long-haired man walks around with a gun at the ready. He pushes a large cake out of his way, and suddenly, music starts to play and a girl pops out of it.

The girl is only wearing a jacket and one of those delightful bits of underclothes called a thong. Her ass is perfectly round as she sways back and forth in time to the music before pulling off her hat and throwing it. The camera pans around to the front, and she opens her jacket, exposing her very well rounded breasts.

"Oh, I like this idea. I would like a surprise cake for my birthday," Xavier says, sitting up straight and watching the movie with more interest, as do the rest of the men.

Lila rolls her eyes, and Brannock shifts the image to a new one. This one has a girl jump out of a cake in a pretty pink outfit, then she and a group of other girls start dancing and singing in unison. This grabs the kraken babies' attention, and they jump up and start copying the moves on the screen. Lila smiles and nods. "That movie is super old, but it's one of my favorites. I do love musicals."

Eventually, after telling us about the carnage during the party games, they get to the bit about Saxon's brother propositioning Xavier. We can tell his betrayal is weighing hard on him. Apparently, Xenos's clan caused quite a scene the next morning as they were escorted by Xavier, Saxon's uncle, and some of the queen's guards to the outpost they have been banished to. Lila is smug, because she convinced the queen to send Radella and Estrella as well—punishment for them trying to get between a blood rose bonding.

"I doubt we will ever be able to mend that relationship," Saxon says quietly, but then he shakes his head and stands, scooping Jack up and whirling him high in the air. Jack squeals and claps his hands. "Anyway, enough sadness. I want to see this new adventure playground you bought for the kids. Who wants to go?" The three kraken babies cheer. Hali and Typhoon clap, but I'm not sure they really know what's going on.

"I want to, but I have rehearsals scheduled all day. I'll take a raincheck though," Lila says, standing up and stretching.

"What time do rehearsals start?" Maxsim also stands, pulling me to my feet and looking to Ghosie, who has basically become Lila's assistant ringmaster, keeping track of her schedule for her.

"You have about an hour and a half," he says, looking at the digital clock on the wall.

"Perfect. Lila will meet you there." My alpha grabs my hand and hers and drags us through the suite to our room.

Lila stumbles but quickly rights herself. "What are you doing?" she sputters as the door opens and he drags us inside.

"Our omega needs us. Get naked," he growls, and although her eyes widen, she waves a hand. She's naked in an instant, and our loincloths are gone.

"Well, why didn't you say so?" A sly smile crosses her lips. "Present for us, omega."

I whine with need and do as they demand.

CHAPTER NINETEEN

Ghosie

"So the schedule will be Cas's group, followed by Magenta and Susie and their new double act." Lila is looking over her notes from rehearsals. I tick off each act against my own list. I love that I have fallen into the role of Lila's personal assistant. It feeds my need for order, and I'm able to contribute to this family. I don't have any skills that can translate into an act or magic that will assist, like Xavier and Zeydan, or medical training like Link. I do have some combat experience, but that's more of the smash and grab style instead of trained military skill like Brannock and Saxon, so it makes me happy that I can contribute in this way.

Poor Lila was looking slightly overwhelmed, and she took on the job that is usually done by the three Adams brothers. Together, we make a great team.

"Then the lightning cats. Minx seemed to fit in well. They are a much more cohesive unit now that Natalia is gone." She jumped down into the ring and rehearsed with them, practicing with the whip that she didn't really need. All of them obeyed her vocal commands, but there needed to be a little showmanship in there, so she cracked it, and Maxsim was unruly and disobedient.

I could see her giggle the whole time he was pretending to be ferocious. Anyone else in the ring probably would have run off, terrified, but she just gave him a scruff on the mane and spanked him on the butt as he turned his back to her. Echo is still performing with them for now, but I'm sure that will change once he gets closer to giving birth. He's starting to show more in the belly, and all I want to do is reach out and rub my hand over it, but I don't want to upset his alpha, so I keep my hands to myself.

There's silence, and I realize Lila is waiting for me to respond. "Oh, sorry, I was thinking about the act. Yes, she did fit in well, and the act was good," I assure her, because I have a feeling she's worried about her own performance.

She taps a finger against her lip. "I feel like we need to change it up a bit. The cats have been with the circus for a few seasons now, so the rest of the galaxy has seen them, but I don't know how to make it fresh."

We're quiet for a moment as we both rack our brains for something, but I have nothing, and it seems she doesn't either. "Don't stress, we can work something out." I reach over and pat her leg. The palm of my paw doesn't have any hair, so it's safe for me to touch her like this. She told me that once her grandmother gets her powers back, she will ask her to fix us or, if that doesn't help, then once she has Vivax's power, she will reverse the curse on the carevasta bears. I live for the day when I can touch my mate without it causing all-consuming lust. I'm sure our whole race will benefit from the change as well.

"Okay, so after the cats are the Nenghe. I was thinking that Oruck could go after them," I suggest. The new acts haven't rehearsed yet, but I think it would be the perfect place to put the rock man.

"Yes, I agree." Lila nods her head, and I tick off two more acts on my list.

I ended up canceling the rest of the auditions before we left Skarr. It upset some of the talent that turned up to try out, but we were happy with the three we hired the first day, and when Lila told me about Phillip and Fiona training the steggies, and that she was going to let them add them to the show, four new acts were enough, not to mention now that the Vilaxians and Aquilians have all returned in some capacity, the show probably would have run too long if we hired more.

"Okay then, so what's next?" Lila looks to me, and I frown.

"Well, the Aquilians were scheduled to talk to us about their performance. It's obviously going to need to be reworked now that there is a different contingency of Aquilians. You vetoed Hali and Typhoon being in the show, didn't you?" I ask, looking at my mate, and she nods her head.

"Yes. Nixie tried to push for it, saying Aquilians matured quickly, but Nikos and I stood firm. They are too freaking young. I'm not sure what she was thinking."

"Oh, I bet she was trying to get back in your good books after blowing you off while Nik was pregnant," I reply, not hiding the anger in my voice. I'm pissed that this female hurt both Lila and Nik.

"That's not the way to do it," she says dryly. "I mean, in my mind, I know she was stuck between choosing to protect her people or us, but in my heart, I'm still hurt. I won't stop her from having a relationship with our babies or Nik, but I am going to be cautious going forward. I should have known better. I've never trusted as quickly as I did when I joined the circus. You would have thought I'd learned from Dylan's betrayal."

Even though I wasn't around when she was attacked by her former friend, I still know the story, and he better pray we never run into each other in a dark corner of space. I may not be military trained, and I don't really enjoy it, but I have no problems getting my hands dirty.

"So where are they?" Lila looks around the circus dome. It's just us and the crew needed to set up. We sent a schedule with rehearsal times to each of the acts, and so far, they have all turned up on time. Caspian's act rehearsed, wanting to allow Malik and Titus a chance to perform. Both of them are going to swap in and out with Caspian and Tirrian if they are needed elsewhere. It went well, and there was lots of laughter and joking, and I could feel some of the tension drain out of Lila as it progressed.

It was the same with Magenta and Susie. They have developed a stunning display that is elegant and death defying. Lila gasped and stood up at one stage, worried for her friends as they fell what seemed like a long way, the silks unraveling, but it was all part of the show, and they were caught mere inches from the floor. The girls giggled and teased her, and she flipped them both off but muttered to me that she was happy they were getting along so well.

"I'm not sure. Hang on, I'll try to reach Nik." I grab the tablet off the chair beside me and open the screen. Each of us have one, and it has all of our direct links on the home screen. I push the icon for Nikos—a stylized warrior merman that he said made him look fierce. The sound of it ringing echoes through the empty dome, but he doesn't pick up. "That's strange. It should have gone to his watch if he isn't in reach of his tablet."

She purses her lips. "Maybe they are in the Aquilian habitat and lost track of time."

There is a commotion by the big doors that allow the crew to bring props out to the stage. Both of us turn our attention to it, and it's the Aquilians and Tirrian. Nikos and Nixie lead the way, and they seem to be arguing about something. Hurricane and his two sisters walk behind them with Tirrian bringing up the rear.

"What's going on?" Lila asks, standing up as they cross the large expanse of the ring. Her voice echoes around the empty space, and the brother and sister stop arguing.

"Sorry we're late, my little clam shell," Nikos calls, and her frown smooths slightly as her lips quirk up in amusement. "Nixie was still trying to convince me to include the twins in the show."

Lila's amusement drops, and she crosses her arms and glares at Nixie. Hurricane growls and steps in front of her like he needs to protect her from Lila. I see Lila flinch like she's been hit, but she straightens her back and stares at the deity.

"I am disappointed that you think you need to protect Nixie from me. I am entitled to my hurt, and I am entitled to be annoyed that she isn't hearing what Nik and I want," she states coldly. I know she wants to have a good relationship with Zeydan's soul brother, but she won't back down either.

He inclines his head. "You are, but I am entitled to protect my mate, even if it is from herself," he replies, and they seem to come to some kind of silent agreement, because he steps back, and Lila softens her glare.

"Hey," Nixie complains and smacks Hurricane on the arm. "What do you mean by that?"

He sighs. "You aren't listening to your brother and sister-in-law. You are showing the very traits you complained to me about your mother. You are not willing to compromise."

Nixie's body sags at his words, and tears glisten in her eyes before she nods. "You are right." She turns to Lila. "I'm sorry. I will not bring it up again."

Lila inclines her head in thanks but doesn't respond.

"Sorry we are late," Nixie continues, "but I had an idea for our performance, and I wanted to ask Tirrian if he would be involved."

Lila's eyebrows jump, and she turns to her dragon mate. "Oh?" I clamp my lips shut so I don't snicker at his fidgeting.

"Well, yes. I mean, we could have gone with the love story angle again, but I figured you are probably going to be too busy to be part of our act and wouldn't want Nik grabbing just anyone out of the audience," Nixie says breezily, and Lila snarls.

"You would be right." Wow, she really is holding a grudge. She isn't softening one little bit toward Nixie. It's going to be a long, hard trek back into Lila's good books. Nixie's smile falls as she seems to come to the same conclusion. Lila is cold and distant.

I look at Nik, trying to gauge how he's feeling, but he just looks at Lila with love and understanding. He was hurt by his sister's attitude too, and while he isn't holding a grudge like Lila, he will support his wife no matter what.

"So instead, I thought we could spin a story about the evil sea beast who captures the young mer females when they are swimming in their animal forms, and the rest of us need to battle them to get them back."

Oh, that is clever. I'm impressed, and Nik looks excited, even though he stays quiet and lets his sister explain.

"It will need to be fleshed out a little, and we can work on that, but I wanted to pitch the idea to you," Nixie continues in a hurry when Lila shows no reaction.

"How do you feel about this?" Lila turns her gaze back to the dragon, who just shrugs.

"It doesn't bother me. It isn't like it's hard to swim around and act menacing."

Lila nods. "Okay, that sounds fine as long as he doesn't get hurt. No real weapons, only stage props, and I want to see the act before I fully approve it. You have two days to get it performance ready. Ghosie will schedule a time for a full performance so we can approve it." She looks at me, but I am already checking the schedule and booking them a slot. I lock it in and send them the details to their tablets.

"We'll be ready, I promise. I won't let you down again," Nixie says quietly, but Lila has already turned her back to her, effectively dismissing her. I see a tear trickle down Nixie's face, and Hurricane puts his arm around her and hurries her out of the arena with his sisters in tow.

Tirrian and Nikos join us.

"You don't think you were a little harsh on her?" Tirrian, of all people, asks, and she just gapes at him.

"Seriously?" she asks, sounding hurt. "You, the king of grudge holding, are going to ask me that?"

He sighs and shakes his head. "It's because I know how badly I fucked up holding that grudge against you, and I don't want you to make the same mistake."

"But it's not the same. I didn't hurt you. I didn't do anything, you just had misinformation. She hurt me, not to mention Nik. We both needed her while he was pregnant, and instead of supporting him, she let her mother walk all over her."

"It can be hard when it involves family," Tirrian argues, obviously thinking about how he took his cousin's side.

"But Nik was her family too, and he was there for her more than her mother ever was." Lila is not giving an inch, and I start to worry this is going to devolve into a real argument, but Tirrian backs down.

"You're right. You are entitled to your feelings. I just don't want you to regret it later." He pulls her into a hug, and she goes willingly into his arms and sags a little. Lila has had to adjust to being in charge on the fly, and it's going to take a toll. We need to remember to give her hugs and reassure her she's doing a great job.

"Thank you for accepting the idea for the new show. I wasn't interested in dragging another woman out of the crowd," Nik tells our wife, and she pulls out of Tirrian's arms and throws her own around the merman.

"No other woman is going to get the chance to

stroke your fins. I would kill them first," she growls, giving him a fierce kiss on the lips. When she pulls back, he has a dopey grin on his face. He's still getting use to how affectionate Lila is with all her mates. He wasn't able to experience it previously when he was confined to the pool during his pregnancy. It gives him hearts in his eyes every time she lavishes it on him. I can't deny I'm fiercely jealous and can't wait until the time when I can experience the same without worrying about causing a galactic pornographic incident.

"Yes, dear," he mutters, and Tirrian snorts, dragging him away so we can continue our rehearsals.

"What's next?" Lila asks, sitting down next to me.

"Intermission is next, but do we want to shift things around and have one more act before it?" I count what we have so far. "Adding the rock man to the first half means we have six acts before intermission, leaving five for the second half of the show."

"They are all quite spectacular acts too, aren't they?" She counts off on her fingers. "The new steggy polo, which I think should be straight after intermission, like Viggy used to be, then the Vilaxians and Thorn who will now help with their act, the larnuks, Meela the Elrug bubble woman, and the fire sheepies."

I laugh at her name for the last act. It isn't what they are called, but she says she can never remember what they are, so that works for her. We will have to get her to come up with a name for the act when she introduces it.

"Yes, that's right," I confirm, and she taps a finger on her cheek in thought.

"Let's finish with the larnuks as usual and put Meela on as the first act after intermission. The steggies, Vilaxians, fire sheep, and larnuks. We will have a full dress rehearsal and see if that works. What do you think?"

I puff out my chest in pride that she values my opinion. "I think that sounds like a perfect lineup."

She grins at my response. "Right, I don't know about you, but I'm hungry. How long until the next rehearsal?" she asks me, and I look at our schedule.

"There's nothing for this afternoon because we hadn't decided on the lineup. I will send the remaining acts their rehearsal time now that we've decided. You're free for the rest of the day," I tell her, and she grins, standing.

"Clear the dome please. You can all go to lunch," she shouts to the crew. I stand up too, but she puts her hand out to stop me. We wait and listen to the sounds of the crew departing for the main levels of the ship.

"Okay, we're alone," she says, and my heart starts to beat faster. Fuck, what have I done wrong? Is this where she tells me she isn't happy about the job I've been doing? At least she waited until they all left before embarrassing me like that.

Her body shimmers, and she changes into her bear form. I gulp as she steps closer to me, pushing me back into my seat and climbing into my lap.

"Have I told you today how fucking sexy it is that

you are my assistant? I have fantasies of you climbing under my desk and servicing me while I'm taking meetings." She starts to writhe against me as my fur begins to work on her. My hips involuntarily thrust up into her as her fur affects me.

Holy fuck. This isn't where I thought this was going at all.

My hands come up to rest on her thick hips as my cock hardens at the feeling of her rubbing against me.

"That's going to have to wait for another time, but right now, I'm going to reward you for excellent service to your employer by servicing you." She slides off my lap and runs a hand over my cock, which has pushed out of its sheath. "Good PAs get their cocks sucked."

She leans down and licks the tip of my throbbing member. My head drops back and my eyes close as Lila shows me who's boss.

CHAPTER TWENTY

Lila

The next few days are pure chaos. There are rehearsals, costume fittings, and memorizing lines, and that's just the circus half of the chaos. We spend time with our children, organize the new family spaces, and deal with the few hiccups that occur from interspecies interaction, which is way more dramatic and violent than I'm used to, not to mention planning the raid on Area 51.

Rehearsals ran less than smoothly, but hopefully that just means the show will run like a dream come performance time. It's actually terrifying when things go wrong. It isn't just a matter of a sprained ankle or possible broken bone. Nope, there are maimings and near-death experiences.

Steggy polo was an eye opener. Phillip and Fiona were finally well enough to rehearse, and together with

Connor, they created a fun and exciting event that our audience members will be able to participate in, but it wasn't without its casualties. Connor's leg was gored when one of the crew members got a little excited and didn't pay attention to where his steggy was running. I just about gagged from the amount of blood and thought we were going to lose Connor, but Mark and Aarin were quick with the healing hands while I just flailed around in panic, forgetting about my own abilities. Then, though, the two of them were basically useless when Susie had an awkward fall from her silks and dislocated her shoulder. Link was able to set it, and I used my own healing capabilities to ease any further discomfort.

We know to have medical on hand during the steggy polo, because while it's relatively harmless, accidents do happen. We are allowing a lot less steggies on the pitch while on Earth as opposed to when we are on a different planet. On Earth, it will only be four on each side in the hopes we can limit casualties amongst Earth circus attendees.

Meela the Elrug bubble woman entertained all of the crew, but she keeps eyeing my men like they are snacks and she has a fierce hunger. Magenta tried to tell me it's because unlike the pampered princes of her world, my men are talented and useful, and she isn't used to seeing that, but I growled that there were plenty more men in the circus, and she should keep her eyeballs and her fingers to herself if she wanted to live long enough to discover other options. Magenta quickly intervened and dragged her off to give her a little private advice. We will see if she lasts a tour or if I will be sending her home on the next shuttle. I've had enough of delusional women to last me a lifetime. They are mated men, have some respect.

When it came time for the Vilaxians to rehearse, I insisted that a net be put under them, even though it's usually just for show on Earth, and luckily I did. It took them a good two rehearsals to get into the swing of the performance. As much as I disliked Saxon's former clan, they were a well-oiled machine. Eventually Thorn and Saxon worked out the kinks, and the girls weren't dropped much after that, which is probably a good thing. Although none of them hit the ground, they were getting pretty hangry from using their abilities to stop themselves from falling. I needed to make sure we had extra blood on hand.

I tried to strike up a conversation with Vanity, but she was aloof and distracted and kept sniffing the air. I have no idea what that was about, but I wasn't going to risk having my neck gnawed on by a hangry Vilaxian, so I let her be.

Ghosie suggested that I could join the act, and while I have tumbling skills, flying through the air like that with no chance to touch ground makes me feel queasy, so I declined Saxon's offer to catch me. I still haven't mastered the Vilaxian form of flying and prefer to use my wings if I have to do any.

The fire sheepies from Bhusta, which are actually called something unpronounceable, were next. Their trainer, whose name was also a tongue twister but insisted we call him Bob, is a tall alien similar to the Earth tale of the slender man. His head is elongated, his limbs and torso are long and slender, and his skin color is a pale blue. His race is peaceful and nature loving, and it turns out the Bhusta are one of Zeydan's creations. Bob fell to his feet and started crooning a high-pitched prayer sounding noise when he came face-to-face with his creator.

Zeydan was gracious, picked him up off the ground, and had a conversation with him in his mother tongue before carefully inspecting his fire sheepies as requested by Bob. He lavished praise on them, and Bob puffed up with pride before putting the sheepies through their paces. We only burnt the first row of one side of the dome, and Xavier and Zeydan were able to combine their magic and put it back together. Bob apologized profusely, swearing he was nervous in front of the great and noble Zeydan. He said he will be better next time. I can only keep my fingers crossed that this is the case and have crew at the ready with fire extinguishers. Even though those sheepies are bred to fight fires, they were much too excited when the fire got out of control and ran around bleating, spitting more fire. It was a low-key disaster, and I told Ghosie to schedule Bob for a couple more rehearsals with Zeydan front and center. We can't have him injuring our audience because he is nervous.

When it was time for the larnuks to rehearse, Zala grumbled about the smell of smoke that seemed to have drifted into the larnuk habitat from the fire sheepies' habitat. I promised to have maintenance look at the extraction system for her, and she was happy with that response. I got to spend some quality one-on-one time with Shiny. He's not mature enough for me to ride on his back yet, but he had fun prancing around the arena with the other larnuks and then chasing after them when they took to the air. It was so cute that Zala decided to add him to the act. He tossed his head and high stepped like a champion. I rewarded him with an extra scoop of dragon eye gems.

Finally, we were done for the day, and it was dinnertime. I considered going to dinner with the crew when they invited me, but I begged off, pleading that I hadn't seen my children all day and I needed snuggles. Our krakens have become very popular with just about everyone in the circus, winning everyone over with their adorable ways. The mer babies are a little more aloof, and although they are now crawling, they still can't keep up with their older brother and sisters yet, much to Hali's disgust. She spends a lot of time complaining about it at a very high volume. She isn't winning any friends.

Kinga has been run ragged now that we have circus responsibilities, and Hurricane's teen sisters have taken to helping her out. I increased their wages and promised them a huge shopping spree on Earth in payment. This seemed to appease them, if their squeals of joy were any indication, thank goodness. I can't afford to lose my nanny, and until I can hire another one, they are a good solution. I instructed for Ghosie to put out a galaxy-wide advertisement for experienced and qualified nannies. He is fielding all the applicants and setting up interviews for the most suitable ones. They will be shuttled to Earth in a fast craft, and we will hold interviews between shows.

On my way back to our suite, I ran into Aura, who expressed their gratitude in allowing them and their family to return to the Pleasure Inn. Brannock was going to quiz them today about how they got their "entertainment" on and off the planet. Hopefully he has an update for me. We need to know if and how Smith can leave to attend the Syndicate meeting.

My suite is loud with most of my family sitting around the table eating dinner, and nobody notices me at the door. I contemplate joining them, but instead, I activate my warlock powers and teleport to the small pool located next door to Nikos's bedroom. I strip and jump in, letting my original half kraken form wash over me. I sink down to the bottom and close my eyes, trying to ease the chaos in my mind. I know it won't always be like this, but at the moment, I'm feeling incredibly overwhelmed. My mates are all super supportive, but it's hard to share when you've spent so many years bottling all that kind of crap up.

I breathe in, feeling the water slip through my gills and fill my lungs before breathing back out again. I start counting slowly, using it to clear my mind, and eventually, it starts to work. All of my worries lessen with the ebb and flow of the water around me.

I'm not sure how long I float for, but eventually, I push to the surface and climb out using my tentacles. I grab a towel from the basket and dry off before teleporting directly to my bedroom.

I find Silac lying on my bed, not surprised to see me in the least. His eyes light up at seeing my naked body, but he doesn't move.

"Feeling better?" he asks, and I sigh, moving to my closet to find some clothes.

"So much better. I don't know how my grandparents didn't go insane. I understand why they chose to leave me in foster care when my parents died."

"There were three of them, remember? It was easy to spread the load between them, but you are doing well by using Ghosie and not trying to do it all yourself."

I smile, thinking about how, exactly, I have been using Ghosie. Yes, he is an excellent personal assistant, but he is also very good at relieving stress. "He has been a blessing, as have all of you. Don't think I don't know you are helping in your own little ways." When I checked on Kinga earlier in the day via tablet, she and Andre were having lunch at one of the cafes, while Silac and Tirrian took the kids up to the bio level to run around.

Tirrian and the Aquilians are showing me their performance tomorrow, and I'm looking forward to seeing what they came up with, but when I asked him about why he wasn't rehearsing, he said he didn't need to do much but swim around and look scary.

Silac drags my attention back to him. "Xavier felt you when you teleported in and asked me to come check on you. Do you need anything?"

I pull on a pair of fleece pajama pants and a long-sleeved sweatshirt before going over to the bed and climbing onto it. I crawl across to my snake and snuggle into his side.

He presses a kiss to the top of my head and sighs. "Hello, wifey," he murmurs, and my lips lift in happiness.

"Hello, hubby," I reply. Silac is the only one I am officially mated and married to, though the warlock bonding ceremony may count as an official wedding ceremony. I would like to marry them all eventually, even if it isn't legal, because it makes me feel like I've included them all. Could you imagine us going to a little chapel in Vegas and getting Elvis to marry all thirteen of us? Talk about a hunk of burning love.

"I've missed you," I tell him. We've been constantly on the go since we married, and apart from the marriage consummation, we haven't had a lot of time together. I haven't even seen him naked in this form. I roll over and start running my hands over his body, but he grabs them and pins them down.

"You need to eat, and our children aren't going to wait much longer. They were demanding to see Mama during dinner. Caspian distracted them with ice cream, but it's not going to be long before they look for you."

I sigh and look him in his pretty orange and black eyes. "Rain check?" I ask him, and he smirks.

"But of course."

My eyes run down his body, stopping at his crotch area where I know he has two cocks that are all mine hidden behind those tight pants. I sigh in disappointment, but I sit up and heave myself off the bed. I know if I don't move straight away, my willpower will become nonexistent, and I will ask him to show me his one-eyed snakes.

His grin grows even bigger, like he knows exactly how I'm feeling, but he follows me off the bed, removing my temptation. Grabbing my hand, he tugs me out of the room. I grumble and follow him reluctantly, but then I hear the noise from the living area, and I find a second wind. I overtake him, dropping his hand and hurrying out to find my mates are in the process of wiping the kids' faces and hands. Dinner is not exactly a quiet and clean process, but that's okay, I love it.

I don't get anywhere near enough time to spend with my babies. Yes, they are exhausting, but I love them so much more than I ever thought I would. I didn't think I was cut out for motherhood, but I miss them when I don't see them for hours. I can now completely relate to working mothers who don't get to spend all their time with their kids because they need to earn a livable income. It fucking sucks.

I lift Hali out of her highchair and give her a little

snuggle. The mer twins have missed out the most, and I promise to spend more time with them. They are going to start calling Kinga Mama if I'm not careful. Hali squeals as I blow raspberries on her little tummy before slapping my cheeks with both hands and babbling to me. I settle her on my hip before I turn my attention to my little prince. Typhoon is watching me with wide, cautious eyes, and I feel a pang of hurt. Because I've been so busy and I'm not the one feeding them, I haven't bonded with them like I did with the krakens. I make a promise to myself to do better. Tomorrow, before anything else happens, I'm taking them to the Aquilian habitat and going for a swim with them. I've avoided it for the last few days because Nixie is living there again, but I need to stop being such a weenie. My children and our relationship are so much more important than being uncomfortable.

I hand Hali off to Silac, who wandered up behind me. She goes to him, but instead of squealing, she looks at him solemnly. He's in his human form, and she grabs a handful of his emerald green hair and gives it a tug before she starts babbling to him quite seri-ously. I smother the smile that wants to cross my lips as he nods his head and has a conversation with her, apparently making all the appropriate noises because she doesn't get upset.

I turn my attention back to Typhoon and hold out my hands to him. He's a lot more subdued than his sister. She's a bull in a china shop and not afraid to scream to get her way, whereas he seems to analyze everything before making a move. I need to wait for him to come to me and not force him to do it if he doesn't want to.

He seems to come to a decision, and he holds his hands up to me. I lift him and place little kisses all over his face until he giggles. "Mama, stop." He chuckles and pushes my face away, and I freeze.

I look around the room, and everyone is stunned into silence. "Did you hear that?" I ask them, meeting Nikos's gaze.

He nods, his eyes glistening with tears. "Yes, his first real words." He and Hali seem to have their own language that they communicate with, much like the kraken babies did, but this is the first time I've heard Ty say something in English. It's the language we all speak to the babies, because none of them are old enough for communicator implants. We will eventually allow them to have them, but not until their brains have developed more.

"Aw, babe, how does that feel?" Cas asks, and I just about burst with pride.

"So fucking good," I reply.

"Fucking good!" Jack yells and bangs his hands on the table to get our attention. "My fucking turn for cuddles." He holds his hands up, making grabby motions.

There's another stunned silence, and I hang my head with shame as everyone else bursts into laughter. There's no point in scolding Jack, since he doesn't know what he did wrong, and try as I might, I have not succeeded in completely curbing my language in front of them. I have no one to blame but myself.

Cas scoops him up and whispers to him that we don't use that word, but I don't think Jack pays any attention. He wriggles out of his father's arms, slides down his body, and runs over to me, tugging on my pajama pants. "Cuddles, Mama. I missed you."

Aww, I just about melt into the floor. I crouch down, Ty still on my hip, and open my spare arm for Jack. He throws his arms around my neck and his legs around my waist, almost kicking his brother.

"Up, Mama, up," he demands, and I stand with a little help from Maxsim, who gives me a boost from behind with his giant head. I hadn't noticed that he and Echo were in cat form. He licks a strip of exposed skin when my shirt rides up from Jack's legs before he and Echo walk over to the door. Xavier waves a hand, and the door opens, letting them out.

"They wanted to go for a run after dinner. Echo is feeling fat now that his belly is starting to stick out. It's normal, but he's hormonal, more than I would have expected at this stage in his pregnancy," Link explains from the sink where he's stacking dishes into our industrial-sized dishwasher.

"I mean, is it any surprise that his pregnancy isn't normal? Nothing we do is normal," I point out, and he just smiles and nods in agreement.

"Truer words have never been spoken," Tirrian agrees, lifting Callie, while Ghosie grabs Cordy out of her highchair. Both of them wiggle to get down, and they slide down their fathers' legs and make a beeline to me, almost knocking me over.

"Whoa. How about we let Mama sit down, and then she can snuggle with all of you?" Brannock suggests, snatching up Cordy and swinging her around. Zeydan eyes Callie cautiously. I can feel his need to get to know the children, but I don't think he's been around many, and he isn't sure how to act with them.

"Don't be hesitant. They aren't breakable," Xavier tells him, obviously able to feel the same thing I do. "Trust me, with this family, you're going to have to stake a claim, or you're never going to get cuddles." He scoops Callie up and places her in Zeydan's arms before flopping back on the large sectional that is somehow big enough for most of us.

"Right, let's watch a movie. What shall we watch?" Saxon suggests as I take Brannock's recommendation and settle onto the sofa with Xavier, holding Ty and Jack in my arms. Callie and Cordy have both lost interest in me as Zeydan and Brannock also take their seats, situating them on their laps.

"Rain, rain." Cordy claps her hands and bounces up and down on Brannock's lap, and he groans.

"Not rain again," he argues, and I frown.

"What is she talking about?"

He grimaces. "Remember when I showed them that clip from the movie last night with the girl jumping out of the cake?"

My eyes widen as I think about them watching

Under Siege. "That's not suitable for them," I scold, and his eyes widen, and he shakes his head.

"No, not that one, the second one, the musical. Kinga has had it on repeat for them all day."

"Oh, well, that's okay. I love that movie, it's one of my favorite classics," I tell him, and he nods.

"Yes, it's a great movie, and it was one of Chloe's favorites too, but it's been playing nonstop all day, and I'm going to be dreaming of yellow raincoats and black umbrellas," he grumbles, and I giggle.

"But they are so adorable when they watch it," Saxon argues as he uses the tablet to put it on the viewing window screen. We could move to our family theater room, but the fire is on, and it's cozy out here.

We watch the movie, and the older kids jump up and dance, shaking their little bums, trying to copy the movements on the screen for the first couple of dance numbers, but eventually, they start to tire and pick a lap to curl up in. The whole time, Ty and Hali stay snuggled up in my arms, Hali demanding my attention once Silac took a seat next to me.

Eventually, Max and Echo return, laying at my feet in cat form. It's such a perfect family evening, and I can't wait for many more to come.

CHAPTER TWENTY-ONE

Lila

We are about a day out from Earth when the thirteen of us sit down for another strategic planning meeting. We consider inviting Tirrian's brothers, Saxon's cousins, and Zeydan's god brothers to join the raid, but we decide the less people to set off the sensors, the better.

"Teleporting directly into the building is out. Smith will hit the kill switch and poison all the prisoners without even flinching," Brannock explains as we start to plan who will do what with the raid. "And teleporting outside the facility is also out, since they have infrared sensors that will pick up anyone who suddenly appears."

"I'm assuming if we send the message to the Syndicate pretending to be the Madovian, saying we have the orb and demanding a meeting, that this will send Smith scurrying?" Saxon taps a finger on the table as he studies the updated Area 51 schematics with the extra wing that we didn't have on ours.

"Yes, it should do. Liliana said that Vivax complained about him, constantly saying he was a thorn in her side. She couldn't wait to get rid of him the moment she had the orb in her hands, so I'm pretty sure he will be summoned so she can kill him," Zeydan says, reminding us of what my grandmother said.

Brannock growls. "Not before I can get my hands on him."

"So how are we going to get in?" Caspian frowns.

"Did you know that lightning cats don't show up on infrared sensors?" Maxsim muses, and Silac nods his head.

"Neither do snake shifters. We can cool our body temperatures enough that it doesn't register."

"So maybe Maxsim, Silac, and Lila can breach the compound from the outside, neutralizing all the security out there, and then we can mount a frontal assault," Link suggests.

"All it would take is someone hitting the alarm, and the prisoners would be dead. No, we need to think about this sensibly. Also, the galaxy level is not something that is unilaterally known about. You need special clearance to work in that level. We would be alerting the whole facility to its existence," Brannock explains. "It actually has its own exit—an underground tunnel that exits miles away from the facility. The level is sealed off from the rest of the facility, with its own power and water source. The controls for those are midway down the tunnel, but the tunnel is lined with laser sensors." He points out that there are no elevator shafts leading up from the level on the schematics, only one that leads away at ground level.

"Okay, how about this? We teleport to the entrance of the tunnel, then Lila and I will go in mist form and cut the power. That will disable any defense system the level has. Although it will put the guards on high alert, it should be easy enough for us to incapacitate them if we aren't worrying about anyone tripping the fail-safe." Xavier leans forward in his seat, and I can feel his anticipation and excitement.

Brannock purses his lips in thought before giving a small nod. "Yes, that should work. Mist form won't set off the laser sensors, and once you cut the power, all defenses will be rendered neutral, but we will need to watch out for trigger happy guards. Once we are in the facility and have incapacitated the guards, Ghosie will use his powers to go through the sealed and locked door and open it from the other side. Only Smith's handprint and eye scan will open it from the side we will be on, and he won't be around to use."

"That's a shame," Tirrian says dryly.

"So we're all going then?" I ask, biting my lip and worrying about my mates.

"I won't for obvious reasons," Echo says, pointing at his belly.

"Neither will I," Nikos says. "I'll stay behind with our children."

Cas nods. "I will do the same. You have plenty of fire power and magic, so you don't need me. We also need to keep up the appearance that we are with the circus pod in Asia in case they have any spies. I propose that Silac and I head down with that so we're seen by the crew, and if anyone asks, we will tell them you are making preparations elsewhere and will be with us shortly."

"That's actually a good idea. What about you, Link? Coming or staying with the circus?" Saxon asks my cyborg who looks torn.

"What if any of the aliens need medical attention? Maybe I should go with you."

"We have Lila and her magic healing abilities," Tirrian reminds him.

"But what if she runs out of power using all her different abilities?"

"She shouldn't. Now that she doesn't have to change forms every time to tap into her abilities, she shouldn't drain so quickly. It's the mimic changing power that drains her energy and requires her to power up through sex. Tapping into her powers is a goddess power, and while she is only a quarter and a bit deity" —Zeydan winks at me as he explains— "it should let her do everything she needs to during the mission, including healing any injuries."

My cyborg visibly relaxes. "In that case, I will remain behind as well. I don't enjoy conflict as much as all of you." He really is a gentle soul and well suited to being a healer.

"And if we have any problems, we can have Mark and Aarin on standby to beam down and assist us with healing," Brannock suggests. "We know neither of them are moles for the Syndicate."

"Good point," I agree and make a note to speak to them. "So who does that leave then? Brannock, Saxon, Ghosie, Xavier, Tirrian, Zeydan, and I. What about you, Maxsim? In or out?"

My alpha cat is torn. His need to protect Echo is warring with his need to protect me. We keep doing this to him, and it isn't fair. Hopefully this will be the last time he has to make this choice.

Before he can reply, Saxon claps him on the shoulder. "You stay and help protect the children. We will make sure nothing happens to Lila." The tension drains out of the big male as he quickly agrees. Saxon deciding for him was the right move, and he can be guilt free now if anything goes wrong during the incursion—not that it's going to.

"Okay, I say we allow the hologram program to run in Singapore, and the circus pod leaves before we breach the compound. That will ensure most of the crew is on the surface, leaving only a skeleton crew on the ship, which will make it easier for us to transport to Nevada without being seen," Brannock decides. He's been the main planner for this, as we all know he is ready to bust heads and get his daughter back. It has kept him focused.

"And we should send that message to the Syndicate as soon as we hit Earth's orbit, which will give Smith time to leave before we invade," Xavier adds.

"We need to monitor how he leaves. Aura assured me that it is easy enough to cloak a small shuttle vessel and hide behind the galaxy ship. That's how they get illegals on and off the planet," Saxon explains, and I frown.

"Why hasn't the bridge ever picked up ships in the vicinity when they've done their scans?" I question.

"We've never noticed because we never scanned for other ships. None were supposed to be in the vicinity." Saxon looks as skeptical as I feel.

"It's a shame we didn't know when there were ships shadowing us, because we can't compare it to the duty roster for the bridge. I suspect that we have a mole," Link muses thoughtfully, his genius brain expressing exactly what I was thinking.

"Well, now that we know it's happening, we can keep a discrete eye on it." Silac uses the console in the war room to do something, his fingers flying across the screen in a way that makes me slightly dizzy, so I look away. "I've created a backdoor link into the outside sensors of the ship. I will monitor them from my tablet so we can see exactly if and when Smith is retrieved."

"If we have a mole, we need to have the Madovian or the Filani she was posing as be seen by some of the crew members so they don't grow suspicious that she hasn't been seen," Caspian points out. "Orion's Belt is opening again, and she will be expected to perform. Nobody knows about the Madovian incident because Xavier wiped it from everyone who was in attendance. As far as they know, they just saw a Filani perform."

"Yes, the mole doesn't know we know about her. I'm sure the Syndicate will ask them to check if she really is on board once we advise them of having found the orb—or I would anyway," Brannock says.

"So I need to make an appearance at the club as the Filani stripper? Shit, I haven't mimicked one of those before. I'm not sure I will be able to without seeing one." I gnaw on my lip with my teeth as my heart rate increases with my panic.

"And some of us can be in the audience scoping out possible moles. I'd really like to know who is betraying us," Maxsim growls, and my eyebrows jump in surprise.

"You want to see strippers?" I ask him, and he looks at me with a frown.

"What? No, I want to know who the mole is." He sounds confused, and I see some of the other guys grin at his naivety, but then he grins and shrugs. "And if it's you stripping, then what is the harm in that?"

Echo laughs at my surprised reaction. "There is nothing wrong with us admiring our mate's naked body," he agrees. "I wish to be in the audience as well."

"Are you two going to be able to control your instincts when you realize other people who aren't your co-mates are also looking at your naked wife?"

Nikos asks before shuddering. "I will pass. I am likely to stab them all in the eye with my trident. No, you can shake your lovely breasts for me in private." He winks at me, and I roll my eyes.

Of course they are probably all going to want a private show after that.

"I'll be in the form of the Madovian too," I remind the cats, and they blanch and quickly decide they don't need to go.

"So we have a plan then?" Ghosie speaks up over the rumbles of agreement, getting us back on track.

"Yes. I say Lila performs tonight, and I will send the urgent message to the Syndicate posing as the Madovian, saying that I know where the orb is and I am planning on retrieving it as soon as the ship lands in Singapore," Brannock confirms, and everyone murmurs their agreement. "Then I will send another message once we are in Earth's orbit saying the timeline moved up, I have the orb, and demand a meeting for three days' time, saying I need that much time to make my escape."

"I'm still not sure if I can mimic the Filani," I remind them, and Silac shakes his head.

"You won't have to. Although she got on the ship posing as a Filani, she was in her Madovian humanoid form during the performance," he reminds me, and I heave out a sigh of relief.

"Oh yeah, you're right, with all those wiggling snakes for hair. Yeah, I can do that, but remember, I get very primal when I'm like that, so you may have to knock me out or sedate me if I do anything you don't like."

"And maybe Silac and Tirrian should stay away. Your Madovian form likes both of them a little too much," Link reminds us, and I grimace. Yeah, she does. I've only assumed it one more time just to practice, but she was obsessed with both reptilian men. She wants the dragon to fuck her in his animal form. Despite the huge gaping hole in her stomach, I'm pretty sure dragon cock would shred her to pieces.

With a plan well and truly in place, we split up. I head to lunch with Susie and Mark and I guess Aarin. I wonder when he's going to grow a set of balls and tell Mark that he is his mate. I hope he like BOGO, because Susie and Mark are a team. There is no way they will give each other up, but I could see Susie happy to have Aarin as a lover as well.

We meet in one of the smaller cafes instead of the large dining room, which is only open for breakfast and dinner, while the cafes are used for lunches. Sure enough, the three of them already have a table when I arrive.

Susie waves me over, and I make my way through the crowded café, saying hello to everyone who greets me.

"Sorry I'm late. My meeting ran over a little," I apologize as I take a seat, and Susie gives me a kiss on the cheek. Mark grins, and Aarin inclines his head.

"Where are my nieces and nephews?" she asks, and I laugh.

"Lunch would be chaotic if I brought all five of them as well. I'd also need to bring some of my guys or their nanny and bodyguard. We would never be able to have a conversation. I swam with them this morning, and they are probably napping now."

She pouts prettily. "Fine, but I want some Aunt Susie time. Maybe we can paint our nails." She wiggles her hands, and I see her polish is chipping.

I wince. "Good luck with that. I'm sure your hands will be a mess afterward." *And my children and the furniture and the walls*, but I refrain from saying it

She waves a hand. "I don't care, that's easy to fix."

"Listen, I wanted to talk to you about something," I tell them, changing the subject. I wave a hand, creating a privacy bubble so nobody can overhear our conversation. I share the details of the meeting, asking Mark and Aarin if they are okay being on standby if any of the captives need medical assistance.

They readily agree and will come up with an excuse to stay behind when the circus pod heads to Earth.

I breathe out a sigh of relief and release the privacy bubble. That's one less thing to worry about. I hear someone call my name, and I look around and find Magenta heading toward us.

"You were late, but she was even later!" Susie laughs.

We watch her come toward us, but she trips on something and falls onto a table, smashing a glass of water.

"Oh my goodness, I am so sorry," she apologizes to the occupants who jump up to help her.

"Wow, that wasn't particularly graceful," I mutter, hiding my smile in case she isn't okay. The occupants help her stand, and as she raises a hand, I see a trickle of blood. Mark stands up, his wings vibrating with his need to heal her, but before he can go to her, there is a blur of movement, and Saxon's clan sister, Vanity, is suddenly standing in front of my Skarrian friend.

She's growling and sniffing the air. "Blood rose," she declares and leaps at Magenta.

In a panic, I lift my hand and throw magic at her. I've never frozen anyone before, but fuck, I hope this works. Sure enough, Vanity is left frozen in mid-leap, and I heave out a sigh of relief.

"Fuck, this is going to be a problem."

Mark and I hurry over to the wrecked table. A waitress is there, cleaning things up, and I apologize again to the occupants who wave us off like it's no bother. Magenta, although not frozen by my spell, is stunned into inactivity. The blood trickles down her hand as she gapes at the frozen Vilaxian in front of her.

Mark heals her hand while I use my watch to send an SOS to Link and Saxon before turning to my friend.

"Well, you were saying you were thinking about

settling down. Congratulations, you just hit the jack-pot," I joke.

Her skin turns paler, and she drops in a dead faint. Luckily Mark has quick reflexes and catches her before she does any more damage.

"What a clusterfuck."

CHAPTER TWENTY-TWO

Lila

By the time Link and Saxon arrive, Magenta has regained consciousness. Saxon takes one look at a frozen Vanity and pales.

"Shit, what happened?" he asks, looking around the now deserted cafe, his eyes settling on the mess Magenta made of the table when she tripped. I asked everyone to move to another cafe while we sorted this out, and they were all happy to comply, but I don't doubt that rumors of what happened are already circling the ship.

"So it turns out that Magenta is Vanity's blood rose," I explain, looking down at my friend who is still on the floor.

Mark's hands are glowing as he checks her out, but they stop, and he sits back on his heels. "You're alright. Your blood pressure plummeted with your shock, causing you to pass out. I'm going to raise your legs to help with that." He gestures to one of the chairs, and Link moves it into place for him, knowing exactly what he wants. "I also healed the cut on your hand from the glass."

Magenta still looks a little pale, and I crouch down next to her, taking her hand. "Are you okay?"

I'm referring to her mental state now that I know she is physically okay. She blinks a couple of times, staring at me without seeing. I look to Mark and Link for advice, but Link just makes a *be patient* hand gesture.

"Mags?" I push, looking to where Vanity is still frozen. "Hey, I think that should last, but maybe we should get Xavier or Zeydan here to reinforce it," I suggest to the others. Susie gives me a thumbs-up and moves to the side to contact one of my power hitters.

"Did she say I am her blood rose?" Magenta asks, her voice quiet and unsure.

I nod my head. "Yeah, she did. Have you even met her?" I ask. I've been so busy that I've only seen Mags during rehearsals the last couple of days.

"I met her briefly during rehearsals when Titus and Malik invited me to watch Thorn rehearse with them."

Huh. Mags was hanging out with Titus and Malik? I hadn't been privy to that rumor yet. Maybe they are keeping it low-key for now.

I raise an eyebrow at my friend, and she blushes. "They've been helping me avoid Nixie since she returned."

That makes me frown. Although I understand it, I think they need to talk, even if it's to clear the air.

She rolls her eyes at my frown. "It's fine, we talked. I'm like whatever. I'm happy she found a mate. She wanted to rekindle things, but I'm not sure I want to. I'm hurt, and I'm not ready to play nice. Malik and Titus are a nice, nonsexual distraction." She stresses the word nonsexual. Hmm, maybe she really meant it when she told me she wanted more.

"Dude, you are preaching to the choir. I completely understand. Trust is going to be a long road walked."

She looks at me with confusion in her eyes, and I realize that maybe my metaphors are unfamiliar to her.

I shake my head. "Never mind. Let's turn our attention to the elephant in the room." I wave my hand at the frozen Vilaxian. "How do you feel about her and this situation?"

"She's not an elephant. Is Lila alright in the head? Should she really be in charge of such a large operation?" I hear Aarin mutter to Mark, who snorts with amusement and shushes him.

"I'm her blood rose," Mags mumbles again, and this time it sounds less like shock and more like awe. "She wants me despite me being Skarrian." She looks to Saxon with hope in her eyes.

His worry softens, and he nods, smiling gently at her. "Yes. She doesn't care who or what you are. You are her perfect match."

Mags smiles, and this time it's blinding. She wriggles, lifting her feet off the chair, and gestures for us to move so she can get up. Link offers her a hand, and she gets to her feet. I follow her when Saxon offers me some help too.

I give him a kiss on the cheek and turn my attention back to my alien bestie. She's staring at Vanity with awe. She reaches out to touch her, but I slap her hand away. She squeaks with surprise and jumps backward before glaring at me.

"What the fuck was that for?" she demands, and I grimace sheepishly.

"Ah, I'm not sure if the frozen state will stand up to interference. It's best not to risk it yet."

Just as I say that, Xavier pops in behind Aarin, making him jump and squeal like a girl. Xavier snickers when the deity glares at him, but thankfully he doesn't say anything. I don't have time for man squabbles.

He inspects the frozen Vilaxian and lets out a whistle. "This is a tight spell, Lila, good job. She isn't going anywhere," he praises me, and my skin prickles with goosebumps at his compliment. "So a bloodsucking girlfriend, Mags? What fun," he says to my friend, giving her a wink, and I roll my eyes. God, could he get any more irreverent?

Saxon glares at him before turning his attention back to Magenta. "Is this something you are open to?" he asks, and I brace myself for her reaction. I wouldn't blame her if she needed some time to think about it, but of course in true Magenta style, that isn't the case.

"Hell fucking yes I'm okay with it. Unfreeze her,

and I'll seal that blood rose bond here and now," she says enthusiastically, her eyes sparkling with excitement.

"But we need the blood rose chalice, and Xenos returned it to the queen when the circus broke up because of John's medical emergency," I say, and her face drops. "Without it, you could die during the process. We're going to have to wait until the queen can send it again."

I hate that I had to pump the brakes. She looked so excited, and I could feel how thrilled she was to be the one who was being pursued instead of her doing the pursuing for a change.

"Hmm," Saxon muses. "I think we might actually be in luck. Sabine sent the blood rose chalice along with Musette and Mehira in case either of them found their blood rose on the tour. She didn't want them to wait."

Magenta's disappointment turns back into excitement, and she bounces up and down, clapping her hands. "Let's do this."

"Do you know what's going to happen?" I ask her, and she shakes her head, her pink purple hair flying everywhere.

"No, but I don't care. I just want to make her my mate."

Aww, that's so fucking sweet. "Well, okay then. How about I teleport you to your room, and then Xavier can bring Vanity while Saxon finds his cousins and grabs the blood rose chalice?"

I look at my two mates, and they seem to agree with the plan.

"Magenta, I want you and Vanity to come see me when you are done. I want to make sure your body makes the same kind of adjustments that Lila's did, just to be sure," Link orders her, and she agrees.

"I'm sorry lunch was a bust. Can we try again soon?" I say to Susie, who is standing off to the side with both Mark and Aarin. She gives me a smile. "Of course," she replies before giving Magenta a thumbs-up. "Get some," she says, cheering, and Magenta laughs.

"Oh, I plan on it." I take her hand, and we teleport to her bedroom, Xavier following behind us with Vanity.

It doesn't take Saxon long to find his cousins and grab the blood rose chalice. I release Vanity from her frozen state and get her to calm down long enough to explain what needs to happen, but she already knows, so we leave them to it.

"How exciting," Musette gushes as we walk down the corridor of one of the residential levels. "I have hope for us now." She gives her sister's hand a squeeze, and Mehira nods.

"Yes, I wish we could go around cutting people, which is an acceptable way of testing someone on Vilax, but I'm pretty sure that won't fly here."

"You think?" I say dryly, looking at my cousin-in-law.

"Don't forget that someone who smells especially

good to you has a higher chance of being your blood rose," Saxon reminds them.

"Yes, and you could always ask them if they would mind being tested," I suggest, and they seem happy with that.

"What are you two doing now?" Musette asks, and I look at my watch. "I missed lunch, and I'm starving, so grabbing a quick bite before I go for a swim, and then I need to get ready for a thing tonight," I tell them.

Musette wrinkles her nose. "Of course, we will leave you to it." The two of them take off without a backward glance.

"Was it something I said?" I ask the guys.

Xavier chuckles. "You said 'a quick bite.' I think they thought you and Saxon were going to bury your fangs in one another."

I giggle and shrug. "Well, I wouldn't be opposed," I reply with a wink.

Xavier doesn't hesitate. He reaches out with both hands, putting one on each of us, and we tumble through space, landing at the base of his bed.

I squeal as the two of them lunge at me and throw me on the bed. I do enjoy a little afternoon delight.

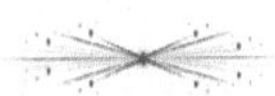

That evening, I'm waiting in the green room of Orion's Belt. Apparently, the bar only has adult entertainment twice a week, and tonight is the first time it's been advertised since the ship left Skarr because, well, there are no strippers on board.

Xavier had to tell Sully and Tully the truth, but then he made it so they couldn't share that truth with the whole ship, which also means he had to return their previous memories. They apologized profusely to me for the previous Madovian, but I assured them not one of us held it against them. After all, she had fake documents that said she was a Filani.

I adjust one of the veils that are wrapped around my body. I have to dance around on stage, removing veil after veil. We discussed what I was going to do when I got down to the last few. I can't very well put on the same show the last one did—it was horrifying—but apparently I can hypnotize them all to believe they are seeing a Filani. I watched a video of what that actually looks like and practiced earlier on Xavier. If I can fool him, then I can fool anyone. He claims it worked, and he better not be lying to me. He says he saw large, bouncing boobs, a skinny waist, and an enticing cunt, which is the opposite of the hot mess of a Madovian I'm pretending to be.

The snakes that are my hair writhe in agitation, and the tiny wings at my back flutter with expectation. I pace back and forth, wrestling internally with the monster that wants to basically set fire to the world. I kind of feel sorry for these women. It must be exhausting being them. No wonder they hire them-selves out for violence and mayhem. I would too if I constantly felt like a raging hormonal psychopath.

"Are you ready?" Xavier enters the room, and I lunge and hiss at him, and he puts up a quick barrier between us. "Fuck, Lila, calm yourself."

I smack against the invisible barrier and yelp as my face stings. That has me regaining some sense. I rub my nose slits, and I feel a trickle of blood run down my chin from where my fangs cut into my lip.

"Sorry," he says, and I wave him off.

"Actually, it helped, thanks," I tell him, grabbing a tissue and blotting at the damage. "I can think a little clearer now."

"Well then, you're welcome. Saxon, Brannock, and Tirrian are in the audience, and I will join them. They are invisible like we were for Silac's wedding, so you won't see us, and I'll be glamoured as a bouncer."

"That's good. We don't want to spook the mole. If they saw the four of you, they would be suspicious since you're supposed to be happily mated and off the market—not that I care if you want to go see strippers. Everyone likes some pretty entertainment. I know I do." Susie and I went to see the Magic Mike show back on Earth, and it was extremely entertaining. Who am I to judge the guys if they want to do the same? As long as there is no touching involved, I don't care.

"Do you suspect anyone in the crowd?" I ask, and he nods.

"A couple of the bridge crew are in to see the show.

Any one of them probably could have made it so the alarms didn't sound or the sensors didn't pick up a ship hiding in our shadow. We made a list for Link and Silac, and they are going to do a deep dive into their backgrounds—way more than we do for regular employees. We're going to check accounts and see if any of them have been paid unusual amounts recently."

"Good thinking. I hope it's someone getting paid and no one with a grudge against the circus."

He winces. "I guess we need to look at family members as well. There are many reasons someone could be working for the Syndicate—grudge and payment being just two of them. It could be blackmail as well. Look at Brannock."

I start to feel annoyed again that someone is betraying us, and the snakes on my head begin to lunge and snap at the air. "Let's get this over with. I don't want to spend any more time in this body than necessary."

He frowns. "Are you going to be okay for the Syndicate meeting?"

I hear his worry, and I nod. "Yes, because there will be an end in sight, and once this is all over, I never have to take this form again. Some of her thoughts make me want to hurl, like how good you would look round and swollen with my eggs, but not as good as you would look nourishing my young, and by that, she means while they are eating you."

He blanches and steps back. "Ah, yeah, that is disturbing."

"Make sure I don't hurt anyone out there," I say quietly, and he gives me a solemn nod before hurrying out. I follow after him, the four inch heels making me taller and slightly unsteady on my feet.

I stand in the middle of the stage, the lights dimmed, when the music starts up and a spotlight illuminates me. The crowd gasps as I start to undulate sensually, sliding the scarves off my body and twirling them around. I begin with the ones on my arms, then the fabric that hangs over my thighs, and the one wrapped around the back of my body.

I bend and snap, showing them my pert round ass and shaking it for them, all the while letting the hypnotizing magic soak into the people viewing the show. Most of them should be seeing a Filani succubus, but in case our mole has an illusion nullifying pendant, we decided it was best for me to be in the Madovian form. All four of my guys are wearing the same kind of pendant so they wouldn't be distracted by my performance and could keep an eye on the crowd.

It's hard for me to see out into it with the spotlight shining directly into my eyes, but when I spin back around and drop to my knees to crawl seductively across the stage, I notice Captain Lester is sitting at one of the small tables near the stage. Behind him are the weapons and security officers. At another table full of jeering, cheering men, I see two of our pilots. Xavier was right, there are a few people we need to look into.

I stand up again, and a hand reaches out to tug at one of the remaining veils. The last two are over my face and the crosscut in my stomach, but a security guard, who I am almost certain is Xavier glamoured, tackles him to the ground, and a brawl breaks out. I take it as my cue to get off the stage. We have our suspects now. We can let Link and Silac do their thing and focus on the raid for Area 51.

As soon as I return to the dressing room, I shed the Madovian form before running to the bathroom and vomiting. Her mind is twisted and sick and not a nice place to be. My own naga form was nothing like that, though she did have the same unhealthy breeding obsession as all of my creatures.

Thank goodness for birth control. If it were up to them, I would be permanently pregnant. We do not have time for that at the moment. I need to finish this thing with the Syndicate and make it through my first season as ringmaster, and then we will reconsider. Maybe by then the grandpas will be happy to come back and help out. I can't command a circus if I'm stuck sitting on eggs as a dragon or having to hibernate like the nagas do. That is a concern for another time though.

I wipe my face and get dressed, then I head out to see how much damage has been done to the club.

CHAPTER TWENTY-THREE

Lila

I stand in front of Magenta's door, chewing on my lip as I try to decide if I'm going to risk knocking or not.

"They will be alright, my sweet blood rose." I almost jump a mile into the air at the sound of Saxon's voice behind me. I thought I'd been stealthy when I snuck away to check on my friend. I whirl around to face him, my cheeks heated with embarrassment. The corridors are filled with excited performers and crew who are all making their way to the circus pod for entry to Earth.

We sent out a ship-wide notification that none of us would be traveling down with the pod because of our children. Instead, we will beam down as necessary so we don't have to leave our children alone because we feel they are too young to travel to Earth.

It's been well received, and lots of people tell us goodbye as they pass.

I lean against the wall next to Saxon and stare at the closed door. "Doesn't mean I don't worry."

He chuckles and wraps an arm around my shoulders. "Magenta is way more prepared for something like this than you were, and you survived just fine. So will she. Come on, the pod is about to leave, and it's fascinating to watch it from the bridge."

I take one more look at my friend's door and allow Saxon to lead me away. He's right, the corridors are a lot less crowded. All of the performers and crew travel down with the pod. The remaining crew on the big ship, the café staff, and retail store workers, as well as housekeeping and such all treat this time as days off. Some of them also travel down with the pod to do tourist things on Earth. The cafes and stores are closed, and the entertainment venues have reduced hours because of the lack of patrons. The large dining area will be used for all meals.

It really is a skeleton crew, so I'm surprised when I get to the bridge and there is almost a full complement of crew and someone projecting their emotions like they are an electronic billboard in Times Square. I just about stumble at the impact, but I manage to keep myself steady—Saxon's hand on my back helped too.

"What's going on?" I ask Captain Lester, and he grunts a greeting before replying.

"None of us wanted to travel down on the ship this swing. We were there recently."

"But can Bubby fly the pod on his own?"

"He isn't on his own, you stupid girl. The pod has a separate crew from this one," he snarls, and my eyebrows jump in surprise.

"Watch how you speak to her." Saxon steps between Lester and me and stares the Skarrian man down. Lester pales considerably and steps back, but he doesn't apologize.

This asshole is on my very last fucking nerve. He has been nothing but rude and combative with me since day one.

"Clear the bridge," I call as Xavier and Brannock walk out from the war room and take up spots on the wall. They obviously heard our confrontation.

The crew members exchange glances but are quick to comply.

"Not you, Lester," I say flatly as he tries to join the rest of them. He stiffens and turns back to face me, his lips turned up in a sneer.

"Look at you, growing a backbone. Well, it won't be enough. You won't be able to replace your grandfathers. You don't have the balls to run this operation."

"Whether I do or not is neither here nor there, but you won't be here to see it. Pack your things, you're fired."

"But I have a contract," he sputters, looking surprised that, yes, I do have those balls he was skeptical of.

I shrug. "I don't care. I will have our lawyers pay it out. I'm done with this shit."

"Who will captain this ship? Broderick Potter can't do it on his own."

"I don't care. I'll find someone," I reply calmly, though internally I'm freaking out.

"I can do it." Saxon moves now that Lester isn't as confrontational. "If I can captain a Vilaxian battle cruiser, then this ship will be a piece of cake."

"Oh snap," Xavier mutters, and he and Brannock exchange a fist bump. I ignore their antics.

"I will arrange for a fast shuttle from Skarr to retrieve you. Until then, you are confined to your quarters for insubordination to your superior."

"Superior?" he scoffs. "You don't even have a ranking."

"Maybe not, but I am the CEO, so until there is a ranking that is suitable for me, say maybe supreme and benevolent beautiful one, then I still outrank you." All three of my guys snicker at my fabulous new title, but again, I ignore them, keeping my focus on the irate man in front of me.

He doesn't say another word as he turns and marches out of the room. The ship begins to shake as the circus pod breaks off and starts its descent to the surface. I'm shaking with adrenaline as I move over to the viewing window and watch in silence. I feel my guys fall in behind me, but they stay quiet while I process my feelings.

I knew everyone wasn't going to be happy with me taking over the circus, but no one has been outwardly aggressive. I've been working hard, and I think maybe some who were doubting me have come to change their minds. I guess Captain Lester wasn't one of them.

I turn away from watching the pod and find that Tirrian, Zeydan, and Silac have joined us.

"I've been monitoring communications since Brannock sent word via the Madovian's communicator that the orb has been located and she is working on retrieving it. There aren't signs of any other ships in the vicinity yet." Silac takes a seat in the vacated security officer's chair.

"Should someone be escorting him?" Tirrian waves his hand in the direction the disgruntled captain went.

I shake my head. "No. I'm giving him enough rope to hang himself with."

All the others gape at me with confusion, except Xavier.

"Captain Lester is quite the projector when his emotions are high," he explains.

"Yes, the minute I walked through the door, his thoughts and emotions hit me like a slap in the face. He was giddy with excitement," I tell them. "Apparently he received a communication informing him of the whereabouts of the orb and to be on standby to transport himself and one other to a specific location."

"He's the mole?" Zeydan asks, starting to follow after him, but I wave him back.

"Leave him. I want to know what he's going to do."

Silac's fingers have been tapping furiously on the

screens in the security officer's station. He's muttering to himself, but he finally looks up. The window has been turned into a giant viewing screen, and on it, we can see a transcript of his communications.

"I found these in his inbox. They were encrypted, but I managed to break the encryption."

Sure enough, in black and white, there are the exact instructions he received signed with a stylish S.

"It doesn't mention how they are going to transport. No teleporting machine is powerful enough to teleport across the galaxy," Saxon murmurs as Silac brings up another communication. This one was sent by Captain Lester last night.

Can confirm Madovian agent is on the ship. I saw her with my own eyes. Will attempt to make contact and ascertain the whereabouts of the orb.

The response is harsh.

Stand down. If you attempt to interfere with their mission, you will be terminated. I'm sure you wouldn't like to be the Madovian's next incubator. Your job is transport only. It's why you were activated in the first place.

"He's obviously a low man in the Syndicate," I remark. "I wonder how long he's been working for them or if it's recent."

"I can't find any more messages to him prior to the circus breaking up. They must have tapped him while he was on hiatus." Silac leans back in his chair, switching the image from the messages to cameras that track Lester as he moves through the ship.

We're all silent as we watch him go into his room. There are no cameras in there, but it doesn't take long for him to reappear with a backpack on his shoulder.

"He obviously already had that packed," Xavier says, pointing at the screen.

"A bugout bag," I murmur.

"Where is he going?" Brannock asks. "I would have expected him to head to the space dock."

The cameras track him back to the elevator, and he gets on it. We have to wait until he makes his descent or ascent before the cameras will pick him up again.

Instead of the space dock, the lift opens one deck below where we are currently standing. On the bridge deck, there is only the bridge and our suite now, as well as the war/conference room. The teleport room was shifted one deck down at the same time my grandpas moved their suite down a deck to free up space for me and my family.

"Is he ignoring instructions and going after the orb? Does he think it's in your grandpas' rooms? Did they leave any of their belongings there?" Zeydan asks me, and I shake my head.

"No, I don't think so. Maybe some clothes, but they took all their personal items home with them."

We watch him walk straight past my grandpas' suite to the teleporting bay.

"What is he doing now?" Tirrian points as he activates the teleporter. "Can you see what his destination is?"

Silac frowns but leans forward and starts typing

again. "Maybe." His brow furrows in concentration, and his lips purse. He looks up. "He isn't going anywhere. There is an incoming transport."

We watch in stunned amazement as Smith appears on the teleporting platform, gun in hand, looking around in awe.

They say something to each other, which we can't hear, before they leave the transport room and head back to the elevator.

"Should we stop them?" Saxon asks me, and I look at my Aaz'axian mate, seeing the pure fury in his eyes as he looks at the man who has held his daughter's safety over his head for so many months. Smith is right within Brannock's reach. I could let him take his revenge now.

Just as I'm about to give the go ahead, my warlock speaks up.

"If we get rid of Smith now, it may tip off the Syndicate to this being a setup."

I heave out a sigh and nod. I hate seeing the disappointment on Brannock's face, so I go over to him and give him a kiss on the lips before wrapping my arms around him.

"Xavier is right," I tell him, even though I hate to say those words out loud.

He sags at my touch but nods. "Yes, I know, but it doesn't mean I don't hate it."

"Me too, baby, but I promise you will get your pound of flesh," I whisper into his ear.

"And entrails and organs. I like to rip out their

heart while it's still beating," Zeydan says, and when I turn to look at my deity mate in shock, his eyes flash red and he glows green, his god powers pulsing.

"Whoa. Slow your roll, big guy. Evisceration is so messy. Getting body fluids out of fabric is tedious."

I gape at my mates talking so casually about murder. Yeah, I am more blasé about it now, and I'll do anything to protect my family, but this seems a little extreme, almost like they enjoy it.

"Oh, don't look so shocked. You know we don't work with the same stunted morals as Earthlings," Saxon tells me, and I gulp in a big breath of air before turning my attention to the screen.

Smith and Lester just exited the elevator in the spaceport. I watch as they hurry toward the closest shuttle. It's my grandpas' personal one, which they left on board for my use. It's how I planned to get the orb to the Syndicate meeting.

"Don't let them steal my ship," I tell Silac.

"It's secure and can only be accessed by you or one of us," he assures me.

We watch as Lester is approached by one of the spaceport crew. He seems to be the only one around, but before he can say anything, Smith lifts his gun and shoots him.

I scream and clamp a hand over my mouth. "Oh my god!"

"Fuck, they really mean business," Xavier growls.

"We're lucky he's a shitty shot." Zeydan points at the crew member. He's down, but it looks like he was only hit in the shoulder. The other two keep moving to the next shuttle. This one is smaller and not as fast as my grandpas' vessel. "As soon as they leave, you can get down there and heal him."

"That's going to take forever to get where they need to go," I murmur as they are more successful this time. The door opens, and the two of them run up the ramp.

"Actually, it won't. My aunt upgraded the technology on those crafts too." Saxon nods at mine and the other three in the hangar. "They all have subsonic capabilities and are probably faster than this ship now. They are small and light and travel at a faster pace."

We're all silent as the shuttle lights up and slowly moves down the hangar, the big bay doors opening, and then it glides out into space. We switch the view so we are now watching it live as it crosses in front of the bridge viewing window. It doesn't get very far before it jumps to warp speed and disappears.

"They are gone," Brannock says flatly, and I squeeze him.

"That was always the plan."

"Come on, man, cheer up." Xavier slaps him on the back and heads for the exit to the bridge, whistling. "Let's go get your daughter."

CHAPTER TWENTY-FOUR

Tirrian

Lila has Link and Mark meet her in the spaceport, where the three of them take care of the crew member Smith shot. Brannock and I go with her when Brannock suggests we should question him before we leave. The others go back to the suite to change into battle gear.

I watch patiently as Link digs out the bullet with his tools, and Mark then uses his power to heal the remaining wound.

"Luckily Smith had an Earth gun and not one of the ones we use," Link says to the crew member, holding up the small metal projectile. "Otherwise, you would be dead."

The pale male blanches further and sways on his feet. Mark grabs his arm to support him. "Maybe a blood transfusion would be a good idea," he suggests to Link, who agrees.

"We will take him up to the med bay to administer it and keep him overnight for observation."

I put my hand out before they can leave. "Did you hear them say anything?"

The crew member blinks at me, slightly dazed from residual pain and blood loss. "Not really." He shakes his head.

Damn, I was hoping they would have given a hint about where they were going. We still haven't been given a location, because Brannock hasn't informed them that he has the orb, only that he knows the location. We plan on relaying that message once we finish rescuing Chloe, his daughter.

They move away, Link and Mark supporting the man, but then they stop. "I heard them arguing as they were getting on the shuttle. The man who shot me said they needed to go to Grichi 517E. Lester said it couldn't be that location because the planet has been desolate since the Aaz'axian and Una's war. Only ruins remain, and no sentient life-forms."

I don't have to be a warlock to feel the rush of shame that hits Brannock when he mentions this.

"Are you okay?" I ask the man, even though I know it's a stupid question. The guilt he's feeling would be pretty fucking bad.

"That was one of the planets our leaders ordered us to decimate. They thought the orb had been hidden on it. Our military leaders were reluctant, since there was no credible evidence that it was on the planet, but they did mine a mineral that our leadership wanted to get their hands on. I always thought it was a convenient excuse to invade."

He hangs his head in shame and walks away from Lila and me. We follow him, but as Lila reaches for him, I stop her. "Give him a moment," I caution her.

I've been in battle, and I know what it's like to relive those memories. That planet had done nothing to deserve the invasion, they just ended up on the radar of bad leadership, and both they and the actual people who were forced to attack suffered.

Our soft-hearted mate can't let one of us suffer in silence. "No," she says with a stubborn set to her jaw. "Our family doesn't suffer alone."

She hurries after him, putting her hand on his arm. "Hey. You aren't to blame."

He jumps, so lost in his memories. "Aren't I? I helped in the genocide of that species," Brannock snaps harshly, but instead of recoiling, Lila just shakes her head.

"Unwillingly. Are you telling me that if you weren't being controlled by the chips inside your heads, the one that has now been removed, that you would have done any of those things you were ordered to do?"

"No, of course not."

"Exactly. You have nothing to feel guilty for, but if I ever find where your leadership went into hiding, then I can assure you, I will cause an incident of mass destruction that they'd wish they had been able to cause. Remember, I will be the goddess of death, and they will answer to me as a death creation."

Her eyes blaze with righteous fury, and her body practically vibrates with her intention. She never looks sexier than when she is trying to gain retribution for one of us. I am truly blessed she forgave me for all my idiotic actions.

Brannock looks at her with stars in his eyes. "You have no idea how thankful I am that you don't judge me for my past. I don't like the person I was then. I should have fought harder to disobey our orders. We all should have."

"You couldn't have, otherwise you all would have died," I argue, and Lila nods.

"You're right. We would have died. They didn't hesitate to use the kill switches in our brains if we defied orders. The Aaz'axian Death Squad was quick on their trigger. They were the team responsible for keeping us all in line. Our superiors, who were right below the council, didn't want to directly stain their hands with blood."

"What happened to them? Do we need to track them down and kill them?" Lila asks, baring her teeth as smoke drifts out of her nose. Her dragon is very close to the surface, and mine is getting turned on by her bloodthirsty ways. Having a dual soul can be terribly inconvenient when you get aroused at inopportune times.

"No, they were captured by the warlocks and

Vilaxians in a joint operation and were sentenced to death. It was telecast across the galaxy. At that stage, I still had not settled on Earth, and me and my team watched the execution on a screen in a dirty, backwater tavern on some desolate planet at the edge of the galaxy. We celebrated for three days straight. It was one of the best days of my life, apart from Chloe's birth and mating you," he tells her, and she smiles sweetly at him.

"Unfortunately, the ten men and women on the ruling council who started the war escaped. I doubt the women survived, because they would have succumbed to the illness that affected all the females of our race, but that still leaves six monsters unaccounted for. With our ability to glamour, they've managed to stay hidden all this time—much like me and my team on Earth, or we had until one of us turned into a traitor and gave me up to Smith. I think I was the only one who was captured. I never saw any of my team in the facility."

"We will find out soon, and if they are there, then we will help free them. If we run into the traitor, we will take his head for you," I promise, and the grin he gives me sends shivers down my spine. I can see the Aaz'axian berserker gleaming in his eyes.

"So it shall be," he agrees.

"Come on. We have a daughter to rescue. Do you think once we get her back, she would like her own room? There is a spare at the end of the hall next to the nursery." She tucks her arms into ours, and we walk back to the elevator. She babbles on about Chloe, giving Brannock a chance to pull himself together.

I am so grateful to fate for putting this wonderful woman in our path. She is everything I wanted and so much more.

"I doubt she's going to want to sleep in the nursery with the babies, but maybe she will want to sleep in your room," she continues, and Brannock murmurs.

"I'm worried she's going to be so traumatized, she'll never recover."

Lila pulls us to a stop and throws her arms around the male.

"She probably will be. Who knows what kind of treatment she has been suffering through? I know if we are patient and give her love and time, though, she will get through this. We also have the Celestian royal family in our pockets, and Queen Tabbris is not only an excellent physical healer, but she also excels in healing trauma of the mind."

"How do you know this?" I ask her, surprised by the information. I knew they could heal bodily ailments, but I didn't know about mental ones.

"I asked Mark. I've been worrying about the mental state of all the alien captives, but mostly Chloe's. I've actually arranged for them all to spend time on Celestia to be assessed before they will be allowed to return to their normal lives. The royal family not only agreed, but they also promised to heal the captives themselves. When Chloe is ready, the three of us will travel there together and make sure she is okay too," she promises Brannock, and he snatches her up and swings her around, tears streaming down his face.

"Thank you," he whispers as he puts her down. "Thank you so much."

I turn away for a moment, giving them their privacy.

She pushes him away, and her face is bright red as she starts toward the door again. "Now give me the four-one-one about your daughter. I need to know what kind of bribes... I mean special things she may like before we leave Earth."

I laugh at her less than subtle change of subject as we use the elevator to take us to our floor and head to our suite to get changed as well.

I'm pacing back and forth in our suite, waiting for the others, when there's an alert at our door. I frown, looking at Saxon. "Are you expecting anyone?" I ask him, and he shakes his head.

"No. Cas, Maxsim, Silac, Nikos, and Link headed down to the circus to make an appearance. Echo is in the nursery with Kinga, getting the babies ready for bed, and Andre went back to their quarters to grab a change of clothes. His got wet while the kids had their baths. He got too close to the tub, and the krakens decided it was funny to splash him with water. He was dripping when he left." Saxon chuckles.

I know Xavier and Brannock are fetching weapons for us from the armory, and Zeydan was up in the bio level recharging, muttering about not being able to wait until he has his full powers back.

"I'll get it." Ghosie appears from his room. He's wearing the same protective leathers as us, and they cover his fur from head to toe to avoid any accidental seduction during the mission. The only bit of his fur that shows is on his face, and it's kind of jarring to see him fully covered like that.

He activates the door, and it slides open. Magenta and Saxon's cousin, Vanity, are standing there, holding hands.

"Ah, come in." He steps out of the way and lets the two women in.

"Van!" Saxon gets up off the sofa and goes over to his clan sister. "Congratulations." He gives her a big hug, kissing both cheeks before turning to Magenta.

"Welcome to the family, sister." He hugs and kisses Magenta too, who blinks with surprise before giggling.

"Thank you," Van says as Ghosie and I also give them our congratulations. "I am very happy. I can't believe I was so lucky to find my blood rose." She looks at Magenta with hearts in her eyes, and Magenta blushes.

"What's going on?" Magenta asks, tugging her Vilaxian over to the sofa and taking a seat. They snuggle so closely together, they appear joined. It's cute, and I can't help but feel happy for them despite the danger we're about to walk into.

"When did the pod leave?" Magenta asks.

"An hour or so ago," I tell them. Magenta and Vanity haven't been read into our mission, just because we wanted to keep it within our inner circle, but now that they are here, I think it would be the perfect time to include them, especially Vanity. She was Saxon's second-in-command on his battleship when he was in the military. He must have the same idea.

"We are about to raid Area 51 and rescue Chloe, Brannock's daughter, and all the aliens being held captive for their breeding program," he explains, and both girls' mouths drop open in shock.

"He has a daughter?" Magenta looks stunned. Obviously Lila hadn't shared that little tidbit.

"They are breeding aliens?" Vanity growls.

"Yes. It's one of the ways Smith was able to capture Brannock and make him wear the control collar he had on when he was first deported. He wanted him to spy for him and used her to manipulate him," Saxon shares.

"He's been feeding him information?" Magenta asks with worried eyes.

"Fake information," I assure her. "Just enough to keep his daughter safe until we could return to rescue her, which is what we are doing now."

"Oh, that poor thing, having to wait so long to do it. Is there anything we can do to help?" Magenta gets up and comes over to me, putting her hand on my arm, and I see her distress and need to help. Before I can answer, though, there is a rumbling growl of discontent.

"You should back away from the dragon very slowly," Saxon says quietly, and I look at Vanity. Her eyes flash red, and her fangs are exposed as she snarls at me.

"And take your whore hands off my husband," another voice adds, and Magenta and I jump apart.

"I wasn't..." Magenta stares at Lila, who has her hands on her hips in the entrance to the living area.

She dissolves into giggles. "You two should see your faces. That was freaking hilarious. I don't care, hug away, but maybe wait until the blood rose bond has settled a little bit." She points at Vanity, who is still growling.

"Oops." Magenta hurries back to her wife and snuggles into her, and the growl dies out.

"She will be sensitive and extra growly for at least a few days," Lila warns Magenta as she comes over and gives her own Vilaxian a slap on the ass, "but they eventually calm down. Don't you, love?"

He starts to growl, and I grin. "Best not to poke a bear, my love," I tell her, and she smacks a kiss on Saxon's lips before coming to me.

"Did that slutty Skarrian violate you?" she coos, looking me over.

"Takes one to know one. Who has twelve mates? Is your vagina even still usable down there?" Magenta retorts, and the two girls giggle.

"Resilient Skarrian vagina for the win!" Lila shouts, and the two of them high five.

Vanity rolls her eyes. "Seriously?"

The girls shrug it off, and Lila sits down on the sofa with her friend and her new mate.

"Congratulations, I'm so happy for you both." She reaches out and squeezes both of their hands.

"The guys were just telling us about your mission," Vanity says. "How can we help?"

Lila shrugs and looks to us for advice.

"Actually, it would be good if the two of you could stay here and help guard the children and Echo. The others had to go down to Earth to keep up appearances. We don't want anyone suspecting what we're about to do, because there is a fail-safe which will trigger and kill all the captives if we're discovered," I explain.

"But who would tell them you're coming?" Magenta asks.

"We discovered a mole. Who's to say there aren't others?" I reply, and Vanity nods.

"Of course. We will guard your young and mate like they are our own."

"Thank you. I will feel much better if you are here with them," Saxon says, and I see the relief in his eyes. I didn't realize how concerned he was.

The door to our suite opens, and Brannock and Xavier return with weapons. Both of them are carrying an arsenal—knives, guns, swords, and throwing stars just to mention a few. Xavier, who usually goes weapons free and relies on his magic, is even carrying a crossbow on his back.

Lila gapes at them. "Are you sure we're going to need that many weapons? Are we planning on killing everyone, or just incapacitating them?"

She sounds worried. "Lila, honey…" Brannock crouches down at her feet and takes her hands. "All of the guards at the facility are trained to shoot first and ask questions later. Smith won't want to risk any of his precious breeding stock getting away. He'd rather they were killed. They will not hesitate to kill us, and we shouldn't hesitate either."

I see the fear in her eyes, and she swallows but nods her head. "Okay. Shoot to kill, okay."

She stands up and takes the two lasers Xavier holds out to her and puts them into the holsters built into her clothing. The rest of us load up, and Zeydan pops into the room, glowing green and fully recharged from the bio level. He takes one of the large swords and slides it into a scabbard resting against his back, and then he tucks numerous knives and throwing stars into various pockets in his own clothing.

"Are we ready?" Saxon asks.

"Yes, let's head to the teleporter room. Andre will return shortly, but don't let anyone else into this room unless I let them touch my vagina with their dick," Lila cautions the two females. Vanity rolls her eyes, but Magenta snorts with amusement.

"Yes, sir." She gives her friend a sassy salute.

"Or it's Mark, Susie, or Aarin. They are staying to

lend medical support to the refugees if they need it," Ghosie reminds Lila.

"Good luck, General," Vanity tells Saxon. "May your mission be bloody."

It's a traditional Vilaxian war ritual to wish for a bloody mission.

Lila wrinkles her nose but keeps her mouth shut.

"We aren't expecting any trouble. I'm pretty sure if there were any more moles left on the ship, they would have left with Lester and Smith, but just in case, stay alert," Xavier says.

"Let's go. It's nighttime in Nevada, and I want to use the cover of darkness to slip into the tunnels unseen." Brannock leads the way down to the teleporter room and programs the coordinates. He's having it drop us a few hundred yards from the tunnel, and we will make the rest of the trek on foot. He isn't sure if they have security cameras covering the tunnels and wants to be certain before we breach the compound. There is no point in setting off the alarms before we even set foot in it.

The team steps up onto the platform, and I see Lila shiver. Xavier puts his arm around her. "Use the emotions and adrenaline to fuel your righteous fury," he tells her.

He can obviously feel her reluctance to kill and is giving her a pep talk. I grab the remote that we need to send us, and then I return again, shoving a couple of extras in my pocket just in case. They are automatically programmed to return to the ship in case of an emergency, you just hit the red button.

My heart races as Brannock steps up onto the platform, his eyes glazed with anticipation and his body primed with adrenaline. He shed his glamour, and his spines shiver with agitation. It wouldn't take much to push him into berserker mode.

"Hold it together a little longer," I tell him, clamping a hand on his shoulder next to one of the lethal spikes.

He nods, and we dematerialize. He's about to see his precious girl for the first time in months, and God help anyone who gets in his way.

CHAPTER TWENTY-FIVE

Lila

We materialize in the desert, setting down at a spot slightly away from the tunnel entrance. The cold, crisp, fresh air hits my senses, and I drag lungfuls of it in as we assess our surroundings. Breathing fresh air again makes me realize just how much my life has changed over the last six months.

When I was getting dressed, preparing to assault a military base and free some captive aliens, it really hit me that my life has changed dramatically. Gone is the drifting, unhappy female who didn't know what she wanted to do with her life, and in her place is a mother, a wife, and a CEO of a large corporation who will defend her family and way of life at the expense of everything else.

I got a message while I was doing up the laces on my combat boots. It was a note from Cronus and

Xylene, wishing us luck on our incursion. It also contained a picture. The photo was of the two of them and the two people I now recognize as my parents. They are dressed up in Halloween costumes as the Scooby gang. Cronus and Xylene are Fred and Daphne, and my parents are Shaggy and Velma. In their arms is a toddler dressed as Scrappy Doo, and Xavier stands in front of them in a Scooby costume with a scowl on his face. Everyone is smiling at the camera but Xavier. His pout would put Hali to shame.

We always came to Earth to celebrate Halloween with your family. We liked to go in group costumes. Xavier was not a fan of this year's costume, but you looked adorable. Your parents would be so proud of the woman you have become, as are we.

A tear trickled down my face as I read it. Xavier's parents really are wonderful, and I'm blessed to be a part of their family.

I studied the photo, smiling even though I don't remember it. My dad was the spitting image of my grandpas, and it was kind of weird to see. He wore his hair slightly shaved at the sides and longer on top, and in this image, it was completely tousled to mimic Shaggy, but his eyes were the same shade of green as mine.

My mother looked to be wearing a black wig. I'm pretty sure Gigi said I was the spitting image of her, so she must have had hair the same color as mine used to be. Her eyes were hidden behind black-rimmed glasses, but I thought they were hazel. She was shorter than my dad and curvy in all the right places much like I am.

Although I was happy to have the image, seeing it was bittersweet. I'm never going to know these people. Looking at them hurt, but someday, it wouldn't, so I saved the image, closed the tablet, and finished my preparation.

"Lila, are you okay?" Ghosie asks me, bringing me back to the present.

"Yeah. Sorry, just getting my bearings and breathing in the fresh air. It's a shock every time," I tell him, and he nods, some of the worry in his eyes fading.

I look around, and the guys are all on high alert. The moon is full and bright in the sky, lighting up the landscape like a floodlight. Brannock has a pair of binoculars in his hands and is looking at something in the distance.

Zeydan is glowing again, drawing in as much power from the earth and surrounding vegetation as he can. He didn't want to drain the bio level, but here on Earth, he has an unlimited resource.

"What's the sitrep?" Saxon asks as Brannock lowers the binoculars.

"I don't see any cameras around the entrance, but I could be wrong. Can you feel with your magic?" he asks Xavier, who nods and sends out a burst of lilac mist. It creeps across the ground like fog, spreading to cover a large area before it drifts in the direction of the tunnels.

"That will alert us to anything in the surrounding area that has an electrical current running through it. It's also searching the ground for land mines and trip wires and deactivating any of them."

A small squeak escapes me before I can stop it, and I clamp my lips tightly together in the hope nobody noticed, but alas, that was not the case.

"Are you okay?" Tirrian asks, smoke drifting out of his nose. His dragon is riding him hard. I bet it wants to come out and eat everyone, but this mission is strictly for two-legged forms.

"Yeah, I guess I wasn't expecting land mines. How naive of me," I reply dryly, watching Xavier's mist move eerily across the space between us and the tunnel entrance.

We wait in silence as it gets to the tunnels and expands outwards, draping the area in a thick fog and obscuring our view. Xavier glows purple, the same color as his mist, and he mutters a few words and does a few complicated hand signals. I don't know this kind of magic, since it isn't anything we've touched on in our lessons yet, but I'm sure we will get there eventually. Suddenly, it all dissipates until nothing remains, like it was never there in the first place.

"Okay, we're clear. There were some cameras, but they have been neutralized," Xavier tells us.

"Isn't that going to alert them to us being here?" Ghosie asks, a frown creasing his brow. I miss all his beautiful fur, but we decided that being fully covered was less of a risk to us during the mission. I live for the day when we won't have to worry about it, and I can put my hands on his sexy body whenever I want without having to worry about scarring anyone.

"No, because instead of destroying them, I created a loop that will show the same image. It won't pick us up as we pass in front of it."

I let a little sigh of relief out as Brannock leads us forward. I'm shuffled into the middle of the group. Saxon and Brannock are in front, Ghosie and Xavier are on either side of me, and Tirrian and Zeydan bring up the rear.

We get to the entrance of the tunnels, our laser weapons drawn. Saxon holds up his hand, making a fist, and we freeze. I strain my ears to listen, pushing the limits of my Vilaxian hearing, but I can hear nothing except for an inconsistent dripping somewhere further down the tunnels. There are no signs of life—no heartbeats, breathing, or rustling of clothing or fidgeting of limbs.

"We're clear," he says.

I heave out a sigh, some of the built-up tension draining out of my body, and stash my weapon in its holster.

"Okay, we need you to head down the tunnel in mist form and cut the power to the top secret level. The rest of the facility shouldn't be any wiser."

"But it will put the remaining guards on high alert, right?" Tirrian asks.

"Possibly, but there have been power malfunctions in the past. I heard guards talking about rats chewing holes in the cables. I'm hoping they will assume the same has happened and send a team to investigate," Brannock explains, staring down the tunnel with longing.

"And we will be ready to take care of them." Zeydan cracks his knuckles, and he frees his tails from his body. The nine animals yip and screech as they gather at his feet, bristling with anticipation for the fight to come.

"Huh, that's handy. We just added nine more to our team," Ghosie whispers to me, and I snicker.

"Is it just the one generator?" Saxon asks, and Brannock shakes his head.

"No. There are two, which is why Lila needs to go too—one on either side of the tunnel and slightly apart from one another. You need to switch them off at the same time. One powers the outer facility, and one powers the one on the other side of the door we need to go through. All the prisoners will go into lockdown and be returned to their rooms, making them easier to rescue."

"You've really thought of everything." I stare at him in wonder, and he nods ruefully.

"I've had a long time to scheme and plan my daughter's rescue. I just never imagined I'd have so many allies to help me," he says solemnly, his eyes shining with gratitude.

"Family, not allies." Saxon slaps him on the shoulder. "Alright, let's get this show on the road."

Xavier and I allow our bodies to turn into mist.

We've been practicing all week between rehearsals, and I pretty much have it down now. The only thing I struggle with is manipulating matter while in this form. I need to get it right today, though, because failure is not an option.

We float down the tunnel. It's weird being in this form. Although I have all my senses, the feeling of my body is gone, and it's slightly disorienting. I smacked into quite a few things before I learned to go around them or use cracks to go through or under them.

I can see and feel the lasers lining the tunnel, but because we are basically vapor, we glide through them without setting them off. We arrive at the first generator. It's a huge unit, the tunnel having been widened on one side for it to reside in.

You do this one, and I'll go to the next one, Xavier instructs me telepathically.

I do a lap around the machine, looking for the off switch. I find it and feel a thrill of success when I open the cover. I just need to wait for Xavier to give the command. My mind is a mess of emotions—nervous anticipation, relief, and excitement all wrapped together with the burning need for revenge against Smith. How dare he do what he's done? How dare he treat aliens like they are his own personal play toys to exploit? To think he was creating an army for his own use. I don't know what we will find behind that door or how successful his program has been.

Brannock said the program is in its early stages, and that it's only been running for about ten years, so we won't have any brainwashed adults to deal with. I made the guys promise that anyone behind that door who comes at us will be incapacitated as opposed to being executed, and we can work out guilty and not guilty once they are all safely back on the ship.

The Celestians are sending a transport to bring them back to their health facilities and are en route as we execute this mission. Link's med bay wasn't going to be big enough to handle the influx of victims we are expecting, so they converted the hologram warehouse to an overflow med bay, setting up beds for treatment of any injuries. We are hoping there aren't many, but who knows? There may be a number of pregnant females. We're preparing for the worst-case scenario.

Okay, I'm in position, Xavier says, and I jolt in surprise but quickly get my shit together as he starts a countdown. *On three. One, two, three...*

I flip the switch on the generator, and the lights and lasers in the tunnel turn off, plunging it into complete darkness.

I reform as I hear the others make the journey toward me. They use their enhanced speed and join me within seconds.

"Good job." Tirrian gives my waist a quick squeeze. They all know how worried I was because my skills were a bit hit and miss.

Suddenly, we hear a shout echoing down the tunnel from Xavier's direction.

"Xavier!" I don't wait, drawing my laser and running toward my warlock mate. I feel the guys on my heels. Ghosie grumbles about not being able to see a thing, and suddenly, a green glow lights up the immediate area.

When I look back, Zeydan has changed into his god form, the green glow making it easier for my bear.

"Thank you," he says while panting. My poor bear is not really in fighting form. I love his dad bod, but he's not really built for speed and stealth, more smash and grab style attacks.

Zeydan's nine tails dart ahead of us, the distance to Xavier a lot farther than I expected. When we arrive, we find the tunnel lit up with pale purple light spheres floating in the air and Xavier battling a host of beings.

"I thought you said there were no life-forms," Brannock growls at Saxon, but he looks surprised.

"There weren't any."

"That's because they aren't alive. These are robots," Xavier growls, slicing the arm off one, but he keeps going.

"Robots? They look real." I look a little closer, but even though they look real, none of them are bleeding.

"Holy shit, are they murderous sex robots?" I ask, taking in their beautiful features and perfect bodies.

"Yes, I think maybe Pleasure Bot Industries may have expanded their capabilities." Xavier grunts as he's tackled by two of the figures. "A little help here, please?"

Zeydan, Saxon, Brannock, and Tirrian join the fight. Ghosie pulls me to the side, puffing slightly, and the two of us stay out of the way while the others quickly take care of the robots. A blow to the back of the head or decapitation, severing their core processor, takes them out. They just collapse in a pile when this happens.

Finally, they are all incapacitated, and the guys are barely winded. "Well, that was a good warm-up." Xavier beams as he puts his sword back into its scabbard. "I wasn't expecting them. They appeared out of nowhere."

"I've never seen them before. Obviously the facility has had an upgrade. I wonder if any of the internal guards have been replaced as well," Brannock murmurs, inspecting a scratch on his hand where one of the female robots got him with her ridiculously long nails. Seriously, who has nails like that in battle?

"How do we tell the difference between them and humans?" Ghosie asks as we shuffle a little closer.

"Humans bleed," Saxon says dryly, kicking one of the incapacitated lumps.

"True." Tirrian stares down the tunnel we need to traverse, his head cocked like he's listening.

"It sounds like we have more coming. Shall we meet them halfway?" He doesn't wait for a response, just bellows a roar and takes off.

"So much for stealth," Zeydan mutters as his tails stream after the dragon, caught up in the bloodlust.

The rest of them follow just as enthusiastically except for Ghosie and me. We exchange a look.

"Do you want to join the fight?" he asks, pointing in the direction they went.

"No, not particularly," I reply, linking my arm with his, happy to touch him freely. "We can guard the rear," I tell him, and he nods happily.

"I like that plan, and by the time we get there, all the hard work will be done."

"I like how you think," I chirp as we slowly meander after the others.

CHAPTER TWENTY-SIX

Lila

When Ghosie and I catch up with the rest of the team, the scene we come across is a little more gruesome. They must have run out of robot sex warriors and sent in the live ones. Blood is splashed all over the walls, and the floor is littered with bodies. Throats are torn out, bodies are clawed up and burnt, and the smell is gag worthy.

"Wow, just wow..." I try not to focus on any one thing, but it's kind of hard. My gaze keeps dropping to the ground. You know that whole traffic accident mentality where you can't just drive by, and you have to slow down to get a good look at what happened?

"They started shooting first!" Tirrian exclaims before blowing fire on one of the bodies. I watch in pure amazement as it crumbles to ashes.

"That's pretty handy," Ghosie says, and I can hear the admiration in his voice.

"Thanks," Tirrian replies, moving onto the next body.

What has my life become? All of them are completely unfazed by death. I fear the day when death doesn't bother me.

A groan has me turning my attention to Zeydan who is holding up Saxon.

"Saxon?" I ask, stepping forward, fearful of what I'm going to see. Zeydan's hand glows green above a wound in Saxon's stomach. I watch in awe as he pulls the bullet out with his magic. When it drops into his palm, he examines it closely.

"This is made of fleitine," he muses quietly.

Tirrian turns his attention away from his cremation for a moment. "Isn't that the metal that contains that mineral from Grichi 517E? Brannock just talked about it earlier. He said they were instructed to attack the planet because the orb was supposed to be there, but he thought it was because the council wanted to get their hands on the mineral."

Zeydan purses his lips. "I am not really surprised. When this mineral is combined with a mixture of the correct elements, it is the one thing in the whole galaxy that can kill any species. Our family created the combination as a fail-safe just in case."

"Is Saxon dying?" I ask, feeling numb as I move over and support my Vilaxian, who is an alarming shade of white.

Zeydan shakes his head before crushing the bullet in his hand and sniffing the dust. "No, the mixture is off. It did some damage, but removing it and giving him some blood should heal him right up."

"The plot grows thicker," Xavier says, standing up from where he was rifling through the pockets of the dead. "Someone gave Smith the recipe, and he created those bullets especially for his guards." He uses a key card he took off one of them to point at the dust in Zeydan's hand. "Thank fuck they got the proportions wrong, otherwise this could have had a whole different outcome."

"Where's Brannock?" I ask, looking around, and Xavier points down the tunnel.

"A couple ran back in that direction. He was going to take care of them."

"On his own?" I ask, horrified.

"Yes. It was only two, he will be fine." As soon as the words are out of Xavier's mouth, I see movement coming toward us through the darkness. When they become more visible, I see it's Brannock, and he's towing two guards behind him by their arms.

"These ones are alive. I thought maybe you might want to make use of their necks." He dumps them at Saxon's feet, and I blink in surprise.

"Aww, look at that, he's offering you a meal. Many species do that to prove they are good providers for their families. How romantic," Xavier teases, and Brannock flips him off.

Zeydan bends down and hauls one of the humans

to his feet. He's dazed and confused but very alive. He freaks out at the sight of Zeydan in his god form, though, and starts screaming. Zeydan ignores him and heaves him into place for Saxon, who can barely hold himself up, let alone support a blood donor.

I put a hand on him to aid him, but the wall he's leaning against does most of the work as he bites into the neck of the screaming human. The human's screams die down quickly as Saxon drains him of all the blood in his body. I look down, and the wound closes a little bit, but not much.

"Next victim," Ghosie says cheerfully, lifting the other human who is still unconscious.

Saxon rinses and repeats, but when Ghosie drags the dead human away, the hole in his stomach is still dribbling blood and not fully closed.

"Stupid, weak-ass human blood," Xavier spits out and turns to our dragon. "Shift! Saxon needs more powerful blood."

Tirrian blinks at him, and just when I think he's going to tell Xavier to get fucked, he nods.

"Okay, that will make cleanup easier. Can you move all the bodies into a pile? My dragon can torch them in one go."

I hold Saxon upright, and the two of us watch as the rest do as Tirrian asked. Ghosie, Brannock, Zeydan, and Xavier gather all the bodies into a large pile, casually comparing kill counts as they move. They tease Ghosie about the fact that he doesn't like to get his fur bloody, and he grouses about blood being so hard to remove, he needs a special shampoo to do it.

I'm literally speechless. How has this become my life? Before I can scold them for their callous regard for human life, I remember that they aren't human, so I shouldn't hold them to the same standards I grew up with. I keep my mouth shut and turn my attention to Saxon.

"Would my blood help?" I ask him, and he nods.

"Yes, but I don't want to weaken you before we see what we are up against. We are going to need your powers before long, and you need to be at full capacity. I will drink from you later if I need to," he promises, and I accept his reasoning.

Tirrian shifts, and his body just about fills the tunnel. There is definitely no way he can stretch his wings out without doing damage, but instead of freaking out, he settles down and looks at us, his dark eyes glowing.

"Come on," I tell Saxon, slinging his arm around my shoulders. "You know he's super tasty, and don't tell anyone, but I think his blood is almost as powerful as Xavier's," I say quietly, but the dragon's eyes gleam, and I don't think I said it quiet enough. "You will feel better in no time."

The others step away, and I hear them discussing the bullet while I remind Saxon exactly where he can sink his fangs into Tirrian without snapping them off. I stroke my hand over Tirrian and whisper words of gratitude and encouragement to Saxon while he drinks. The color returns to his face, and the hole in his stomach closes up, leaving just a jagged rip in his armor.

"Why didn't this protect him?" I ask, pointing at the armor.

"We were just discussing that." Xavier appears next to me and helps Saxon to his feet. He's slightly blood drunk and is going to take a moment to get his bearings. He forgot to seal the wound on the dragon, so I lean in and swipe my own tongue over it, using the healing enzymes in my saliva before placing a kiss on the spot. Sure, I could have used my Celestian powers, but where's the fun in that?

"It seems like this projectile can also penetrate previously impenetrable protection. As I said, this formulation is slightly different from the one my brothers and sisters created as a fail-safe. I wonder if it was deliberately changed so it would penetrate weapon-proofed armor." Zeydan sounds perplexed.

"That would take someone who has a good knowledge in chemical compounds and experimentation, wouldn't it?" Ghosie points out.

"Yes, or someone who is really smart and has a whole lab of scientists and programmers at their fingertips," Xavier says, frowning, but it sounds like he has suspicions.

"What are you thinking?" Saxon slurs, struggling to stand upright as he comes out of his blood stupor.

"I think I know where you're going with this," Tirrian says as he wraps an arm around my body and pulls me against him. "You're a tease," he whispers in my ear and rubs his dick against my backside. I snicker quietly.

"What are you thinking?" Zeydan asks, and Xavier sighs.

"Link's mother has all of those things we just talked about and is very capable of reformulating something to fit another purpose."

"And what purpose is that though? It didn't kill him," Brannock says as the smell of ash reaches my nose. Tirrian's dragon torched the rest of the bodies before he changed back.

"No, it didn't, but it cut through his armor like butter. Maybe that is the purpose. If you can badly wound most of the forces you are fighting against, then it doesn't matter if they die or not if you can go around and finish them while they are writhing around on the ground in pain."

We all fall silent at Xavier's words.

"Shit, now it's even more important that we shut down the Syndicate, especially if Deinara Digicon has been recruited to their ranks," Tirrian mutters. "We need to warn our families. If she is providing the Syndicate with unlimited warrior sex robots, as Lila calls them, who don't bleed or cause pain and have armor piercing rounds, then anyone who goes up against them is going to suffer major casualties."

"Pfft, even with their technological capabilities, they are no match for warlock magic," Xavier scoffs, and Zeydan frowns.

"I wouldn't be too sure. I have a feeling that round contained a compound that would nullify your magic. That's why Saxon wasn't healing. His Vilaxian magic, so to speak, wasn't working. It basically rendered him benign."

"Human," I murmur. "No one would be spared."

"Fuck, come on then, let's get this raid over with, rescue the damsel in distress, and go take care of the big bosses," Ghosie says, jolting everyone out of their panicked musings.

"Sounds like a video game to me," I tease as we head in the direction Brannock came from with his two donors.

"I grabbed a swipe card so we can get into the facility, but I should probably go first to see if there is another team of guards waiting for us," Xavier suggests, and the rest of us agree. He can do his floaty misty thing and give us exact numbers.

When we get to the door, it doesn't take him long, and when he returns, he's smiling. "It looks like there is only a small crew left inside, and they are all mostly panicked about the lack of power. It was guard changeover, and most of their forces were on this side of that door when the power was cut. That's why there were so many for us to battle. There are maybe twenty remaining inside the facility, including a few admin staff as well."

I wonder if that bitchy assistant to Smith is in there. I wouldn't mind showing her the pointy end of my fangs.

"Excellent." Zeydan grins foxily, his tails flowing back into his body to go through the door. He probably figures we won't need the backup.

"Yeah, but the bad news is with the power out, that door is locked down tight. No one goes in or out," Xavier continues, ignoring the god.

"Well, that sucks, but it's hardly a problem since we have our trusty bear here to get us through." Tirrian slaps Ghosie on the shoulder, touching him without having to worry about the properties of his fur. Maybe we need him to wear clothes more often so we can all give him some affection. I'd never even thought to suggest it because he doesn't usually wear any. Unlike my cats, he isn't flashing his goods around willy-nilly, literally in their case.

"Yeah, but I can only take one person at a time, and we will be vulnerable as we step through the door. You won't be able to use your weapons or powers" — he looks at Zeydan— "while we are phasing."

"That's not a problem. I can mist like Xavier," Zeydan announces casually, crouching down and putting his hands on the ground, absorbing more energy from the dirt. "So that leaves only three people who need to be phased."

Xavier nods thoughtfully. "The three of us can mist through the cracks and reform on the other side and cover you while Ghosie goes back and forth. What do you think?"

We agree to the plan, and the three of us that can mist go through. We rematerialize in a dark room that looks like it might be a staff room. There are lockers, a kitchen area, some couches, and a bookcase.

"Cozy," I mutter, pulling my weapon and looking around.

"This area is clear," Xavier whispers. "Most of them are standing around with their weapons aimed at the sealed door that leads to the area that needs special clearance. I heard them muttering about not letting the animals escape. That's their focus for now, but some of the admin are spooked and were talking about trying to get this door open so they could get out."

There's a sound behind us, and it's the same kind of electric buzzing sound that I heard when Ghosie phased with me from the space station onto the carevasta ship. I don't turn around, but eventually I hear Tirrian groan, and when I look, he's bent over with his hands on his knees and his eyes closed.

"That was fucking awful." He gags as Ghosie phases right back through like it doesn't affect him.

I rub his back, pushing some healing into him. We don't need the three of them incapacitated if anyone comes this way. Xavier and Zeydan keep watch. Zeydan lets his tails free again, and the nine of them disappear. I guess they are going to keep watch since he can see through their eyes.

Ghosie goes back and forth two more times, bringing Brannock and then Saxon. I push healing into both of them too, but my worry for Saxon increases. He isn't back to full strength since his wound, and the phasing hasn't helped.

"You need to take some of my blood," I insist, holding up my wrist.

"We don't have time for you to orgasm, Lila," Brannock hisses. I forgive him for being an asshole because he is super close to being reunited with his daughter. Any other time, I would have said a cutting comment and given him a withering stare—not to mention he is also right.

"Make it hurt," I instruct my Vilaxian, and he must feel pretty fucking awful because he doesn't argue, just takes my wrist and bites down.

"Holy fuck," I whisper-scream as the pain pierces my nerves and shoots through my limbs. Each mouthful is agonizing as he seems to rip the blood from my veins. Tirrian reaches for me, but Xavier stops him.

Xavier puts his hands on my head, and I'm instantly projected somewhere else. The two of us are standing in the grotto of the place where we sealed our intimate bond.

"What are we doing here?" I ask him, and he shakes his head and smiles.

"We're not really. I just took hold of your mind to distract you. You wouldn't have lasted without scream-ing, and then everyone would know we are here." He leans in and kisses me, or I guess he manipulates my mind to think we are kissing, but it feels so real, so I just go with it.

"Lila," Saxon calls, and Xavier releases my mind, and I return to reality. Saxon's skin is back to its normal color, and his eyes are clear and bright. "Thank you." He kisses me, and I cup his cheek.

"Anything for you, my love." It's the truth. I would carve out my heart for any of these men.

"Okay, what do you say we bust some heads and rescue us some aliens?" Xavier slaps Brannock on the back, and the two of them take the lead.

Zeydan studies me closely, making sure I'm okay, before he follows. Saxon, Ghosie, and Tirrian hang back with me, and we bring up the rear, our weapons at the ready.

CHAPTER TWENTY-SEVEN

Lila

My body is wound so tightly, my muscles ache as we slowly make our way through the facility. Zeydan's tails are spread out, supplying us with all the locations of the remaining staff. We are adjacent to the door to the office area where Smith took us to sign all the paperwork for Brannock the one time I had been to the facility.

Back then, I thought they were a legit agency trying to keep the knowledge of aliens on the down-low from the general public, and maybe, once upon a time, it started like that, but Smith's corruption poisoned a once credible agency. Now, we know better. Now, we need to wipe out the rot and clean house, then install trusted personnel to return it to the agency it needs to be—one that provides support and help to all extraterrestrials making Earth their home for now.

We've taken out a lone guard who I think was trying to make a run for it. He didn't even put up a fight. Before any of the guys could kill him, I froze him and told the others we would deal with him when we had seen to the others. I couldn't, in good conscience, just kill him, especially since he surrendered, wide-eyed and terrified, at the sight of the six aliens escorting me.

Now, Xavier has sent out probes and knows there are six admin staff inside that area. I'm sure they are all military trained in this kind of complex, but I want to give them the chance to surrender, even Bitchy McBitch face. Maybe they don't have a choice in where they work or who they work for and have no clue what is truly behind the secret door.

"On my command." Zeydan waves a hand, and his magic explodes the door inward. The sounds of gunfire are loud in the quiet hall, the muzzle flashes competing with the red glow of the emergency lighting, which must be on a different system from the generators. It literally must be the only thing that works, though, because it is stifling hot inside, so the HVAC system must have been taken offline as well.

I wipe my sweaty brow as we wait for the furious barrage of bullets to stop. They are just firing randomly, and none of them are even close to hitting us.

Finally, we hear the telltale sound of empty weapons clicking and the panicked whispers of them saying they are out of bullets. Zeydan sends his tails in. The shouts of fright are loud, and we can hear terrified movements. The seven of us follow, and when two of the three females and one male see my escort, the shouts turn to screams and pleading for their lives. Of course, Bitchy McBitch face has to put on a show.

"You," she sneers, glaring at me with undisguised hatred. "Smith knew you were going to be a problem. He's going to take great joy in killing you. I will get a promotion for handing you over."

I give her a little finger wave and see her reach for a letter opener on her desk.

"Uh-uh," I tut and point my weapon at her, gesturing for her to join the other three cowering on the ground. They made the right decision to surrender.

"Is this the same Smith who fled Earth and is now currently halfway across the galaxy, trying to save his weaselly ass?" Tirrian asks casually, but smoke drifts out of his nostrils, and his wings flare up high, causing the three on the ground to cower with their hands over their heads.

"He wouldn't leave me behind," she argues, shaking her head. "He promised to take me wherever he went."

"He lied," Brannock says flatly, and she turns pale at the sight of him.

"You! Oh my god, we're all going to die!" She starts to shake, and tears drip down her face.

"Yes, you are," Saxon says, baring his fangs at her. They all scream and cower in terror.

"How many prisoners are in the restricted wing?"

Zeydan asks the three who are sobbing uncontrollably and mostly useless.

"We don't have a restricted wing," the guy answers, snot dripping down his face.

Zeydan scoffs at his answer, unable to hide the disgust in his eyes. "You are all pathetic," he growls, and I smell that one of them wet their pants.

I mean, he isn't wrong. We haven't even done anything yet.

Bitchy McBitch face smirks. "Doesn't matter, they'll all be dead by now. The first thing I did when the power was cut was hit the kill switch."

I lift my gun and fire, hitting her between the eyes. She blinks in shock, but it must be a reflex, because she's dead before she even hits the ground, her brain splattered on the wall behind her.

"So, um, understandable," Xavier says, nodding at her dead body, "but we could have used the information."

"What does it matter if they are all dead?" I say flatly, turning my back on the others and walking out. I'm numb and furious at the same time, and the urge to paint the walls red with the remaining guards' blood is riding me. My alternate forms were mostly silent during the raid, not wanting to distract me, but now they are baying for blood.

"What do we do with these three?" Ghosie asks, and I hear Brannock reply.

"Kill them or don't, it doesn't matter, but if my daughter is dead like that bitch just said, then I will come back and slaughter anyone who remains." His fury burns in the air as hot as mine.

I hear the others mumbling as they decide what to do with the three in the room, but I'm not stopping. I walk down the corridor to the door. I feel Brannock at my heels, but we don't talk, because there is nothing left to say.

"I thought you said the kill switch couldn't be activated without power?" Tirrian asks, and the others catch up.

"It shouldn't have been. In the event of a power failure, that area hermetically seals. They are trying to create bioweapons from some of the aliens as well, so it's a fail-safe so nothing escapes into the base or worse, gets out into the atmosphere."

"Bioweapons?" Saxon growls.

"Yes, the guards are a chatty group, and I overheard two of them talking about it during the raid on the Pleasure Inn. They were hoping to round up some new and interesting creatures to experiment on."

"Fuck, they all need to die," Xavier growls. "Can we agree all of them need to die, Lila?" I can hear how exasperated he is with my human sensibilities. Xavier is the one who has always been impatient with that part of me, but he has nothing to worry about now. I've gone all psycho Cheryl on them, and shoot to kill is now my motto.

I raise both guns as the noise increases, and we find a dozen guards milling around the restricted door. They seemed to have calmed down somewhat and are arguing about how they are going to get through to make sure all the experiments are contained.

I don't even wait for them to notice us before I start firing my weapons, one in each hand like a gunslinger from the O.K. Corral. Three are dead before the others even realize what's happening. Xavier could freeze them, and it would be like shooting fish in a barrel, but that isn't any fun. The five of them stream past me with Ghosie once again staying with me to protect my back from anyone we may have missed.

"Watch out for those bullets," he reminds the others, but it's unnecessary, since none of them can get their weapons up before they hit the ground in bloody, dead messes. Brannock is a ruthless killing machine, and the other four aren't slouches in that department either. I think it takes less than ten minutes, and the guards are all dead. None of them surrendered, so we didn't spare any of them.

I watch, detached, as they are dragged into a pile off to the side. We don't want any children who are behind the door to see them and get frightened.

"We need to hurry. We cut off the power, and the HVAC system isn't working out here, so it means air is not circulating, and with that area being sealed, they are all going to run out of oxygen very quickly." Brannock stares at the sealed door like he can melt it with his mind.

"How about we go back and turn the generators on? We need to power up the transport room anyway," Tirrian suggests.

"Let's wait until we clear that area of personnel. There are probably scientists and guards in there too, right?" Saxon suggests.

"I'm not sure if they go home in the evenings or if they live in, so yes, we should probably wait and clear that area before we turn the power back on," Brannock agrees and steps back so Ghosie can do his thing. This time, the three of us can't squeeze through the cracks because it's sealed—Xavier tried.

Instead, I strip off my armor and change into my carevasta bear form. I don't want to destroy it, and my chunky bear body is not going to fit into it.

Ghosie grins at me as he looks me up and down, and I wink at him. We don't have time for fun, but he has gotten to know the quirks of this form quite often over the last week. Stress relief with my PA for the win.

"We'll take Xavier and Zeydan through first, and the two of them will use their magic to protect anyone else coming through," I tell the others, who don't like that I'm going to be in danger, but there isn't much they can do about it, so they keep their objections to themselves, which I appreciate.

Stress relief wasn't the only thing Ghosie and I spent time doing during the week. We also practiced phasing in case I needed to do it on the mission. It's the freakiest fucking feeling in the world, and I killed a few inanimate objects before I got the hang of it and attempted it with a live creature. I started with a chicken, just in case, and when I proved I could take a chicken through walls, then Tirrian bravely volunteered to be my guinea pig. Well, I say bravely but he extracted a bargain from me before he agreed. After this is done, we have to spend a week shopping for things for my dragon vault. I know, right? How dare he expect me to spend money in exchange for his help!

I wrap my arms around Zeydan while Ghosie does the same to Xavier, and we step through the door. Zeydan squeezes his eyes shut, and I hear him growling low in his chest, his tails pinned tightly against his body as we move through the door. I look around the other side for danger before releasing my phase. If they were to shoot at us while we were phasing, the bullets would pass harmlessly through us, but the minute we stop phasing, we are in the line of fire again.

The area is clear. It's another corridor, but we knew that from the plans Brannock drew us. I was expecting security to be banging on this door as well, but they aren't. Maybe they are having trouble containing their captives.

I grin as we drop out of phase, and Zeydan steps back, shuddering.

"That is awful," he mutters, and he runs a hand over his ears and face in agitation, like he's feeling to make sure everything went back into place.

Xavier is pretty collected when he and Ghosie appear, though he does look a little queasy. "What is that evil grin for?" he asks, pointing at me. "It's even scarier in that form. You look so cute and cuddly, it's kind of psychotic."

He eyes me warily, and I laugh. "I was just imagining that the captives are causing a little uprising and getting some of their own back. I'm guessing that's why there is no security here." I wave my hand around, and he nods thoughtfully.

"You may be right. Our job may have been done for us already."

"We will go get the others. We'll leave Brannock for last because he isn't going to want to wait while being this close to Chloe," I tell the others, and Xavier puts out his hand to stop me.

"Lila. You need to be prepared for what we might find," he says quietly, and I frown in confusion, looking between him and Zeydan.

"What do you mean?"

The two of them exchange a glance.

"Despite the lack of the kill switch, I don't doubt the guards and scientists in here have some form of protection. The prisoners are probably wearing collars like Brannock did," Xavier warns me, and I still don't get what he's saying.

"What he's saying, Lila, is all the captives may already be dead," Zeydan states flatly, and I stumble back, gasping.

"Oh my god!" I slap a hand over my mouth to stop the scream that wants to escape. I shake my head. "No, no, no. Oh God, what if they are? He will never forgive any of us."

Xavier nods solemnly, pulling a syringe from one of the pockets in his armor. "That's why I have this. Link gave me a sedative in case of that scenario. We will freeze Brannock and administer it before he can go berserker on us. None of us, not even you, would survive."

Tears stream down my face, and I want to scream and rage, but I nod. "Okay, that was smart." I wipe my face and take a deep breath, trying to get my shit together. I don't want to set him off before we've even discovered the truth.

"Should we even bring him through?" Ghosie asks, looking at the door we need to return through.

"At this stage, I don't think we can avoid it. He'll only hurt himself if we don't," Zeydan says, his focus down the corridor. He wears a small frown on his face, and his cute little fox ears twitch like he's listening to something, but then he smiles—or at least I think it's supposed to be a smile. It's kind of hard to tell on his foxy features. "I think we are going to be okay. Go get them, we have work to do." He practically pushes us through the door.

Ghosie and I bring Tirrian, Saxon, and Brannock back through. Brannock doesn't wait to recover from the phasing before he has his weapon in hand and is storming down the corridor. I quickly change back, put my armor on, and hurry after him.

We move swiftly down what is quite a lengthy corridor, my stomach in my throat as I brace for what we are about to find. When the corridor ends, we come to a large, open, circular space with about fifteen closed doors lining the outside and a large medical facility opposite us. In the open space are a couple of guards and scientists, and they are all arguing about how they are going to get the doors to the rooms unlocked.

They don't even notice us in the low emergency lighting. "We need to keep one or two alive so we can question them about everything that has been happening in this facility," I hiss at Brannock, and he gives me a curt nod of assurance. I look to the others. "Do you understand?" I check with them, and they all nod.

"Which one was in charge?" Xavier asks, and Brannock shrugs. "I don't know, I was never kept in this area."

I tune into the thoughts of the panicked staff, who alternate between banging on doors and shouting demands.

"That one." I point to a woman in a white lab coat. "She's the head scientist. Even with all that is happening, her mind is still excited about running tests on an infant who was born recently," I growl, really wishing I could eviscerate the woman, but I know we need her.

I keep scanning the minds. "And that one." I point out a male in a white lab coat. "He is actually sympathetic to the captives and wishes he didn't have to be here. He will spill his guts. He's only here because his idiot brother, who is a guard, made some bad bets, and he's paying off some kind of debt for him."

"And that one," Xavier growls, pointing out one of the guards. "He likes to use that cattle prod on the children. I want to torture him for information." Xavier's words cause a violent reaction from the other five men. They seem to growl in unison like a pack of wild animals, and this finally gets the staff's attention.

"Fuck, they've come to kill us," a guard shouts and takes off through the medical facility to a door on the other side.

"Yes, we have, unless you choose to surrender. Lay your weapons down, and you will be spared," I offer. Some of these people may be like the man whose mind I scanned—not here willingly. One or two of the scientists drop to their knees and put their hands behind their heads, but I watch in shock as the head guard Xavier picked out points his gun at them and takes aim. Before we can react, he kills all three of them.

"Dirty fucking traitors," he growls, and then all hell breaks loose.

CHAPTER TWENTY-EIGHT

Lila

Xavier waves a hand and freezes the three we want to save as the rest of them open fire on us. My guys engage the enemy, and I know it's only a matter of time before they are victorious, but I'm worried about stray bullets taking out the three frozen captives. I'm almost certain Xavier's magic isn't going to stop them from dying if a bullet hits them.

"Come on, we need to protect the ones that need to be questioned," I call to Ghosie. We use telekinesis to move them together, and then I wrap a magical shield around them, hoping that will protect them

Suddenly, there is a blinding pain in my shoulder, and I scream, knowing I've been hit or stabbed. I reach for the wound, and my fingers come away bloody.

Ghosie roars and starts to vibrate, and then he begins

to grow. I lose all interest in my wound as I watch in awe as he grows rapidly bigger, bursting out of his armor. His fur becomes longer, shaggier, and brighter, and it's almost like he's hulking out. His muscles bulge, his mouth fills with huge teeth, and his claws become monstrous. He swipes at the person who injured me, and I hear a wet squelch. When I whirl around, there is nothing left but a lump of mangled flesh at my feet. I gag and sway a little, the pain in my shoulder spreading through my body.

"Lila," Ghosie roars, and I feel him pick me up. This must be how Ann felt when King Kong carried her to the top of the Empire State Building. I'm but a mere flea compared to his bulk.

"Oh my god." The pain in my body starts to morph into pleasure, and I begin to squirm in his arms. Shit, his fur is doing its thing, and I am going to beg him to fuck me within moments. In this state, he would rip me in half. Hell, I didn't even know he had this form. I don't think anyone did. I turn to call for help from my other mates, and they are staring at Ghosie in awe.

"Easy, buddy, you did well, and she's safe, but we need to check out her wound. Her having an orgasm right now isn't optimal." Tirrian tries to talk the bear down, his rolling growl running through my body where I'm pressed against his chest.

"There's always time for orgasms," I pant as all rational thought leaves my mind.

"You're going to have to knock him out," Zeydan

shouts at Xavier. I want to warn Ghosie, but I feel Xavier take control of my mind.

Sorry, my sweet. I know what you were going to do, he apologizes inside my head, and I curse him creatively. He laughs as some of the sex fog clears now that he's controlling my body.

I can't see what's happening clearly, but when I turn my head, it looks like Xavier passes a needle to Zeydan and one to Saxon. Huh, I guess he must have had more than one, which makes sense if Brannock was in berserker mode. One probably wouldn't do the trick, or maybe he was prepared to sedate any of us.

"How about you put our girl down so we can take a look at that wound on her shoulder?" Brannock asks Ghosie, holding up his hands in a nonthreatening way.

"You told us how much you hate getting blood in your fur, and she's bleeding all over you," Tirrian chimes in.

Steady, Lila, Xavier croons in my mind as I start to squirm in Ghosie's arms again. *You are bleeding quite badly. We really need to get that wound looked at. I'm thinking maybe the knives are coated with whatever the bullet was made of, because you aren't healing like you should be.*

"I was stabbed?" I shout, and Ghosie tightens his grip on me, holding me closer to his body.

"Now!" Saxon shouts, and Ghosie flinches before letting out an ear-splitting roar. Within moments, I feel his hold on me loosen and Brannock lunges and snatches me out of his arms as he falls to his knees and then flat on his face, out cold.

"Ghosie," I mumble, reaching for him as Xavier frees my mind, but the drugging effect of his fur is wearing off, and the pain from my wound returns.

"Ow, fuck, that hurts," I grumble as Brannock places me on the ground and peels down the top of my armor so he can take a good look at the wound.

I grit my teeth as he pokes around in it, but it's like lightning striking me, and I can't stop the scream that escapes.

Out of the corner of my eye, I see beings staring out of the small windows in the locked door. Thank goodness I have a sports bra on, otherwise everyone would be getting a good look at the girls.

My guys surround me, and they are all blocked from view.

"Yeah, just as I expected, it isn't healing. Drag one of those live ones over here, will you?" Brannock says over his shoulder, and Saxon crouches down with us.

"I can feed her," he offers, but Zeydan shakes his head.

"No, you only just recovered from your own injury. She can drain a human or two, and if that doesn't work, she can drink from each of us." He points to Xavier, Brannock, and himself. Tirrian's out because he fed Saxon, and we don't want to over tax him, and Ghosie's out because his blood is now filled with sedative.

Saxon grumbles but concedes quickly, so he must still feel pretty crappy, even though he won't admit it.

"There's blood in the fridges," a voice says from somewhere, and when I look around, Xavier has unfrozen the male scientist who hadn't wanted to be there. "We have two Vilaxians in the breeding rooms, and there's a child in the soldier program. We have to keep him well fed so he doesn't attack the other soldiers." He looks kind of green when he says this, and I gasp in horror.

"Get them," Brannock demands, his eyes blazing.

Xavier releases the man, and he hurries over to some industrial-sized fridges and grabs an armful of blood bags before returning to me.

"These are all taken from the captives. We found that human blood was too weak to sustain the vampires." He passes them to Xavier, not wanting to get too close to any of the others.

I don't blame him. He's being smart, and it may keep him alive. Xavier brings them over to me, and I pierce a hole in the top of the first bag, draining it. It's tasty but not as tasty as one of my guys. I drain two more bags, and I feel my wound start to heal, but it's still sluggish.

Brannock passes me the last bag of blood, and I stare at it in wonder. It looks like it has glitter flakes floating in it. I pierce my fang through it and slurp it down, and I just about burst out of my skin. Holy fuckety fuck.

Power zings through my body, and I jolt in

surprise, looking at Zeydan. I haven't drunk from him yet, but I bet this is what his blood feels like. It's fucking powerful.

"Wow, look at that wound heal," Tirrian mumbles behind me.

"I've never seen something heal so fast. That must be very powerful blood."

Zeydan frowns and takes the empty bag out of my hand, peering at the label. "Subject twenty-three, female. Species unknown. Who did this blood come from?" He shakes the bag at the scientist, who shrinks back in fear.

"One of the females. No matter how much she was tortured, she never divulged anything, much to Agent Smith's disgust," he sneers, his own repugnance at Smith evident. "The weird thing is, anyone else probably would have died from the torture, but she just kept regenerating. They talked about decapitating her and shredding her heart, but they didn't want to risk that she wouldn't regenerate. She's a favorite and has been forcibly bred. Smith desperately wanted an army of invincible soldiers."

"She was raped?" Tirrian growls, and the man visibly shakes.

"Yes, but there was only one alien male who volunteered for the job. All the other male captives were repulsed by the suggestion, and some of the guards also had a go. She is very attractive and doesn't seem to have any strange body parts. They said it was no hardship."

"She didn't fight back?" Saxon sounds ill, and the scientist shakes his head.

"She was restrained, and we have a chemical that blocks alien powers."

"Who was this male?" I ask, wriggling in Brannock's arms so he will let me stand. I feel fucking amazing—homicidal but amazing—and now I want to know who to aim my divine wrath at.

"He's in the next breeding block, through that door. He looks just like him." He points at Brannock. "But, well, with his anatomy, we couldn't allow him to destroy the breeding stock. The only reason Smith let him was because the female healed the damage the male did when he found his release."

"Oh my god." I feel sick. That poor female. She would have been ripped to shreds. Hell, I'm ripped to shreds, but my body is made for it, and it feels good. It must have been pure torture.

Brannock roars, and his body switches from his normal form to his berserker form, and all the other guys back out of the way.

"Oh fuck, Lila, you have to do something, or he will kill everyone in sight," Xavier shouts at me as Tirrian drags Ghosie out of the path of Brannock's rage.

"But what? Only fucking worked last time. I can't do that now," I shout.

"Fucking or fighting," Saxon shouts. "Quick, which way to the male who participated in the rape," he demands of the scientist.

"Through the next door, there's another room like this. He's in breeding room twenty-six. He is on his own at the moment because he can't be trusted with any of the other females."

Brannock roars and starts heading for the two frozen captives.

"Lila, we need those two alive. Distract him." Zeydan goes to step in front of Brannock, but he just bats him away like he's an annoying fly. Zeydan, eyes wide with surprise, flies through the air and slams against one of the breeding room doors with a thud. He groans as he slides down it, looking dazed when he stops.

I wave a hand, and my armor disappears, leaving me naked. I let my Aaz'axian form wash over me and jump in front of my rampaging mate, drawing his attention.

"Whoa, what is she?" I hear the scientist ask, but everyone ignores him in our desperate need to deal with the rampaging alien.

"How do we open the cell?" Tirrian asks, running through the medical facility to open the far door.

"His handprint." He points at the frozen guard. Saxon doesn't fuck around, he draws his sword and slices off the man's hand, catching it before it can hit the ground.

"Here." He holds it out to me.

"Fuck no," I shout.

"Toss it to me," Tirrian calls, and Saxon yeets the hand across the room. It flies like a bullet, and Tirrian snatches it out of the air, the droplets of blood landing on the spotless white floors and pristine metal benches.

"Go, Lila, go! I'll stay here and keep an eye on Ghosie until he comes around," Xavier commands, and I back away from berserker Brannock, knowing it's going to trigger his predatory instincts. Sure enough, he bellows loudly and comes at me.

I squeak and run, my surroundings a blur at my speed, but I reach the next breeding room and screech to a halt. Tirrian has already used the hand to open cell twenty-six. Another male Aaz'axian steps out. He's in his natural form, and his color is duller than Brannock's, but he has one of those control collars around his neck. I bet this is the asshole who gave up Brannock and Chloe. Karma really is a glorious bitch.

His eyes lock on me and widen before narrowing with undisguised greedy glee. "A female. They found me a female. Get over here, bitch, so I can ruin your cunt. I won't have to wait for the little one to get older," he demands. Is he talking about Chloe? Oh fuck, I'm tempted to attack the male myself, but an ear-splitting howl sounds out from behind me.

"Mine," Brannock screams and steps between me and the other male.

The glee in the male's face vanishes, and I see him swallow nervously. "Brannock?" he asks, but Brannock has lost all reason. He charges the male, swiping with his claws. The male doesn't even get a chance to raise his hands to defend himself before his stomach is eviscerated. His innards become his outers, and his screams are horrifying as Brannock slashes and claws him until there's nothing left that is recognizable. He turns to me, his body covered in blood, and starts to stalk toward me.

"Damn it, Lila, do something," Tirrian says. "Why didn't that appease the berserker?"

"He's moved onto the fuck portion of the schedule," I say, not taking my eyes off him. "I'm going to try to distract him. I hope this works, otherwise we're going to put on quite a show for the viewers." I slide my eyes to the doors, and sure enough, I see other beings watching. Some look terrified, but others seem to cheer us on.

"Brannock, you need to calm down," I tell him, holding out my hands. "Chloe needs you." I hope her name will snap him from his rage. He stops, and I hold my breath.

"We need to find Chloe," I repeat, and he shakes his head, and his whole body twitches. His berserker form melts away, leaving him blinking with confusion at his bloody state. Changing forms is disorienting when coming down from a berserker rage.

He looks down at the mess of flesh at his feet. "Relgrael," he snarls and spits on the remains. "I guess I got my revenge."

"And then some," Tirrian mutters as he pushes off the wall. "Let's go talk to the scientists and find out where the cells for the children are. I'm ready to burn this facility to the ground and be done with it."

I go to hug Brannock but stop, not wanting to

cover myself in gore. "And let's find you a shower. We don't want Chloe seeing you like this when you're reunited."

The three of us walk back the way we came, silent and lost in our own worlds. This is really unacceptable, and if the Galactic Council was to learn about this, I'm pretty sure they would go full *Independence Day* on the Earth. We need to find a way to deal with this and get the outcome we need. I'll have to ask the guys for advice. They are all diplomats, after all, so I may as well make use of their skills.

CHAPTER TWENTY-NINE

Lila

Ghosie is still sleeping with the fairies when we return to the first group of breeding cells. Zeydan, Saxon, and Xavier have been busy. They have unfrozen the two other humans and are trying to question them. The male is cupping the stump of his arm and sobbing, and the female is glaring at my guys.

"Everything okay?" Xavier smiles as we return, scanning Brannock and nodding. "Looks like you got your revenge," he comments.

Brannock grunts. "Part of it. I need a shower."

Xavier waves his hand and uses his magic to clean Brannock. Brannock nods his gratitude, turning his focus to the female. She shivers under his intense stare, but then she sees me over his shoulder.

"Oh my god, a female Aaz'axian. I thought they

didn't exist," she mutters, eyeing me with greedy hunger.

I let the form drop away, then I conjure my armor, covering my naked body. She blinks, and that greedy hunger intensifies. "What are you?" she sounds awed, and I ignore her, satisfied with her going to her death without ever knowing what I am.

"Nothing you're ever going to get your hands on." Saxon bares his fangs at her and hisses.

"Where are the children? Have you brainwashed them?" Zeydan asks, and she clamps her lips shut, losing interest in me in the face of his god form.

"Bitch isn't talking?" Tirrian asks, and Saxon shakes his head.

"The younger ones aren't, but a few of the older ones have started being programmed," the helpful guy responds. "I will take you to them, but you will have to be alert, because the older ones may attack, though I'm almost certain there is a trigger word."

"Shut your fucking mouth!" the female scientist screams at him.

The guard just moans, and I come up with an idea. I make my way over to the chair he's tied to and crouch down in front of him. "I can fix that for you if you want," I tell him gently, and he cracks an eye open. A drop of sweat trickles down the side of his face. "I can probably even reattach the hand." I cross my fingers that I'm not lying. "But you need to give me something. What's the trigger word for the soldier kids?" I ask him, and he mutters something I can't hear.

"Don't you dare, Phil," the female scientist shouts. "Shut your fucking trap. We will be rewarded with our loyalty. Smith promised us powers."

Xavier snorts with amusement. "Smith is halfway across the galaxy. He left you to fend for yourselves. He can't give you shit."

"He's going to bring water back from the planet Skarr. It was one of the things that woman promised him when they made a deal." In her panic, the woman is blabbing Smith's plan to us without any prompting.

"What could Smith have given Vivax that allowed him to bargain with her?" Zeydan murmurs quietly, but the female hears it and starts laughing hysterically before spewing more information. It's then I realize Xavier has worked his magic and manipulated her emotions so she has no inhibitions and the secrets are pouring out. She's kind of giddy, like she's high.

"She wanted him to kill a couple of the aliens years ago, but Smith had other ideas. He decided he was going to capture them and experiment on them. They were the first of our breeding program. We've gathered a lot more since the originals. They were duds anyway. It was only recently that they managed a successful breeding. Smith tried all sorts of combinations, but the male was never able to get another female pregnant, and the females were never fertilized by other males."

"Was everyone in this facility raped?" Tirrian growls, and the female blanches and shakes her head. "No, the control collars have a needle that injects a chemical compound into them," she says.

"It's basically GHB," the male scientist says with disgust. "They were mentally and chemically manipulated into fucking each other. None of the aliens are to blame in the least, except for the one he obviously took care of." He nods in Brannock's direction.

"What is GHB?" Zeydan asks, and the rest of my guys look confused as well, even though my righteous fury is slowly starting to build again.

"GHB is a date rate drug. It's illegal, but it's popular in the party scene. It produces feelings of euphoria, confidence, relaxation, and sociability, which is great if you knowingly take it, but it gets slipped unknowingly into drinks, making the consumer susceptible to things they may not be interested in if they were sober."

"Yes, and all of the aliens had a low tolerance to it, so it made them horny. Getting them to fuck after administering it to them really wasn't an issue." The male sounds ashamed.

The guard in front of me mutters something, and I have to lean closer to hear it.

"Kitrubu? What does that mean?" I lean back on my heels. Why isn't my universal translator translating it? "Do any of you know?" I ask, wondering if my translator is broken with all my changes today.

All of them shake their heads. Well, shit.

"It's Sumerian for sacrifice," the helpful scientist offers. "It makes sense that they'd use something nobody else is familiar with."

"How do you know?" I ask, perplexed at this random bit of knowledge.

"Dead languages are my specialty. It was why I was tapped for this program. Some of the aliens don't speak any known language, and Smith wanted me to create a dictionary of sorts."

"That's bullshit. All aliens who reside on Earth or come here for a vacation are required to have a translator implant. You've been conned," Saxon tells the man who nods and grins.

"Yes, I know that now, and you know that, but the rest of these idiots don't."

I'm growing to like this guy. "What's your name?" I ask him, and he blinks in surprise. "Doctor Matthew Raynor. My wife, Melissa, works in the soldiers' cell block, looking after the children. Please don't kill her," he begs. "I promise to tell you everything you want to know."

"He certainly has been helpful," Zeydan agrees, and Xavier and Saxon concur.

"Okay, Matthew, I'll tell you what's about to happen. We are going to release all of these aliens. We are then going to escort them to our ship where they will be assessed. If any of them point the finger at you for being involved in any form of torture or maiming, I'll kill you without blinking, but if none of them have a bad thing to say about you or Melissa, then I'll let the two of you live and possibly offer you a job when we're done. Okay?"

He quickly agrees, and I stand up and back away from the male guard.

"Hey, my hand?" he croaks, his voice broken from his screams.

"Oh, I lied. I saw in your mind what you did to all of these beings and you, sir, are a sick fucker who deserves all that is coming to you."

He starts shouting, and I freeze him again. The woman also starts complaining, so I give her the same treatment.

"Xavier, we'll go back to the door, and I will phase you through so we can get the power started again. Then we will start releasing some of these people."

He agrees, and I turn to Brannock. "I hate to ask you to wait, but I'm assuming Chloe's in the soldiers' wing, and I don't want to release those children until we can reunite them with their parents.

He heaves out a sigh. "I hate it, but I understand."

"When the power comes back on, we need to turn on all these terminals and transfer the information to the ship so we can comb through it all. When we are done and everyone is evacuated, I want Tirrian to shift again and burn this place to the ground. It's a secure level, so the rest of Area 51 should be none the wiser. We will police our own people now, and Earth politicians can go fuck themselves. Agreed?" I ask, and my mates who are conscious respond in the affirmative.

I look at Ghosie. "I'm not sure what to do with him. That must have been a super strength sedative."

Xavier chuckles. "It would have knocked Viggy out."

"And you used two?" I screech, hurrying over to check that my bear is still breathing, but Saxon catches me as I move past him.

"He's fine." He brushes a hand over my hair. "He's sleeping like a baby and will likely stay that way for a few more hours. We will use telekinesis to move him to the platform and take him home."

"Why is he still that big?" I ask, pointing at his giant shaggy form.

Xavier shrugs. "No clue, but we expect him to go back to normal when the sedative wears off and he wakes."

"Let's hurry up. This place is giving me the heebie-jeebies," Tirrian grumbles, smoke wafting out of his nose.

"Imagine how all of them feel," Brannock says, gesturing to the closed doors. I can't see anyone watching us anymore, but I don't blame them. They could be jumping from the frying pan and into the fire. For all they know, we're worse than Smith.

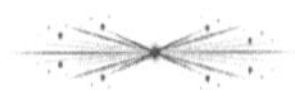

It doesn't take long to get the power up and running again, and we release the first room of prisoners. The prisoners are reluctant to come out, and when Xavier announces who he is and that the Galaxy Circus is here to rescue them, it doesn't get any better.

"Why should we trust you? We were told that the Adams brothers sold that bastard Smith a list of all aliens on Earth," a voice calls from inside one of the rooms.

"Like fuck they did!" I exclaim.

"Shut up, blood sucker," another voice calls. "You know that isn't true." I spin around to find a female exiting the breeding room, tears streaming down her face. "Is it true you're getting us out of here?"

"Absolutely. We are going to transport you to the Galaxy Circus and then the Celestian royal family is sending a ship. You will travel to Celestia to be assessed by their medical professionals, both physically and mentally, and once they clear you, you are free to leave. We will ensure you are escorted to wherever you want to go. We have the full backing of not only the Celestian royal family, but also the Vilaxian and warlock leaders." I wave to Saxon and Xavier. Xavier gives a little finger wave, and Saxon dips his head in greeting. "Not to mention the dragon royal family from Fluxx, the leading streak on Iceen, and the support of the crown prince of Aquilia. I also have the heirs of both Pleasure Bot Industries and the suva trade in my pocket."

The female purses her lips and whistles. "You have some heavy hitters."

I nod, taking her hand and giving it a reassuring squeeze. "Yes, and they are all dedicated to seeing the people responsible for your imprisonment get punished. Most of the people in this facility are already dead. We haven't gotten as far as the nursery yet, but everyone else was taken care of."

While Tirrian and I were busy with Brannock, Xavier used his handy people dissolving spell to dispose of all the dead bodies.

"And it's only a matter of time before we catch up with Smith. I guarantee he will pay in blood for what he has wrought here."

"Come out, everyone, she's telling the truth," the female calls, and I blink in surprise.

"You can tell that?" I ask her, and she nods.

"Yes. One of my Skarrian abilities is to discern people's motives and whether they are being truthful or not."

"You're from Skarr?" I ask, feeling tears build in my eyes.

"Yes, and I knew the Adams brothers weren't responsible. I could feel the lies the scientists and Smith told, but I also knew them personally. I was friends with their son and daughter-in-law. We were neighbors once upon a time, and I was the one who looked after you when they had their accident." Her eyes blur with tears. "Lila, you've grown into such a beautiful young woman."

I'm stunned into speechlessness.

"Lila's memories were manipulated, and some of them have not returned yet," Xavier explains when I can't talk because the lump in my throat is so big.

"Yes, I know. I was the one who called your parents when it happened and summoned them to Earth. Xylene and I cried buckets of tears the day we handed you over to child services. I wanted to keep you, but they insisted it was what your parents wanted. Thankfully they did, because I was captured roughly a year after their deaths."

"You've been in here for almost twenty years?" Saxon sounds incredulous, and the woman nods.

"Yes, I didn't think I was ever going to leave."

"I'm sorry, I don't remember your name," I say to the woman, and she smiles gently.

"I'm Amanda, but you called me Mandymoo."

Something prickles in my mind, and a memory of a younger Amanda pushing me on a tire swing in the backyard of a large home flutters through my mind.

"Are any of the children yours?" Zeydan asks gently, and her eyes widen slightly at his appearance.

"Babe, do you want to maybe reel in the whole godly being thing now?" I suggest, and I can see him think about it.

"You're a god? Which one?" Amanda asks.

"I am Zeydan, the earth elemental god."

"Come with me." Amanda grabs his hand and tugs him through the medical facility. I hear the rest of the occupants in the first rooms start to chatter amongst themselves, and I realize they had all ventured out while we were distracted. Most of them are humanoid in appearance, which was one of the conditions for being able to reside on Earth, since they needed to blend in, but I can't tell you what species they are.

"Go," Brannock encourages. "We will get these people to the transporter and catch up. The others are all back on the ship and ready to receive the refugees. Link, Mark, Susie, and Aarin are all on standby."

"Thank you," I call to him and follow after Amanda and Zeydan. The others remain behind to assist the shaken captives who all seem incredibly emotional now that they know they are being rescued. I think Xavier will probably need to do some mood stabilizing to get them to cooperate.

I reach the other room and find Amanda staring down at what remains of Relgrael. She gives him a vicious kick with her toe, and I shudder. I wonder if she was one of the ones who was forced by him. Her resilient Skarrian vagina may have survived sex with him, but it would have hurt.

"Do you have any children?" I ask her, and she shakes her head. "No. Skarrian children only happen once you have bonded with your chosen mates, and everyone in the mating circle needs to be involved," she reminds me, and I grimace. She gives me a small smile. "Thankfully in here, mutual orgasms were not a frequent occurrence, and they didn't know how to force me to bond, so I avoided having any children. Others were not so lucky." She looks at me with haunted eyes, and I feel so much pain coming from her and, funnily enough, compassion. I don't get a chance to question it, though, before she points at one of the doors. "Open that one."

I grab the amputated hand and hold it over the sensor. The door opens, and Amanda hurries in. I hear some whispering, and then there's a shout.

"What? He's here?"

I go on high alert as a woman with blindingly red hair rushes out of the room. She's thin in a malnourished way, but her stomach is obscenely round. She is very, very pregnant. Hell, I don't think I was even that round with the krakens.

She stops and stares at Zeydan, who is frozen, his mouth dropping open in shock. Her eyes literally blaze with fire, I instantly know who this is, and my stomach sinks. Smith has really screwed the pooch. We will be lucky if Earth is unmade. This poor woman. I'm going to go out on a limb and guess that she's pregnant with an Aaz'axian deity hybrid.

"Sanshia?" Zeydan's voice breaks as he whispers her name.

The woman bursts into tears and flings herself at my mate. He gathers his sister in his arms and holds her tightly, speaking to her in a language that doesn't translate for my ears. This is where that last batch of blood came from, I would put my money on it.

"Death is too good for Smith. He will suffer an eternity for this," I promise out loud before turning to Amanda.

"Thank you," I tell her, but she just shakes her head sadly.

"Don't thank me yet."

CHAPTER THIRTY

Lila

Amanda and I release the rest of the captives in the second room, while Zeydan and Sanshia have a quiet conversation. I don't interrupt them, because we can take care of introductions later. I'm pretty sure they are exchanging stories, but every now and then, I feel eyes on me.

We herd the tearful, relieved captives into the first room so they can be escorted to the ship. Silac, Link, Musette, and Mehira all transported down to the facility. I guess they must have been read into the mission. Well, that isn't a bad thing, since we need all the help we can get. There are a lot more captives than we guessed. In most of the rooms, there were "couples."

"Hey, what are you two doing here?" I ask my guys as they swoop in and give me relieved hugs.

"I came down to transfer all the information, and

Link is here to assess the two pregnant women and the woman with the infant who are in the next two rooms," Silac explains, moving back to the computers. I'm sure nothing they have here is so hi-tech he can't hack into them, so I turn my focus to my cyborg.

"How do you know about them?" I ask him. We haven't gotten that far yet, and Amanda hasn't said anything.

"One of the other captives in the first group said I should come down, and that one of the pregnant women is due to give birth any day," Link says, gazing at the group milling around.

Musette and Mehira are gently guiding them toward the other half of the facility to transport to the ship.

"Oh yeah, she sure looks like she's going to explode at any moment. It's Zeydan's sister, Sanshia."

"The goddess of fire?" Tirrian must have heard me with his shifter hearing, and I cringe, wondering how many more of these people just heard me announce that.

Shit. I look around, but most of them are occupied with their own trauma. "Yes."

"Saxon told me she's been raped repeatedly. I'm assuming the child is a product of that?" Link asks quietly, his eyes dark silver with concern.

"I don't know, but I would guess so. Look, at the moment, the priority is getting everyone out safely. We can worry about anything else after that," I suggest, and he nods and then gasps.

I turn around, and Zeydan is supporting his sister as they walk toward us. Her hand is on her belly, and she is panting. Seeing her is really a kick in the teeth, because she looks so sick. I want to put my hands on her and heal her, but I don't have that kind of experience. I'm hoping Mark and Aarin will be able to give her what she needs.

"She's in labor. I think the surprise of seeing me triggered it," Zeydan calls, and Link jumps into action.

"Let's go. We need to get her to the ship stat. She's malnourished, and I want her on an IV as well as a pain killer before I can assess the labor. Pick her up and carry her," he orders Zeydan, who obeys without argument.

"Can she transport in labor?" I ask, and Link flinches.

"Fuck, no, she probably shouldn't—not this far along and not in active labor. When you did with the krakens, there was no worry you would go into spontaneous labor."

He looks around the room, blanching at the cold, sterile area. "Okay, get her on one of those beds. Let me check their supplies." Link points at the bed, which looks more like a torture table than a birthing bed, but beggars can't be choosers.

Zeydan carries his sister over there and lays her down, and Link starts searching through cabinets.

"Matthew," I call, getting the scientist's attention. "We need your help. Can you assist Link and show him where your birthing supplies are? I assume these labs are equipped for births, considering that was the whole purpose of this section of the facility."

He quickly agrees and hurries over to show Link the supplies.

"Melissa is a midwife. Can someone go get her? She has helped most of the females birth their young," he tells me, and I assure him we will do that.

I watch as Link squirts gel on Sanshia's stomach and prepares to give her an ultrasound. Zeydan holds her hand and pushes her hair back from her sweaty face. He's such a good male.

"Brannock," I call him over, gesturing for Xavier and Saxon to join us as well. "Right, the third room is going to have to wait. We need to get to the child soldiers. Link needs the midwife's help."

Brannock perks up, and his spikes bristle with what I'm assuming is anticipation. "Finally," he murmurs, his eyes shining with unshed tears.

"Xavier, go in first and check out what we are dealing with. There are supposed to be a couple more caregivers in there, but I'm not sure about guards. Once we know what we are dealing with, we can formulate a plan. Not one of those children will be hurt, even if they start something."

Tirrian approaches us and hands out guns.

"What are these for?" I ask him, horrified at the idea that he wants us to shoot the young ones.

"They contain tranq darts just in case. Child dosages. There are two areas—one for children under five, and the other for those older than five. The children under five should be easy to subdue, but the ones over five won't necessarily be as easy. Remember, we don't know what species these kids are, and even though they say they are all under ten, remember a lot of them age quicker and could appear older. Don't hesitate to sedate them, and we can sort it all out when we get them to the ship."

I guess the guys had been busy. Not only have they been moving captives, but they also grilled them for info too.

"Let's go." I can feel Xavier's impatience to get to the children. It's as great as Brannock's. Even though he has a fearsome reputation as the mighty warlock, he also has the biggest, softest heart and is a sucker for kids.

We let Brannock lead the way, bypassing the other breeding block and heading straight for the soldiers' ward. This door is reinforced and has handprint access as well.

"Are the staff locked in with the kids?" I growl as Tirrian returns for Phil's hand. When he gets back to us, it looks a bit worse for wear. It's been discarded on the floor a number of times now. There's no way to reattach it no matter how good my healing powers are. Someone must have stomped on it, because a couple of the fingers look broken.

Now that the power is back on, the rooms are no longer sealed shut, so Xavier turns to mist and creeps under the door. I expect him to return within seconds, but he doesn't. Brannock starts to pace back and forth, and his form flickers.

"Uh-uh." I clamp my hand on his arm and give it a shake. "No berserking out on us. We don't have time or another body for you to mutilate. Take a deep breath in then breathe it out," I order as I push feelings of calmness and serenity on him. It works, and his body relaxes slightly, his form no longer flickering.

"Not long now," Saxon tells him, patting him on the shoulder.

Brannock breathes in and out again as Xavier's mist floats back under the door, and he reforms with a frown on his face.

"Is everything okay?" I ask him, and he cocks his head to the side.

"I'm not sure," he replies.

"What's wrong?" I ask, and he waves a hand at the door.

"It's weird. It looks like they don't even know the facility is under attack. The children are all in their beds. It's dorm style, with two different areas separated by age like you told us. There are five staff members in there— three women and two guards. The women are all asleep in their beds. Two of them are with the younger children, and only one is with the older ones. The guards are playing cards. All of them look none the wiser. Could they be on another generator?" he asks Brannock.

"What if they are on a different system because

Smith didn't want to lose his prized soldiers if he had to hit the kill switch?" Saxon suggests.

"That makes sense," Tirrian agrees. "Do we think the women are hostiles? Are we going to take care of them?"

"No!" I shout. "We need the midwife, and I say we incapacitate them and scan their minds before we kill anyone. We may need their help. If they are the only contact the children have had since they were removed from their parents, then we're going to need them."

"Lila's right. The women didn't have any weapons that I could see, and I took care of the guards already, so let's move, shall we?" Xavier waves at the handprint scanner, and Tirrian puts Phil's hand against it with a sickening thump.

The door opens, and he tosses it to the side once more.

"Hey, we're going to need that one more time," I remind him, and he grimaces but picks it up and tucks it into one of the pockets on his armor.

We creep through the silent ward, looking around in surprise. The main room is set up like a classroom, but there is a play area on one side with a TV and a gaming system as well as books, blocks, and other assorted toys. On the walls are educational posters showing the alphabet and numbers, as well as posters of foreign countries. I guess they were learning something other than how to be good soldiers. At least that's something. We follow Xavier, and he takes us to a kitchen. The large dining table, which has the two guards slumped over it, would sit maybe twenty-five people.

"They have this many children?" I whisper, and he nods. "Damn it, hopefully all of their parents are out there, and we can reunite them."

"Hopefully their parents want them," Tirrian mutters, and my stomach sinks.

Past the kitchen, there is a hallway with three doors. "Young kids, slightly older, and bathroom," Xavier says, pointing out the corresponding doors.

"Let's go in and get the younger ones first. You said there are two women in there? They should be able to help us, right?"

We go to the left door and push it open.

"Freeze. Don't come any closer," a woman hisses, and we hear the sound of a safety flicking off.

Xavier forms two balls of light in his hands and tosses them into the air before erecting an invisible shield in front of us in case she gets an itchy trigger finger. Hopefully the bullet isn't one of the special ones, which can nullify magic and pass straight through.

"Easy," Brannock says. "We're the good guys and have come to break you all out."

"Oh, thank God," she sobs and lowers the weapon.

"I'm Lila Adams from Galaxy Circus. We have released all the adults and transported them to our ship. We'd like to reunite their children with them, if possible."

"Yes, yes, of course. Hettie," she hisses, and her

friend sits up. I guess she was just pretending to be asleep. "Wake the little ones and get them dressed."

"No time, we just need to get them out of here. We can come back for things later," Tirrian says, and I bite my lip.

"Maybe grab their most special things now." I glare at him, daring him to contradict me. I know he's going to torch this facility as soon as we are clear.

"Okay, but make it quick. I'll get the girls to help. We're going to need it," he says as the fifteen small children start to wake up. Most of them look at us with wide-eyed amazement, but one or two start crying."

"The older children will help. I'll go wake them," the woman with the gun says.

"Are you Melissa?" I ask her, and she nods.

"You are needed in the first cell block. One of the women is in labor." I don't use her name in case that isn't what she goes by.

"Oh dear. Poor thing. She hasn't been very well during this pregnancy at all." She hurries away, and Brannock grunts and looks around.

"I bet it's doing to her body what it did to my wife's, but she managed to withstand it because she's a goddess."

"I would say that is a pretty good bet," Xavier replies as Hettie starts to gather the children.

"Can you see Chloe?" I ask my Aaz'axian, but his face falls, and he shakes his head.

"Maybe she's in with the older ones. Let's go wake them," I suggest, giving his hand a squeeze.

"I'll stay here and supervise this group," Saxon tells me, and I give him a quick kiss on the cheek. "Shout if you run across trouble."

The four of us move to the next room. The woman in this room is fast asleep, and I don't want to startle her, but there aren't many other options. I flick the light on and stand in front of the guys. I, at least, look human, and the other three aren't even close, but then maybe that isn't a bad thing.

There looks to be ten children in this room, and all of them are awake and alert the instant the lights turn on.

"Who are you?" A boy of about ten jumps to his feet and puts his hands on his hips, placing himself just in front of the rest of them.

"I'm Lila, and we're breaking you out of here," I tell him.

He frowns. "Does Smith have a mission for us?" he asks, and a sob escapes the mouth of the silent guardian. She slaps her hand over it when my eyes move to her.

"No. Smith is never going to be involved in your lives ever again," I promise him.

This causes his frown to grow even deeper, and the children behind him mutter amongst themselves, but the guardian gets to her feet.

"Oh, bless you! That man is evil and his plans for these children are just as bad."

"Gather your things. We won't be coming back, and anything you can't carry will be replaced," Xavier tells the group of children, who amazingly don't argue, just follow orders like good little soldiers. My soul weeps for them.

"Why should we go with you?" the boy demands, and I have to admire his stubbornness.

"Because your parents are already on our ship, and we are going to make sure you can be together again and be children, not soldiers," I state plainly.

"We're going to sea?" one of the other boys asks, his eyes lighting up with excitement. "I've never seen the ocean."

I wince. "Actually, when I said ship, I meant spaceship."

His lips purse, and his eyes bug out. "We're going to space? Oh, I've never done that either." He starts to shove things into his backpack quicker, and I stifle a smile.

"Chloe?" Brannock calls as he studies each of the female children. "Where's Chloe?" he demands harshly, and his form starts to flicker again.

Both Xavier and I put a hand on him and push calming vibes into him.

"Chloe? What do you want with her?" The head boy crosses his arms and widens his feet, his body tense with aggression.

"Easy, son, this is Chloe's father. He's been looking for her," Tirrian tells the boy, and this time, he doesn't stay calm, his eyes widening too.

"Her dad? She said you would come and you would rescue us all. She's in with her foster parents.

They just had a baby, and Smith promised if she behaved, she could spend some time with them for a few days. That should be in the last cell block before here." He gives up the information and starts to pack his own bag. Obviously, he trusts Chloe and Brannock by association.

I heave out a sigh of relief. This has been a lot easier than I anticipated. Thank goodness we didn't need the sedatives.

"Once you are packed, can you help with the little ones?" I ask, and the children are quick to agree.

"How have they all stayed so well natured?" I muse, and their guardian hears me.

"I'm Francine. Smith didn't have a lot to do with them day to day. It was mostly me and the other two ladies. He would come in once a month and spout off propaganda, which basically went over most of their heads, so we raised them normally, schooling them and letting them be kids before he could turn them into super soldiers. We wanted to instill some kindness and good morals into them."

"Well, you have done an admirable job." I squeeze her hand.

"What's going to happen to us now?" she whispers.

"Don't worry, we will protect you. We can arrange for you to start new lives anywhere in the world or you can come with us if you want. If you decide to stay on Earth, you will need to have the fact that aliens exist locked in your mind. It won't hurt you, you just won't be able to talk about them."

"I've always wanted to move to Australia, and that's fine, I understand why." She goes back to her packing.

Finally, we have all the children organized, and we herd them through the complex. Xavier, Tirrian, and Saxon go with them, while Brannock and I stop at the final breeding block to release all of these captives.

CHAPTER THIRTY-ONE

Brannock

Lila and I open all the doors in this block, and when the doors open, I can't wait any longer.

"Chloe," I call, my voice husky with emotions.

"Daddy?" a small voice replies hesitantly.

I spin around to where the voice came from. "Chloe?" I ask, clenching my hands into fists in an attempt not to rip the door off the hinges and barge into the room. I don't want to scare the people the boy called her foster parents. What is with that?

"Daddy?" My daughter appears in the doorway, flanked by a man and woman. The woman has a baby in her arms, and the man has a hand on Chloe's shoulder. A growl rips out of my lips before I can stop it, and my spines bristle aggressively. "Daddy, it is you! I knew you would come."

She throws herself at me, and I pick her up and

swing her around. She's in her human glamour. Her dark hair is in two braids, and her crystal blue eyes sparkle with happiness. Her plump cheeks are round, and I can feel through her clothes she has been well looked after.

"Oh, my baby. I promised you I would."

I stop swinging her and hold her in my arms, just looking at my baby girl. She looks older in the few months we've been separated, and I feel a violent need to kill Relgrael again. Thankfully, Aaz'axian children age at a normal rate and she's not suddenly a teenager. I'm not sure I would be able to handle that.

She puts her palms on my cheeks. "What took you so long?"

"See the pretty lady over there?" I nod at Lila. Chloe's eyes shift to her, and she smiles.

"She has pretty hair," she whispers.

"That's Lila, and she's going to be your mom. Her grandpas own a circus, and we are all going to go live with them, but they needed help first, so that's why I took so long," I tell her solemnly.

"Did you say circus?" the man from Chloe's room snaps, and I turn my attention to him.

"Yes, the Galaxy Circus," I tell him. He's obviously heard of it.

"Oh my god." The woman next to him sways, and he wraps an arm around her shoulders and pulls her closer as she mutters something.

I study her, and my eyes widen in shock. "Holy shit," I mutter, and Chloe slaps a hand over my mouth.

"You need to put a dollar in the swear jar, Daddy," she says.

I'm not paying attention to her though. Instead, I'm watching her foster parents who are staring at Lila like she hung the sun.

"Liliana?" the man says, and Lila turns to him

"I go by Lila. Liliana is my grandma," she says, but her words trail off and her golden skin pales like she's seen a ghost.

"Dad? Mom?" she asks hesitantly. "You aren't dead."

Lila's mom, Alina, gasps as tears stream down her face. "Oh my god, you're alive."

"Look at our baby, all grown up," Lila's dad, Marcus, mutters, sounding just as shocked as both females.

The three of them move toward one another almost in unison. They collide in a clash of limbs, and I hear a wail as the baby in the woman's arms starts to cry. They all freeze and look down at the infant.

"You have a baby?" Lila murmurs and runs a finger over the small being's cheek. It's maybe four months old, slightly bigger and chubbier than a newborn.

"This is your brother, Bastien," Alina tells her.

Lila sobs, and tears stream down her face as she stares down at the little boy in awe.

"Why are they crying?" Chloe asks me, dragging my attention back to her.

"That's Lila's mommy and daddy, and they have

been apart way longer than you and I were," I tell her, and she frowns.

"That's so sad, but they should be happy, not crying," she says, watching them.

"When your emotions are too big for your own body, sometimes crying is the only way to let them out," I remind her, and she nods.

"I was so sad when I first came here, and I couldn't stop crying. That's why they let me live with Marcus and Alina. They would give me cuddles and make me feel so much better," she explains, and even if these two weren't my wife's parents, I would never be able to thank them enough for what they did for my girl.

"What's going on?" Xavier approaches from behind. "Lila's emotions are all over the place." I step to the side so he can see what's going on.

"Fuck me," he mutters, his eyes going wide. "Is that Alina and Marcus?"

"You need to put a dollar in the swear jar," Chloe says pertly, and he turns his attention to her and grins. It's that grin that no one can resist. I see her disapproval soften, and she smiles back at him.

"I will make sure we have one at home. God knows your new mommy is going to fill it in no time," he tells her, giving her a pinch on the cheek. "And aren't you a beauty. I'm Xavier, and you're going to come and live at our house. We have five more kiddos at home, but you're going to be the best big sister. Does that sound okay?"

"I'm already a big sister," she says, pointing to the

baby, "but I'm a good big sister, so I will look after the others as well," she promises and seems no worse for wear despite her ordeal.

Behind us, Tirrian and Saxon explain to all the others what is about to happen before shuffling them all through the complex to the transport.

Lila and her parents talk quietly, but she looks up and sees us watching. We're the only ones remaining, and we are just waiting for the three of them.

"Mom and Dad, I'd like you to meet two of my mates. This is Brannock, Chloe's dad, and you might remember Xavier from when we were smaller."

Alina gasps. "Xavier Colest?"

Xavier gives her a small wave. "Hey, Alina, it's nice to see you alive. My parents are going to be so pissed with themselves that they didn't search for you and trusted the police report."

"That's another dollar," Chloe sings, and I smother a grin.

"Two of your mates?" Marcus says slowly. "How many do you have?" He's frowning, and I chuckle, knowing his fatherly instinct is rearing its ugly head.

"Oh, ah, um... I mean, it's not that many, right? The other mimic I met had twenty," Lila stammers, and both of her parents gasp.

"You're a mimic?" Marcus asks, sounding awed.

"Yup, and I have whisperer powers," Lila tells them, and they stare at her with pride and amazement in their eyes.

Alina beams. "Our little girl is so freaking powerful!"

"Why doesn't she have to put a dollar in the swear jar?" I hear Xavier ask Chloe, who shakes her head stubbornly.

"Freaking isn't a swear word," she tells him.

"I noticed you didn't answer my question," Marcus prompts Lila, and she sighs.

"Twelve," she mumbles quietly.

Marcus frowns. "I'm sorry. I don't think I heard you correctly." He chuckles, looking at his wife. "I thought you said you had twelve mates, that would be ridiculous."

Alina isn't laughing, just looking at her husband with pity in her eyes.

"Nope, you heard right. Lila has twelve mates. Come on, there are a few more out in the main area. I'll introduce you, and we kind of want to blow this popsicle stand. The family lizard is going to torch it for us." Xavier waves his hand in the direction we need to go.

"Liliana," Marcus growls as Lila starts to move.

"I go by Lila now, Dad," she growls back, and Alina sighs. Xavier and I snicker like children, and our wife glares at us.

"Can we maybe do this later? I don't know about you, but twenty years in this hellhole is long enough. I don't want to wait until you have a man tantrum to get out," Alina scolds her husband.

I turn my head and hide my laughter in Chloe's

neck. She giggles. I like Lila's mom. She's feisty, just like Lila is. I can see where she gets it from.

"You're going to be in so much trouble," I mutter to Xavier as we leave the cell block behind. Chloe is tucked into my side, and I have no plans of letting her go anytime soon. She plays with my spikes and giggles, waving at the others behind us. "Lila's going to kick your ass."

"As long as it isn't Marcus. I remember what his Skarrian powers are, or one of them at least. He has the ability to throw lightning. I bet that shit hurts." He winces.

"Don't forget she can do the same thing in her cat form."

"Fuu... dge," he finishes, sneaking a side glance at Chloe.

When we arrive back to the first cell block, it's in chaos. Some of the children are reuniting with parents, and there are tears of joy. Musette and Mehira, along with Tirrian and Saxon, are trying to get them to leave.

In the medical facility, a woman is wailing. Zeydan's god form is gone, and he is wiping sweat from his sister's brow.

"Lila, I need you now," Link yells at her. "Celestian form. I have to do a cesarian. She can't give birth to this baby naturally. The spikes are preventing it."

"Chloe's mom wasn't able to either. Thankfully we had access to Savannah when it was time," I say, remembering that dark time and feeling sad. Hopefully Sanshia survives, though even if she doesn't, she will reincarnate, but then we won't be able to return her powers to her. Shit.

"Lila, she needs to live so we can deal with the orb," I remind her as she starts to strip off her clothes.

"I don't know how to do a cesarian," she says as her father snaps, "Lila, put your clothes back on now, there are children around."

She ignores him and changes into her Celestian form, wincing as her wings break through her skin. Xavier waves a hand and clothes her in one of their traditional gowns. She hurries over to the bed, her hands glowing with power.

Her dad just stammers as his wife rubs a soothing hand on his back, her baby cradled against her. I realize he's in some kind of sling.

"I'm doing the cesarian, I need you to heal her once I have the baby out," Link says, holding up a scalpel. Next to him, the midwife is waiting with a blanket to receive the baby.

I look around and find Ghosie leaning up against the wall, snoring peacefully. I move over to him. "Chloe, this is my friend Ghosie. He was very tired and needed a nap. Can you look after him for me while I help the others?"

She nods, sticking her thumb in her mouth as I put her down on the floor next to him. "Carebear," she mumbles around her thumb and climbs into his lap, making herself comfortable. "I'll watch him, Daddy."

Secure in the notion my daughter is safe, I hurry

over to the bed. "You know the baby isn't going to look like a human one, right?" I ask the midwife.

"Yes, it's fine. Some of my charges have alt forms. Sometimes I wonder if I'm raising children or a zoo," she jokes, and I step out of the way. I wouldn't want her to drop it in surprise.

"Can I do anything to help?" I ask Link, but before he can reply, Zeydan speaks to me.

"Put your glamour on please. I don't want Sanshia reliving her trauma." His tone is terse, but I'm not offended. I just wish I'd have thought about it myself. I change my form to the one I'm most comfortable in anyway after having lived with it for hundreds of years.

"Can you please just help the others clear the base out? We have it all handled, but I would like to move as soon as the baby is born. Sanshia needs more help than this base can give her," Link requests.

"Don't let her die, Lila. We need her to return her powers to her, and we don't have time to wait for years for her to reincarnate," Zeydan reminds her, and Lila's eyes widen with panic.

"Okay." She holds her hands up, at the ready.

"As soon as the baby is out, heal her," Link instructs. "She's hemorrhaging from the baby, and she really needs a blood transfusion, but I'm not sure if normal blood will be suitable."

"Tap me." Zeydan holds out his arm, and Link shakes his head.

"Not yet. I need you to talk to her and keep her

conscious. Brannock, send word to the ship that Aarin and Hurricane need to donate as much as they can."

I hurry over to the console Silac is still sitting at, and he presses a button. Susie appears on the screen, looking slightly harassed.

"What, Silac? We are a little busy."

"Susie, Link has asked for Aarin and Hurricane to donate some blood. We have their sister Sanshia here, and she's hemorrhaging. He's worried nondivine blood won't be suitable, and Zeydan is too busy keeping her conscious to donate."

Susie drops her annoyed look and gives a small nod. "I'll draw it myself."

"Tell Mark we are incoming with a malnourished female who has just given birth and will need blood transfusions, IV nutrients, and painkillers. Prepare a bed for her," Link calls across the room as his blade slides across Sanshia's stomach.

"Oh my god!" Alina blanches at the sight as Link then cuts through layers of muscle and fat to get to her uterus. He breaks it open and puts the scalpel down before reaching in for the baby.

He grimaces. "Get ready, Lila. The baby has made a mess of her insides. I hope it doesn't permanently scar her. Hopefully once she regains her full god power, it will all heal as it should," he says as he pulls out a perfectly formed Aaz'axian baby, complete with all their tiny little spikes and membranes.

Sanshia has fallen silent, and when I glance at her face, I think she might be unconscious.

"It's a girl," the midwife announces as she takes the baby and rubs it all over, cleaning off the blood, and the baby starts to wail.

"A girl?" Sanshia mutters, opening her eyes slightly to take a peek.

"Do you want to hold her?" the midwife asks the goddess, but she turns her head away and closes her eyes again. A wave of sorrow hits me, but I don't blame the goddess.

Lila is busy healing Sanshia, her powers glowing bright white as they work to mend her broken body. First, the internal organs, and then each layer of muscle, fat, and skin until she is whole once more.

Lila is panting by the time she is done, and she stumbles as she steps back. I leap forward to support her.

"Good job," I whisper and give her a kiss on the cheek.

"We need to move," Link says, pulling his gloves off. "Zeydan, you get that end of the bed, I'll take this one."

They don't stick around, hurrying the gurney down the corridor to the transporter.

CHAPTER THIRTY-TWO

Lila

"What about the baby?" Melissa holds up the squealing infant.

"Pass her to me," Brannock offers and takes her from the woman. He looks down at the precious girl with awe. "It's hard to believe that not twelve months ago, I considered this baby's father one of my best friends. It's bittersweet to hold her while his remains are splattered in the other room because of me."

"Don't feel guilty. He deserved it," I assure him, and he shakes his head.

"Oh, I don't feel guilty. I'm just sad that she will probably suffer because of the kind of man he was," Brannock remarks, alluding to the fact that Sanshia couldn't even look at her.

"Don't worry, there are plenty of us to love her, and it probably isn't a bad thing if we take her in. You can teach her all she needs to know like you did with Chloe." I lean in to have a look at the bundle in his arms. "She's super cute," I tell him, running a finger over one of the spines sticking out from her shoulder blades, wondering if our baby will be as cute one day.

"Do you think Nikos could feed her as well as the twins?" he asks, jiggling the bundle in his arms when she starts to fuss.

"I'm sure he won't mind. We'll ask him."

"Ask him?" Marcus and Alina join us. "Who are you talking about?" My dad is all kinds of confused, and it's really not a surprise. He's been trapped in this basement building for a long time, so he's probably forgotten about a lot of the species in the galaxy.

"One of my mates is Aquilian," I tell him, bracing for the blowup. He isn't coping well with all this news, but Mom's eyes light up with knowing.

"And he has children?" she asks, obviously familiar with the possibility of Aquilian males having babies.

"Yes. He and I have two, and we have three more with another of my mates."

My parents exchange a surprised glance.

"You have five children?" Dad stammers, and I can feel Brannock's sympathy for him, but I'm not so kind.

"Congrats, you're a grandpa," I announce, giggling as he turns pale.

"I'm too young to be a grandpa," he mutters, and Mom just laughs.

"Especially since it seems like they may be the same age as your son. I am also willing to take the little one.

I'm still breastfeeding Bastien, and they can grow up together."

"Thank you for the offer. I'm not sure if your nipples would be able to cope with her teeth," Brannock tells my mom, using a finger to show us that she has a row of teeth, unlike a gummy human baby, and her eyes widen comically before she winces.

"Ah, yes, I hadn't considered that."

"Nikos is used to it. The merbabies have them too," I tell her, but I know the truth—Brannock is already attached, and if her mother doesn't want her, I'm pretty sure our family just grew by one more. I definitely need another nanny now, possibly two.

"Okay, I'm done," Silac declares, standing up. "Tirrian can torch the place now."

"Xavier, can you do your thing and make sure no one is left behind?" Saxon approaches and pulls me into his arms, giving me a kiss. It's funny to watch Dad's eyes bulge out of his head.

"I know you! You're General Saxon of the Vilaxian army. We met at a diplomatic dinner your aunt hosted for the circus when we were on Vilax one year."

"I remember. It's nice to see you again, sir." Saxon inclines his head politely.

"He's older than I am!" Dad explodes, stabbing a finger in Saxon's direction. "And he's one of your mates?"

"Oh dear..." Mom sighs, and I roll my eyes.

"I think my dad's brain just exploded. Someone sedate him until we can get on the ship, otherwise this is going to take forever," I suggest, patting Saxon's armor for another tranq.

Dad gasps and looks at me with hurt, but I don't care. If he's going to be a drama queen, I'll treat him like one. "Lila, that's not how you speak about your father," he scolds.

"It's not a terrible idea," Mom muses, and he turns his attention to her, looking hurt.

"Here, sir, can you hold the child? I need to grab Chloe and Ghosie." I watch with awe as Brannock hands my father the child, effectively distracting him from his man meltdown. I am so giving him a blowjob when we get back to the ship. I blow him a kiss, and Mom gives him a thumbs-up.

"He's a keeper," she murmurs to me as she jiggles my brother in her arms. Holy shit, a brother. I still can't believe it. He's uncle to my kids, and he's the same age as them.

"What about us?" a voice behind us asks, and we find the four human staff members who are still alive waiting. The guard and the female scientist are not around, but I'm assuming they are either not breathing or are in cells back on the ship, waiting for us to question them.

"You are free to go, or you can come with us, and we can relocate you." Xavier returns from doing his mist check of the facility. "Apart from us, there are no life-forms in the building, though I did find an interesting room filled with more cyborg sex warriors."

"We all want to go, even if it's just so we can see

what a spaceship looks like," Matthew replies, speaking for the four of them. He sounds giddy, and I can't blame them.

"Okay, well, get moving. Head in the direction they went with the gurney. Is there anything you can't live without? It isn't going to survive the next half hour," I tell them, and they shake their heads and move in that direction. They all have backpacks, so they must have packed their own stuff earlier when the kids did."

"Guys, can you show Mom and Dad the way?" I frown at Ghosie, who's still unconscious in the corner. "Do you think he will wake up if I heal him? He's too big for us to move." Chloe is sitting on his lap, singing to him and braiding his fur. It's so cute, but I don't want him to scare her if he wakes up.

"Nonsense, I've got this." Xavier waves a hand, and purple magic wraps around them, and Ghosie levitates in the air. Chloe startles and looks around, but then she giggles and claps her hands as Ghosie turns into a flying carpet.

"Look at me, Daddy!" she cries.

"Let's go. We will see you back at the ship, love." Saxon gives me a kiss and steps away, and I nod. Silac, Brannock, and Xavier also give me kisses as Tirrian steps up next to me and grabs my hand.

"One, two, three, four, five?" my father mutters.

"Don't forget the bear. He hulked out on us earlier and needed a nap," Xavier tells him, and I'm just about ready to hulk out on him myself.

"Why aren't you coming?" Mom asks, ignoring her husband.

"I'm going to give Tirrian a hand in burning this place to the ground," I tell her, excited to let my dragon out of my skin.

"How are you going to do that? C4?" Dad asks, and Tirrian and I exchange a glance.

"Nope, dragon," I tell him, and he gapes at the two of us.

"Dragon shifter?" He looks at my mate who started wearing his human form around the kids because they wanted to touch his wings.

"Yeah." Tirrian drops the glamour, and wings burst out of his back through the slits in his armor. I don't know why I didn't get a pair that has wing slit holes. It would have made things a lot easier than stripping every time. It was poor planning on everyone's behalf, but then I still needed to strip for my carevasta form anyway. Le sigh.

"We met the dragon royal couple one year when they came to the circus. Lovely people," my mom muses, and Tirrian smiles.

"I'm sure Mom and Dad will be happy to hear that."

"More royalty!" she exclaims, looking at me, and I wince.

"You have no idea," I mutter, and Saxon and Xavier distract my parents, telling them they need to go. They disappear, and only Brannock remains.

"Give us fifteen minutes, and then you can torch

the place. Radio the ship when you are ready to return and hit the locator beacon."

He points to the button on Tirrian's armor. "Yes, Dad," Tirrian teases. "Now go give your daughter more cuddles if you can tear her away from the teddy."

Brannock gives me another kiss and leaves, and suddenly, the room is silent and blissfully peaceful. I rub my temples, my head throbbing with the combination of stress and emotions. I wonder if I can heal myself. I try to activate my powers, but they don't work, damn it.

"How are you doing?" Tirrian asks, scrutinizing me carefully.

"It's been a lot," I reply wearily, and he scoffs.

"That is a slight understatement."

I head toward one of the open doors and peer into the cell the breeders were in. It's better than I expected. It's set up like a studio apartment. There is a bed and a small living space with a food preparation area and a door on the back wall, which I'm assuming leads to a bathroom.

"Wow, they really were encouraging them to play happy family."

"Matthew said they would rotate people if they ended up not being compatible or attracted to the person they were with," he tells me, leaning against the doorframe.

"Well, some of them must have been. There are twenty-five kids who prove they had some success."

"Talking of success, how do you feel about your

little brother?" he asks cautiously as I continue to poke around, grimacing when I notice cameras in the corners of the rooms.

"I wonder if they got to be themselves. You know, let their inner alien out occasionally, or if they were completely trapped. I'm surprised none of them didn't go mad."

"We don't know that they didn't, that's why the Celestians are assessing them before letting them out in the wild. We don't want to release unstable predators into the galaxy."

I put the books I had been using to distract myself down and turn to face my mate.

"I'm happy, of course, but also pretty devastated that he came into the world in these kinds of circumstances."

"Your parents look fairly attached to him," he says as I move out of the room, brushing past him on the way. I guess he must be thinking of Sanshia's reaction to her baby.

"Yeah, they did, but they obviously had a solid relationship before they got stuck in here. Thank goodness that stayed strong and didn't break."

"Your dad seems to be struggling to adjust to having an adult daughter." Tirrian follows behind me as I move through the facility, heading toward the children's quarters again.

"Yeah, it must be a bit of a shock. I was about four when they died. They only have memories of me at that age. It's going to be a big adjustment for us, but I can't wait." I gasp and whirl to face my dragon.

"My grandparents! They are going to be so happy. Not only did they get their wife back, but now they will have their long-lost son and daughter-in-law with a bonus grandson. Oh, and Bubby. He's going to be pissed he missed this."

We didn't tell Bubby of our suspicions about Lester. He's probably sitting pretty in the circus pod, thinking everything is normal.

"Okay, how about we get these fireworks on the road? I don't know about you, but a nice flight through the dark Nevada desert might be just what we need to distract us from all this." Tirrian waves his hand around, and I sigh.

"Sounds freaking perfect." I throw my arms around his waist and give him a hug. "Let's hope they don't pick us up on the Area 51 radar."

He laughs and gives me a kiss. "That's just keeping them on their toes. I'm sure there hasn't been a credible UFO sighting in years."

"They are called UAP now, thank you very much, and lord knows we are pretty damn phenomenal."

I remove the dress Xavier conjured, and Tirrian's eyes narrow with lust, and he takes a step closer.

"Easy, tiger, we have a hidden facility to destroy. If you keep it in your pants now, maybe before we hit the handy-dandy button, we can fool around a little." I pluck the button off his armor. I left mine in my armor in the other room and won't be able to grab it once I'm in dragon form, but at least we have one. Now how am I going to carry it? I remember one of the tricks Xavier taught me with warlock power.

I wave my hand, making a couple of gestures, and when I feel the interdimensional pocket form, I tuck the button into it, ready for when we finish flying. Tirrian's eyebrows jump.

"That's pretty damn handy," he tells me, sounding impressed. "Can you put these in there too? They are my favorite." He hands me two swords that he pulls from the scabbards on his back. I saw him wielding them before, and he was fierce. He then proceeds to strip off the rest of his weapons—knives, guns, and grenades—handing them to me. I roll my eyes but put them all in the hiding space, ready to retrieve at a later time.

Finally, he's done, and he pulls off his armor and stands naked in front of me. "Well, I mean, I guess we have a few moments," I say and step closer, running my hands over his body.

"Yes, absolutely. We can be quick," he assures me and pulls me against him, his rapidly hardening cock pushing against my front as he takes my mouth with his.

It's been a stressful day, so sue me for wanting to take a little stress relief.

CHAPTER THIRTY-THREE

Maxsim

The ship is complete chaos when we return in the evening. Lila and the rest of the guys beamed down to Earth and raided Smith's facility, and the med bay and the overflow med bay are full of rescued aliens.

None of them are lightning cats, thankfully. Earth is too warm for any of them to reside there, not to mention without a glamour charm, we can't pass as an Earthling, but there are plenty of people in need. They all look slightly shell-shocked, and we do our best to comfort them, but it isn't easy. We aren't equipped for this many captives.

The Celestian ship is on its way, and Mark says they are about an hour out and are fully equipped to handle the influx of refugees. We thought maybe there were a few alien captives, but there are almost a hundred beings here. How did they all slip under the radar, and how did Smith get away with keeping them captive?

I was discussing it with Caspian and Nikos. Once the aliens arrive on Earth, they became their responsibility, and the circus never once checked in with them unless they requested assistance. Once upon a time, there was an off-worlder as a liaison, but they all went by the wayside when Lila's parents were killed. They were the last liaisons, and the Adams brothers never replaced them, trusting Smith to police the aliens, but that was a big mistake.

"How did he get away with this for so long? How didn't anyone pick up that he was such a cretin?"

There's a signal to say another group is ready to beam aboard. I've been controlling the transporter room because there isn't much else I can do, and we are still trying to keep the ship's crew as in the dark as possible. None of them have ventured to these two floors since the circus pod departed and Lila discovered that Lester is a traitor. She locked access just in case there are more traitors. She will unlock it in the morning when all of the captives have transferred to the next ship. It's just lucky the med bay, transporter room, and hologram deck are all on the floor below the bridge. She told everyone it was for family privacy in the evenings, and they all accepted that excuse just fine.

The second lot of refugees that beamed had children spread between them. They all stared at me with awe as they were shuffled out of the transporter room. When we returned, we brought Titus, Thorn, Nixie,

Hurricane, and his two sisters back as well as Saxon's two cousins.

We need the help, and we trust all of them because they are family and new to the circus. Mehira and Musette went down to the facility to assist, and the rest stayed here to help with the influx.

Echo remains safely on the deck above with the children, Kinga, and Andre. I know he wants to come down and help, but I won't risk him. I think we're going to need Magenta and Vanity, but I'm not sure Vanity is stable enough yet after bonding to risk it. Better off leaving them there for now.

The transporter hums, letting me know there is another incoming transport. I check the security ID. Huh, that's Captain Potter's ID. Why is he coming back to the ship?

I hit the button to approve the transport, and it fires up. Within moments, Broderick appears on the platform with a thunderous look on his face.

"What's going on?" he demands, striding off the platform and approaching me. I consider growling at him, but I know this anger comes from fear and not knowing. "Imagine my surprise when I go to find Lila or one of her mates to ask a question about the concession hiring, and I couldn't find any of them. Someone informed me that they were returning to the ship in the evening to be with their children. Okay, fine, understandable, but then one of the trapeze riggers asks me if I could find any of the new fliers, since they had some tech question, and when I sent out a pod-wide call, there was no response from any of them. I sent a message to Malik and Titus, wondering if they knew where any one was and didn't get a response, but then I remember Nixie is back, and I went in search of her, and she was nowhere to be found, and neither was her mate or his sisters. Something is definitely fishy."

I snort at his unintended pun, and he glares at me. "So, kitty cat, I want to know what happened."

Before I can answer, the transporter hums again, and the incoming ID code shows Link's name. I hit the button to approve the transport. Susie messaged me, saying that he was bringing an incoming trauma and to be on standby.

"Get out of the way, Rick. This one is coming in hot, and it needs to get to the med bay," I tell him, and his lips round in shock, but he's quick to obey. The transporter activates, and Link appears on the platform, along with Zeydan, a medical gurney, and an unconscious woman.

"We need to hurry. Lila healed her internal organs, but she still lost a lot of blood, and she's underweight like she hadn't been looking after herself. Whether she couldn't keep anything down because of the baby or they were starving her, we won't know until we can speak to her," he tells Zeydan, then he notices Rick and me.

"Oh, good. Can you two walk ahead and clear the halls? We can't afford to be delayed," he asks us with a tone that isn't going to accept a no.

We do as he asks and escort them to the med bay,

but Rick is not happy. "What in the blue blazes is going on, and why wasn't I read in? Where is Lester? Why isn't he helping with all of this?"

We pass a group of refugees who are waiting outside the holo deck to be assigned a bed and assessed. They all move out of the way. Some of them mutter words of sympathy to the woman on the bed as we go past, while all of them look concerned.

"We have a lot to tell you," I explain. "Lester was one of the moles inside the circus. He was also assisting illegal aliens on and off the planet by masking ship signatures on our radars when they would use the shadow of the galaxy ship to hide their presence. They were able to transport on and off without going through the proper circus channels. It's also one of the reasons so many of these captives were able to be taken without anyone knowing, because they weren't on Earth through legal channels, so nobody knew they were missing."

His mouth drops open, and he is stunned into silence as we arrive at the med center and the woman is wheeled into the bay. Susie and Mark jump into action, placing IVs in both arms. One is a blood transfusion, direct from Nixie's mate Hurricane, and the other one is a clear bag of fluids. Link grabs a syringe of something and injects it into the bag of liquids. The woman in the bed doesn't move the whole time as Susie hooks her up to monitors.

"Where did you find her? Why is she like this?"

Hurricane demands from Zeydan, staring at the woman with a scary kind of fury.

"She was one of Smith's breeders. Seeing me triggered her labor, and the pregnancy was not an easy one, nor was the birth because the baby was not compatible with her body."

"What the hell kind of baby did she have?" Susie exclaims as she gives the woman a sponge bath. Both Rick and I stand back, but we want to hear what happened.

"She had an Aaz'axian baby, and it wasn't through a consensual arrangement," Zeydan explains, running a hand over his head. His long, white hair is in disarray, and his foxlike ears twitch in irritation.

"Brannock?" Aarin, who is sitting in a chair also donating blood, asks.

"God no," Link denies, shaking his head. "He would never do that to a woman."

"No, he wouldn't, and he actually got revenge for her when he eviscerated the one who did do it. He was the same one who turned him and Chloe in. Karma bit him on the ass, and he was a breeding captive too, but they wouldn't let him breed many of the women because he ripped them apart on release. Only Sanshia survived because of her power to regenerate, and I think possibly a Skarrian woman who helped us, but because they need to be bonded to conceive, it never took," Zeydan says, taking a seat.

"Oh my god," Rick whispers in horror.

"Okay, we're giving her fluids and a painkiller. The

blood transfusion will help, but she's probably going to need another bag." Link looks at the bag of blood, which is almost empty.

"Take some of my blood too. If you don't need it, Lila or Saxon can have it," he tells Susie, who quickly sets him up.

"You better get back to the transporter, Max. They were just about finished and will be returning. Lila and Tirrian are going to remain behind and torch the facility." Link rubs his eyes and watches the monitors carefully, nodding at what he sees.

"Isn't that going to alert the rest of the facility that there was a secret level?" Rick points out, and Zeydan shakes his head.

"No, it's completely sealed off from the other level. No one should be any wiser, and they will close the tunnels after they are done, but even if anyone does discover it, Silac wiped the computers, and nothing will survive Lila's and Tirrian's fire."

"Her heart rate is stabilizing, and her blood pressure is slowly getting better. Hopefully she is out of the woods physically. Now we just need to worry about her mental state." Link turns to study his monitors and nods, looking pleased.

"We need her to be okay. She needs to take her powers from the orb," Zeydan says quietly. There are one or two other refugees here getting treatment, and they all seem to be sleeping, but you can't be too careful.

"I'm sure Tabbris will see her before the ship leaves

if you ask her to. She may want the memories removed permanently from her mind, and Xavier can do that for her or, if not him, then his parents, but that means the little girl will need a family to raise her," Link assures him, putting a hand on his shoulder and giving it a squeeze.

"She didn't want her child?" I ask, feeling sympathy for both the woman and child.

"Sometimes women who have conceived through rape don't want the baby. It is understandable, but it isn't the baby's fault, and we want it to grow up without being subjected to hate from its mother," Susie explains, and I nod my understanding.

"Echo and I will take it," I offer, feeling such overwhelming sorrow for both parties. "We would be honored to give it a home. Nobody should ever feel unwanted." I know that Echo sometimes feels like this —not from his family, since they loved him with all their heart, but because of the general consensus for male omegas that Mazlan perpetuated. My mother is working hard to banish that stupid idea, but it is a work in progress.

"Thank you, Maxsim." Link nods at me. "I think Brannock has already suggested that Nikos could feed her because he is feeding Hali and Ty and is used to babies with teeth." His gaze slides to Rick, and he winces. I don't think anyone would notice, but I was paying sharp attention to the pretty cyborg whom Echo wants to join us in bed. He is an admirable and capable man whom I would be happy to share my omega's heat with, not to mention attractive. "There was another woman there who was feeding an infant, and she offered, but she is Skarrian and not used to infants with teeth."

"Is this the same woman who was raped?" Rick sounds furious, and Link shakes his head. "So there are two Skarrians? Two illegal Skarrians?"

"Actually, both of those women were known to the circus, but it was unknown that they had disappeared off the radar for reasons you will understand. Head back to the transporter room and wait for them. I think you may know one of them, Rick," Link says mysteriously, and I want to question him, but he gives me a small shake of his head. Rick takes off, not wanting to ask any more questions.

"Go with him, he may need some support," Link says. "Lila found her parents. They aren't dead."

Susie gasps, dropping the tray of tools she was moving, and they clatter to the ground. "Her parents are alive? Oh my god, were they tortured too?" she asks as Mark hurries over to help her.

"Poor Lila," he says, waiting for Link to answer.

"I don't know if they were tortured. They looked healthy enough, but I know they were forced to try to breed with other captives."

"Forced?" Aarin asks, his eyes not leaving his sister. "How does one force someone to breed?"

Is he really that naive? We all look at him with speculation, and he waves his free hand. "I mean, I know there are ways, drugs and all, but would human drugs work on any of us?"

"Apparently yes. Something called GHB. All the captives had a low tolerance for it, and they used it regularly," Link says flatly. "Go, Maxsim. Broderick and Marcus were best friends, and I think Rick was courting Alina when they died. I'm not sure he's going to take this well. He will blame himself. Xavier thinks his parents are going to do the same. Smith is a dead man walking."

I hurry after Rick, my mind swirling with this new information. Lila's parents are alive. She must be so happy but also completely devastated. They have been gone twenty years, which means Smith has had them for that long. I can't stop the growl that rumbles from my chest in one continuous long sound. People in the corridor see me coming and get out of the way, the smell of their terror tainting the air around them.

When I get to the transporter room, it's already humming. I stand next to Rick and wait for the incoming travelers. The screen shows Xavier's ID. When they materialize, he gives us a jaunty wave, but his eyes are weary and strained.

He, Saxon, Silac, and Brannock are standing in front. Brannock has a baby cradled in his arms, and I clench my hands as the urge to grab it takes hold of me. Wow, that's an interesting reaction. Until Lila had the krakens, I was indifferent to babies. I knew Echo wanted them, but it wasn't a priority for me. It was all about keeping him safe. Things have certainly changed, though, and I am just about as crazy about our children as he is. The thought that this little one is going to miss out on her mother's love because she was created in such a horrible way hurts my soul. It's better for her to be raised by us, people who can love her unconditionally, and it's not like one more is going to make a difference at this stage.

"I'm just going to show the humans to the holo deck. We can get them settled, and they can decide what they want to do. I may need Matthew's help going through all that data." Silac steps down from the platform and waves a hand. Four wide-eyed humans follow after him, one male and three females. Their eyes get even wider when they catch sight of me.

"Whoa, what are you?" the male asks boldly, and one of the women smacks him on the arm.

"Matthew, that's so rude," she hisses. "Please excuse my husband. We haven't seen one of your species before, and his scientist mouth talks before his brain can stop it."

"I understand, I am not offended," I reply, and Xavier chuckles.

"Wow, Maxsim, that is showing real growth. I am so proud of you," he teases, and I flip him off, very much liking the Earth gesture.

"Fascinating," Matthew mumbles, and his wife just huffs and tugs his arm as they follow Silac, the two other women hurrying to keep up.

"Hey, so is there a spare bed in the med bay? Ghosie needs to take a load off." Xavier waves a hand behind him. The three of them part, and there's the bear, flat on his back, levitating above the ground with a small child sitting on his chest, combing a finger through the fur on one of his arms and singing about a whole new world. Behind him are a man and a woman who has a baby cradled against her chest in a sort of sling contraption.

"Holy fuck," Rick mutters. "Marcus? Alina?" He sounds like he's been hit over the head with an ice axe.

I look at the couple again, and my eyes widen when I get a better look at the woman. She could be Lila's slightly older sister. These must be her parents. My heart double thumps with happiness for my mate as the couple turns their attention to Rick, and their faces light up. They push past the sleeping bear and the rest of Lila's mates and hurry off the platform at the same time Rick moves.

The three of them collide. There are tears, laughter, and mumbled words, and then Rick bends down, pulls Alina toward him, and kisses her hard before grabbing Marcus with his spare arm, tugging him closer, and switching to kissing him.

"Oh, I did not see that coming," Xavier mutters to Saxon. "Good for Rick."

"How long will Lila be?" I ask, turning my attention away from her parents and to my co-mates. I know she's staying behind to do what needs to be done, but I am impatient to see her.

The three of them step down from the platform, Ghosie's body and the little girl floating behind.

"Probably at least an hour. I think Tirrian muttered something about taking her for a flight before returning," Saxon answers.

"And they will probably fu..." Xavier breaks off, looking down at the small child before continuing. "Do that thing that Lila's animals all like to do so much."

"She had to change forms quite a few times, and she healed Sanshia, which looked like it was a lot of work. She's probably down on power, so I agree with X." Brannock stops in front of me, and I get a look at the adorable little baby.

"Hey, little one," I coo, running my finger over the baby's cheek and admiring her little spines.

"It's a girl," he tells me.

"Does she have a name?" I ask, and he shakes his head.

"Not yet. We're not sure if Sanshia wants to name her or not."

"Well, she's still unconscious, but Link has her hooked up to a lot of things, so I'm sure she will come around in time," I tell them.

"Doesn't mean she will want to name the baby," Saxon says. "How about I show Lila's parents to a room, and you can take the little one down for Link to check over?"

"I know where our room is on the ship." Marcus must have heard us, and he breaks apart from a scene that was really too intimate for us to be witnessing.

"Ah, yeah, no." Rick runs a hand through his hair

but leaves one arm wrapped around Alina who has tears streaking her face. "The ship has gone through an extensive remodel. Your suite became Lila's when she joined us and, well, it takes up the entire top deck."

Marcus frowns. "Where are my fathers? Their suite was up there too." Marcus doesn't know that his mother has been found either, but that isn't something I plan on telling him. I'll leave it to Rick, but Rick grimaces and turns to us with pleading eyes.

"Pussy," Xavier coughs.

"Your parents are back on Skarr. They have decided to retire and handed the circus over to Lila," Saxon explains.

"Retire? My dads?" Marcus sounds shocked, and Rick clears his throat.

"Yeah. They recently reunited with your mother, and they are trying to make up for lost time."

"My mother?" Marcus repeats, his voice breaking. "She isn't dead?"

"Nope. Turns out that's happening a lot recently." Xavier chuckles, and Rick glares at him.

"They still have a suite, but it's on this level now. I can show you to it if you want," I offer, but Rick shakes his head.

"They can come to mine. It's just down the hall a little ways. We can get some food and talk. I'll tell you everything that's happened." He turns his attention to me. "Does your nursery have a spare crib we can use?"

I nod. "Yes. We have two for Echo's babies, but we have no need for them for now. You can have one, and we will use the other for this little one." I point to the babe in Brannock's arms. "I'll have it brought to you in a little while," I assure him.

"Thank you." Lila's mom smiles gently at me with curious eyes. "Are you one of Lila's mates?" she asks, and I nod, smiling at her.

"I am. I am Maxsim."

"It is lovely to meet you," she replies, but Lila's father grumbles, "Twelve mates, Rick. How could you let that happen?"

Rick and the rest of us laugh. "You don't know your daughter if you think any of us let her do anything," he replies, and Marcus scowls.

"No, I really don't, but that's not my fault."

We fall into an awkward silence.

"Way to kill the mood." Alina smacks her husband's arm. "Ignore him. He must be getting space sickness, though he was grumpy before we got here, so it might just be him. Come on, Rick. Bastien is getting heavy, and my back could use a break." Just like that, she breaks the tension. Rick hurries them off without a backward glance, leaving us alone.

"Well, I guess we should get the cribs. Lila and Tirrian won't be back for a while. I don't know about you, but I could use a drink." Xavier waves his hand, and the floating Ghosie starts to move. "We will drop him off, and then I bet Chloe would like to meet her brothers and sisters." Xavier looks down at the little girl, but she's ignoring him and staring at me with wide eyes.

"Kitty!" she shouts and lifts her arms like she wants me to pick her up. I look at Brannock to make sure he's okay with this, and he gives me a smile.

"Please do, she won't stop nagging until you do. She always wanted a cat, and now she has two very big cuddly ones."

I pick the girl up in my arms. She is wearing her human form, and she pokes a finger at one of my ears before using both hands to lift my top lip and look at my mouth. "Big fangs. Can you go roar?" she asks, and I feel my heart melt.

I give a small roar, and she laughs and claps her hands before sticking her thumb in her mouth and resting her head against me. I start to purr as we walk toward the med bay to drop off the bear.

"And another one bites the dust," Xavier comments behind me. "She'll have us all wrapped around her little finger before Lila even returns."

CHAPTER THIRTY-FOUR

Lila

When Tirrian and I return to the ship, the Celestians have arrived, and Smith's alien breeding captives are in the process of being transferred to their ship. All of them thank us for saving them as they pass us. I'm so happy to see children reunited with at least one parent, if not both.

I stick my head into the med bay and find Sanshia there being monitored by Mark. Aarin, Hurricane, and Zeydan are all piled into chairs surrounding her bed. They look weary, but the three of them glow with their special power—green for Zeydan, blue for Hurricane, and white for Aarin—the radiance surrounding their sister. I'm sure it's probably some kind of healing.

I scan the room and find Link farther down, standing over Ghosie. I tiptoe past the gods and sidle up next to my cyborg, giving him a kiss on the cheek.

He gives me a weary smile, and I see bags under his eyes. He really needs to rest. I can't remember the last time he did. Maybe when we were on Vilax.

"How is he?" I whisper, looking at my bear who is still in his hulked out form.

"My scans show he's fine. The sedative is starting to wear off, but it may be another hour or two. That was a Viggy size dose because we weren't sure what would stop Brannock in berserker form."

"Well, it stopped a bear in hulked out form too," I tease. "I'm heading home. I'm exhausted. Make sure you get some rest. We're going to need it. I want to put plan B into action once we've all had a little sleep."

"I will once Ghosie wakes up. If it's much longer, I'll give him a reversal, but I'm reluctant to do that in case he stays hulked out with the adrenaline boost."

I say goodbye to him and go on my way. I stick my head in the holo deck to make sure that none of the captives are left behind and find Susie, Magenta, Vanity, and Nixie as well as the four humans whose lives we decided to spare. None of them have a wicked bone in their bodies, and while Matthew is curious, he isn't malicious. The women only care about the health and well-being of the children. I actually have an idea on what to do with them, but first, I need to figure out why the atmosphere is so tense.

I wonder if maybe they were having some kind of argument, but then I spot a young boy behind them. It's the boy who stood up to us when we first found them.

"What's going on?" I ask, entering the room, Tirrian trailing behind me. He waited while I went into the med bay, not wanting to disturb any of the patients.

"Oh, Lila, thank God." Susie is wringing her hands. "Logan doesn't have any parents to go with. His mother died giving birth to him."

"What about his father?" I ask, looking to the humans for information.

"Logan's mother was fertilized via IVF. Smith wasn't happy with how slow his program was. I'm assuming his father is Vilaxian as well, because he hasn't shown any hybrid qualities, only pure Vilaxian traits," Matthew explains.

"But his bloodlust is extreme at times, and he has trouble controlling his temper," Melissa says, brushing a hand through the boy's hair. His eyes blaze with anger, and his lips are clamped together.

"Are you hungry now?" I ask him, and he nods.

"This is why we should be his guardians," Vanity says, and Magenta nods while Nixie shakes her head.

"Hurricane and I will be happy to take care of him. It would be better for him to have some male company."

Oh fuck, I know what's going on here. I'm not sure that I want to get into the middle of a pissing contest. This isn't about the boy at all, and I'm annoyed at all of the parties involved. Susie looks at me with pleading eyes, and I decide not to back away slowly, but thankfully Tirrian steps in before I can say anything.

"I'm sorry, Nixie, but I'm going to agree with Vanity. He needs to be with someone who can help him with his bloodlust, and while I know Aquilians don't mind a bit of blood when they bite, you don't drink it like Vilaxians do. Vanity and Magenta will already have everything they need for him in their fridge." My dragon is totally getting a reward blowjob as soon as I get a spare five minutes.

"But Vanity only drinks from Magenta now," Nixie sneers, pointing a finger, and I can hear her jealousy. Damn, this is going to be a mess.

"But we still have blood in our fridge in case we feel like something different," Magenta argues, hurt in her voice. Nixie is just making everything worse. Did she really think she could convince Magenta to give a relationship with her another go? She has a lot of hurt to make up for before she would even consider it. That's even if Vanity is open to Magenta adding more to her bond. It is the Skarrian way, but will Vanity be as okay about it as Saxon is?

"Right, Logan will go with Magenta and Vanity for now. I will have Silac dig through the files and see if we can figure out who his father is," I say, backing my mate up.

Matthew bites his lip like he wants to tell me something. I consider pulling it from his mind, but I want to see what kind of man he is and whether or not I can make the idea I have a reality. I look at him, and he gets the hint.

"Smith had another few males that he used for breeding stock, but a woman came to visit once to see his program and took a liking to a couple of the males and demanded he turn them over. He was happy to because he had product from them to continue trying to implant the women with."

"Do you know who this woman was?" I ask him, and he shakes his head.

"Could you describe her?" Tirrian requests, and the man nods enthusiastically.

"Oh yes, she was something else—kind of other-worldly beautiful in a perfect way. She had copper-colored hair and eyes, and I'm not talking human copper, but bright, burning copper like freshly poured metal. She was tall and wore sky-high heels and had the look of a professional, like she was in charge of a corpo-ration or something. She held herself with confidence."

The description rings some bells, but I just can't place it. I don't remember seeing or knowing anyone like this, but a lot has happened in my life recently, so it's no wonder I don't remember everyone.

"I'll let Silac know, and he can dig into the files and see if there are any records of the transaction," I tell him. "Right, that's settled. Magenta, why don't you and Vanity take Logan with you? I'm not sure which living quarters you're staying in, but let Link know so he can give Logan a checkup when he gets a free moment. We will arrange to get you a bigger living space now that you've bonded, but it won't be until we stop at a space port somewhere," I explain, and both women assure me it isn't an issue for now.

They leave, and I almost let out a sigh, but then I see Nixie looking at me with hurt in her eyes. Well, it's too bad. She hurt me just as much, and I don't have time to coddle her, nor is this even about that. This is about what's better for the boy.

"Nixie, could you please show these people to some living quarters? They are making a decision on what they would like to do next," I tell her before turning my attention to them.

"You can choose to return to Earth, and our lawyers will set you up with new identities and make sure you are settled someplace new, or you could choose to stay with the circus. My family is rapidly expanding, and my poor nanny is run ragged. She could use some help, and since you three have experience in that department, I would like to offer you the position. We also have need of teaching experience to assist with the education of all the ship's children, which are my five current ones, as well as Chloe, Logan, Bastien, and the new baby who needs a name. A few of the other performers and crew have their children with us this season as well. It will probably be between fifteen and twenty children needing education, especially when our new ones arrive in a few months."

I can tell the idea intrigues them, and Melissa grabs Matthew's hand and squeezes it excitedly. "I don't know about Hettie and Francine, but Melissa and I already talked about it, and we want to stay," Matthew tells me.

"I would love to be your nanny, and I'm sure Matthew can make himself useful in some sort of way. He's very smart," she says, and I smile at the couple. They are kind of adorable, and I hope we become good friends.

"Won't we be in danger with all the aliens around?" Francine sounds more cautious, which is understandable.

"Not intentionally, but sometimes things get out of hand, and children have less control over their powers than adults. I may have something that can help with that, but I want to know if you're committed or not. We can work on a trial period, and then I can tell you what my idea is."

I'm thinking about offering them water from Skarr. It activated Susie's latent DNA, so I'm hoping it would do the same for these humans too, but I don't want to give it to them and then have them return to Earth. "For now, I can ask my warlock husband to create charms to give you a personal shield, which should hold up against the children's mishaps."

The two other women agree, and Nixie takes them to some spare rooms, glaring at me as she leaves, but I ignore it. I don't have time for hurt feelings because it's time to plan our next step.

"Come on, I want to see the kids before we make

our next move," I say to Tirrian, who wraps an arm around my shoulders and leads me to the elevator.

"I'm sorry about Nixie and Magenta. I know their drama is bothering you," he murmurs, and I lean my head on him.

"Yeah, but I can't even begin to get involved. It's something they need to sort out on their own, and we have enough to worry about. Brannock needs to send the message, and I need to ask my grandpas where the orb is. It's time to finish the Syndicate."

We spend the rest of the walk back to our home in silence, both lost in our thoughts. Everything that happened today was overwhelming, and I just need a moment. The minute we get in the door of our suite, I strip down and hurry to our pool, diving in and letting my mer form wash over me. I can't think of anything I want more than ten peaceful minutes at the bottom of the pool. Hopefully I'll get it, but if I know my mates, I won't get a minute longer.

I'm right, and it's only a little longer than ten minutes before Cas and Nik join me at the bottom of the pool. They don't speak though, which I'm grateful for, just wrap themselves around me, making a Lila sandwich, and hold me while we float. The tears I'd been holding at bay start to flow, and once they do,

I can't stop them. I sob uncontrollably, and the two men whisper words of comfort and caress my body. My parents were stuck in that hellhole for twenty years. My poor grandparents are never going to forgive themselves for trusting the police report and Smith. It's a clusterfuck of epic proportions, and I hope for all our sakes it's one we can move past quickly.

I finally get myself together, and we surface. We dry off, get dressed, and meet the rest of my mates in the living area for a meal. It's the middle of the night, and the kids are still asleep, so we take a moment to ourselves.

Ghosie is finally awake and back to his normal size.

"I'm so sorry," he says and reaches for me but then stops. "Ugh, I hate this," he growls and stomps away, disappearing to his room. My heart aches for him, and I start to follow, but Link shakes his head.

"Give him a moment. I'm worried about him. He's completely touch starved. He's going to start becoming aggressive if we aren't careful."

"We need to kill Vivax and end his curse," Echo shouts, startling everyone. Maxsim starts purring to soothe him and rubs a hand up and down his back. My poor sensitive omega wants to fix everything, and not being able to is making him unusually irritable. It isn't good for him or the babies.

"Why don't you go cuddle with him?" Maxsim suggests, and we all stare at the alpha in shock.

"That's cruel, Maxsim. You know what happens

when we touch his fur," Echo scolds him, and Maxsim shakes his head.

"So, my love? You are needy, and he can tend to you just as well as I can. We've seen his cock. It has all sorts of interesting ridges and bumps. It might soothe your need for a knot."

I'm unable to stop my mouth from dropping open in shock. Oh my sweet alpha cat. I think I just fell a little more in love with him.

"You won't care?" Echo asks, and Maxsim shakes his head. "I just want what's best for all of my family, and you both need it."

The rest of us are quiet, but I get up and go sit in my alpha's lap. "Why don't you both go? Goodness knows he needs it, and none of you are needed for the Syndicate takedown. The three of you can watch the children."

Maxsim shakes his head and gives me a kiss before standing up and putting me on the ground. "I will help tend the bear, but I will be coming on the mission. My mother is sending cats, and I am to lead them."

"What if we are meeting on a planet like Rilu?" I argue, and he shakes his head.

"No matter, I will still be joining the fight, even if the rest of the cats can't." He gestures to the amulet around his neck.

I accept his argument and the two of them leave to look after our bear. I would really like to be the filling in that delightfully furry sandwich, but it's going to have to wait.

"I say Brannock sends that message confirming we have the orb and asks for the location of the meeting. Once we know, we can tell your grandparents and our allies, and we can all rendezvous." Xavier watches Maxsim leave with envy in his eyes and I smother a smirk. Such a manwhore, but I can completely relate.

Brannock is sitting on the couch with Nik, who is feeding our new infant. She's guzzling milk, and I think she might be a bit rough in her hunger, because Nik keeps wincing.

"Are you okay, Nik? I smell your blood," Saxon asks. He has blood in his cup, but I can smell that it's Xavier's.

"Yes, the little one is very hungry and is not being very careful, but I am used to it. Hali is the same way." He smiles down at the baby and runs a finger over one of her spikes. "She is very cute, but she needs a name. We can't keep calling her baby or she or her."

"My sister didn't even want to discuss it," Zeydan says wearily. I'm worried about him. He looks the most exhausted of us all. I may suggest he teleport down to Earth to absorb more power, because he's going to need it with what is to come.

"Well then, I think you should decide," Caspian says to him. "And it's good that we are raising her. She is half god, after all."

The room falls silent, and I hear Xavier whistle.

"She could take the goddess of death's powers," I mutter, but Zeydan shakes his head.

"I'm not sure she could. She will have elemental god powers, and they are slightly different from death and life powers."

My heart sinks. I hoped that there was someone else who could take them.

"But Lila, there is another option," Link says. He looks as tired as Zeydan, and I am going to make both of them go to bed very shortly.

"Who?" I ask, not sure where he is going with this.

"Your father is half god, which is more divine than you. He would be more than suitable to take death's powers."

Zeydan sits upright, all signs of being tired disappearing. "Yes, you're right. His life genes would make him compatible with death's powers, like Lila is. I would think he is an option, but I would have to discuss it with Liliana and, of course, he would have to be asked."

"No," I state firmly, shutting down that idea without a second thought, and Link gives me an understanding nod. "He's been through too much. We aren't going to ask him. Let him live his life free from captivity without having to add worrying about numerous planets and races under his control."

"Your brother, Bastien, is a choice too. Maybe your dad could be the keeper of the powers until Bastien is old enough," Xavier suggests, and I glare at him.

"Actually, whoever gets the power won't have to

worry about planets and races. Most of them have been free of our influence for so long that we are not planning on announcing our presence. All of us have made lives for ourselves in other ways," Zeydan explains. "Well, all but Sanshia, but she is free to do the same thing. We don't want to disrupt that any more than the Galactic Council wants us to make a reappearance. No, we all plan on staying on the peripheral of our creations and only stepping in again if we need to."

"Someone will need to keep an eye on Sanshia for a while. We wouldn't want her to become bitter and twisted like Vivax did. If there was ever a trigger for cruelty, rape and an unwanted pregnancy would be at the top of the list," Nikos muses as he puts our new baby over his shoulder and gently pats her back.

"What about Ember?" Tirrian suggests. "I always liked that name for a girl. It has fire connotations, and that seems suitable since she will be half fire goddess."

We look at Zeydan, and he smiles at my dragon.

"That is a lovely name. Does everyone else agree?" he asks, and we are quick to give our affirmative.

Ember burps, and it's loud and very unbabylike, and we all burst into laughter, some of the tension melting away.

"We will make sure your sister is looked after. I'm not sure how yet, but we will," I promise my god, thinking that maybe my grandma will be the best person to rope into helping out.

"How about we all get some sleep, and tomorrow, we kick some Syndicate ass?" Cas suggests, standing up and stretching, and my kraken wakes and gives me a push. She wasn't happy that we didn't start anything in the water, and she wants to love on him a little. After all, I could use a power top up, and instead of arguing with her, I agree.

I'm going to need all the power I can get for tomorrow. Tonight just might be a musical beds kind of night. I'm not sure I'm going to get much sleep, but luckily with my extra Vilaxian and god bits, I don't need a lot.

CHAPTER THIRTY-FIVE

Lila

We gave up all pretense of trying to run a circus the following day. A lot of the acts were up in space with us, so I gave the crew and performers a four-day vacation on Earth and warned them not to get into any mischief. Xavier passed out glamour charms like they were Halloween candy, but I think we managed to make everyone happy. Minx squealed with excitement and said they were going shopping. Trace, Sim, and Fuse didn't look so enthused about the possibility, but I told them Singapore has amazing food, and they weren't so reluctant after that.

Back on the main ship, I called a meeting for the extended family and held it in the main cafeteria. It was the only place that could fit us and that included the children, because I wanted to introduce my parents to my babies. Breakfast was a chaotic, loud mess with tears, laughter, joy, and sadness all at the same time, but finally, it was time to settle down and finalize plans.

"Just like we suspected, the meeting will be on Grichi 517E, which is worrying because that's the home to that metal compound we found on the bullets and knives the guards had," Brannock says now that Kinga, Andre, and the three human women have taken all the children away. Matthew remained behind in case he could offer any Smith insight. "We've been instructed to bring the orb there and turn it over, and the Madovian will get paid."

"I advised the queen of the destination and time, and she is coordinating with the rest of our allies to rendezvous there and cut off any escape by surrounding the whole planet," Saxon adds.

"At least we don't have to worry about civilian casualties since the planet is deserted," Zeydan points out. "Anyone at the meeting will have ties with the Syndicate, and we can kill or detain them at will."

"I would prefer we detain and find a deep, impenetrable cell to stick them in to live out the rest of their lives," I tell them, not really looking forward to killing the members of the Syndicate no matter if galactic subjugation is their agenda.

"What about creating something on Husadavia? Even if they escaped their cells, they couldn't get off the planet, and the vegetation and animals would take care of the escapees," Ghosie suggests. He emerged from his bedroom with a spring in his step and smile on his face this morning. Both Maxsim and Echo looked like they'd been ridden hard and hung out wet. I know exactly how they feel. Ghosie's fur is some potent shit, and it would be easy enough to sex yourself to death with it.

We look at Zeydan who shrugs. "I don't see why not. I have no need for it."

"I kind of like the idea of using it as a getaway where no one can disturb us," I tell him, pouting at the thought that I won't be able to have fun by the hot springs with my mates anymore.

"I'm with Lila," Tirrian agrees. He's the one I fucked by the hot springs.

"What about Grichi itself? If the metal has a property that inhibits powers, then creating cells from the mines would be ideal. Anyone we put in there would not be able to use their powers to escape," Xavier suggests, and his idea gets a lot of interest.

"That's if it survives when we distribute the orb's powers. With the meeting being held there, we won't have to worry about the fallout," Zeydan murmurs, which really doesn't make me feel better.

"Someone would have to be warden, and we would have to make sure they have their basic necessities, like food and water," Link remarks, showing his compassion.

"Someone incorruptible," Aarin grumbles. "That's going to be nearly impossible to find."

"Actually, I've been thinking about that." Silac steeples his fingers together and swings his chair back and forth. "Tirrian told me about the sex robot warriors you came across."

Link winces at this. "I'm almost certain my mother is involved. She has to be responsible for the robots being on Earth."

Oh snap. I gasp. Could Link's mother be the person Matthew described yesterday? The woman who took some of Smith's breeding stock? But why? She has an entire catalog of sex robots at her disposal, so why would she need living ones?

"But couldn't we use them to guard the prison? They wouldn't be able to corrupt them because unless they reprogram them, the robots wouldn't respond to bribes." Silac looks to Link who nods.

"In theory, yes, but if my mother is involved, then she would be able to reprogram them."

Silac sags in defeat.

"Not necessarily. Those guards were pretty simple, and we were told they weren't programmable, unlike the sex bots. They were a budget version because they were guards and could be destroyed," Matthew chimes in, and Silac's hope returns.

"I like the idea. I wouldn't want to have to appoint a sentient being to guard them. That would be hell," Xavier agrees.

"Okay, so we have a plan on what to do with them. Now we need to figure out how to capture them with the least casualties," Rick says. He, my mom, and my dad have barely been able to keep their hands off each other this whole time. I kind of feel like gagging. You don't see me being all demonstrative with PDA with my mates in front of them.

You know your mom and dad bonded him last night, Xavier says in my head, and again, I feel sick.

How do you know? I ask him, and he smirks at me.

I can feel it, and you could too if you tried.

Pass, I reply flatly, not wanting to feel any of the emotions emitting from my parents right now.

You'll have to start calling Rick Papa, he teases, and I flip him off mentally.

"We already have a plan, and we are still going ahead with it. Lila is going to pose as the Madovian, and with Tirrian and Silac as her escorts, she is going to take the orb to the meeting. We need all six gods in the same room at the same time to redistribute the powers and destroy it," Brannock tells Rick, and that gets my dad's attention.

"The orb? You're destroying it? How? It can't be done."

I guess they were too busy bonding last night for Rick to catch Mom and Dad up on everything.

We spend the next half hour updating my parents on everything they missed. Nothing like saying congrats, your mother is a god, so you're half god, to shock a man into silence.

"Wow," my mother says once it's all out, and my father seems to be having a small stroke, sputtering nonsensically next to her. "You have had quite a few months, haven't you?" She's gazing at me with awe, and I want to squirm under her scrutiny, but I manage to stay still.

"You have no idea. After we deal with the Syndicate, we will sit down for a long talk, I promise," I tell her. I'm sad that we can't take the time to do that yet, but I don't want this hanging over our heads any longer.

My dad jumps to his feet and yells, "I forbid you! We just got you back, and you are not putting yourself in danger. Why are you doing it and not one of your mates?" He looks around at my mates, glaring at them in fury. "Why are you letting her do this?"

Xavier whistles and steps back, holding his hands up. "Nope, dude, you're all on your own with this one," he says as a rumble escapes my chest and smoke starts to drift out of my nose.

"Xavier's right, we don't let Lila do anything," Link says, crossing his arms and giving my dad his own glare.

"She's right there. Why don't you ask her yourself?" Brannock says, smirking because he knows what's about to happen.

Everyone else in the room watches with undisguised glee. Echo is purring, trying to soothe a growling Maxsim, his tail flicking back and forth with his annoyance.

"Is it bad that I wish we had some popcorn to go with the show?" Susie whispers to Magenta, who giggles.

"And drinks. This is going to be good."

"Nobody tells me what I can and can't do," I tell my father, trying to stay calm, but it really is a stretch. I know he is worried, I would be too if it were one of my kids, but he doesn't get to walk back into my life and throw his weight around like he gets a vote.

"Hey, kiddo, I'm sure you think it will be easy, but you don't know the kind of beings you will be up against. They may have all manner of life-forms in their little group, and how are you going to get out without getting hurt or worse, losing the orb to them and becoming a captive yourself?"

I stand up and start to strip off my clothes. I'm in a Galaxy Circus shirt and a pair of sweats this morning, wanting to be comfortable while we planned.

My dad starts to splutter. "Lila, what have I told you about keeping your clothes on?"

"Relax, Dad, everyone here has already seen what I have to offer. It's nothing new." His mouth drops open, and he splutters a little more.

"Lila..." My mom sighs with disappointment, but everyone else laughs.

"I certainly haven't, nor do I want to," Aarin grumbles, and Mark shushes him while Susie mouths, "Sorry," to me. That threesome is going to be funny to watch. Aarin seems a little tightly wound, which is definitely not the definition of my girl Susie. Mark might fall somewhere in the middle, though, so maybe they'll be okay.

"Seriously, why are you taking your clothes off?"

My dad crosses his arms and stomps his foot before blocking Bubby's view, which I'm kind of thankful for, to be honest. Wow, I'm pretty sure I saw Jack behave exactly like that the other day when something didn't go his way.

"Because, Dad, I don't really want to go through new clothes every time I shift forms," I reply and let the first form wash over me. I choose the Celestian one, which he has already seen. Xavier lifts a hand to conjure me an outfit to cover my body, but I shake my head.

"Don't bother, it won't last," I tell him before shifting into my Aaz'axian form, then my carevasta, then to my kraken and naga. I shift through all of them except for my dragon and mer forms because they won't work in this environment. I finish with my Madovian form. Silac and Tirrian jump up as I hiss aggressively at my dad, who has gone pale and dropped into the seat behind him.

"Oh my god." My tail slides back and forth as he stares at the crosscut hole in my stomach. "My poor baby," he stammers, and I try to lunge for him, but Xavier freezes me.

"Shift back, Lila," Tirrian demands, and I shake off the aggressive presence and shift back, putting my clothes back on. I'm a little shaky from the show, but I think it's adrenaline. I really gorged on my mates last night, so my well of power seems kind of endless at the moment, and I think my dad got the idea.

"And not only can I use the powers of each form, but I can also use them in whatever form I'm in thanks to Gigi's blood," I tell him as my mother whispers something in his ear.

"She's more powerful than you know, Marcus." Rick gives my dad's shoulder a squeeze. "She, along with help from her mates, is more than capable of doing what needs to be done, and we'll all be on standby to bust in if needed." Bubby has a stubborn set to his chin, and I know I'm going to have to pick my timing carefully if I want to stop them from coming.

"Fine, you can wait with the grandparents," I concede for now as I redress.

"Everyone waits until Lila gives the signal. The warlocks are going to go in first and freeze the whole meeting, while the rest of us will take out anyone guarding the perimeter. Then, we will escort everyone out of the meeting except for Vivax and get clear of the planet. Liliana, Lila, and the rest of the gods will do their thing, with Lila taking Vivax's power," Brannock continues, outlining the plan for everyone.

"What about the bit she still holds?" Hurricane asks. "We all retained some of our power."

"Vivax's and Liliana's powers are only Skarrian in nature. It's why she has been so desperate to get the orb back. When Liliana managed to free all four of us elemental gods, she sacrificed her and Vivax's powers completely to the spell. They retain nothing of their former god powers except for the ability to reincarnate, and that's why it took so long," Zeydan tells him. "Vivax really is no more dangerous than any other Skarrian, and being amongst the fleitine should render that null as well. She will be impotent."

"And if we manage to do that, we can all go home and live our lives in peace with the threat of the Syndicate and galactic domination from them hanging over our heads," Caspian says blithely.

"And if we don't win?" Titus asks, sitting closer to Malik than is possibly acceptable for *just friends*.

"Let's not think about it, because I'm sure it would be nothing good." My deity mate shudders at the thought of Vivax ruling over us, unstoppable with everyone's powers at her fingertips.

"If it comes to that, I may have a backup plan, but it would mean abandoning this realm," Xavier says slowly.

I think about where we cemented our intimate bond, wondering if it would indeed shelter us and how many of us they could save—probably the whole warlock race, but I don't see them taking any others. That would mean leaving our families behind, and I'm not prepared to do that.

"It's not an option, so I plan on kicking this chick's ass and then heading back to Earth and being the best damn ringmaster that circus has ever seen. Are you with me?" I ask my surrounding friends and family, and without even hesitating, they all cheer. It warms my heart and soothes some of the tension.

"Okay, we need to make a move. Who's coming

with, and who is staying behind?" Brannock asks, and that starts a whole other argument.

I sigh. It's going to be a long ass day.

CHAPTER THIRTY-SIX

Lila

The trip to Grichi 517E would normally take us three days, but with the improvements the Vilaxians made, it should only take thirty hours in my grandpas' personal shuttle. Because of space restrictions, we had to limit who went with us. Of my guys, it's Brannock, Zeydan, Maxsim, Saxon, Xavier, Silac, and Tirrian. The others wanted to come too, but I said no. If anything were to happen to us, our children needed someone, so I put my foot down when Nikos and Caspian tried to join the excursion. It's bad enough that Maxsim wouldn't take no for an answer, which could possibly leave Echo as a sole parent to raise our cubs, but the others promised to look after him. I made them promise not to fall apart and to stay together as a family and find someone else to love if anything happened to me. They scoffed and said the right things, but I don't think any of them meant it.

All three gods are joining us. Sanshia is healed, but she hasn't spoken to anyone since she woke up. Her brothers explained what is happening, and she agreed to come, but apart from that, she hasn't said a word—not even to ask about Ember, who is firmly ensconced in our nursery with the other babies, and Chloe, who is a major hit with her younger siblings. They think she is amazing, and she can get them to do anything. I doubt it will last, but we'll make the most of it for now.

Brannock asked Ghosie to raise her and Ember if anything were to happen to him, and Ghosie cried and promised to love them with all his heart.

Link was torn. He wanted to come, but in the end, he stayed back with the others. He has no interest in confronting his mother if she is one of the Syndicate leaders, but he spoke to his father who warned him that she had been outed from Pleasure Bot Industries and was on a warpath. Both gave their blessings to deal with her as we see fit and told us not to spare her on their behalf.

My parents insisted on coming, and I as much as I wanted to deny the request, we allowed it, leaving Bastien behind with Bubby. I couldn't help laughing at the deer in headlights look on his face when he arrived to wish us off with Bastien strapped to his chest in a harness. Kinga promised to give him as much help as he needs, as have the three human women who have been a pleasant surprise. The humans are fitting in nicely, and I think it's going to work out for the best.

We haven't told my grandparents that my parents are alive yet, since they have enough to worry about. They will have a nice surprise when they get there.

Rounding out the group are Titus and Thorn, who both have combat experience, and Musette and Mehira. They are going to coordinate their family's troops for us, much like Maxsim is doing for the lightning cats. Thankfully, Grichi 517E is a desolate planet that's cold and inhospitable, so the cats should fit in just fine.

The tight squeeze in the shuttle isn't great, but it's only thirty hours, so we can deal with it. We're going to rendezvous with the fleet of allies just out of sensor range. The others will beam aboard the Vilaxian battleship, and Tirrian, Silac, and I will continue on our own.

We say our tearful goodbyes, and I'm about to board the ship when Link stops me.

"Lila, are you forgetting something?" he asks, and I look around, patting my pockets. I don't have anything in them because I'm going to be in my Madovian form anyway.

"No, I think I'm good." I tip my head to the side in confusion. "What am I missing?" I ask when he actually laughs out loud.

"Why are you going, Lila?" he asks me.

"To return the gods' powers from the orb... Oh, the orb. Fuck!" I shout, panic gripping me. "Where the fuck is the orb? I've been so busy, I didn't think to ask my grandparents."

"You don't know where the orb is?" My dad comes back down the gangplank, and I shake my head.

"No. The grandpas were going to tell me, but so much has happened we haven't gotten around to it."

He smiles and takes me by the hand as my mother catches up to us. "Get the shuttle running, General. We will only be ten minutes," he tells Saxon, and the two of them hurry me to the elevators.

"Where are we going?" I ask them when Mom pushes the button to the top deck, which has my family suite and the bridge.

"You took over your grandpas' rooms with all their stuff, right?" my father asks me as the doors open and we walk out.

"I mean, kind of, but it's all been refurbished since then," I reply as they lead the way to our front door.

"But you have all of their circus things? Their costumes and everything?" he asks as I let us in the front door.

"Well, sort of. I have my own set that they made for me. I'm not sure what happened to Eric's and William's. I think they probably took them home or maybe kept them in their smaller suite downstairs." I'm so confused, but I answer his question.

"But you have the cane? The one that will change into a whip for the cats, with the pretty glowing gem on top?" Mom asks urgently.

"Yeah, it's in my closet, I've been having trouble

managing the whip. Heck, I didn't even know it was one until Eric showed me how to use it. It's pretty clever," I tell them, feeling a little embarrassed that I still can't get a handle on the whip. I keep tearing holes in my pants, and my ass has a permanent scorch mark.

I lead the way into my bedroom, open the door to my walk-in closet, and grab the cane. There is a button on the side, which will transform it to a whip. I hold it out, showing my parents.

"Cronus created that for your grandpas, infusing magic into it so it would switch between both things. He overheard Eric grumbling about ruined costume lines when he had to carry both things and came up with that solution." My mom smiles fondly at the memory as my dad takes it from my hand. The beautiful gem at the end pulses like it has life in it. I always marveled at the way it did that, but I never thought anything of it. Dad gives it a twist, and there's a click, and it falls into his open hand. He holds it out to me.

"Behold the orb of power."

I stare at it, blinking in surprise. "You have got to be shitting me. They hid it in plain sight?" I screech so loudly they both wince. "And they didn't fucking warn me?"

"What can I say? My fathers are interesting men." My dad shrugs like it's no big deal. I snatch it out of his hand and storm out of my bedroom and back through our home, muttering under my breath the whole way. Thank goodness the kids are down in the pool, going for a swim. Chloe was dying to see the big pool. Xavier promised he would find a way for her to swim with her brothers and sisters when he returned, and I bet he will be able to as well.

"When I see those damn men, they are going to get my foot up their asses so hard, and I swear if Eric even thinks about snickering at me, I'll make his damn face flat like that damn dog Muttley," I mutter under my breath, but obviously not quietly enough.

"Oh dear, I think maybe we should warn my fathers," I hear my dad say.

"Oh no, dear, I'm pretty sure they are going to get exactly what they deserve." My mom doesn't sound worried in the least.

"It is so nice not being the only female in the family now," I call back to her. "I missed you, Mom. I'm glad you're here," I tell her, and there's silence before I hear a sob. I stop and turn around, and she's wrapped in Dad's arms, crying.

"Oh shit, I'm sorry. I didn't mean to upset her," I apologize, but Dad just shakes his head and smiles.

"She's not upset, baby. She's just super happy we're back together and equally sad that we missed so many years. Luckily for us, we have many, many more to enjoy to make up for it."

I give them a quick group hug before I continue on my way. "Especially after Gigi teaches you to shove some of your essence into Mom and Bubby, and they become immortal like you."

Again, there is silence, but this time, I don't stop.

Note to self—I have to pick more appropriate times to announce such major things like immortality.

We get to the elevator, and as we move to the shuttle bay, I take a moment to shove the orb into my interdimensional safe space. Mom and Dad gape at me in surprise. "Having a warlock husband is handy," I tell them.

"I'll say. Do you think he could teach me that?" my dad asks. "It would be a great place to store some weapons and a snack."

"Yes, that's exactly what I said," I say, and he holds up his hand for a high five. "An emergency snack is always a necessity."

My mom just rolls her eyes at us.

The hangar is empty, and the engines on the shuttle are glowing blue. The three of us run up the gangplank. "Hit the hyperdrive, Chewie," I shout as the door closes behind us.

"Huh?" Everyone looks at me strangely.

"Did she hit her head wherever you went?" Saxon asks, looking at my dad.

"Nice *Star Wars* reference." He holds up his hand for another high five, and I indulge him while beaming at him.

"Oh no, they are bonding. We could be in trouble," Xavier whispers to Brannock, who just bats him away because he's practically sitting in his lap.

"Did you get the orb?" Zeydan asks, looking me up and down.

"Yup, sure did. We can leave now." The three of us find seats, and Saxon starts to maneuver the shuttle out of the hangar. This one is bigger than the one I flew into Fluxx and is designed more like a luxurious lounge than a plane. There are also a couple of cabins for sleeping and a large galley for meals. Thirty hours is a long time, but we shouldn't go hungry, and we can take shifts napping.

Dad has taken the copilot seat, and I am next to my mom. "Are we sure that's a good idea?" I ask her, nodding in Dad's direction. He is doing something to the controls and chatting to Saxon.

Mom's eyebrows jump. "Marcus is an excellent pilot. Why would you be worried?"

"Bubby told me exactly how good of a pilot he is. Apparently he crashed this shuttle before in the middle of space where there was nothing or no one, and I'd like to arrive in one piece."

"The bit of space junk came out of nowhere. Damn that man, he has never let me live it down," my dad growls over his shoulder, and Mom's peals of laughter echo around the shuttle. It is music to my ears, and I find myself grinning with unrestrained joy. I'm on a mission with my parents who I never thought I was going to see again. Life is freaking good. Now, we just need to survive the next forty-eight hours, and we can start enjoying the rest of our long lives.

We're all a little irritable and crabby when we rendezvous with the fleet. We played one too many card games where I'm almost certain Xavier was cheating. As we approach the fleet, a lump develops in my throat of the sight of it. These ships are unlike anything I've ever seen before. They put the Galaxy Circus ship to shame. These are flying cities and wouldn't look out of place in an Earth sci-fi movie. In fact, the Vilaxian battleship looks very similar to something you might find a stormtrooper on. I wonder if one of their tech advisors was an alien.

I thought everyone was going to have to beam aboard, but Saxon just flies the shuttle right into the belly of the giant spaceship. There's a greeting party once the doors open and the gangplank releases.

"Lila!" Cronus shouts. "It's so good of you to join the party." He holds up a glass of something. Hmm, a little early for him to be drinking, but I guess he may need to calm his nerves.

I hear a chuckle, and Xavier steps up next to me. "Pray he didn't hear you think that, or he will never let you forget you doubted his nerves."

Sabine and Aleister wave and engulf their girls in hugs. I hear them telling their parents all about Vanity finding her blood rose.

Astrea and Jalin are also there, and they greet Maxsim by hugging him and rubbing noses. It's freaking adorable.

"Boys! There you are. When Tallon said you joined the circus, I thought she was joking!" Tysar greets all three of his sons jovially. "But I guess the joke's on me. Come over here and hug me. I missed you, and we have wonderful news. Your mother is nesting."

I snicker as all three of them wince. Brannock and the gods stand off to the side, keeping a barrier between Sanshia and everyone else.

"Lila, don't you have a hug for your old grandpas?" Eric appears in my sight, and he's smirking that maddening smile at me. He's flanked by William and John, and all three of them look like years have been taken off their lives. I don't even want to think about what might have caused that. Nope, no way.

I run down the ramp and tackle them, hugging them like it's been years instead of barely over a week since I saw them, but I got so used to having them in my life, I missed them fiercely.

"Be careful with her, she still has a task," my grandma scolds as she approaches us and also gives me a hug.

"I have so much to tell you," I blurt out, but before I can tell them everything, she catches sight of her family.

"You found them!" she exclaims, tears welling in her eyes at the sight of the elemental gods.

"We did, but be gentle with Sanshia, Gigi. She isn't in a good place." My grandma pales and takes a step toward them, but before she can get farther, my parents appear in the door of the shuttle.

"Holy fuck, I have had too much to drink. I'm

seeing ghosts." Cronus stares into his mug. "What did you put in this, Xylene?"

"Oh, so I see you're still blaming your beautiful wife for all your mistakes. Typical." My dad grins at his best friend who turns white and then falls backward in a dead faint.

"Ha!" Xavier laughs and points at his dad. "Please tell me someone is catching this on film. I want a copy. He's going to be mortified. The great and mighty warlock king in a dead faint." He doubles over laughing, and Xylene hisses at him.

"Marcus? Alina?" All of my grandparents are staring at my mom and dad like they can't believe they are here.

"Smith had them. Well, don't just stand there, go hug your son and daughter," I tell them, and there's a split second where I think I'm going to have four more unconscious people, but then there's a mad rush up the ramp. All four of my grandparents and Xylene tackle my parents, shouting and crying and laughing as I crouch down next to Cronus and slap him on the cheek. "Come on, Dad, you're missing out. I have another one now, so the competition is on for which one is best."

That has him moving quickly. He bolts up and puffs out his chest. "Please, I have magic. What does he have? Pretty lights." All of a sudden, a bolt of lightning streaks across the room and strikes Cronus on the ass. He screams and clutches his butt cheeks, glaring at my dad.

"Damn you, asshole. I missed you. It's so good to see you." He stomps up the ramp and joins in, tears streaming down his face. Later, he'll claim it was because he was happy, but Xavier will claim it was from the hit to the ass.

Silac and Brannock step up next to me, and each grab a hand. "This is nice, isn't it?" Silac murmurs, watching the drama with a small smile.

"Are you okay?" I ask him. He and Brannock are the only ones without family here, and I know Brannock's made peace with it for a long time, but Silac's father's betrayal is fresh. All of this happy family stuff could be rubbing salt into an open wound.

"Yeah, I'm good. My mother and siblings are safe, and I have a new family that loves me unconditionally. I'm probably the happiest snake in the galaxy." He presses a kiss to my cheek.

"Well, hold onto that feeling, because it's going to get worse before it gets better, and being a Madovian's captive isn't going to be a walk in the park," Brannock warns him. "Even if you are that Madovian's husband."

CHAPTER THIRTY-SEVEN

Silac

Unfortunately, we are on a deadline, so any further celebrations are going to have to wait until after the mission is complete. The hangar is cleared out of everyone but Lila, Tirrian, and me, as well as her parents, grandparents, the gods, and the warlocks.

"Lila, when you make your entrance, make a big scene that will allow the three of us to enter the room unseen in our mist forms," Xylene instructs.

"Whatever happens, Vivax can't get her hands on the orb. If she does, all is lost, so don't show it to her until the last minute," Gigi tells me.

"Keep her talking while our forces take care of the perimeter guards," Cronus instructs. "Once that is done, Maxsim will advise Xavier, who will let the ship know, and the Vilaxians will beam down and do their thing." Saxon is responsible for tagging everyone inside the complex with transporter beacons. Musette, Mehira, and their parents will take care of any forces outside. "Then you guys will do your thing." He nods to the gods.

"Yes, you need to make sure she is frozen too. Hopefully she didn't think to wear a nullifying pendant. If you don't, she doesn't have the power to do any damage to us gods, so she will aim at Tirrian and Silac to cause a distraction," Liliana warns, and I see Lila swallow nervously.

"Maybe they should stay behind, and I'll do this on my own," she argues.

"No," Tirrian and I snap.

"No way. We are with you until the end," he tells her.

"And in the case that she isn't frozen, both of us are very capable of defending ourselves. I'll be in half form anyway, and I can always mesmerize her if I need to," I add, feeling confident.

"But you can't torch her," Zeydan tells Tirrian. "I don't want to wait another five hundred years until she returns, not to mention we have no idea who or what she would reincarnate as. I think the only reason she came back as Skarrian this time is because her and Liliana's essences were tied together. Next time, she could come back as one of her own creations, and we'd never find her."

"I won't. I want this over and done with," Tirrian promises.

"Here." Xavier holds out a couple of collars with leashes attached to Lila. She takes them, looking at him quizzically.

"We've embedded them with a type of shield that will activate if Vivax tries to harm them."

"These are for the guys?" she asks, turning them over in her hand.

"Yes. Madovians don't have mates, they have captive breeding vessels. Tirrian and Silac are yours, but Madovians are very possessive of them because they carry the future of their race within them, and they don't let them get far away. They also continue to use them for sexual pleasure until their eggs hatch, kill, and consume the incubators," he tells her, smirking at the dragon and me. Smoke wafts out of Tirrian's nose, his annoyance at our warlock very visible, but I don't care. I like the idea of being owned by Lila, just not the eaten vessel part. She turns her attention to me.

"Change forms," she says, and I do, stripping off my clothes and tossing them to the side before letting my half form take over. When I've finished changing, I'm staring down at her, and she looks up at me with a smile. "I can't quite reach you. Bend down a little?" she asks, and I do as requested. I'm face-to-face with her, her sweet breath brushing over me as she places the collar around my neck and tightens it. I grunt and pray my cocks behave. Now is not the time to have dirty thoughts about these collars.

We can keep them for later if you want. I startle when Xavier's voice sounds in my mind, and so does

Lila. He must have projected the words to both of us. I see Lila nod her head, and she smiles. I have to think nasty thoughts so I don't embarrass myself in front of her family.

Once she's done with me, I return to my normal height and watch as she attaches a collar to Tirrian. He's already in half form, but Xavier makes him remove his shirt so, as he puts it, all his pretty muscles are on show. He also rubs some kind of oil over his chest so he glimmers like a jewel. Tirrian grumbles the whole time, smoke wafting around him and Xavier, but he lets him do it.

He doesn't want to admit it, but the dragon likes the collar as well as having my hands on him. I see some fun times in our future, he murmurs inside my head.

He is such an asshole, but one day, revenge will be sweet. I will bide my time.

He steps back and gestures to the two of us. "Attack them," he tells his dad who doesn't hesitate to throw magic at us. Shouts fill the air, and Lila leaps forward, like she's going to put herself between us and the magic, but it's too late. She isn't fast enough, and the magic barrels toward us. I put my hands up as if to stop it, but suddenly, a shield activates, and the magic bounces off it harmlessly.

"Oh good, it works." Xavier and his father look pleased, but Lila shrieks.

"It works? You weren't sure it worked, and you attacked them?" Her voice is high-pitched, and she whirls on Xavier and his father, glaring at them.

Xylene steps back, muttering about idiot husbands and sons.

"Oh dear, I think you're in trouble," Cronus says to his son, who puts his hands up and looks at our wife pleadingly.

"Now, honey, I was positive Dad and I knew what we were doing. It isn't the first time we've created a spell like that, just the first time we've used collars to hold it."

"You didn't think to, you know, test it on yourselves first? You idiots. What if it hadn't worked? They would have been hurt." She's still livid, and Cronus takes his life in his hands by brushing her anger away.

"Oh no, it was fine. That spell would have only given them space pox."

"Space pox?" she screeches. "How about I give you a dose of space pox?" She holds up her hands, and they start to glow purple.

"Lila, calm down. Now is not the time to get even. He will keep." Alina pats her daughter on the shoulder, and tension flows out of Lila. Everyone breathes a sigh of relief.

"Ho-ho, I'd forgotten about your mood stabilizing powers. Very handy in a family like yours," Cronus complements Alina, who just glares at him.

"Xylene, do you think maybe you could gag your husband so the adults in the room can talk?"

Cronus looks affronted, and Marcus chuckles while Xylene just rolls her eyes and sighs with exasperation.

"Ah, fun times," William mutters. "I forgot how the four of them were when they are together."

"Maddening," Liliana agrees.

"Can we get back to the mission please?" Aarin asks, sounding frustrated.

"Yes, once everyone is frozen and we appear, the rest of the occupants of the planet will be beamed back to this ship using the transponders that Saxon and his family will have placed on everyone" —Zeydan holds up a small transponder beacon that the transporters lock onto— "getting them safely out of the way for us to deal with the orb. Justice can be dispensed after our powers have returned."

"And once the room is clear we will start the spell that will give our powers back. Only the five of us, Vivax, and Lila can be present. Everyone else must get clear of the planet in case anything goes wrong," Hurricane says, a frown on his face. "Way clear."

"What the fuck? No." I start to argue, and so does Tirrian and Xavier, but Liliana holds up her hand, stopping us before we can voice our opinions.

"I'm sorry. It is the only way."

With the plan finalized, we take a moment to get our bearings, and Lila needs to change forms. The three of us, with the warlocks in mist form, are going down to the surface in the shuttle, while the rest will beam down when it's time.

The gods, grandparents, Lila's parents, and Xavier's parents all huddle off to the side and give the four of us a moment together.

"I have to change forms, I just wanted to give you all a kiss and apologize for anything this form might say or do when I am wearing it. It's the hardest form to control. If I try to force you to do anything you don't want to, knock me out. Mission be damned. We can try again."

I shake my head. "No way, I will take whatever she does as long as we can complete this mission and get back to living our lives."

"I agree, but it doesn't mean I won't put up a fight," Tirrian says.

"We will freeze them as soon as we see the opportunity. Vivax should be frozen as well. We just need to be prepared in case she's wearing some kind of protective charm too. Our intel says she has a warlock on her payroll, but our hope is that he's no match for our combined powers." Xavier sounds worried, and Lila leans in and gives him a kiss on the cheek, murmuring to him about how he is the most powerful being in the galaxy and they should be fine.

I ignore all that, my attention on the other group. They are whispering and sending us side glances. I'm pretty sure they are hatching a backup plan. Just when I try to listen closer, Lila steals my attention by grabbing me by the collar and tugging me down to kiss height. She kisses me soundly, and then her body shimmers and sparkles and she's in her Madovian form. We all back up a little as she stretches her body and the snakes on her head start hissing and striking out.

She runs her hands over the top of her body and

strokes her tail against my own. My cocks harden beneath my scales at the feeling of her rubbing up against me, even though she isn't in naga form. Fuck, it's going to be a long evening.

"Lila," Tirrian hisses. His eyes are wide, his pupils are huge, and his own cock is hard beneath his pants. "Reel in the pheromones, otherwise we aren't going to get anywhere," he growls, and Xavier waves his hands around.

"Holy fuck, that is potent. I want to jump your bones, and I'm not attracted to that in the least." He points at the cross-hatched slit in her stomach that seems to be undulating.

"Let's go," I say through gritted teeth and move away from her and into the shuttle. She follows, and the warlocks and Tirrian take up the rear. We don't say goodbye. We've all said what we needed to, so now we are mission focused. The warlocks turn to mist in the ship, so their life-forms aren't sensed on any radar, and Lila takes the pilot's seat, resting her large body on it with her tail behind her. The door shuts, and Tirrian and I find seats far away from her.

"Fuck, that is awful. I simultaneously want to fuck her brains out and run screaming," he mutters to me, and I nod with a grimace.

"It really is disturbing. The pheromones seem to want to keep you on edge to confuse their prey. It would be more than horrifying to find yourself as an incubator for a Madovian and not remember anything."

"Or worse, remember it all." He looks ill when he says that. "I have no desire whatsoever to take the Madovian form for a spin, as Xavier would say."

Neither do I, Xavier mutters in our heads. *You would have to be psychotic to want to.*

"Here we go," Lila warns as the ship moves out of the hangar and she sets course for Girchi 517E. "We will be within sensor range within the next ten minutes, so the act starts now. We don't know if they have spying capabilities and can listen to our conversation. I don't want to blow this mission before we've even landed," she warns, and we all murmur our agreement.

The shuttle is fast, and with the modifications the Vilaxians made, we are in the planet's orbit in half an hour, and in the lower atmosphere another five minutes later. The communicator pings with an incoming call.

"Yes?" Lila answers, her words sibilant in the Madovian form.

"We have you on our sensors. Why are there three occupants on your shuttle?" a distorted voice demands.

"I have two incubators with me. You know a Madovian won't leave her eggs unattended." There's an awkward pause, and the voice comes back over the speakers. They sound uncomfortable.

"Please be advised, we will be searching your incubators for weapons."

Lila scoffs. "By all means. I am not stupid enough

to allow them weapons, even if they are docile and completely in my thrall."

She looks at us pointedly, and we both know how we have to behave—blank looks and no reactions but fawning over her.

"We have programed your ship with the coordinates. Fly into the open space and land. Come out so it can be searched. If we see any signs of weapons, we will shoot first and take the orb from you."

"You can try," Lila hisses, unwilling to concede to the voice on the radio. The communications cut off, and I heave out a sigh of relief. That went well, or it seemed to. We will only know when we land, which is about ten minutes later.

Lila navigates to the meeting coordinates and sets the ship down in what looks like a large open mine shaft. She engages the landing gear, and the ship bumps down. She turns it off and slithers toward us, grabbing the leashes and giving them a tug. "Come on, boys," she says, her tongue flicking in and out, the snakes on her head hissing in agitation.

Lila is not wearing anything over her breasts. Madovians are proud of their half forms and wouldn't dream of covering them. Lila has come a long way since she first joined the circus and was afraid of showing everyone her goodies, as she likes to call them. Now, she doesn't even blush at the thought of everyone seeing them and pushes them out with pride.

The leashes tighten as she moves down the ramp, Tirrian and I walking docilely behind her. The collars not only give us a shield if needed, but also glamour both of us to look unlike ourselves. We weren't sure who was a part of the Syndicate, and both Tirrian and I are known throughout the galaxy as not only Lila's partners, but as the dragon prince and heir to Snakebite Logistics. Tirrian's glamour makes him look like a blue dragon, with long flowing hair almost down to his ass and gold glitter across his wings. I look like a basilisk, dull green in color with horns all over my head instead of my hood. The mouthful of fangs isn't particularly pleasant either.

My tongue wants to flick in and out with agitation too, but I have to pretend to be docile, so I clamp my lips shut and stare adoringly at Lila.

There is a door in the wall of the cliff, and it opens before fifteen guards run out, swarming us and the ship. Lila pauses and acts bored as they search the ship, Tirrian, and me. They return and stand behind the commander of the team who waits patiently in front of Lila. His face is calm, but we can see the terror in his eyes.

"All clear," one of the guards announces robotically, and I slowly turn my head to look carefully at him. That sounded slightly artificial, and sure enough, when I look closely at them, I notice they are all soldier bots like Smith had on Earth.

"Mistress, we must search you too," the commander insists, and I can tell by how he smells that he isn't a bot. He smells like terror despite trying not to show it. The rest of the guards smell like nothing but machine oil and computer chips, and it isn't a nice smell like our cyborg, who smells like electricity before a storm.

"Get on with it," she hisses. "I have better things to do than hang out here all day."

He waves the robot forward, and he gives her a pat down, even though there is nowhere she can hide anything since she isn't wearing clothes. The robot eyes the slit in her stomach, and all of the snakes on her lunge forward, their mouths open. The robot doesn't flinch but looks at the commander who visibly shudders.

"Leave it." He waves the robot back, and he steps into line. "If you will follow me." He gestures us forward, and Lila follows, tugging our leashes. The commander stops. "You can leave your incubators here. They will be safe while you conduct business."

She hisses and rumbles her displeasure. "My incubators do not leave my sight until they are dead and my babies are consuming their corpses—or would you like to take their place?" she threatens, and the slit in her stomach starts to writhe like it's going to open.

He swallows nervously and shakes his head. "Fine, bring them, but they will be shot if you try anything."

"If any harm comes to my incubators, you will replace them," she warns him, and he hurries forward through the door in the side of the mine. It's dark in here, but none of us have trouble seeing because we all have excellent night vision. Tirrian's arm brushes against mine in reassurance, which I don't need but appreciate. The door bangs closed behind us, sealing us off completely. I don't turn back to look, but I can hear feet following behind us. It's not as many as there were, so I'm assuming some of them remained behind to guard the ship.

The path winds its way downward into the mine. I think this is probably the old living quarters of the original miners, but it smells musty and unused, like no one has been here in years.

"How long has this base been stationed here?" Lila asks the commander.

"It's housed the Syndicate since the first days," he says proudly. "Right under the Galactic Council's noses without anyone being any wiser."

It's strange that I don't hear very many heartbeats within the compound. Only a large door at the end of the corridor has any sounds of life. We reach it, and the commander presses a button. It opens into a bright room. Lila hisses and shrieks as she is temporarily blinded by the bright light. It's a clever tactic to keep both your enemies and allies off-kilter.

When our eyes adjust, we are ushered through a large room to a seating area at the front of the room. I smother the surprised gasp that wants to leave my mouth. Seated is a who's who of people Lila has pissed off over the last few months, but in the very center is her grandmother's sister, Vivian, who we now know as Vivax. On one side of her is Smith, who's looking smug as fuck, and on her other side is Deineira Digicon, Link's mother. We suspected both of them, but the people fanning out on either side really aren't a surprise either.

None of them are looking at us with recognition, though, so I think for now, we are in the clear.

"Mallabar, I was worried you were dead or worse, had been discovered when I hadn't heard from you for so long. You have the orb?" Vivax asks, and Lila nods.

"Yes."

"Where is it?" Vivax demands. "You and your ship were searched, and it wasn't found."

"I have it, but I don't see my payment." Lila looks around. "Where is what you promised me?"

When we were going through past communications, I discovered something truly disturbing. The payment for this Madovian retrieving the orb wasn't in money or precious metals or gems—it was in male flesh.

Vivax waves a hand, and off to the side, a group of men in shackles are nudged forward by more soldier bots. There are ten of them of all species, and they don't look like they are in the best condition. I wonder if some of them are the missing aliens from Earth. The Vilaxian showing his fangs might be Logan's father.

Lila hisses. "I said they had to be in prime condition. My sisters can't breed damaged stock." She rears up on her tail, becoming larger and more intimidating. "Are you trying to go back on our deal?"

"Some of them put up a fight and needed to be subdued. A deal's a deal, now where is my orb?" Vivax stands up.

"Very well, but if any of them don't survive the implantation, I and all of my sisters will be coming after you. Our species is on the verge of extinction," Lila threatens.

She reaches a hand into the slit in her stomach, and Vivax watches with greedy eyes. She is so focused on the movement, she doesn't notice the mist pouring into the room, and neither does anyone else. It is very clever of her to pretend the orb is hidden there. Suddenly, everyone is frozen, including Vivax. I guess she thought she was safe deep inside her mountain fortress.

"Ew, you put the orb in your stomach slit?" Cronus appears in front of us, looking at Lila with horror. Her form shimmers, and she changes into her original form and doubles over in laughter as Xavier covers her in her armor.

"No, but it was a good bluff, right?"

"No!" He still looks traumatized as we all turn to study the Syndicate with detached interest.

"Well, Lila, I would think it's safe to say everyone you ever pissed off has joined forces to see that you pay," the warlock says to our wife flippantly, but she ignores him.

"Call the others and let's get this done." I can't wait to see them all pay.

CHAPTER THIRTY-EIGHT

Lila

Xavier isn't wrong. I study the Syndicate and feel a pang of sorrow.

Lester, of course, is next to Smith, and it's no surprise to see Destir and a scarred and bored looking Dylan. I would have put money on them being on the *we hate Lila* train. Hanging off Dylan's arm is none other than the dragon loving bitch Zilla. The purple streaks that signify her bond with a larnuk are gone, and instead, those parts are gray and brittle. In fact, all of her looks slightly brittle. She's lost weight and looks way older than before.

I turn my attention to the other side and feel a pang of sorrow for Link. We suspected his mother was involved, but seeing it confirmed is a real kick in the ass. I'm not sure if the fleitine will handicap a cyborg, since they don't contain magic. We need to figure out another way to render her benign. With the ability to manipulate nanobots, she could conceivably escape quite easily, and if she is able to override the soldier guards, then we would lose all of our prisoners. Maybe keeping them all together in the same prison isn't a great idea.

Next to her is another blast from the past in the form of Natalia. I don't think Maxsim had been informed of her escape, or if he had, he hadn't thought to share it with me. We will be having words if that's the case. She looks a little worse for wear too, which makes me irrationally happy. She looks like she has some sort of mange. Her fur is patchy, and her skin is red in places where there is no fur.

I slide my eyes further along and recognize one of the warlocks, but not the other. One is that upstart asshole Aryan, Cronus's aide. I'm assuming the other one is his father.

"Ah, so that's where that asshole Atrax got to." Cronus points at the man on the end. "Why am I not surprised? I knew it was too much temptation for Aryan to stay loyal to me instead of his father. I bet he's wishing he had now." The warlock king chuckles and rubs his hands together in glee. I don't envy either of them one little bit.

"You know, I'm kind of disappointed. This is the feared Syndicate?" I say. "How were we scared of this?" I ask, shaking my head.

"I think maybe we managed to take a few of them out during our travels. The basilisk showed heavy involvement with them when we went through their files," Silac tells me.

"So was Mazlan. I guess Natalia is her replacement," Xavier points out. "Not to mention the cyborg we took care of and both Estrella and Radella. All had been actively recruited. Josa was recruited previous to the circus going on hiatus, but Estrella and Radella were after it. That's why they insisted on the clan dissolution trial, but it backfired on them. We got that information from them when we were transporting them to the outpost."

"My father is going to be devastated by this." Tirrian waves at his uncle. "The man has never been particularly pleasant, but to conspire against the throne and the galactic council, well, it's going to break his heart."

I heave out a sigh. "Call the others down. It's time to finish this," I tell Xavier, and he sends the agreed upon signal. Within seconds, the gods, my father, and the Vilaxians appear. Saxon races around, placing transport beacons on all the Syndicate members except for Vivax and the captive men. The others disappear to take care of the guards outside and anyone else who may be in the complex.

"Make sure Brannock is given access to Smith. I promised him," I tell my father who approaches me.

"Yes, he and I have had an in-depth discussion on exactly what will happen to Agent Smith. I'm just sad I'm not going to be there to see it," he tells me, and I frown.

"What do you mean?" I ask him but before he can answer the Vilaxians return.

"All life-forms are accounted for, but everyone outside of this room wasn't sentient. There is no Syndicate army, just one full of bots," Sabine sneers.

"Okay, all beacons have been placed. Prepare to beam," Saxon says into his watch, contacting the control deck of the Vilaxian battleship.

Zeydan approaches me and wraps me in his arms as my grandma approaches her sister with a sad look in her eyes.

I watch with worry as Sanshia approaches Smith. I did promise him to Brannock, but I am sure he would understand if she killed him. All she does, however, is spit on him.

"Rot in hell," she growls.

Zeydan places a kiss on my temple. "It's time, love. Get the orb," he tells me, and I pull away from his embrace and reach into my safe space and retrieve the orb. When I pull it out, it flares brightly like a beacon, and I feel the power inside it as it shudders in my hand.

"The power wants to return to its rightful homes," Liliana tells me as she approaches me, Vivax floating behind her.

"How are you going to stop the power from going into her instead of me?" I ask. They were never clear on that part.

She holds up a knife that gleams much like the one I was stabbed with on Earth.

"That has the correct fail-safe formula I told you

about." Zeydan points to the weapon. "When we stab it into her, it will block her from receiving the power, and the power will seek out the next suitable host."

"Me," I confirm, but the gods surround me, and I start to feel a moment of panic. "What's going on?" I demand, and Zeydan steps back to join his brothers and sisters, mouthing, "I'm sorry."

"Beam now," Saxon shouts, and I feel my body start to dematerialize. I scream in horror at my last view before I become particles, the gods and my father remaining behind.

"No!" I scream as my body rematerializes in the hangar of the Vilaxian ship with all the other beings wearing transport beacons.

"What have you done?" I scream at my mates. Tirrian, Saxon, Xavier, and Silac are all trying to talk to me. "Send me back now. I will not let my father do this. He has sacrificed too much." I hit them as they surround me, caging me between their bodies.

"Lila," my mom's gentle voice calls, and I turn, tears clouding my vision, to find her pushing her way between Saxon and Xavier before pulling me into her arms.

"It was what your father wanted," she tells me. "You've been through enough and have twelve mates and many children relying on you."

"But he has you, Bubby, and Bastien," I sob, and she shakes her head sadly.

"Us being bound to Bubby is what made him make the choice. Bubby and I should survive if anything were to happen to him. Don't cheapen his sacrifice by being angry," she tells me, and I feel a wave of guilt as my grandpas join us.

"We will be out of range in a few minutes. Do you want to watch by the viewing window?" they ask, and I grimace.

"What are we going to watch? Our loved ones destroying themselves?" I snap, and Eric shakes his head.

"No, Lila! The rebirth of old gods is not something you see every day and shouldn't be missed." He doesn't sound worried in the least, so I go with everyone to the viewing deck. The Vilaxian military takes care of the remaining members of the Syndicate and the poor men who had been slated as Madovian incubators.

Brannock disappears in the direction Smith is taken. They are all still frozen by warlock power, and it's easy to handle them and less noisy. I wouldn't want to be those soldiers when they unfreeze. Shit will hit the fan.

We reach the viewing window, and we can see the planet in the distance. We're joined by the warlock and Vilaxian royal families. Saxon wraps his arms around me and whispers, "I'm sorry." I sigh and sag back into him. It wasn't his fault. I should have guessed they were planning something.

"Your dad wouldn't take no for an answer," he tells me. "And Zeydan was completely on board. I was outnumbered."

"Don't blame anyone. This is how it is supposed to

be. It's all going to be fine, I can feel it," my mother says, grabbing my hand and giving it a squeeze as a small glow appears on the planet.

"It's starting," John whispers, and we fall silent as the glow grows bigger and bigger until it encompasses the whole planet.

"Whoa, isn't that going to destroy the planet?" I ask.

"No, they thought that because it was full of that metal they use in the fail-safe compound, it would be resistant to the power, and it would have no choice but to flow back into their bodies, which is what it will want to do," William explains, not taking his eyes off the view in front of us.

The white glow starts to change color and break off—white, red, green, blue, pink, and black. Each of the colors grow until they explode in what looks like a burst of fireworks, each color blending with the others. Mom and I scream, and there are gasps of horror around us.

"No!" I sob as the fireworks clear, and there is nothing in sight but the planet still in one piece. "What happened? Did it go wrong?"

"I would say it all went very right," an other-worldly voice says behind us.

As one, we all spin to see where it's coming from. Standing there in their god forms are the four elemental gods. Zeydan is in his familiar form, but it's hard to look at him because he's so perfect now. Aarin has the same wings and a head like a bird. Hurricane floats in the air, his mer tail shimmering with blue and silver sparkles as his hair drifts like it's underwater, a giant trident in his hand. Sanshia is the most different. Gone is the emaciated woman, and in her place is a curvy goddess with black eyes and dragon wings, and she is surrounded by flames that don't burn anything they touch.

"Dad?" I ask Zeydan, and he smiles, and the four of them part. I can see my grandmother and father behind them. They are both in what I'm guessing are their godly forms. Gigi looks like herself but on steroids. She's almost too beautiful to look at, and she radiates a sereneness that makes you want to bow down in her presence. She has glossy, white fairy-like wings. My father, on the other hand, looks like he's had a glow up. All his features have sharpened, and his form flickers between that and a hooded being that when you look too closely inspires pants-wetting fear. He holds a scythe and has black fairy-like wings.

My mother walks right up to him and throws her arms around him. "Marcus," she murmurs with relief, and I smile as they kiss like they are the air each other breathes.

"So I'm assuming it worked?" Xavier asks, slinging an arm around my shoulders. "I knew it would."

I consider smacking him, but I'm too darned relieved to bother. "Yup, you were right," I say, giving him a kiss instead.

He smirks smugly, and I hear his mother scoff behind me.

"Well, now that that's all done, don't you have a circus to run?" William asks after the three of them hug my grandmother tightly.

"Jesus, Dad, pushy much?" my father jokes, pulling away from my mom.

I hold up a hand and wave at the six of them.

"Is this a permanent thing now? Because it's kind of hard to look at." All of their glows dim, and they return to their normal forms. Five of them are fully clothed, but we all turn to stare at my dad, who is completely naked. He looks down at his body and gives us a sheepish grin as I shriek and put my hands over my eyes.

"Sorry, it's going to take a bit to get used to these powers."

Cronus chuckles, and I'm assuming he clothes my dad, because I feel someone pull my hand from my eyes, and when I look, he's grinning at me, fully clothed.

"Payback is a bitch, isn't it?"

"Let's agree here and now never to get naked in front of one another again," I tell him, and we shake on it while everyone else laughs at us.

In the end, the great and scary Syndicate was actually a bit of a letdown. Most of their troops were robot soldiers Deinera contributed to the cause, unbeknownst to her husband and the rest of the Pleasure Bot Industries board. The only live beings were the ones we captured. It was decided to let the Galactic Council deal with them. We handed them all over, minus Smith, and I doubt any of them will see the light of day again.

Smith was tortured repeatedly, and in the end, my father and Brannock gifted him to Sanshia, and she turned him to ash with a flick of her wrist. She seemed a lot happier after that, but she still doesn't want anything to do with Ember, and we respect that. Maybe one day it will change, but we will make sure she is loved and cared for until that time.

"The Syndicate really was pretty lame—a group of disgruntled beings gathering and bitching about all the wrongs that had been done to them. They had no real plans except getting the orb," I comment to Cas as we watch the kids climb all over my grandparents and parents. They returned with us to the circus when it was time to leave. Chloe has fit into the mix like a dream. She accepted me with no trouble and I'm already in love with her, as are the rest of my family. It was such a relief after all the other stress.

"It really is, though they would have been a problem if Vivax managed to get her hands on the orb," he replies, wincing as Jack tugs on my dad's now super long hair. He's kept it that way, and I keep seeing him swish it around like some kind of historical romance novel hero. Bubby and Mom seem to like it though. You think he would learn to tie it back around the children, since I've seen Bastien grab hold of it like that too.

"I don't understand how any of them thought she would share the power with them though. It was obvious to anyone with half a brain that she was going to be a dictator, and I'm sure they would have all ended up dead if they hadn't caved to her plans," I murmur.

"Cas, come on, we need to finish getting ready, and I need someone to rub oil into my chest," Silac calls. "I hate feeling it on my hands." I smirk as Cas gives me a kiss on the head and pulls away, hurrying to help Silac and Tirrian oil themselves up for the first act.

"How are you feeling?" Ghosie asks, wrapping his arms around me from behind, and I sigh, sinking back into his fur. One of the first things dad and Gigi did was fix the carevastas and Aaz'axians.

This means Chloe and Ember are now both safe from whatever was killing the Aaz'axian females, and Gigi and Dad promised they are going to figure out a way to rebuild both them and the Una's races. They did it one time, so why can't they do it again? It is a work in progress though. Both want to spend some quality time with our families before they disappear to do godly things.

We've had reports from Ghosie's dad that men spontaneously changed back into women, and so did half of the children. It's been a confusing time for the carevastas, but they are working it all out and happy for the change. Apparently, they are trying to go legit too, and some of our allies are reaching out to them to hire their services. Ghosie has been over the moon and basically tackling anyone who will hug him. I even found Cronus hugging him the other day when they arrived with the rest of our extended family, insisting they needed to see my first show as ringmaster.

That leads us to tonight. I pull out of his arms and smooth my hands nervously over my outfit. It's the one from the first day—red coat jacket with a black collar and cuffs with gold accents, black booty shorts, fish net tights, and knee-high boots. I have a top hat on my head and the cane minus the orb, but it was replaced with a large dragon eye gem that my mine conveniently gave up and sent along with Zala. She was waiting for the right time to give it to me per instructions from her all-knowing grandmother. Much like the previous gem, this one glows happily in its place at the top of my cane. All dressed up, I certainly look the part. Let's just hope I can pull it off.

"Five minutes. Five minute call," someone shouts, warning the performers, and my stomach feels like it's in my throat.

The staging area is bustling with crew, and my grandpas approach me as everyone else who is not performing files out, wishing me luck. They are going to take their seats in the arena. We have a whole blocked off VIP area for everyone, and the children are

wearing glamours so they can attend their first performance too.

"We are so very proud of you, Lila," John says,
grabbing my hands and hugging me tightly.

"So thankful you have come into our lives and
made them so much better," William tells me, also
giving me a hug, and I can feel he's struggling to hold
his tears back. Their pride and love fills me with confidence, and I smile as I turn to Eric.

"And for Gigi's sake, girl, give it a little showmanship." He waves his fingers and then gives me a quick
hug before they turn me around, and I face the stage
door. I swallow nervously as I hear the rumbling sound
of the audience, but then the lights go down, and the
room falls into a tense, anticipatory silence.

I take a deep breath before teleporting to the
middle of the dome and striking a pose that should
make Eric's little showman heart sing as the spotlights
light me up.

"Ladies and gentlemen, boys and girls, welcome to
Galaxy Circus."

AFTERWORD

We did it! We made it to the end. I hope you are as satisfied with ending as I am.
Please think to leave a review if you enjoyed it.

I doubt I will ever be completely done with the Galaxy Circus, I plan on writing bonus scenes for the up coming omni's and special editions, as well as so many potential side stories. But for now I am moving on to wrapping up another series and some new things for next year.

If Galaxy Circus is your first Lexie Winston Series you can find all of my other offerings by scanning the link below or searching for them on Amazon.

www.lexiewinston.com

ACKNOWLEDGMENTS

To my cover designer Jessica, of Raven Ink Covers. Thank you for making the covers exactly what I envisioned, you nailed it and all of them.

Thank you to Jess at Elemental Editing. My book is pretty and readable thanks to you.

My ever reliable and faithful beta readers Kerry and Tegan... You da bomb xxx

Special thanks to Amanda Murray who is like the Galaxy Circus whisperer and made sure I didn't stray away from previous books. Your assistance was invaluable.

I wrote the last sentence of Ovation and promptly burst into tears. The series was a labor of love but it was intense, so many characters and major world building to keep straight at times I struggled. So it is with equal parts relief, sadness ,and satisfaction that I say goodbye to Lila and the gang for now. I doubt I will ever truly be done but I have another series I need to wrap up and many new ideas I want to work on next year. But make sure you are a part of my Facebook readers group or are subscribed to my newsletter because they will be the first place you hear about any new Galaxy Circus whispers

And lastly to you guys the readers. I love what I do, and probably would do it regardless if anyone read them or not, but you guys make it that much sweeter so thank you.

Until next time, happy reading

Lexie

9 781763 622845